To Nick

Enjoy the Journey!

Seer
of
Souls

Susan Faw

Cover Design by Greg Simanson
Edited by Pam Harris

This is a work of fiction. Names, characters, places, brands, media, and incidents are either the product of the author's imagination or are used fictitiously. Any resemblance to similarly named places or to persons living or deceased is unintentional.

PRINT ISBN 978-0-9953438-0-1
EPUB ISBN 978-0-9953438-1-8

Dedication

There are many people who cross your path in life, and some, especially these days, you may never meet in person.

But they have the power to inspire you from afar. They can suggest an idea, spark a phrase, and help you remember an emotion, an event in your life that inspires a scene.

I wish to dedicate this, my debut novel, to two very special people.

Firstly, I wish to thank Tabby Dermody, who I met online playing a silly children's game but who, through that game, showed me the soul of a true friend, and has been my buddy and constant supporter through all of our trials. Thank you Tabby, for all your beta read suggestions and for believing in me as an author, and by the way, I have some great suggestions for new characters in our game!

Secondly, or perhaps in a tie, I would like to thank my childhood friend, Geoff Miller, who has also championed Cayden and Avery's journey, and who has supplied a constant stream of encouragement, wit, and a swift kick in the ass when my motivation lagged.

To all who dream of a life beyond, welcome to the journey.

Perhaps, together, we really can see beyond this reality. It's worth the peek, don't you think?

GET THE PREQUEL, SOUL SURVIVOR FOR FREE!
http://susanfaw.com/soul-survivor-prequel-free-download/

Prologue

THE BABY GAVE a feeble, barely discernable kick. Its twin had ceased movement but not with the natural stillness of slumber. Poison moved through their premature bodies, oozing along their tiny veins, a burning acid in their blood.

Mordecai lifted his hand from the woman's sweaty forehead. Gwen's panicked eyes locked onto his sad grey ones. She clutched her distended belly as another wave of pain ripped through her.

"It must be poison! This is more than simple birthing pangs." She coughed and the motion made bile rise in her throat. Gwen clutched at Mordecai's left hand, gripping it so tight the knuckles of her hand whitened. "It's reaching the babies! Mordecai, what do we do?"

Straightening his lanky frame, he released her hand and wandered over to the tall mullioned window of the bartizan room. His sweeping brows pinched together in a frown as he gazed unseeingly at the silent courtyard below him. Purple wisteria climbed the ashlar walls of the castle, revealing their stark outlines. A fresh breeze stirred the heavy tapestry curtains as lightning flashed, highlighting the roiling clouds, puffing in eager anticipation of the storm breaking over the castle.

Her seclusion was for her protection. Gwen's grief over Prince Alexander's failure to return from his most recent patrol with the Kingsmen twisted in her gut, accentuating the pain of the poison. The prince and all of the Kingsmen in his unit had been slaughtered by Primordials in a sudden vicious attack. This sorrowful news had arrived on the heels of the king's death from a heart attack a week prior. The kingdom was reeling from the double disaster. *And now it's my turn. I am the target,* she thought.

Gwen coughed and froth formed in her mouth, drowning her thoughts. Her lungs attempted to fill but failed. Intense pressure gripped her chest as though a large man with a booted foot stood on it compressing it. She pushed aside her discomfort and staggered over to join the wizard at the window. She clutched a handful of his grey robe sleeve, partly to gain his attention and partly to keep from sinking to the floor.

"Please, Mordecai, I must save my babies! What can I do? There has to be a way to help them. Between your magic and my heritage, there *must* be a way."

Mordecai's mouth drooped beneath his long white beard. "I can only think of one solution, Gwen" he said gently. "You must pass the mother bond to me." Tears sparked in her almond-shaped eyes as he locked his to hers. "I think we both know that you cannot survive this poison." He squeezed her hands. "We need to convince Alcina the babes have died with you."

Gwen's liquid green eyes searched and found steely resolve reflected in his grey ones. She nodded once and unconsciously rubbed one hand across her protruding belly, where the foot of the lone stirring child pushed against the thin protection of her skin.

"We need to do this quickly, Gwen. The birth will take most of your remaining strength, and they must be born alive in order to pass the bond."

She groaned again as a hard contraction took her. The twisting pain of a poison-filled cramp left her gasping for air as she sank to her knees beside the wizard. She raised her head, panting. "I do not think that is a problem, Mordecai."

Mordecai gently eased her onto her back, on the cold stone floor. Reaching inside his pocket, he took out a clear crystal stone and placed it between her cold hands, clasping them with in his own. Together, they began to chant.

*   *   *

The late-day sun streamed through the garden-view windows of the bartizan room. Dust motes stirred in a breeze heavy with the smell of damp earth and wisteria. A few trailing clouds scuttled across the sky in an attempt to catch the storm moving off to the east, low rumbles fading softly into the distance.

With a groan, Mordecai sank back to his knees on the polished floor beside the princess. Gwen's sweat-soaked brown hair curled damply over her curiously shaped ears. Dark circles shadowed her eyes; eyes that stared back at him from a deathly pale face.

She lay on the floor, her bloodstained gown bunched to one side. Beside her, wrapped in cotton swaddling, were two newborn infants, a boy and a girl.

Both children were dead.

A tiny red birthmark, resembling the shape of an oak leaf, adorned the right side of each smooth cheek. The tattoos faded away before his eyes. Mordecai smiled a grim smile and trailed a thin finger down the soft cheeks where the tattoos had appeared so briefly, sensing the residue of magic under the skin.

Gwen lifted her hand and caressed the cheeks of her two babes. A hot tear trickled out of the corner of her eye. She would never know them, nor they her.

Mordecai lifted the children and placed them in her arms. She hugged them and wept silently, tears streaming down onto the cherubic face of the closest child.

Gwen's mournful eyes lifted to the man standing beside her.

"Are they truly safe now, Mordecai?" Her weak voice shook with supressed emotion.

"They are as safe as we can make them, Gwen."

She touched his sleeve. "Thank you," she murmured weakly. "You have been a true friend." She stiffened, sucking in a hard breath that ended abruptly. Her eyes widened as the soul in their emerald depths faded away. Her hand slipped from his sleeve and thudded to the floor.

Mordecai gently closed her eyes, squeezing his own shut to dam the tears sliding down his whiskered face.

"Sleep well, Gwen, and welcome the peaceful embrace of the Mother."

He staggered to a chair by the open window. Leaning out over the stone ledge, he saw a dead eagle on the stones below. He dropped back into the chair beside the window and gazed out at the setting sun. The last of the storm clouds faded into the distance. Little did they know that they carried the hopes and dreams of the world in their midst.

Pain stabbed into Mordecai's chest and he sucked in a deep

breath. If his calculations were correct, he had little more than a half hour left. The poison was completing its job.

Well, his task was finished. What would be would be. Eyes opened wide, he watched the sun creep toward the horizon. The rays of the setting sun blazed through the retreating clouds, glowing pink and orange. His lips curved with satisfaction. It was done.

* * *

The tall, regal woman burst into the room, cruel eyes sweeping the creeping shadows. Her contingent of guards with lanterns held aloft quickly encircled her and then spread out along the sides of the room.

She gazed around at the scene before her. "Search the room for others. Check to see that no one is alive," she snapped at the guards.

She marched up to the woman lying on the floor cuddling her two babes. Frowning, she stepped around the bodies and moved over to the man in the chair.

He sat staring glassy-eyed out the window. She felt for a pulse in his neck and located a faint pulse under the curve of his chin.

"The wizard still lives!" she screamed. "Find the mage. Hurry!"

She snapped her fingers, calling the two guards standing closest. "Pick him up, and move him to the lower dungeon. Secure him with two guards on the door at all times. His head is to be shaven before he awakes and it must remain shaven or his powers will return."

She grabbed Mordecai's whiskered jaw in her long-nailed hand and shook his slack face. "Poor bald wizard," she murmured to him. "You hoped to be dead before I arrived, didn't you? Soon, you will tell me all your secrets, starting with this room. I will know the truth of this before you die." She released his face. "Take him away!"

Whirling around, she barked to the other guards crowding the room. "Burn the bodies—immediately! There will be no Remembrance Eulogy for them. They are unworthy of the honour. It is reserved for true royalty"—she nudged Gwen's body with her toe—"and she is not royalty! Filthy heathen!"

Furious, she stormed from the room, her black silk skirts

snapping in her wake.

Chapter 1

ZIONA ASPENWOOD STOOD at the edge of the glade in the shadow of an ancient oak tree watching the blond-haired young man. Dressed in rough woolen pants and a bleached linen shirt, he sat on a rocky outcropping, whittling a length of wood.

He paused to examine his work, holding it up to his right eye and peering down the long shaft and then turned it over in his hands, running his fingers along the hollows he had carved into the body of the wood.

Satisfied, he picked up a long narrow awl, a useful leather tool that now doubled as a whittling knife, and with deft movements tunnelled into the shaft of wood, starting at one end then working from the other until a tube formed through its length.

He shook his hand and shavings fell to the grass at his feet. He blew into one end and peered down the tube once again. Grunting his satisfaction, he smoothed the center of the piece with the sharp awl.

Suddenly he glanced up, his piercing green eyes staring directly at Ziona. They pinned her to the spot. She flinched back to take cover even though she knew human eyes were not as sharp as a Primordial. Still, his focused concentration made her believe he had spotted her hiding place amongst the trees.

He stared at her like a deer scenting danger for a moment and then picked up his project once again, deciding the danger had passed.

Ziona drew back into the gloom of the woods and joined her companion. Sharisha Fernfell was dark-skinned for a Primordial with brown eyes bordering on black. Her sharp cheekbones and permanent frown provided a stark contrast to Ziona's leafy green eyes, set in a heart-shaped face and framed by sun-kissed hair.

"Did he spot you?" Sharisha crossed her arms over her chest, annoyed by the lingering of her younger companion.

"No, I don't believe so," said Ziona, shaking her head. "I thought he caught my scent, but there is no possibility of that, is there? Perhaps one of his sheep alerted him to our presence."

"We need to be careful," Sharisha huffed. "The escalation of the war has made it unsafe for Primordials to be seen in human lands. Surely you know this, Ziona!'"

"Yes. There is no need to remind me, Sharisha," snapped Ziona.

Sharisha frowned at the younger woman and instead asked, "So...what do you think? Is he the one we seek?"

Ziona was silent for a moment, thinking. Was it possible he was the one? He seemed to fit the parameters, but, on the other hand, he seemed so simple...so common...not at all what she had anticipated.

They had been watching him and his sister on and off for a week now. Other than an affinity for nature, they had not exhibited any skills or talents out of the ordinary.

"I don't know, Sharisha. I just don't know. The elders speak of an undeniable sign that will show them true. I guess we should continue to watch him. If he is the one then eventually he will show us proof of his true nature. The spring equinox is almost here. If a sign is to come, it will be then, when the Goddess returns to bless the land. I think we should wait until then."

"Agreed," said Sharisha. "We will wait and watch."

Sharisha led the way back through the woods to their campsite deep in the forest. She moved without a sound on soft moccasin-shod feet. Ziona followed, slipping into the shadows.

* * *

Cayden Tiernan glanced up from his whittling, staring at a flash of something in the oak grove at the far end of the clifftop pasture.

He stared at the spot, focusing his senses on the spot, searching for anything out of the ordinary. He thought he sensed a presence beneath the ancient oak tree, which stood tall and proud where the field of tall grass ended. He smelled a fresh calming scent, reminiscent of his sister. Someone or something was definitely watching him.

He whittled without focus, his senses attuned to the spot. There. The movement was as graceful as a doe in the trees, so fleeting that the average person would miss it.

Now, the presence was gone.

Who are they? What do they want with that particular spot?

Cayden pocketed his flute and affected a casual stroll toward the ancient oak. As he entered the shadowy circle formed by the canopy of the tree, the lower branch quivered and a slender figure dropped onto his back. He staggered sideways, not as a result of the negligible weight but from the arm that snaked around his skull in a squeezing headlock that blocked his eyes and made spots swim behind his eyelids. His foot caught on a thick tree root that rounded out of the soil. The combination was too much and he tumbled to the earth with a thump that dislodged his attacker, tossing her over his shoulder and rolling away.

Cayden winced at the sharp spear of pain in his knee and looked up to see his twin sister, Avery, lying flat on her stomach, head twisted to the side. Her arms were sprawled to either side and she jerked spasmodically. Alarmed, he lurched to his feet, one hand soothing the friction burn on his face and the other brushing stones from his knee, as he stumbled to her side. Sinking onto his uninjured knee he grabbed her shoulder and flipped her over. Fear tightened his throat and he croaked, "Avery! Are you OK?" His shout trailed away as her face was revealed. Avery was laughing so hard that her shoulders shook and she swiped at the tears streaming from her eyes. A full-bellied laugh burst from her lungs and she rolled onto her side, curling into a ball and hugging her middle.

"I have a stitch in my side," she hiccupped and continued to laugh and hiccup in an alternating pattern that eerily echoed the tune that had just been playing in Cayden's mind.

Miffed, Cayden stood up and stalked away. *She is always doing that, trying to scare me.* His hands drifted into his pockets, checking that his flutes were intact as his eyes quickly scanned the surrounding forest, but whatever had caught his attention earlier was long gone.

Cayden rolled his shoulders, easing the tension there and also relaxing the sore point where Avery's knee had impacted. He turned back and offered her a hand up. "If you are quite through…?"

Avery accepted his hand and he hauled her hiccupping to her feet. She brushed grass and leaves off her tan pants and picked a twig out of the turndown at the top of her boot.

"What were you doing there, Cayden?" She poked at his pocket. "Carving another flute?"

"Shh!" Cayden put a finger to his lips, hushing her question, with an involuntary glance at the suspect shrubbery. He strode to the area that had caught his eye and searched the underbrush for telltale signs of a human presence but found no evidence of anyone having stood there.

Cayden walked back to the ancient oak tree, Avery trailing in his wake. Kneeling at the base Cayden pulled back the pile of oak leaves nestled in the crook between two large surface roots, exposing a small, hollow crevice under the tree. He reached inside and pulled out a deerskin bag, loosening the drawstring. Inside were ten carved flutes.

So the strangers were not here for my flutes, he mused.

Cayden tightened the drawstrings and slid the bag back into the hollow at the base of the tree, deep in the crevice. He replaced the leaves in and over the hole, obscuring it from view and then erased his tracks by covering them with more fallen leaves. He studied his handiwork for a moment and satisfied that their hiding place was perfectly concealed, he perched on his favourite outcropping of rock in the pasture once again.

Avery watched her brother's actions, a bemused expression playing across her features. She followed him to the rock and climbed up beside him, flopping down on her stomach on its warm smooth surface.

"What do you plan to do with all those flutes?" she asked, chin propped in her hand, watching him work with the slim stick of wood.

Cayden didn't answer. The truth was that he didn't know why he carved them. Avery was the only person who knew they existed. Magic in any form was banned, and his flutes would be perceived as magical. Of that he had no doubt. Avery was the only person who knew of his magic, and he knew she also harbored similar magical talents, although hers were more easily hidden.

The warm late day sun made the slab of granite a very pleasant perch for watching the sheep. His bow rested against the base of the rock, a quiver of arrows within easy reach.

Taking out his partially completed flute, Cayden examined it again. A bubble of excitement welled up inside him. He had been working on this flute for the last three days and it was near completion. Each one he had made was slightly different than the one before. Some were longer, some shorter, some fatter, some thinner, some slightly curved. All were decorated with spirals or lines carved into the surface.

He was not sure why he decorated them so, other than it seemed to change the sound and pitch of the tones produced. And the end result? It was completely unpredictable.

Cayden studied the flute in his hands and inspiration struck. Picking up the awl, he deftly carved sinuous lines lengthwise along the shaft of the flute. At the base, he carved his signature mark, a towering oak tree. He always carved in sight of the tree. It seemed magical to him. It gave him the wood to carve and so he wished for it to witness the creation he made with its gift. The oak tree limbs swayed slightly in silent acknowledgement. It was not the first time they had done so.

"Cayden? Do you think it's true, what they say about the war?" Avery's question broke through his concentration.

Cayden grunted and glanced quickly at her before returning his attention to the flute. "What are they saying? I have heard so many different rumours that it's difficult to know what to believe."

"Well do you believe that the Primordials are invading?" Avery frowned at him. "The queen's criers are saying that the Primordial clans plan to come across the Highland Needle and raid the farms. They say that travellers are being snatched and are never seen again. They say that strange creatures have been spotted, dark monsters that suck the soul from people. They say that the Primordials are cursing the sheep that graze closest to the pass, and lambs are being born with two heads. Two heads! How strange is that?" Her words tumbled to a halt.

Cayden snorted. "Do you really think any creature can survive with two heads? It sounds like stories made for telling around a solstice fire."

Avery frowned at Cayden's response. "Well it can't all be stories. What about the McKinnons? They had that two-headed calf born last spring, remember? It actually lived for a few days."

Cayden grimaced and nodded. Curious, he had gone to see it, before it died. He had snuck into the barn just before dark and there it was, in the stall beside the cow which had given birth to it, complete with two heads, one larger than the other. The heads had competed with each other to nurse first and within a few days it had starved itself to death. He shivered involuntarily; the memory was creepy.

"They burned the calf body," Cayden said, picking up the story, "and the McKinnons moved away. The queen's guards were going to arrest them for witchcraft, Pa said so."

It was Avery's turn to nod. "Cayden, I am afraid of anyone learning of our magic." She fidgeted with a few stalks of tall grass as she spoke, braiding them together. "We must be very careful, with the legions on the move."

"They wouldn't want us! We are shepherds. I don't think they even know where Sanctuary-by-the-Sea is located." He waved the flute in her direction. "Here, take a look at this one."

Avery scooted over the rock to his side and peered over his shoulder at the flute in his hands. Pleased with the result, Cayden took a soft cloth and a small container of linseed oil from his pocket. He opened the lid and dipped a folded corner of cloth into the pot, then wiped it onto the flute, working the oil into the raw wood surface. It glowed as the oil was absorbed into the body.

He put the lid back on the container then stowed both the cloth and the pot of oil back in his pocket. His eyes searched the field one more time checking that they were alone, and then he placed the flute to his lips.

A hauntingly soft but reedy sound came from the flute. He tried a couple of other notes, up and down the pipe. Settling his back against the rock outcropping, he played the tune that had been bouncing around in his brain, eyes wandering lazily over to an ewe and newborn lamb, cropping the short grasses a foot or two away. His eyes drifted closed while he played, listening to the tone of the flute. The melody lingered in the air when he finished.

He opened his eyes to find snakes crawling out of rocky dens where they had been hibernating. They crawled toward them and gathered beside him on the rock, seemingly bewitched by the sounds coming from the flute.

He was not surprised, and neither was Avery. Strange things happened around Cayden's flutes, usually involving some creature or another. The only surprise left was what kind of animal the flutes would summon.

He continued to play and the snakes swayed in time to the music. Cayden counted fifty snakes around him of every type known in the area from poisonous black adders to common garden snakes. None showed any aggression toward him at all.

He stopped playing and the snakes slithered up beside him, coiling on the rocks. Their gentle hisses were not words, but he grasped their meaning. He sensed they meant him no harm. His talent was sufficiently strange that to outsiders, especially those who rigidly followed the queen's edicts, it would appear that magic or witchcraft was being practiced. Cayden agreed; the way the music of the flutes attracted creatures to him did seem magical. Magic had been outlawed as long as he had been alive and the queen sent regular patrols to scour the kingdom for signs of its use.

The older men of the village, however, loved to recount tall tales of a time when magic permeated every corner of the world, of the Old Gods and Goddesses, of a time when magic ruled supreme; a time before the Falling; a time before the War of the Gods. It was all very thrilling, the orators' voices rising and waning, the spooky quality heightened by the flickering light of the roaring bonfire, which marked the close of the festival to welcome spring.

The flute he had carved last week had summoned several packs of wolves, the appearance of which panicked the sheep causing them to bolt away, bleating their terror and scattering into the trees. The wolves paid the sheep no attention at all, instead coming to sit right at the base of the rock, their heads cocked to one side listening, expressions of extreme intelligence on their faces. Tongues lolling out of their mouths, they had stayed until Cayden had stopped playing and then slowly faded back into the trees.

Cayden had spent two extra hours gathering up all the sheep, which, of course, had made him late for dinner that day. The lie that he had fallen asleep in the warm sun did not convince his father, earning him a stern lecture and extra chores.

Even stranger still, after each of these encounters with the animals called by the flutes, Cayden felt a bond with them, as though an echo of the song still played in his head. They became a large extended family that never left his side, yet no one ever saw.

Scooping up ten garden snakes, Cayden placed them in the pouch at his waist. They writhed and wiggled and squirmed in the bag.

"Come on, Avery. We need to get back to the farm. Father will be waiting for this flock to come in. The faster we finish dousing the sheep, the sooner we can head into town and check out the festival."

Avery slid off the rock and whistled for the sheep. "I can't wait to check out the decorations. Let's hurry!" She ran off into the pasture, gathered the sheep into a loose bunch and began herding them toward the lane. Grinning, Cayden whistled to gather the few stragglers and headed for home. He had a plan for these snakes.

Chapter 2

AVERY TIERNAN TOOK A DEEP BREATH. She sat cross-legged on the ground out back of the chicken coop, eyes closed, hands resting on her knees, palms up. Exhaling slowly, she let every part of her body relax.

She drew another deep breath, this time holding it until it seemed her lungs would burst with the need to exhale. Spots floated before her eyes, but her senses sharpened and she focused on those smells that came in the deepest of relaxed states.

It made no sense to her, how she could smell so acutely when she wasn't breathing at all, but somehow she knew it wasn't an actual smell she smelled. It was more like an impression of a smell, a memory of a smell. Often it wasn't even a scent she had ever smelled before.

She had discovered this ability quite by accident one day. About six months ago, she had taken a fall from her horse (*of course, it was the horse's fault; she had been perfectly balanced standing on the back of the horse!*) and landed quite painfully on her back, knocking the air from her lungs in a great whoosh. She lay there for several seconds, gasping for a breath that wouldn't come. Like an overturned turtle, she'd lain there, staring at the canopy overhead. Verdant leaves vibrated with every colour and hue, and the rarified air trembled and danced in her vision.

She smelled the scent of an earthworm, wriggling on the soil of the overturned rock that had caused the horse to stumble in the first place. But even more impressive to her, she could sense her horse's surprise and waning fear of falling. Avery watched as her horse,

Sunny, wandered back to nudge her with her nose, snorting. She understood Sunny's thoughts simply from the horse's smell...or what she called a smell.

Sitting up slowly, Avery had patted her mare's nose in comfort.

The smell today was nothing she had ever smelled before. It was the sweet aroma of a wildflower that grew only in the sacred lands to the north of the mountain ranges in the land of the Primordial. How she knew this she did not understand, but she knew it to be true.

She sensed the land knew it too; the trees whispered of the flower and its powers to heal and to soothe. Avery thought the flower had the ability to heal mortal wounds if administered in time.

She shook her head at her crazy thoughts. She knew she was right, though. She would be branded a lunatic and a heretic if she were ever to speak those words out loud. By the queen's decree, she would be declared a witch and the queen would certainly have her burned at the stake were she to even voice the thought. So she kept her dawning abilities to herself and practiced when she had quiet moments alone.

A twig snapped.

Avery's eyes flew open. With her enhanced senses humming, she pinpointed the location, and spied two figures standing about one hundred paces away. They froze and then melted back into the trees and were lost from view.

*   *   *

Ziona allowed the branches of the dogwood to relax back to their natural position, cutting off her view of the curly haired young woman. Sharisha continued to watch her, a slight frown creasing her brow.

"Did you see an aura around her while she was meditating? It pulsed like a living thing! I have never seen such strength of spirit before. She was glowing blue as a midsummer's sky! Look, it's pulsing from her in waves. She is the one, Sharisha, I know she is!"

Sharisha studied Avery, as Ziona walked deeper into the trees. "It is one of the signs. The boy, her brother, must be the other one, even though we did not witness his spirit yesterday." Sharisha silently withdrew from her place of concealment and allowed a rare smile to soften the rigid set of her lips as she caught up to her companion. "We need to keep a close watch on the pair of them."

"So now we split up." Ziona matched her strides to Sharisha's. "I will keep watch over the boy and you can aid the girl as we planned."

"You must not interfere with the boy, Ziona." Sharisha frowned at the younger woman. Ziona bounced along at her side, her excitement evidenced by the way she thrust a low-hanging branch to the side. "He must come to know his powers on his own. We cannot interfere in his trials."

"I know we cannot interfere, unless it is a life-threatening situation." Ziona shrugged her shoulders. "But it doesn't mean I can't talk to him. He will never know who I am or what I do until it is necessary."

"Remember, Ziona." Sharisha gripped Ziona's arm, halting her in mid stride. "The prophecies of the Elder Scrolls make it very clear that the Goddess will give aid when the time is right. They must come to know the strength of their magic by their own hand, not ours."

"Yes, yes. I understand the plan." Frustrated, Ziona changed the topic slightly. "She saw us. Her eyes are much sharper than the boy's."

"Perhaps."

They arrived at their camp, tucked under a slab of granite fallen millennia ago from the mountain soaring above their heads. The edges were worn smooth with time and a perfect cave had formed that protected any inhabitants sheltering there from the weather on three sides. A crack in the rock provided a natural chimney through which the smoke of their campfire escaped.

They kept their fire small, using some thin sticks and a nest of last year's grasses as kindling. A meal of dried berries, nuts, and flatbread was washed down with spring water from a waterskin.

Dinner complete, Ziona picked up a brush and braided Sharisha's waist-length hair, winding it around her head to cover the tips of her pointed ears and then secured it with wooden carved combs from their packs. Sharisha did the same for Ziona.

Next, they focused on their faces. Human faces often had slanted eyes, but not the sharp angular eyebrows of their heritage. Picking up a knife from their meal kit, Sharisha carefully shaped Ziona's brows to a more human curve.

Finally, they took out clothing they had purchased a few villages back and changed into the style of clothing appropriate to a good wife or a merchant of the area. Skirts of woven wools (green for Ziona and brown for Sharisha) topped with white blouses of good cotton and cloaks of wool. Sturdy walking shoes completed the ensembles.

They unfolded their bedrolls and crawled under the coverings. Humming a Primordial melody of rest, they drifted off to sleep.

Chapter 3

ALCINA CURSETAG ENTERED THE GRAND HALL, ignoring the ripples of movement from her personal attendants as she marched across the tiled expanse to the balcony doors at the far end of the room. Heads bobbed on the men and women curtsied low, but for Alcina they might as well not have existed. Her elite guard trailed along in her wake, trotting to keep up with her long strides. She pushed open the heavy glass doors and stepped out onto the stone balustrade, which overlooked the ceremonial parade grounds below.

It was swollen with rank upon rank of soldiers, jammed shoulder to shoulder between the stone walls of the compound. All stood rigidly at attention, even though the hour was early and the wait had been a long one. They stamped feet in an attempt to keep the cold from seeping into their boots.

Their captains, lords of the land all, restlessly shifted position, having been roused from warm beds and stoked fires out into the crisp morning air. Puffs of frozen breath drifted above the assembled men.

The queen's legions were made up of men recruited from across the kingdom. The original guard of Cathair had contained fifteen hundred men. That number had now swollen to close to ten thousand—some barely old enough to shave and then only once a week—due to the queen's decree commanding the conscription of able-bodied youths sixteen years of age and older.

Alcina surveyed the assembled men, her expression haughty and cold.

A young man, a youth really, near the front of the line of men caught sight of her and nudged the soldier next to him. Both straightened their postures, eager to impress the regal woman above them.

"These would be new recruits," said Alcina to the lord general of her personal guard standing at her shoulder. She gestured toward the young men with a flick of her hand. "So fresh and eager to see battle. Well, I should not disappoint them, I think. Wouldn't you agree, Cyrus?"

Cyrus clasped his hands behind his back and glanced at her out of the corner of his eye, speculation on his face. "What did you have in mind, my queen? The eastern campaign?" he rumbled in his deep-timbral voice.

"All those peasants have been escaping their duty for far too long, hiding on their little farms in the hills by the sea. You may send a small contingent to the area. But I have better plans for these troops. How many legions have you called here today?"

"The First and Third Footmen and the Sixth Cavalry Elite, my queen. They are a full five thousand strong. While there are many new recruits amongst the regular soldiers, these are mostly volunteers and not the usual scum we find with the conscription services. Their commanders are the best we have in the field."

"Is that so? Well then, they should have no difficulty with this assignment."

She held up her bejeweled hands to quiet the men. When silence fell, she raised her voice to carry over the crowd.

"Brave men and soldiers of the realm, a great honour is to be granted to you this day. You have been chosen as the elite of the realm to serve your queen. Honour and glory such as men have only dreamed of are to be yours for never in the history of the world has an army been blessed with such a quest.

"The time has come to avenge the people of this great land against the Primordial infidels plaguing this world. They hide and cower on the other side of the Highland Needle, practicing their pagan beliefs and customs, which all know are an abomination to the true faith. It is time to wipe out these heretics once and for all."

A murmur rose from the helmeted men below at these words. The seasoned soldiers shook their heads, knowing this task was nigh impossible.

Alcina raised her voice, drowning out the grumbling. "I do not need to tell you this will be perilous. These he- and she-devils practice magic and other foul rituals in order to corrupt the nature of the divine. Has not our mage said it is so?"

More murmurs rose to her ears. Soldiers butted their spears on the ground, a rhythmic pounding to show their approval of her words. The sound swelled in the confined space. The hooded mage to her right bobbed his head in acknowledgement, his rheumy eyes peering out at the crowd.

"Ours is a righteous battle!" Alcina shouted, and her eyes gleamed in the firelight of the wall torches. "We will triumph! It is the will of the gods! I have seen it! In a glorious dream, the Great Goddess came to me and commanded me to not leave these heathens to pollute the land. The land cries to be cleansed, to be bathed in righteousness. If it must first be bathed in blood, your sacrifice paves the path to freedom for all lands and all peoples. Are you hungry to serve the Great Goddess? Or are you to be counted with the cowards and the heathens?"

A roar accompanied her words as the soldiers thundered their solidarity. Alcina painted a shallow smile on her face and then raised her hands to touch her forehead then her lips, and then pressed her open palms over her heart, the ritual blessing of soldiers. The mage joined in and together they blessed the assembled men. He spoke for the first time, in a squeaky, high-pitched voice. "Go forth! Know the Great Goddess guides your swords. Be proud of your calling. Be proud of your destiny! Her glory is yours! Kill the infidels!"

Alcina dropped her hands. "Attend me, Cyrus." The mage bowed to her as she departed.

She stepped off the balustrade and into a side meeting room of the Great Hall. The room was warmed by a vigorous fire dancing in a stone fireplace on the far wall. Cyrus pulled closed the gilded double doors behind her. Alcina placed her lacquered-fingered hand on his face, tapping his cheek. His eyes found her pitiless ones.

"My queen, our spies have located the primary Primordial force. They are camped at the pass to the Primordial lands on the north side of the switchback trail that leads to the highland village of Sanctuary-by-the-Sea. They lay in wait for our armies."

She dropped her hand and poured herself a cup of blueberry tea from a tall copper flask beaded with moisture and then gestured to Cyrus to help himself.

"I hope the mage's foreseeing is correct. This battle should eliminate the usurper of the throne forever. We must find him before he can begin to gather a following. Cursed prophesies. " Her mouth twisted in an ugly grimace. "The mage believes the prophesied one was born near the lands of the Primordials. We will never gain entry to search the Primordial lands as they guard the mountain passes and our spies have not located him yet outside of those lands." She paced in front of the fieldstone fireplace, and it cast a distorted shadow that flickered like the Ancient Ones of the Dark.

"Of course, I would prefer to face the insolent pup myself, but so far he has eluded my conscription ranks. We know from the mage's foreseeing that he is of an age to be recruited, and we also know from prophecy that he will be reluctant to kill another being. If we can pull him into the ranks of the legion, he should be easy to identify. Recruit all boys his age, I commanded. Scoop him up with the recruiter's net, and yet my legions fail me in this one, simple task; FIND THE BOY AND BRING HIM TO ME. It is a simple request."

Frustrated, she slammed her cup down on the table as she paced past it.

"Fools and children of fools! How I want to be the one to locate him!" She paused in front of the window to the balcony, arms folded across her chest, back rigid, and then she sighed and dropped her arms. "But I must rise above such petty self-indulgences. I expect you, Cyrus, to bring me the head of this saviour. I would have it as a trophy, stuffed and mounted in my throne room for all to see."

"It shall be as you say, my queen." Cyrus bowed to her stiff form then left the room, leaving the queen contemplating her plans.

Chapter 4

CAYDEN SLIPPED BEHIND a couple of quenching barrels, tucked into the shade at the rear of the blacksmith's shop, ducking low and running crouched to avoid detection. He spied his best friend Ryder, through the open casement window, as he draped the neck strap of his smithy apron on the wooden peg at the rear of the shop.

Clearing the window undetected, Cayden stopped at the rear door and placed the squirming bag on the ground. The bag writhed and flopped as the snakes squirmed over each other, seeking an escape from their confinement.

Cayden lifted the lid off the washing barrel, picked up the scoop for dipping and hung it off the side of the barrel rim by the curved handle. He placed the lid back down on the barrel. Loosening the drawstrings, he placed the bag of snakes upside down inside the bowl of the scoop and quickly stepped back behind a container of rough iron ingots and waited.

The door opened and out stepped Ryder. A huge yawn cracked his jaw as he stretched, then he bent down and picked up the lid to the water barrel. With his other hand, he reached over to pick up the water scoop. Noticing the bag resting in the scoop, he pulled it away from the bowl. Ten tiny green wiggling snakes dropped out of the bag. Some fell back into the spoon, the rest spilling over the sides to the ground below. All hissed in warning.

With a yell, Ryder threw the scoop at the wall and fell backward to the ground, doing a swift crab crawl on all fours away from the snakes.

Cayden burst into laughter as he watched his six-foot-two muscular friend scramble away from the tiny snakes, a high-pitched girly scream echoing down the alley. Cayden snorted and gasped for breath as he tried to stop laughing. He felt twinges of his earlier pains from Avery's prank, he was laughing so hard.

"If you could see your face," he wheezed. His cheeks hurt from grinning so hard. His chest hurt from holding in his mirth. "It's priceless!" He barely got the words out between snorts of laughter.

Ryder hesitated for only a moment and then punched him in the stomach. Cayden's eyes bulged and his laughter cut off abruptly as he doubled over, gasping for air in truth this time.

"Good Goddess, Cayden, you scared the life out of me! I should hand-feed you to those snakes bit by bit! What are you trying to do, frighten me to death?"

Still gasping for air, Cayden straightened up and grinned weakly. "Man, you sure can punch hard, Ryder. Remind me to never get on your bad side, eh?"

Ryder grinned back. "Where did you find so many snakes? Why are they out of their dens at this time of year? It's way too early."

Cayden pretended to be searching for escaping snakes, reluctant to meet Ryder's gaze. He couldn't tell Ryder about what happened with his flutes. He decided on a piece of the truth. Reaching into his pocket, Cayden pulled out the flute of carved oak he made earlier in the day. He handed it to Ryder.

"I was sitting on the rocks playing my flute when suddenly I noticed some snakes. Maybe they were disturbed by my playing?" His mouth twitched into a smile. "Maybe I was too loud?"

Ryder inspected the flute. It was about seven inches long, shaped and rounded to fit comfortably in the hand. The holes were saucer shaped and smooth, the right size for Cayden's hands but much too large for his sausage shaped fingers. A small oak tree was carved into the bell-shaped end of the flute. He handed it back to Cayden.

"They were sunning themselves, curled up and still as rocks." *And listening to me*, he thought to himself. He shrugged his shoulders sheepishly. "I know, it sounds weird, eh? Well, I decided I couldn't leave them all there, so I brought you some. I know how much you like snakes."

Ryder grinned. "I loathe snakes." He could not stop himself from checking that all the snakes had slithered away.

"Some dashing knight you will make," said Cayden. "You will throw your horse, before the horse can throw you, the first time you spy a snake out on patrol!" He ducked as his friend made to grab him in a headlock.

Laughing, Cayden nodded his head in the direction of the inn. "Fancy grabbing a pint before we head home? I saw strangers in town earlier. They must be here for the festival."

"OK. Let me wash up first. You don't have any more snakes hiding around here do you?" Ryder's suspicious eyes raked the area around him.

"No, that was it," Cayden chuckled. "Hurry up. I'm thirsty!"

Stripping off his shirt, Ryder quickly dunked his head into the barrel and poured water over his muscular chest and neck. Grabbing a towel, he dried off and then donned his shirt before joining his friend.

***

Avery lifted her long skirts and carefully placed her booted feet on drier patches of ground as she crossed the street. The spring air dampened her dark ringlets and they glistened around her fine features. Stepping up onto the boardwalk, she opened the door and entered the baker's shop, setting a bell to tinkling. The smell of baking bread filled the air. Sniffing appreciatively, she approached the display counter.

"Good morning, young miss!" said the portly owner of the shop. "What can I get for you this fine day?"

"Six of your honeyed sticky buns, Master Hampton, and a loaf of raisin braid bread."

He wrapped the goods in brown paper and handed them over the counter. She tucked the items into her bag. Placing the proper payment in his waiting hand, she thanked the baker and left the shop.

Preparations for the spring festival were well underway. The village square was buzzing with people setting up a large central stage in the round for the traditional resurrection plays. Large striped canvas booths were being erected along the sides of the square for games and challenges. At the far end, a strong man erected a tall pole. Brightly striped in green and red, the strong man's pole contained multiple weights suspended by ropes and run through a series of pulleys on a cross arm. These ropes were guided through and secured to sets of metal eyes that were grasped by the hands of the contestants.

A *silly pastime*, she mused, but one the men of the village seemed to eagerly anticipate almost as much as the archery competition which was set up in the open field behind the blacksmith's building.

She drew the hood of her cloak up around her head and continued on toward the inn.

Her ears registered the sound of horse hooves ringing on the occasional paving stone of the street. She drew back into the entranceway of a building and watched as the procession approached. Men on horseback, clad in dark red metal breastplates and matching helmets, rounded the corner and entered the square.

They were riding three abreast and five rows deep. A man to the right of the central figure carried a flag, red background with a white circle in the middle. A black hand clutching a golden sceptre was centered in the disk.

Behind the riders came several rows of men on foot, all wearing leather vests dyed dark red and sporting matching leather caps. An arrow quiver was visible on each of their backs and unstrung bows were held in their hands. Behind them came a similar group of men, but these carried broad shields and two swords were strapped to each of their backs in crisscrossed scabbards.

Surprised, Avery withdrew even further into the shadows of the doorway. Something smelled wrong about these men. The very air around them brought to mind a festering swamp full of leeches and rotting vegetation. She shuddered and raised a sleeve to cover her nose. She didn't think it was the actual odour of the men, but more a sensation of decay that crept along with them, causing the hair to rise on the skin of her arms. They seemed to be an abomination to her soul, an offense to her very being. Gagging, she slipped into the alley between the buildings to either side. She kept to the shade in order to avoid detection.

The central horseman of the front row was dressed similar to his men; however, he also wore a dark red cape lined with black silk held in place by a silver clasp over his armour. The same symbol as on the flag was embroidered on the left breast of the cape. Steel gauntlets covered his forearms and his lower shins were also encased in armour.

As he strode past, his head swung in her direction. For a brief moment, she felt his eyes rest on her. She sensed open hatred in the gaze. The cold of a murderer stalking his victim assaulted her senses. His gaze roved over the inn and fixed on an object in his line of vision.

Turning her head to follow the direction of his gaze, she saw her brother Cayden about to enter the inn on the other side of the green with his friend Ryder. Cayden glanced up and their eyes met. He grinned, waved to her, and continued on into the inn. A blue glow emanated from his skin. The glow brightened, growing stronger to her eyes as she watched. She first noticed it about six months ago. No one else seemed to be able to see it except for her.

She slipped out the back end of the alley and ran back toward the direction she had entered town. She recognized the flag carried by the bearer to be the Queen's Guard, and there was only one reason for them to be in town. They were there to recruit.

Hiking up her skirts, she ran.

Chapter 5

CAYDEN AND HIS SISTER'S EYES MET, worry shadowing them. He saw a blue glow surrounding her. *Does she know she glows like that?* No one else seemed to notice but he.

He followed Ryder into the inn. As he did so, he saw the riders entering the village square. *Military men, the Queen's Guard for sure,* Cayden thought. He pushed Ryder in ahead of him and entered the inn.

Eyes followed Cayden, he was sure of it. He felt the intense gaze of the man at the head of the column. Cayden glanced back and found himself pinned by the man's hawk-like gaze. A sudden fury rose in him and he glared back in challenge.

The door swung shut behind them, shutting off the noises and view of the street. Cayden tried to shrug off the feeling of foreboding that followed him into the room. Ryder was also looking apprehensively over his shoulder.

"Did you see those guys? They're legionnaires, without a doubt," Cayden said.

Ryder nodded and quickened his pace, heading for the bar at the end of the hall. "They are probably heading here for a meal and a drink. First village they would have seen for days, right? I bet that is all it is." He shrugged, as though not convinced of his own words.

"What will it be, boys?" The sweaty innkeeper, Hans, was mopping his brow on a soiled apron tied to his generous waist.

The inn was busy with the usual dinner crowd and swollen with the addition of merchants and tradesmen recently arrived for the festival. It was the only reputable inn in the village. The only other place to stay was old Molly Bechard's boarding house if you needed to rent a room, complete with bedbugs to keep you company at night.

"Two pints, if you please." Cayden set the coppers on the counter in exchange for the beverages and then picked up the pints and settled into a booth near the rear door of the common room. "Hey, why don't we have a bit of fun with them tonight?"

Ryder paused with his mug of ale halfway to his lips. "What did you have in mind?"

"Well, it would be fun to check out their camp. See what it is like. I have never seen a soldiers' camp before, have you? And they can't all stay here. The inn is too full. I'll bet only the officers stay at the inn and the true soldiers set up camp in Geordie Frenchman's hayfield out on the south end of town. It's the closest cleared ground to the creek. It's a natural spot to set up camp." Cayden took a hefty swig from his pint and set the beaded mug back on the table.

Ryder scratched at his five o'clock shadow, considering. Grinning, he leaned in closer. "Well, what if we made off with a couple of their swords? Or better yet, a couple of their horses?"

Cayden frowned. "That would be stealing."

"No, it wouldn't!" Ryder waved vaguely in the direction of the next town. "They stole it from some farmer further up the road along with all their food supplies and metals for melting down into more swords. The merchants tell stories of what happens when one of these legions come through. They take everything of value. We would be giving them back a taste of their own."

Cayden nodded in agreement. He had heard the stories. But Ryder had lived them.

Ryder burned with hatred and longed for a chance to set right the wrongs being carried out in the name of the queen. He had lost his parents to such a raid when he was five years old and had been sent to this village, Sanctuary-by-the-Sea, to be raised by his aunt. Ryder still remembered the smell of the smoke, the stench of burning flesh and blood spilled, and the cries of his friends as they were burned alive.

The soldiers had descended on the town on an afternoon not dissimilar to this one. The mayor had stepped out to greet the strangers, and before he could do more than say "Greetings, my fine fellows, how may we help you?" the lead soldier had run him through with a sword from horseback. While the mayor lay bleeding to death on the ground, the remaining soldiers spread out through the town, rounding up all the citizens they could locate and herding them to the central square. There, they were held and selectively questioned about their beliefs and if there were any witches or healers in the town. When the townsfolk failed to produce a witch for burning, the soldiers separated out all the young men who appeared to be of military age, between sixteen and twenty-five and took them off down the road. The rest of the people, women, children, and men over the age of twenty-five, they forced into the village inn and barricaded them inside. Then, they had set fire to the building.

He had witnessed it all from the spot where he had hid when the slaughter had begun. Ryder had been running some errands for his father, the smithy, and had been sent down into the basement storage under the floor to fetch a small file for his father when he heard the commotion start. The door to the shop banged open as though someone had shoved it, hard. His father shouted out and began to argue with some heavily booted men and then scuffling erupted, the men crashing into a barrel. It either toppled over or was moved onto the trap door Ryder had gone down. In retrospect, he thought his dad shifted the barrel during the fight in order to hide the entrance from the men who were confronting him. His father was attacked and eventually dragged out into the square, but not before he had taken out two of the soldiers himself with his bare hands. It had taken three men to hold him, even while beating him.

Ryder had watched everything through a ventilation hole carved out of the framing under the porch steps. His father was the first used as an example of the cost of resistance. His throat had been slit in front of Ryder's eyes. Ryder had screamed and screamed, but no one could hear him. Eventually he fell asleep, having screamed himself into exhaustion, curling up on the straw-covered floor in an old work shirt of his father's, burying himself in a cocoon of his father's scent. It was a full day later before the few surviving villagers who had escaped the guards initial search had located him, still curled up in his father's oversized shirt in the storage room under the shop.

Ryder shook his head to dispel the sad memories. He grinned at Cayden. "I would like nothing better than to cause some havoc at

their camp. Drink up and let's get out of here before any of them
come inside."

They downed their beers and left through the back door of the
inn, taking the hallway leading out of the rear of the common room.

Cayden and Ryder headed for the stables at the back of the inn.
They opened the stable door and trotted through the dim interior of
the barn. They exited via the wooden double doors at the rear onto a
paddock which edged a rough lane leading back to the forest road.
They followed the lane until they found the deer trail skirting the
edge of the forest. Walking for about half a mile, they crested a hill
and suddenly they spied the legion's camp.

They ducked into the trees so they wouldn't be spotted and
slipped through the underbrush of silver leaf dogwood, keeping
well-hidden in the leafy ground cover. Dropping to their knees
and eventually their bellies, they crawled to the edge of the forest
and stared.

The camp appeared to set out in squares. Each unit contained a
series of ten tents, which surrounded an area in the middle where
horses were hobbled.

Cook fires were set up every four squares, and men lined up to
receive their evening meals served from a large kettle hung from a
collapsible roasting rack. In the center of the camp was a larger tent,
which was topped with the queen's flag announcing the command
tent. On the forest side of the camp, a row of pits had been dug into
the ground. *The latrines,* Cayden thought from the smell emanating
from the area.

"There must be three hundred or more men in that camp,"
Cayden whispered to Ryder, turning his head. Ryder nodded in
agreement.

"They don't appear much older than us. Do you think they are
all new recruits? I mean, would you settle in all comfy like that if
you had been snatched away from your family recently?"

Ryder growled low in his throat. "I would never settle in. Try to
recruit me and I would fight them with every fibre of my being. I
would never stay." He lowered his eyes. "They would end up killing
me before I ever gave in. They are pigs!" He spat in the dirt in front
of him to emphasize his words.

Cayden nodded his agreement. The very thought of being forced into the legion appalled him.

"I will never serve the queen. I will die first, by the gods, I swear it!" Ryder said his fists clenched so tightly his knuckles whitened under his skin.

"So...where do you think we should strike? I like our chances with the unit over there by the latrines," said Cayden, attempting to lighten the mood. "They are trying to stay as far away from their post as possible probably because of the smell." Cayden sniffed the air and pointed at the bored-looking soldiers stationed to their left at the base of the hill.

Ryder studied the latrines and then his eyes wandered over the hillside, scanning the perimeter of the camp. "Do you see any sentries? Shouldn't there be some patrolling the area here too?"

"No...wait, yes, on the far side, inside the tree line." Cayden pointed across the field to a man who was standing in the shadow of a cottonwood tree, bow in hand and arrow nocked but not drawn. "Can you see any more around?"

"No. Nervous bunch, aren't they?" Ryder said. "Why post sentries in the daylight? Who is going to sneak up on them?"

"People like us, Ryder!" Cayden grinned. Ryder grinned back.

Suddenly, they heard a sound like metal sliding over metal above them, the sound of swords being drawn.

Rolling over, they froze in horror. Cayden sucked in his breath, and Ryder swore under his. Three men stood behind them, swords drawn and pointing at their throats. All three were Queen's Guard scouts.

"I think we found the other scouts, Ryder."

Thunder rumbled overhead.

Chapter 6

ROUGH HANDS GRABBED CAYDEN AND RYDER by their arms and pulled them to their feet. "Well what do we have here? It looks to me like we got us a couple of volunteers." His two companions laughed. "So nice when we don't have to go searching for them. It lets us get back to our gaming that much faster!"

"We are not here to volunteer," Cayden said quickly. "We wanted to see what the camp looked like, that's all." Ryder nodded his head in agreement, keeping his gaze on his boots. He strained to control his temper. Panic bubbled in the pit of his stomach. He felt like a lit firecracker fuse. Ryder tensed against the two men holding him.

"I'm afraid that qualifies as volunteering, lad. Now get moving." Rough hands shoved them in the direction of the camp. That was all it took. At the soldier's touch, Ryder snapped. With a bellow, he swung at the man holding him, his ham-like fist connecting with the man's right ear, knocking the soldier to his knees. Ryder kicked out with his right leg, sweeping the soldier's legs out from under him. He fell into the second scout who was bowled over. The scout's head hit a rock and he didn't move.

Cayden swung around and grappled with the scout holding him, right hand grabbing his thick-whiskered throat and his left hand wrapped around the weapon-wielding wrist forcing his flailing sword above his head. Cayden squeezed with all his might as the scout struggled. The man's eyes bulged. His grip on his sword weakened and it dropped to the ground. Cayden continued to squeeze, until the man's eyes rolled back in his head. Cayden let the man drop. He did not want to kill him; he only wanted to incapacitate him.

Turning, he saw Ryder's original attacker rising to his feet again. Cayden picked up the sword on the ground. He smashed the hilt of the sword down on the head of the strangled scout who was stirring and he crumpled back to the ground.

The last soldier advanced on Cayden, arms outstretched, wary of the blade in Cayden's hand. Cayden shifted his weight from one foot to the other, nervously watching the scout. He had no intention of using the sword. *What possessed me to pick it up?* Cayden wondered as he adjusted his stance, as a malicious grin spread across the face of the scout.

"Drop the sword, little boy," sneered the scout. "You will accidently cut off your own fingers, and then how will you fight? I promise you, if you continue this futile resistance, I will make sure you pay." He looked around at his companions. "In fact, I think you are already in deep trouble. You do know the penalty for attacking a member of the Queen's Guard? No?" His eyes taunted Cayden, noting the trembling in his arms. "Let me inform you. First offense is five years in prison in Cathair. I hear the rats are better fed than the prisoners."

While the scout's attention was focused on Cayden, Ryder scooped up a fallen scout's sword. A bright red flush covered his neck and cheeks, the combination of fear and adrenaline causing a roaring in his ears. His eyes were wild, so wide open that the whites dominated and his nostrils flared as he sucked in huge amounts of air. Yelling, he launched himself at the guard, swinging wildly at him. The blade was heavy in his hand and he tripped over a body as he swung, nearly falling on the blade himself as he tumbled to his knees on the rocky ground. The guard laughed and ignored Ryder.

"Sit down, boy," the scout said to Cayden, "while I dispatch this one. He seems eager to battle. I will deal with you in a moment."

Still on one knee, Ryder watched the scout approach through a mist of anger. Panic seized him and with a bellowing roar, Ryder hoisted the heavy sword with both hands and swung it in an arc curving upward meant for the sword hand of the soldier. However, at the last minute, the soldier turned, and the upward swing of the blade instead found the meaty throat of the guard, slicing the man's jugular. Ryder felt the momentary resistance as the sword caught in the flesh of the man's throat, and then bright red blood sprayed out from the gash, pumped at an alarming rate by a heart that did not know it was doomed. The scout's head flopped to one side and he tumbled to the ground.

Cayden stood stock still, watching as the man's blood pulsed out onto the soil, darkening the stones as it spread out in a pool.

Ryder's shocked eyes looked at the sword in his hand, slick with blood.

Cayden grabbed Ryder by the front of his shirt and pulled him. "Come on! We have to get out of here! Quickly!" he yelled. Turning, he ran back into the woods, as though the hounds of hell were on their trail. Ryder followed in equal haste, the swords in their hands forgotten in their panic to flee the scene of their skirmish.

They ran for roughly a mile, eventually joining up with the stream that had made for an ideal campground for the legion. Keeping to the water-slicked rocks along the edge, they headed up river toward Cayden's farm. Lightning flashed and fresh rumbles of thunder were accompanied by the skies opening up. A heavy downpour followed them, soaking them from above, while the river took care of the rest. They left the stream about two miles past the Tiernan farm, dripping from head to toe and cut across the pastures Cayden knew so well. Cayden led Ryder to the cliffs by the sea and to a cave he had discovered long ago, a secret place known only to him and Avery, and now Ryder.

The cave faced the ocean and was hidden to any who did not appreciate heights. A rocky goat path was the only access and Cayden led Ryder along the outcroppings, showing him the handholds and footholds that were true in the rocky slide. The cave opening was a tall and narrow slit in the cliff face. When they entered, the bats that made this cave their home screeched and swooped around before settling back down to perch upside down from the cave ceiling.

"The bats are great sentries," Cayden said, as he dropped to his knees in the egg-shaped room. The tall slit allowed enough light to see their surroundings in a twilight grey. Ryder collapsed down beside him on the cool rocks, gasping for air, swords clanking as they dropped them. Cayden groaned and rolled onto his back, staring at the roof of the cave. Ryder hung his head; his eyes squeezed shut, body still quivering with nerves and fright. *I killed a man*, Ryder thought to himself, shuddering with the memory.

Cayden reached over, grabbed Ryder's shoulder and shook him. "Are you OK, Ryder?"

Ryder swallowed hard and opened his eyes. "I didn't mean to kill him. I panicked, Cayden, and the sword was in my hands and I swung it. I didn't mean to kill him, only wound him. Good lord, what have I done?"

He squeezed his eyes shut again and his big hands clutched at his head. "I was so scared! I was afraid to be taken," he shuddered. "I was five years old again and trapped in that basement, helpless and terrified. I snapped." His eyes opened again, regret shadowing in their blue depths.

"We can't go back to the village. That much is obvious. They will be searching everywhere for us," said Cayden. "I think they will round up everyone and will try to force them to identify who is missing. Ryder, I am scared of what will happen if the villagers resist."

Ryder straightened up. "Then maybe we should go back to the village? If someone is missing and they cover for us, then the soldiers will burn the town again like before."

Cayden plucked at a hole in his sleeve, thinking. "If we go back, they may find out it was us and capture us. Killing a Queen's Guard is punishable by death. They could kill us instantly or, worse yet, force us into their army. If we return, Ryder, we will be giving them what they want. We can't go back there now. It would be suicide."

Ryder began knocking his head against the rock, groaning. "What can we do? We have to do something. Gods, what a mess!" They lapsed into an uneasy silence, thinking.

Suddenly, Cayden sat up and pulled Ryder up beside him.

"What if we were to volunteer now? No, hear me out," he said holding up his hands as Ryder opened his mouth to protest. "What if we return to the village before they discover the guard's death? Maybe it would throw them off the scent. They can't know it was you, Ryder, who killed that soldier."

"But how would that protect the town?"

"If everyone was accounted for at the beginning, then they might conclude the person they hunted was a soldier in their midst already or it was an outsider to the village who had slipped away. The town might be spared either way."

Ryder idly picked up a stone from the floor as he thought over Cayden's words. "But if they do think the murderer is in the village, why would they let everyone go?"

"Because their mission here is to recruit soldiers, not to avenge a soldier whose death may be the result of one of their own. They would have to look at all the possibilities and, who knows, maybe those scouts have some enemies. Maybe someone owes them some money. The one did mention playing cards; perhaps they cheated someone in a past village, and that person confronted them. They can't know exactly what happened." Even to his ears, the argument sounded weak.

Cayden sat for a moment, plucking at the tear in his shirt sleeve, thinking things over. "Only one of us need volunteer and I think it should be me," he whispered and then shook his head when Ryder protested. "Listen, if I volunteer I can finally see some of the world, you know go on one of those grand adventures we always talked about." He grinned at Ryder, brightening at the thought. "I have always wanted to visit Cathair." He gaze lifted towards the bats in the cave, his mind imagining the trek to capital city. He felt an irresistible draw to the king's city, which now housed the queen. "You know I have always talked of going there. But you, if you get sucked into that legion, you will never realize your dream of becoming a knight. You will never get away. They don't recruit blacksmiths by the queen's decree, so you are in the clear, even if they did discover you killed the guard. But that doesn't mean they won't take one that volunteers, and that service will be for life."

"No, I would be soon dead if I was forced into that legion." Ryder snorted in disgust. "Cayden, there is no king, so how can I be a knight anyways? It was only a childish dream."

"It won't always be this way, Ryder. You will see. Someone will overthrow the queen." Cayden sighed. "So, it is decided. I will volunteer for the legion. With their quota fulfilled, they will leave town. And you, you must go back to the blacksmith shop. You are safe there. You are too valuable a resource for the queen's legions."

Ryder grabbed Cayden's sleeve. "Cayden, don't do this! We will think of another way."

"We don't have the time to sit here and plan, Ryder. With every minute that passes, we endanger the town. It's the only solution I can think of. We have to give them a reason to leave, to look no further. If you can think of another plan, some other way to save the town, I'm listening." Cayden looked hopefully at Ryder, and then as Ryder remained silent, the hope faded and his expression became somber.

Ryder's sad eyes locked onto Cayden's resolved ones. He shook his head. "I never meant for this to happen."

"I know," said Cayden softly. "Slip into the village by the back way and go home. Climb in a window so no one sees you returning. I will grab some clothes and supplies from the farm and make it appear that I was on my way to volunteer."

Cayden got to his feet, brushing off his clothes.

Ryder rose to his feet and took his friend in a long fierce bear hug. Tears sparkled in his baby blue eyes. "You make sure you take care of yourself in there. Learn all you can. It will keep you alive. Try to get away in time. I will find you some day. You can count on it." He grabbed Cayden a second time, crushing him, and then he exited the cave.

Chapter 7

QUEEN ALCINA TURNED THE CORNER of the corridor and walked briskly toward an alcove filled with bright sunlight, the stained-glass windows casting a distorted wave of colour across the tiled floor.

She pushed open a painted oak door that led to a little-used chamber, barely as big as a broom cupboard, used to store old carpets and tufting materials for repairs. She bypassed the clutter and passed through a curved opening in the back wall, which opened into a dark circular room with no windows and no doors.

"Great Mistress?" she whispered, peering around anxiously at the creeping shadows that lurked the corners of her vision.

Suddenly, the room filled with a heavy, oppressive presence. The little light remaining in the room fled and the darkness became complete. Alcina dropped to her knees, trembling as the presence filled the room, shutting out all other sounds.

"Alcina, what do you have to report?"

"Great One, we have picked up a trail that may lead us to whom we seek. We have heard rumours of a presence in the north country by the sea that could be promising."

The shadows trembled. "Rumours do not produce the prophesied heir. I feel that your motivation is not strong enough in this matter. Perhaps a demonstration is in order?"

"No!" gasped Alcina. "No, Great Mistress! I desire to find this usurper to my throne! I will not stand to have our plans...I mean, your plans...derailed at this time! I long to serve beside you...I mean beneath you," she hastily amended at the growl of the Goddess, "for all eternity!"

She panted, trying to slow her racing heart, fear prickling along the nerve endings of her hair, which tried to stand on end in response.

"See that you do not forget who the goddess is here, Alcina. I will grant immortality to those who serve me well. As for those who do not, they will also live forever. But I do not believe that they will find it a pleasant experience." She chuckled and the sound was as if she dragged her fingernails down a chalkboard. The sound shrieked through Alcina's soul, deafening her to all but her own fear.

"I will not fail you, Mistress!"

"See that you do not," the goddess replied as she faded from the room.

***

Cayden eased himself out of the cave and stood facing the sea. He breathed in deeply, eyes closed, tongue tasting the salty tang in the air. He exhaled, seeking calm and courage in the shushing of the waves over the rocks below. He reached out with his senses and found the shadows of those animals now bound to him by his flutes and felt at peace with his decision.

Opening his eyes, Cayden climbed back to the ridge, then examined the forest ahead, as he crossed the clearing. He saw the crown of the ancient oak towering above the rest of its prodigy on the forest floor. He trotted toward the matriarch to retrieve a flute or two to keep him company during his travels, wherever the legion took him.

Reaching the base of the tree, he knelt down and scooped away the leaves and branches hiding the entrance. Reaching inside, he retrieved the brown bag and untied the drawstrings.

He took out the longer, thicker flute, the base of which he had carved with a symbol vaguely reminding him of a paw print. The other one he selected was narrow and thin, delicate like the bones in the wing of a bird. The song of this flute was the cry of an eagle on the hunt.

He left the remaining flutes in the bag and secured it back under the roots, carefully covering the opening with more leaves and sticks.

His feet retraced the familiar, well-worn path home that he had trod most of his life. As he approached the farm's boundary, the sheep in the closed pasture bleated to him in greeting.

He entered the squat cabin, took a leather satchel from a post by the door, and then hurried into his room. He grabbed a coil of string used for snaring and a hook with line used for fishing, shoving both into a pocket of his oiled leather duster. In the other pocket, he put a short-bladed knife and sheath and a piece of flint and striker stone. Into the bottom of his satchel, he put the two flutes he had retrieved and the one he had carved that day, wrapping them with his woolen socks.

Next to go in were two wool sweaters, two lightweight shirts with leather lacings, and a spare pair of pants. A bar of soap and some shaving supplies followed the clothing. He took one last look around, before throwing his duster on over his clothes.

As he turned towards the door, his eyes fell on the blue agate stone his sister had given him. She had sworn she could always find him if he kept it on his person. He had laughed off her claims as childish fantasies, but in light of his own abilities, he decided to take it with him. Besides, it would help remind him of home and why he was choosing to join the legion in the first place. He tucked the stone into a hidden inner pocket of his shirt, close to his heart.

The next stop was the kitchen, where he grabbed some dried beans, dried mutton, a small cooking pot, and a leather waterskin. These were also placed in his satchel.

He snatched up the quill and ink jar, lying on the table, unstoppered the jar, then retrieved a piece of parchment and a quill and quickly scrawled a note. Dipping the tip in the ink, he wrote:

"Father, I know this decision of mine will seem sudden to you, but you have always known of my desire to see the world and especially Cathair and joining the legion seems the perfect opportunity to do so. Know that I choose this of my own free will and do not follow me. Take care of Avery. Give her my love. I will send word when I am able." All of the above was a lie, of course.

Cayden knew his father would see through the ruse, but he was afraid to leave a more personal and incriminating note. He signed his name and placed the note under the kettle sitting on the counter.

Picking up his bow and quiver, he committed this last view of his childhood home to memory.

Closing the door behind him, Cayden left the cabin.

Chapter 8

"What is the price of freedom? What is the cost of war? As the storm crashes against the mountain so shall be the salvation of the world."

— EXCERPT FROM THE *TOME OF SALVATION*

CAYDEN STEPPED ONTO THE DUSTY ROAD at the outer edge of the last farm, leading his horse. An eerie quiet hung over the town as he entered in sharp contrast to the Beltane bustle present a few hours earlier. The reason became evident as he rounded the corner of the building leading to the village square.

The buildings making up the village had been emptied and everyone herded to the village square. A ring of soldiers, swords drawn, surrounded the men, women, and children huddled together with their heads bowed. Cayden spied Ryder in the group, head bent in a submissive posture. Ryder avoided his eyes, although Cayden could feel his gaze.

Cayden stopped walking. His gaze swung to the tall man he had seen earlier on horseback, who was gripping the front of Cayden's father's shirt. Blood trickled from his split lip and he spat to the side.

"I told you. I have not seen my son since noon, my lord," Cayden's father said quietly.

"He is the only person not accounted for in this hellhole of a village. I will know where he is or this town will rue the day he was born. Now tell the truth!"

The two men holding Cayden's father's arms tightened their grip in anticipation of another blow from the lord.

"I am here!" Cayden cried out. He strode toward the small group of soldiers.

At his words, heads swung in his direction, and he felt his father's sorrowful face following his path, full of disappointment. A contingent of soldiers detached themselves and with weapons drawn, surrounded Cayden, as he walked up to his father.

The high lord grabbed Cayden by his coat front. "Where have you been hiding, boy?" he snarled.

"I haven't been hiding anywhere. I was at home gathering some things together to volunteer for the queen's service."

"No one volunteers for the queen's service from these parts," he snarled into Cayden's face. "Volunteer service is for ten years. Conscription is for an additional five years, and a liar's service? That is for life, as we make sure they do not make it through the fifteen years." The soldiers surrounding Cayden barked a laugh, eyeing the skinny frame of the new recruit. "Now tell me again. Why would a farm boy like you volunteer?"

Cayden's father, Gaius, blinked in confusion. Pride shone from his eyes, shadowed with worry.

I'm sorry, Father. Cayden apologized with a mental grimace for the lie, as he opened his mouth to respond. "I have hated the farm my entire life. Who wants to chase sheep for the rest of their days?" Cayden announced loudly. "I have yearned to travel and see the world. What better way than in the Queen's Guard?"

At that moment, a rider from the legion camp galloped into the village, dirt flying beneath his horse's hooves. Hauling his sweaty mount to a halt, he saluted. "My lord! One of the scouts has been murdered, my lord. His throat was cut on patrol. The other two scouts say two men jumped them in the woods and fled after they were confronted."

"They have tracked these men back to their camp?"

"No, my lord. They said they followed their trail to the river where they lost them."

The high lord grimaced and waved the guard away. "Likely they were thieves attempting to rob the camp, scavengers from this sorry, godforsaken backwater." He returned his focus to Cayden and hatred of his duty transferred to the fresh recruit in front of him. "Since you are so eager to join our ranks, you will return with this rider to the recruitment tents. Guardsman, escort our fine new volunteer back to camp."

Saluting, the mounted guardsman prodded Cayden with his booted foot. "Get moving, recruit," he said, pointing in the direction of the camp.

Cayden's father made to grab him, but the lord promptly struck him across the face, knocking him to the ground again.

Cayden's heart lurched. "Please, Father, accept my decision. I will write when I have time." Cayden mounted up and joined the soldiers. He did not look back.

***

Avery watched from the midst of the huddled people in the middle of the square. Mothers clutched their children to their skirts and the men's eyes darted around, anxiously watching the sharp swords surrounding them.

Avery's heart sank as she watched her brother walk up to her father. She could not hear his words, but she saw her father's expression. She knew. It was as she had foreseen.

Her brother glowed with a soft blue aura that never left him. The light pulsed with his feelings. She sensed a riot of emotions although outwardly his face was calm. He was fury mixed with fear, but overriding it all was concern for their father.

The elder lord struck her father again and Cayden's aura pulsed angrily even though his face remained expressionless. *He is hiding his true intentions*, she thought to herself. *Why? And why is he carrying his satchel as though he planned...No! He is planning to join them?*

She stifled a cry as he rode away in front of the mounted guardsman. Cayden picked her out of the crowd and grinned at her. She felt waves of reassurance coming from him.

He has my stone, she realized suddenly.

"Release them!" the lord snapped to the guards who still surrounded the villagers. "They are of no further use to us. Report back to camp."

The men sheathed their swords and swung into saddles. Forming up, they clattered back down the street, following Cayden and the lone guardsman.

The lord addressed Avery's father. The men holding Gaius let go of him and he collapsed to the dirt of the street. With a final kick to the ribs, they left him lying curled in a ball and, laughing, mounted their waiting horses and rode away.

Avery ran over to her father and knelt down beside him, grasping his shoulder and rolling him over onto his back.

"Are you OK? What did they want with Cayden, Father?" Avery said, running her hands over his ribs checking for broken bones.

"They were searching for new conscriptions and Cayden was missing. I tried to hold them off, but then Cayden walks right up to them and volunteers! What in the world was he thinking? He should have hid until they left."

Avery glanced in the direction of the road that had swallowed Cayden's form. "I don't think they would have left, Father. I think they were determined to take away one person from this village. Cayden is up to something. I know it."

Gaius sat up, wincing at the pain in his side. Avery helped him to his feet. Gaius did not understand the connection between the twins, but he knew it was real. He had observed it from their first breaths. His wife used to say it was like they drew the same breath. And yet, they were very different. If Avery said Cayden was up to something, he was.

Turning, she helped him back to the inn and onto a chair by a table inside the door. Ryder Briarman walked in right behind them and paused by their table. His face was stiff, lips compressed into a straight line.

"I need to speak to you both. Not here not where we can be overheard. Join me in the corner booth by the fireplace?"

They nodded, claiming the table in the corner, sliding onto the bench side by side. Ryder strode to the bar and ordered three mugs of ale. Collecting them from the barmaid, he carried them to the booth and placed a mug of beer before each of them. Gaius accepted gratefully, taking a tender sip. He dabbed at his split lip with a handkerchief from his pocket. Ryder slid onto the bench across from them, eyes downcast.

Avery starred impatiently, mug untouched, and waited for Ryder to speak. Reluctantly, he met her eyes.

"You know what is going on with Cayden," she stated. "You know what this is all about. Cayden would never volunteer for the legion. He hates violence and everything to do with it. He is afraid of violence. What's going on, Ryder?"

Ryder opened his mouth and, voice soft, told them what had happened.

Gaius frowned and Avery gasped, flinging hands over her mouth to stifle the sound. Ryder hung his head and his voice quivered when he reached the part where he admitted to killing the guard. Gaius bolted to his feet jostling the table in his haste. Avery pulled him back down with a quick glance around the inn. Thankfully the room was empty as the villagers had gone home with their families.

"It was the only solution we could come up with, at the time." Ryder's shoulders drooped. "I didn't want him to do this, but he insisted. He did not want a repeat of what happened to my village all those years ago."

Ryder hugged his body, his beefy arms bulging with the effort to hold in his pain. His fists clenched, the veins in his arms bulging with tension. *My best friend is gone. When will I ever see him again?*

Avery reached across the table, unfolded the fingers, and took his big rough hand in hers in comfort.

Gaius's face was pale and etched with sad lines. He took a deep breath.

"We know you did not want him to go alone." Frowning, he voiced his thought aloud. "Do you think the other two guards will recognize Cayden?"

Ryder's heart jumped in his chest with fear. He groaned, guilt wriggling in his chest as though the snakes of Cayden's prank resided there. "Oh lords! What will they do to him if they realize he was with me?"

"We will have to trust Cayden to this," Gaius said. "He is a smart lad. He will figure out a way to survive in the legion. One thing is certain. We must play along with his ruse or we will draw attention to the timing of his choice."

Worry etched all their faces as they contemplated the reality of all that had transpired.

"Did they take any other boys?"

Gaius shook his head. "Not from this village. I heard they took two boys from Maiden's Head a week back, but I know of no others."

Gaius stood, drawing Avery up with him. "It's time to get back to the farm, if we are to arrive before the sun sets. Thank you for telling us this." He gripped Ryder's shoulder for a moment and then they were gone.

Ryder watched them both leave the inn. He had never felt so alone in his life. Not since those early days so long ago. Cayden was gone and Ryder had no idea when he would ever see him again. Ryder put his head down on his arms. His great shoulders shook with pent-up grief.

Chapter 9

THE PEOPLE OF THE VILLAGE of Lower Cathair watched from windows and doors as the formation of the Queen's Guard marched past the town in orderly rows, their pikes and halberds stowed on backs bristling like porcupines. Most of the watchers were grey-haired men, backs curving with age, weary-eyed from their toils of the day in the hot spring sun.

The soldiers paid little attention to the villagers as they marched past. This town had been cleared of young men long ago, as its proximity to the castle gate assured men of conscription age had been identified and secured for the throne.

Dust stirred in the wake of the stomping boots and drifted in a cloud behind the thousand or so troops, as they disappeared over the rise of the hill.

Denzik frowned and lowered the pipe from his mouth, watching the retreating backs of the soldiers.

He was a good Kingsman, when such things had been allowed, and he still considered himself such. No kingdom should be ruled by a queen and especially not one acquiring power in the manner of the current one.

He had not reached sixty years of age without having seen a thing or two in his time. Rumours or no, the power of the land was held by the queen, and it seemed might made right…for now at least.

Glancing down, he noticed his pipe had gone cold. He reached inside his pocket, took out his tobacco pouch, and pinched enough to fill his pipe bowl between his forefinger and his thumb. He used his thumb to compact it in place and then leaning over, took a small stick and lit it in the fireplace by his side. He brought the glowing end to the bowl of his pipe and puffed it into flame. Smoke curled up to form a haze around his head.

He opened the front door and stepped out onto his porch. By the central well stood the village baker, Fabian Tavish, and beside him was Nelson McDermid, the owner of The Kings Steed, the village pub and inn. Denzik stepped off his porch and walked over to join the two men.

Fabian was short and as round as the sticky honey buns that had made him famous across the valley. Many rumoured he sampled every batch he made to be assured they were the finest. Denzik mused that it might even be true; however, it was best not to judge the baker by his girth as he had been one of the best captains ever to ride in the King's Cavalry, before their abrupt dismissal.

Nelson was equally as short but skinny and leathery as though the food served at his inn was not fit to eat. That did not stop the locals from flocking to the inn before heading home in the evenings to gossip and share news of the day over a cold pint. Nelson ran his inn with a strict hand. The pub and inn were scrupulously clean, the food served piping hot, and the ale chilled in the stream behind the inn where Nelson had hollowed out an underground cellar and plumbed in water to act as a cooling system. The underground room also served as a cold cellar where he refrigerated his food supplies. It was the envy of the town. Sometimes he even managed to make iced creams, a delicacy reminding Denzik of sweetened butter.

Nelson ran his inn with a military flair, having learned his skills in the army camp kitchens. In the King's Army, he had been the head of supply and his contacts across the realm were secondary only to the king's scouts and better than the king's own spy system.

Denzik frowned at the memory. Had the king's spies not betrayed him, then the king would still live. *But*, he thought to himself, *who spies on the spies?*

Reaching the pair, he raised his hand in greeting. "Enjoying the parade?"

Nelson spat in the dirt at his feet and then realizing what he had done looked around surreptitiously.

"Dirty grovelling worms," he growled. "All dressed up pretty, but not a one knows a damn thing about soldiering. Young whelps. Should still be on their mother's apron strings, I say."

Fabian gazed off in the direction where the soldiers had disappeared. "I doubt they had any choice. Likely they were conscripted into the service, their heads stuffed with stories of the glory of serving the queen in some divine task or another. She'd have patted them on their collective heads and then shooed them away to root out the 'heretics of the realm.'" Fabian snorted his disgust.

Nelson grunted and spat again in the dirt. "They will be dead inside of two weeks with arrows of Primordials stuck in their chests, if they don't starve to death first. Their families will never know what happened to them. Bloody mess the queen is making of things."

Nelson checked to see if anyone was listening then lowered his voice. "The king would never have done such a thing. He was working to unite all peoples, not slaughter them. I suspect that's why he was assassinated. Queen Alcina is my first suspect. Her hands are dirty in this."

"Shush, you old fool!" Denzik hushed. "We do not know who listens in this village. We were told to wait, to watch, and to prepare. You know our mandate. We must go about our lives, knowing someday *he* will come. In the meantime, we must play our roles well. The information we gather daily is vital."

Fabian leaned in and muttered in a barely audible whisper, "When do we meet next?"

"I will let you know before time. It is the safest way to be certain we are not surprised or tracked," murmured Denzik quietly.

"Agreed, I had better get back to the inn," Nelson whispered.

In a louder voice, he announced, "Tabitha is likely overcooking that glorious side of mutton again. Thinks none of us have teeth, she does." Grumbling under his breath, he walked off to the inn.

Fabian twitched into action. "I had better get back to baking. These foot soldiers clean me out every time they pass," he grumbled, "and the set before last didn't even pay me. Told me I was lucky and I could keep the rest of my fingers to keep baking with." He held up his right hand with the missing index finger and waved it in farewell. He subconsciously rubbed at the missing digit's phantom pain as he walked away.

Denzik walked back to his own dwelling. Dusk was falling now, and lights flickered in the windows of the various dwellings as lamps were lit.

Entering his own home, he trimmed the wick on the lantern by the door and, using the same stick he had used to light his pipe, lit the lamp, waving it to extinguish the flaming tip and placed the stick back on the mantle.

Denzik carried the lamp into the small kitchen area of his cabin and pulled out bread, cheese, and some leftover ham from his cold storage. He sliced off two slabs of bread, a hunk of cheese, and a piece of ham. Wrapping them back up, he placed them back in the cold storage.

*Cold storage...*he snorted at the thought. The only way it stayed cold was to either leave the door open to the cabin or to put cold water in a pitcher in the cupboard. He had put a small hole in the back of the cabinet to allow cold air to seep into the chamber and cool the contents, and for three seasons of the year it worked fairly well.

Sitting down in his overstuffed chair, Denzik mechanically ate his dinner, giving no thought to the food. He mulled over the last seventeen years in his mind. All of the men in this village were misfits. The majority were ex-Kingsmen who had been ousted from the castle on threat of death. He remembered it still, the memory slap as sharp as the day it happened.

The coup had been silent, really. They were on their regular assignments within the castle when Cyrus, the Lord General of the Kingsmen, had called them all to attendance in the main yard. He stood on the balcony of the royal apartments and addressed the assembled men.

There, he had announced the king was dead, as were Prince Alexander and his consort, Gwendolyn. No cause of death had been announced, and the future queen, from her self-imposed isolation, had commanded Lord Cyrus to gather all the Kingsmen to hear her decision. The Kingsmen were to be disbanded across the realm. The official version was that as the perpetrator was still at large she feared being surrounded by potential assassins. That so great a tragedy could occur within the castle grounds and without an alarm being raised was a shame on all the Kingsmen and she had refused to place her trust in any of them.

Lord Cyrus's voice had boomed from the wall top, reverberating off the walls across the parade ground. "Effective immediately, I will be taking over command of the newly formed Queen's Guard for the queen-elect. You are hereby ordered to pack the few belongings in your possession and collect your final pay at the gate as you are leaving the castle grounds, which you will do immediately." On the last word, doors on lower level opened out marched an army of new soldiers, all dressed in the queen's colours.

An outraged cry had arisen from the men in the courtyard. The strange men in new Queen's Guard uniforms fanned out and surrounded the Kingsmen. Pikes were lowered and swords drawn. Swords were drawn amongst the Kingsmen too, the blades making a ringing sound of steel on steel as they were drawn from their sheaths.

Lord Cyrus had spoken in a loud voice over the grumbling of the Kingsmen. "You will be escorted in groups of ten to your barracks and then to the gate. This is the only warning you will receive. If you resist in any fashion, the new Guard have been advised to cut you down where you stand. You are to be removed from the castle grounds and released to go wherever you wish. You are never to return to the castle. You may not come within a two-mile radius of Castle Cathair or the village of Upper Cathair. If you do, you will die. This is the royal decree and so it is law."

Turning, he left the balcony and re-entered the royal chambers.

The Kingsmen had found themselves outside the castle gates within two hours. A contingent of Queen's Guards ten deep and the width of the main avenue to the gates had formed up as the last Kingsman exited under escort. The gates swung shut behind them and were sealed.

The men headed up the road, two hundred of them in total. Most carried on up the road and settled in villages along the way and were absorbed into the bigger towns away from the capital.

About twenty of them, Denzik, Fabian, and Nelson in the group, settled in the first hamlet outside the radius, a fly-speck village called Lower Cathair. They virtually doubled the size of the town that night, but the choice of location was not random. As longstanding members of the Kingsmen, they had explored every nook and cranny of Castle Cathair during those twenty-five-odd years of service. They had gone places no one knew existed.

One thing was always consistent about being a Kingsman. On those long cold winter's nights guarding the outer walls, there was nothing more welcome than a nice shot of brandy in your flask. *Of course,* Denzik thought, *only those foolish enough to volunteer for that duty had any right to know the secret.* He smiled to himself in memory.

The small room Denzik had discovered when he was twenty-seven had actually been shown to him on his promotion to captain of the guard by the former captain, Jonathan O'Reilly. He, in turn, had learned it of it from another retiring Kingsman. He warned young Denzik to not reveal the presence of the sealed room to anyone else. It was a sacred trust, and it had to be kept a close secret.

The hidden room was in a false wall off the exercise courtyard for the prisoner cells. Denzik suspected it was originally used to hide high-profile prisoners or political enemies of the crown. During his years in the castle, it had never been used by the royal family, and he believed they had forgotten about it. The only memory of this room remained with the captain of the Kingsman guards, who retained this knowledge as a trusted servant keeps their masters secrets. This secret had been passed down from captain to captain, since there the beginning of the Kingsmen.

Of course, during his time in the Kingsman guard, they had used this room to hide the barrels of brandy they smuggled into the castle for the men of the wall. It had a secret door cleverly concealed in the stone wall at the rear, which led to a tunnel system under the castle.

Denzik had never had an opportunity to fully explore all the tunnels, although he suspected they were extensive. Likely the system had been designed as an escape route for the royal family should the castle ever fall under siege or if the walls be breached. The royal family had to have been aware of some of the tunnels. He did not believe the queen or her counsellors knew of the ones he had used, however. The tunnels they had used had led to the inner city, outside the castle proper but still inside the city walls.

Fabian had suggested the plan as they were marching away from the castle that fateful evening seventeen years ago. They had started planning the very next day, after scabbing together some temporary lodgings. Over the next few months, they purchased a collection of abandoned buildings and lands from the absentee land owners with the dismal balance of their dismissal pay, buildings strategically located. They wasted no time launching the tunnelling underground, aiming to connect with the smuggling tunnel, and it had been their life's work ever since. If they found the tunnels he had used to store those barrels in, all those years ago, it would give them secret access to the castle…and to the queen. The entrance was within the two-mile boundary set by the queen. It was pretty much under her bedroom window.

They were close now.

Finishing his meal, he brought his empty plate to his small kitchen. Sitting back down, he put his feet up and pulled a book entitled *A History of the Royal Family of Cathair* from the table beside him, opening it to his bookmarked spot.

The real work of this day would begin in another couple hours when the main residents of this hamlet were safely tucked into their beds, oblivious to the work being performed under the inn by the river. Denzik settled down to read.

Chapter 10

ZIONA TIED THE LEATHER THONGS of her pack closed. Hefting it onto her shoulder, she took one last look around the cave. All evidence of anyone having camped in the hollow had been eliminated. The fire ashes had been swept up and buried outside.

Sharisha's horse stamped its hoof. Sharisha, already mounted, headed off into the trees, selecting a deer trail leading in the direction of the village. Ziona secured her pack to the back of the saddle and then clambered aboard her roan mare and followed.

As they drew parallel to the farm, Sharisha guided her grey gelding to a path emptying out beside the main gate to the farm. Ziona felt urgency about their task, like an itch behind her shoulder blade she could not scratch. Something felt wrong this morning, as though her quarry were dissolving like a mist before the morning sun. She followed Sharisha, yet her instincts told her she would not find the boy when they arrived.

A shaft of sunlight pierced the yard as they rode through the gates. A man, hearing the chickens clucking in the yard, came out of the house, a walking stave in hand. There was no hesitancy in his step; the stick was obviously not a cane.

Eyeing the two women, he stepped off the porch and approached them.

"Good morning, ladies! What brings you to my place so early this morning?"

Sharisha spoke first. "We have come to speak to your children, kind sir."

"And what business could two strangers possibly have with my children?"

"We believe they are two people we have been seeking for a very long time. You see, we are Primordial kind." Sharisha tucked back the braided coils on her head to reveal the tips of her ears.

Gaius stared at her for a moment. There was no surprise in his expression. With a resigned shrug to his shoulders, he motioned for them to dismount. He took the reins from each mount and tied them to the hitching post at the side of the house.

"This is not a conversation to have out in the open." He gestured toward the stairs to the house. He left the front door open in invitation to enter as he passed through the doorway.

The interior of the cabin was cozy and comfortable. Several overstuffed chairs were set to take advantage of the light coming in from the windows on either side of the rectangular room for reading. They flanked a broad fireplace serving as the main cooking arena, a braided rug warming the floor.

Gaius waved them toward the fireplace. "Tea?"

Nodding their acceptance, Sharisha and Ziona settled into the chairs.

"Avery!" he called. "Would you come here please? We have company."

Avery entered the room a few minutes later, her eyes settling immediately on their guests. They widened as she took in their fair features.

"Please make some tea for our guests. Now, ladies, if you would be so kind as to advise us as to why you are here?"

Avery filled a kettle with water at the small sink in the kitchen, pumping the pump handle to draw the water. She hung the kettle on the cast iron hook suspended above the hot coals left from their morning breakfast in the open-hearth fireplace.

"We are here because of an ancient sacred text of our people called *The Divination of the Divine*. Our Elder Scrolls speak of the birth of two individuals who will have the ability to intercede in the events of the future, who will be the key to preventing the destruction of this world," Sharisha explained. "We do not understand how or why they are important, but certain key events have been foreshadowed and have brought us to this time and place."

Avery hung on every word. Pulling the tin of loose tea from the shelf above the fireplace, she opened it and filled the tea ball with fragrant crushed herbs. She then gathered four mugs and poured tea, passing a steaming cup to each of their guests and then one to her father. Avery settled back on the rough carpet, sitting cross-legged, cradling the warm cup in her hands.

"Where is your son?" Ziona glanced around the room once more.

"He is gone."

"Gone? What do you mean, he's gone?" Ziona said sharply.

"He volunteered for the legion last night."

"What?" Ziona shot to her feet, tea sloshing over the sides of her cup.

"He had no choice. The legion had dragged the entire town out of their homes and shops and was systematically sorting through the assembled people for young men of recruitment age. Although I must say, Cayden came to town prepared. He intended to volunteer."

"Why would he volunteer for such service?"

"I believe he was in some kind of trouble." Gaius was intentionally vague. He was unsure how much of Ryder's confession he should share with these strangers. "You have still not explained why you are interested in my children," he said, his eyes now sharp on their faces.

Instead of answering his question, Sharisha turned to Avery and commanded, "Look at me, child." Avery obeyed, startled by the request. "What is the first memory you can remember? No matter how vague, how shadowed it may seem. What is the first thought you can remember since your birth? Relax your mind and think."

Avery frowned and thought. What was her earliest thought? What was her first memory? She closed her eyes and relaxed her mind. The familiar sensation of being able to smell the mood of things around her filled her. She smelled anxiety on her father and excitement and curiosity from the two Primordial ladies in front of her.

Avery relaxed her mind even further, her breathing slowing, her senses expanding. Lighter than a breeze, softer than a feather, she floated out the door and into the meadow beside the barn. She sensed the industriousness of the ants crawling over the decaying apples fallen from the tree and the serious concentration of the spider spinning a new ground web in the tall grasses near the ant hole.

"Concentrate, child," Sharisha whispered, "and think back to the beginning."

Avery let her mind wander down the familiar path of her childhood memories, moving backward in her mind. Her earliest memory...she sorted sensations and emotions overlaid with thoughts and conversations...and suddenly she had it.

"I remember a storm-filled night," she murmured. "I remember flying. I remember a candle in a window. I remember holding my brother's hand. I remember joy and pain...but joy and pain twice." Avery's eyes shot open. Shock rippled through her and she grabbed her father's hands. "I remember us being born, but I remember it twice! How is that possible?"

Sharisha and Ziona stared at each other, surprise written on their faces also.

Gaius walked over to the fireplace and leaned an arm on the mantle, staring into the amber coals, lost in thought. "Let me tell you the story of their birth," he said in a voice barely above a whisper.

***

Thunder rumbled high above the sheer rocky cliffs of the cove. Lightning flashed in the leaden skies above and the waves of the sea below churned in concert, sending plumes of water into the air then splashing back to the stormy sea.

A tiny light flickered in the window of a small wooden cabin facing the sea, the window open to tempt a cooling breeze. The candle sputtered but then settled back to burning clear and bright.

Gaius swiped a nervous hand across his sweaty brow and glanced out the window. Lightning flashed again and a sonorous boom sounded.

At exactly the same moment, seemingly in concert, his wife Melle screamed in the next room and low murmurs reached his ears, soothing sounds of the woman assisting her. He heard his wife's agonizing wail once more and then...the sound of a baby crying.

He ran to the bedroom and opened up the door. Inside he saw not one, but two babies, lying at the foot of the bed. The last one was being gently wiped down by the midwife and wrapped in a clean blanket. She picked up the two babes, placed them in his wife's arms and stepped back.

He walked quietly over to his wife's side. Two bright-eyed children stared back at him. He saw intelligence sparkling in their eyes, and something more, something he couldn't define.

Gaius gazed down into his wife's beaming face. Her hair was in sweat-soaked tangles and her eyes were tired but gleaming with pride. "Two babes, Gaius, a boy and a girl, and both as healthy as can be!"

As he gazed down at his children, lightning flashed again.

With their faces highlighted in the sudden glare, he noticed a birthmark in the shape of an oak leaf on each of their right cheeks. The lightning faded and with it the birthmark. He bent to take a closer look. There was nothing to see.

***

Gaius sat with elbows on knees, hands clasped, and head bowed. Silence followed his words.

Avery remembered it as clearly as if it had just happened. But she also remembered more. There had been another woman and man, another room, a room of stone. Her senses told her that woman was also her mother. She shook her head in confusion. How could it be? Yet she knew it for the truth...she *felt* the truth of it.

Sharisha and Ziona exchanged glances. They did not understand it either, but one thing was evident. Gaius had spoken of a birthmark which had faded away after a glance. Could this be another of the signs they sought?

There could be no doubt these two children were the ones they had travelled to locate.

And now one was being carried away into the mouth of the beast.

Ziona stood up abruptly. "I must go," she stated. "The legion already has too great of a lead on me."

Sharisha stood also. "How do you plan to approach him?"

"I will attach myself to their travelling supply train. It is the simplest answer. I shall present myself as a merchant seamstress who can sew uniforms for the new recruits. It should allow me access to most of the camp. I will be able to follow them the entire time."

Sharisha nodded her acceptance of the plan.

Ziona stood and bowed to Gaius and Avery. Avery blushed in surprise. "Until we meet again, Mistress Avery. Sir. " Ziona left the cabin, closing the door quietly behind her.

Sharisha directed her words at Avery. "You must come with me back to my homeland. Only there can I protect you."

"Protect me from what? What is it we are supposed to be in danger from? I don't understand any of this. Who are you anyways? And what is she"—Avery pointed at the recently closed door—"going to do with Cayden?" Avery took the seat vacated by Ziona and waited, arms folded across her chest defiantly.

Gaius looked up from the contemplation of his hands. He appeared years older suddenly.

"There were always little things with them both, right from the beginning. Avery, on her second birthday toddled over to her mother's side where she was hanging laundry on the line, jabbering away that Cayden was about to get hurt. She saw Cayden playing with a rattlesnake which had crawled out from under the rock pile to sun. The odd thing was, it seemed as if the rattler and Cayden were having a conversation. There was no aggressive behaviour in the snake. She shooed it away and it left. Cayden later said the snake was watching over them. He babbled on about his guardian snake for days afterward. We thought it was childish talk at the time..." His voice faded off in thought.

"And then there was the time Avery warned me of the thieves who intended to rob us as we came back from town one evening. A couple of bandits, a man and a woman dressed as common folk, were at the side of the road, pretending to fix the wheel of their wagon. The wagon was blocking a good section of the road, enough to cause us to stop or go around. Avery was about four and she was sitting in front of me in the saddle. She said to me very clearly, 'Papa, those people want to hurt us. Their wagon is not broken.' I watched the pair as they waved at us to assist them. It was then that I spied the third person, hiding under the canvas in the wagon with bow drawn and arrow knocked. I heeled my mare and we leapt into the woods at the side of the road. The arrow lodged itself into the tree beside my head as we gained the cover of the woods. How she knew, I never figured out, but she was right and she saved both of our lives that day. The thieves were gone by the time I was able to return with help."

Avery remembered the incident too. "There were four people, Papa. Another man was hidden on the other side of the wagon. They were slavers. They were after children to kidnap and sell. At least that was what I felt from them."

Both Gaius and Sharisha stared at her.

Avery gazed back at them and shrugged, plucking at a pull in her sweater.

Gaius rose abruptly, decision made, placing his cup on the table beside the chair.

"I need to make arrangements for the farm." Gaius rose from his chair. "We will leave in the morning."

Sharisha nodded in acceptance.

Avery stared at him, dumbfounded.

Gaius picked up his hat from the peg by the door and left the cabin.

Chapter 11

CAYDEN RODE BEHIND THE SCOUT. The riders formed up and followed them out of town, soon overtaking them, kicking up a cloud of dust as they passed. Cayden coughed and covered his nose with his sleeve until the dust settled. The scout ahead of him was keeping his mount to a brisk walk.

Cayden longed to enter the dense trees. It would be so easy to slip away into them and forget about this hair-brained scheme, but he knew others would suffer if he did so. So he kept his eyes on the horse in front of him and followed placidly.

They crested the hill and the camp spread out like lava on the slopes of the valley below. There were a few merchant wagons set up along the roadside, their canvas sides rolled up to display their merchandise for sale. They cried out in loud voices at the mounted men riding toward the camp, hawking wares from needles and tobacco to knives, flint, and candy. The riders did not slow until they had entered the perimeter of the camp.

Cayden slowed his mount in order to take in the goods on display. There was little that would be useful to a soldier on the march. A broad rim hat of dyed calf's leather in a dark green shade caught his eye. It would be very useful for keeping the sun out of his eyes. Perhaps, when he earned some pay in the service of the queen, he would return to buy it.

"Magnus, I have a new recruit for you," called the scout to a beefy man standing inside the main entrance of the boundary containing the camp. Magnus walked over to where Cayden had dismounted. He walked around Cayden, sizing him up. He paused in front of him, turned his head and spat at the ground. A stream of foul brown liquid jetted from his mouth. He rolled the chew of tobacco over to the other side of his mouth, tucking it in his cheek and then leered at Cayden, showing yellowed teeth.

"Scrawny thing, but we will soon toughen him up. Ranolph!" he bellowed to another man standing over his shoulder. "Get over here and take the new recruit to the supply tent. Find him a uniform to wear that doesn't fall down around his knees. Bunk him in with the recruits from the last village."

"Aye, sir!" said Ranolph with a quick salute. "Follow me."

Cayden followed Ranolph to the eastern side of the camp, wending his way between tent pegs and cooking fires. The men in the camp seemed a well fed but surly lot. There was no laughter, no music, and no camaraderie. The men sharpened their swords, polished boots, or tended their cook fires but all with an air of workers sharing the same drudgery. Boredom seeped from every pore. Suspicious eyes followed Cayden's journey through the camp. The men sported various injuries and somehow Cayden did not think they were all a result of battle. Many a man was wrapped in bandages, while others used roughly carved crutches to hobble about the camp. *If these are not battle wounds, they can only be training or brawl related,* Cayden thought. He shivered. He thought all it would take was one spark and the camp would erupt like a firework dropped in a campfire.

Cayden was relieved when they reached the supply tent without incident. Drawing the flap aside, he entered the dim interior. A man was seated behind a makeshift desk, making notations in what appeared to be a supply catalog.

He squinted at the newcomers through spectacles perched on the end of his nose. The reading glasses slipped a little as he harrumphed, "New recruit?" He eyed Cayden up and down and then rose and walked over to a trunk. Opening the lid, he pulled out a tan shirt, a pair of dark brown pants, and a belt. He closed the lid of the trunk and then opened an identical one sitting beside it. He pulled out a brown cap and a leather jerkin from its depths. He glanced at Cayden's feet and then reached into the portable cupboard behind him and produced a worn pair of work leather boots. He handed the bundle of clothing to Cayden and jotted the transaction into his ledger, dismissing them with a vague nod of the head.

Cayden followed Ranolph out of the supply tent and then a short distance away to a long horse picket. Ranolph indicated that he tie his horse to the end of the line.

They then approached a low tent off to one side, much larger than the ones surrounding it. Ducking inside this tent, Cayden saw two rows of sleeping mats laid out, ten in total. Each mat had a blanket. All the mats were currently occupied with the exception of one right at the entrance flap, the coldest and noisiest spot in the tent.

"This is where you will sleep. Roll call is at six o'clock every morning. Change into your uniform and come outside. I will take you to your new mates."

He changed quickly and then followed Ranolph out into the camp again. They passed the latrines he had spotted from their earlier spy trip and ended up at the edge of the camp where a practice battle range had been set up.

At the far end of the field they entered the practice range. A group of men about Cayden's age shot arrows at straw targets. Closer in, men worked with practice swords under the careful eye of a trainer. Closer still, Cayden picked out men working with pikes and halberds, dodging the wrapped blades.

Ranolph handed Cayden over to the training sergeant, a balding man with arms and legs like an elephant. His shirt strained across his chest. "Well, well, boys! Look here. We got ourselves a rabbit."

The others stopped their practice and sauntered over, raw aggression evident in their stiff gait.

The sergeant bared his teeth in a predatory smile. "Rabbits run, boy. I suggest you get going."

With a holler the entire practice yard raised weapons and ran at Cayden. Cayden yelped and grabbed a wooden staff from a nearby barrel. He fled out of the yard, only to find his path blocked by more soldiers.

Cayden shot off to the right, toward the practice dummies, the men behind him yelling and catcalling, waving their various weapons at him. He ducked behind a practice dummy, which shuddered as a sword was thrust through it, the tip of the blunt wooden blade stopping a bare inch from Cayden's belly.

He leapt back in shock, but not in time to avoid a blow from a wooden practice mace to his head. His ears rang and the world spun. Staggering away, he launched himself into motion again, this time running toward some wooden boxes arranged in another corner of the yard.

Reaching the boxes, he jumped on top of them and brought his staff around in front of him. With a wild swing, he pushed the five men in front of him back. Two more closed in from the right side, one with a wicked looking blunt steel-tipped spear. The man jabbed the spear at Cayden, catching him on his thigh and ripping a gash in his pant leg, quickly soaking it in blood.

Cayden yelped and swung the staff clumsily once again. A man on his right stabbed at him with a short sword, catching him on the left knee. Cayden hopped back in pain and failed to see the man right in front of him who lifted his own staff and jabbed Cayden in the stomach. Cayden doubled over in pain, gasping for air. A fourth man stepped up to him and with the blunt end of his sword, struck Cayden on the head. Everything went black and Cayden toppled from the crates to land face down in the dirt.

Cayden came to, eyes creeping open to see a pair of polished black boots in front of his nose. He groaned, the light making his head pound. He pushed himself to a sitting position. Sergeant Perez stood in front of him, his icy smile freezing him in place. Cayden reached back and found a large lump on the back of his head. The sergeant sniggered.

"Every morning you will report to this yard. You will be taught defensive skills during the course of the day. Every evening at quitting time, you will become the rabbit. You must not only survive in this arena for ten minutes. You must also take out a minimum of two of your opponents. If you fail, you will repeat the process the next day...and the next day until you learn to defend yourself. Only then will you be taught offensive skills."

Cayden counted the other men. They stood smirking. There was no compassion on any of their faces. He knew he would receive no mercy from this group.

"The day is done. Dismissed!"

The assembled men stored their weapons and walked away.

Cayden got woozily to his feet. His knee was bleeding and blood trickled down into his boot. He limped after the men. He needed to be stitched if there was any kind of healer in the camp.

Ranolph met him as he came out and with a curt nod indicated that Cayden was to follow him again. Cayden limped behind him to a large central tent with a flag hanging limply from a pole by the entrance. The flag fluttered and Cayden caught a glimpse of various leaf shapes imprinted on the flag. This was the healer's tent. He gestured for Cayden to enter the tent. "I will leave you here."

Cayden opened the flap and entered. A middle-aged woman was standing at a scrubbed table, mashing the contents of a stone bowl with a pestle. She added a little water and continued mashing. "Have a seat in that chair by the lamp."

Cayden did as instructed, groaning softly as he eased himself into the chair.

Grumbling to herself, she added a few more drops of water and then turned to face Cayden.

"Always the same time every day, always the same ones." She stopped in surprise. "You're new. When did you arrive?"

"About an hour ago," Cayden said. "About an hour too soon I think."

She laughed, kind eyes twinkling. A slow smile twitched on Cayden's face.

"I'm quite the mess." Cayden sheepishly gestured to his thigh and knee.

She walked over to him, setting the bowl down on the small table holding the lamp. She knelt beside him and inspected his wounds. She stood up and drew his shirt off over his head, examining the bruise on his stomach and probing with tender hands. She then examined his head, Cayden wincing at the slight pressure she applied while searching the wound. She pulled open one eye and then the other.

"My name is Laurista. It appears you will survive, although I would recommend you strive to not take any more beatings like this. The head is a very fragile thing and a man can die from too much head trauma."

Cayden shook his head ruefully, causing the world to spin. "My name is Cayden. And it was not my idea. They tossed me in there with no warning."

"Yes, that is how it is done, and I get stuck with trying to patch everyone back together. It's brutal, yet oddly effective, I think, when it comes to skills training. I am not much of a fan of the attitudes spawned by it, however. You need to watch yourself in this camp. None will call you friend."

"Why would they have a grudge against me? I just arrived," he growled defensively.

"They view all from this area as outsiders. Your villages are so far removed from the capital and your people from the main fighting for so long, that they see you as cowards, cheats who have somehow ducked their duty to the queen. They think it is their right to teach you a lesson. They think you believe yourselves to be better than them, above them. They hope to prove otherwise, I am afraid. You can expect no mercy."

Laurista reached down and scooped up some of the poultice she had been mixing. She gently spread the greenish mixture on both cuts and then applied a wrapping around each location. The mixture stung as it entered the wound and then faded, taking the pain with it. Cayden was caught by surprise. "Hey, that works really well!" He gingerly moved his limbs. "Thank you."

Laurista's lips ghosted a smile at him. She reached into a travel cupboard set on the table, withdrawing a bottle of purple liquid. She added a few drops of the liquid with some water and returned to him.

"Drink this. It will help with the dizziness."

Cayden drank the liquid, which tasted like berries. His vision steadied.

"I'm finished with you. You should go get something to eat and rest. It is a narrow window when they serve meals." She collected up her bowl and vial and set them back down on the table.

"Thank you again. I really appreciate it and the advice. I will take it to heart and head." He grimaced. "Until next time?" Grinning, he stood and waved a friendly goodbye and sauntered out the tent.

Laurista watched him go, a tiny frown creasing her forehead. There was something different about that boy, something very different indeed.

Chapter 12

AVERY FOLLOWED HER FATHER and the Primordial woman through the twisting path created by the stream bed. Their horses gingerly picked their way amongst the loose stones at the side of the stream.

Reaching a fainter path created by some animal, they ascended into to the wooded mountainside, the foothills of the Highland Needle range. Far above, Avery saw a cleft in the rocks, a natural divide backlit from the far side by a sun that had not yet reached the zenith of the mountain.

The animal trail meandered back and forth on the climb, finding the best purchase for an animal with hooves. The morning dew clung to the branches and leaves of the underbrush and soon soaked through their clothing. Avery drew her cloak tighter as she shivered.

They had been travelling for several days now, always during the early morning hours when the dew was fresh. Sharisha had said little more about their purpose in going to the Primordial lands and Avery's father had been equally withdrawn and tight-lipped, as though he didn't want to know what would be revealed there.

Avery sensed the worry and anger he held tightly. Ever since her mother died when she and Cayden were little, their father had protected them with an almost religious fervour, allowing nothing to come too near them, human or animal.

The day her mother had died, she had gone alone to collect blueberries from the scrubby plants that loved to nestle amongst the rocky hillsides. She did not return. The next day, her father had found the body. Her mother had been attacked, torn to shreds by some animal or animals they had never seen or been able to find, although her father and some of the other villagers had attempted to hunt it down. Avery had been five years old.

From that point on, he refused to speak of it to them, but her father had changed that day. Something other than her mother's death had scared him; Avery sensed it. She shook her head. Why was she revisiting that memory this morning of all mornings? Perhaps it was the rocky terrain recalling the time to her. Suddenly she realized her father was thinking these thoughts also and as she dwelled on that idea, his thoughts nearly congealed into a solid form right in front of her.

"Papa, are you thinking about the day Mother died?"

Her father gave a surprised start in his saddle, his head whipping around.

"How did you know that?" he challenged.

Sharisha's dark eyes settled on Avery's green ones.

"I...don't know...," Avery puzzled. "I saw a mental image of what you were thinking."

Sharisha watched the exchange, her cool gaze hinting at hidden knowledge. She twisted back around in her saddle. "Come. The pass is just ahead. We can easily reach it by noon. We will break for food there."

***

Cayden unconsciously shoved his blankets off to his knees. He rolled onto his side and settled back to an uneasy sleep filled with dreams. Thunder rolled, lightning flashed.

An eagle soared in the midst of the storm, carrying a blanket woven of curly goat hair in its beak. The eagle dived through the tempest, alighting on the stone sill of a window set in a cottage wall. The ghostly bird hopped down into the room and onto the shadowed arm of the tall thin man who greeted the eagle like an old friend. He carried the shadow eagle over to where a woman in the throes of giving birth writhed in a bed, clearly in pain. The bird lowered the shimmering blanket to the floor.

The shadowed old man murmured a spell that enveloped the body of the woman. A midwife knelt at the foot of the bed, giving no indication she saw the man or the eagle.

She eased the children from the woman's body and one by one, placed them on a soft blanket folded multiple times and placed on the floor in front of the eagle she could not see. The midwife dipped a cloth into the bucket of warm water and began to bathe the twins. She wrapped the infants in soft blankets and then left them while she ministered to the mother.

Cocking its head to one side, the eagle gazed at the children.

The wisp of a man then began to utter a rhythmic prayer, pulling a vial of liquid from his robes. He dipped his finger in the vial and traced the outline of a leaf on the cheek of each child with a stroke of his finger. The outline flared blue and faded, as the chant continued.

The eagle screeched and hopped closer to the children. It swayed to the rhythm of the chant, bobbling its head and flapping its wings.

Suddenly, the man clapped his hands and the thunder crashed, shaking the cottage, its sound echoing off the polished logs. Blue lightning flickered into the room and touched each of the inhabitants, including the eagle, bathing the room in an effervescent glow.

When the lighting faded, the eagle flew back to the window, blanket in its beak and hurled itself into the storm. Lightning flashed once again, striking the eagle. The blanket vanished. The eagle plummeted into the waves below.

Cayden rolled over once more. His breathing steadied as the storm overhead departed. He did not remember the dream in the morning.

Chapter 13

CAYDEN WOKE TO THE SOUND of movement in the tent. The other men were already dressed, stuffing their belongings into packs and rolling up their sleeping pallets and blankets. Cayden scrambled up and dressed quickly.

"Are we breaking camp?" he spoke aloud to no one in particular.

"No, we are going on a picnic," a pockmarked face sneered. *Powell is his name,* Cayden thought. Laughter filled the tent.

The flap opened and in stomped Sergeant Perez. The men in the tent snapped to attention. Cayden went rigid.

"You have two minutes to report to the central practice grounds. Last man to report in will be taking the place of one of the pack mules that has come up lame." Sneering at Cayden, who was standing with one sock on and the other still in hand, he left the tent.

The tent emptied faster than a stirred hornet's nest. Cayden tugged on his boots. Gathering up his gear, he left the tent for the horse lines. There, he found his mare mixed in with the army's horses. As he went to fetch his saddle and gear from the storage tent, a soldier stepped up to him.

"You cannot take that horse, son. It is now the property of the legion. Don't you have a squad you have been assigned to?"

"Yes, sir."

"Then I suggest you form up with them."

Frowning, Cayden trotted back to the practice grounds. He was the last one to arrive, much to the glee of his bunk mates and the sergeant.

"Will you look at this? The rabbit has volunteered to replace the mule," scoffed Perez. "Get over here so we can get you harnessed."

Cayden walked toward the wood-sided wagon piled high with gear. Attached to the front yoke, where normally a pair of mules would have stood, was a freckle-faced lad Cayden's age. He was one of the men sharing Cayden's tent. He stared at his feet, face red as his hair.

Perez grabbed Cayden's arm and shoved him in beside the other young man. Rough leather straps were wound around his shoulders and across his chest and buckled behind him. Attached to either side of the harness was a set of reins which were looped around a piece of wood on the front of the wagon.

Sergeant Perez bellowed for the men to form marching units. He clambered up the side, rocking the wagon with his weight then settled onto the rough seat. One beefy hand took up the reins and the second picked up the horsewhip.

With an exaggerated flick of the reins, he shouted a command to leave. The whip whistled through the air and snapped the tip of Cayden's ear. Cayden cried out, clasping a hand over the reddening curve, protecting it from further harm. Cayden swore loudly and pulled on the straps. The other lad did the same as they strained to get the wagon into motion. The whip flicked out again and this time the lad beside Cayden yelped and jumped. The whip had caught him on the side of the forehead, leaving a swelling welt.

Cayden's anger flamed and his face reddened. The rest of the camp was in various stages of preparation to leave. It appeared they were the first group to actually do so.

As they strained to start the wagon rolling, random soldiers lifted bowls of steaming food to them in a mock salute. Cayden's stomach rumbled loudly. Others laughed and pointed. Perez smirked and flicked the whip again. Cayden's shoulder stung. Cayden kept his gaze fixed ahead on the path straining against the straps to climb out of the meadow and into the trees. Sweat broke out on his brow and his blood thundered in his ears. He felt a surge rise up his neck and into his face but not from exertion. Fury hummed along his veins, adrenaline pumping.

"My name is Cayden. What's yours?" he said to the lanky lad yoked beside him, trying to distract himself from his anger.

"Darius," the lad answered hoarsely.

"How did you end up here beside me?"

"I didn't get the sergeant's boots polished in time."

"You polish his boots? Why in the world would you do that?"

"Well, because otherwise I will end up as the rabbit." A brief grin flashed across his face.

"Oh," said Cayden, nonplussed. "I guess that's a good reason. It is my honoured position right now, at least until someone new comes to camp."

"I doubt it will make a difference even then." Darius glanced back over at Cayden, adjusting his grip on the leather straps on his chest for better leverage. Cayden thought he saw pity in his grey eyes.

Frowning, Cayden gazed sightlessly down the road they travelled.

"Why should I be singled out? I just got to camp. I haven't even had a chance to prove myself."

"It doesn't matter what you do, Cayden. You are from the cliffs. You are automatically classed as an outsider. You will never be allowed to advance. You will never be given rank. You will be pushed and punished until you break." Darius shrugged uncomfortably at his own words.

"Then why accept my offer to serve? That makes no sense."

"No one from your area ever volunteers for service in the legion." Darius tilted his head at Cayden quizzically. "Why did you? There is no way it's because you love the legion. No one would believe it even if you swore on the queen's crown."

"No, it was not for love of the queen." Cayden thought quickly. "I want to see the world outside of the cliffs because, as you said, no one ever comes away from the cliffs to see the world. I thought this would be a good way to do it. Food, a place to sleep, you know, some wages to go with it along the way?"

"And the occasional skirmish where you get to stick your sword in someone. Yeah, I know." Darius was grinning openly now.

Cayden shrugged again, the movement restricted by the leather harness. He was not thrilled by the idea of sticking his sword in anyone. He felt a sick squirm in his stomach at the thought.

"Why did you join?"

"Well, I am from the plains at the base of the Highland Needle, you see. It is grasslands mostly and not a tree to be seen. It's always dry, even desert-like in some areas. My folks, they have nine kids. I am the eldest. Last year was a hard year. The crops never sprouted as the spring rains didn't come until it was too late. My pa scraped together a grub stake and gave me my clothes, a good hunting knife, and a skin of water and told me it was time to make my own way in the world. I left that very night and haven't seen them since."

Darius paused, thinking. "Then about six months back, near starvation and thinking I would need to steal food from the farms I passed, I bumped into the legion. Well, in actual fact, I passed out in the middle of the roadway and they nearly ran me over. When I came to, I was in the healer's tent and being shoved into a uniform as soon as I could stand. Guess I got recruited while I was passed out. It's not such a bad life. I get regular meals and my clothes are taken care of. I get to train on weapons, which is fun…as long as I don't get stuck by anything. I haven't seen any real fighting yet." He paused, his forehead wrinkling, concerned at that thought, but continued his story. "Not sure how that will go, to tell the truth. I was a farm boy. I don't know anything about fighting, only about vegetables."

He lapsed into silence. Cayden felt sorry for him. Although he wasn't much older, he felt ancient in comparison. He grinned over at Darius. "I could use a friend and who better than the guy being forced to help me drag his sorry carcass all the way to the next camp?" He jerked his head back at the sergeant lounging in his wagon seat.

Not surprisingly, Perez guessed at the conversation. The cruel whip flicked out again and this time it cut Cayden's cheek below the eye, his head still turned in Darius's direction. Cayden's hand jerked to his cheek, pulling it away to show a bloody smear.

Darius snapped his head back straight and focused on pulling the cart.

Cayden glared back over his shoulder, his hatred naked on his face. Perez grinned evilly as he pulled out his short knife and proceeded to scrape dirt out from under his fingernails.

Cayden whispered fiercely, "We will come out of this fine, Darius. You'll see. Don't let them get to you. If I won't break, you are not allowed to either. We are a team, you and me. OK?"

"OK," whispered Darius.

They lapsed into silence, each alone with his thoughts. Dust puffed under their feet as they walked.

Chapter 14

THE AIR AT THE TOP OF THE PASS was cool and thin. Avery took a deep breath and still wanted more. The horses didn't seem bothered by the thin air, but the short exercise of gathering firewood from the scrub brush around their campsite had her wheezing like the bellows at Ryder's forges.

Sharisha put a kettle over the fire to brew a pot of tea. From his saddlebag, Gaius retrieved some dried mutton and some flatbread. Avery retrieved some dried berries from her saddlebags, which with the addition of water plumped back up in a few minutes.

Sharisha walked away into the trees and collected some bright green fiddleheads and a full bowl of wild mushrooms, which she then added to a pot with the dried mutton and water and set it to simmer on the coals.

Avery lowered herself to sit on a blanket on the ground near the fire. She was quiet, thinking about the last conversation.

Sharisha had brought her horse up alongside of hers, matching her pace.

"What you do is a very rare gift, my child."

"What is it I do?"

"You have the ability to sense the feelings of others. You can also sense their truths, their honesty, or their lies. You can tell if they believe what they are saying or whether they lie to themselves and to others. This can be a two-edged sword. The fanatical do what they do, convinced what they believe is the truth, even if it is the most diabolical of actions. The radical will kill in the name of the lesser gods to please them and the same men will spare wicked lives to avoid the attention of the Great Goddess of the Dark. Knowing what they believe is not necessarily knowing truth and acting on what you believe to be their intent can cause grief beyond measure. This is in part why we are bringing you to Faylea, our capital city. We have elders there who are able to help train you in your abilities and give you guidance. The head of our order, the Spirit High Priestess resides there, and of course the Shining Temple is at the very heart of Faylea. Faylea is the home of the Spirit Clans."

Gaius rode up on Avery's other side and focused on Sharisha. "Why does she have them, these special abilities you mention? Where did they come from? Is it something genetic?"

Sharisha gazed solemnly at him. "I cannot say. I do not have that knowledge. The elders will know. They will be able to say for certain. I am merely a Seeker sent to search for those who may be spoken of in our prophecies. We are trained from birth and made to memorize the Elder Scrolls so that we may perform this sacred duty."

Avery checked the stew. She took the pot off the coals and ladled the bubbling contents into wooden bowls. She handed them around, not meeting either set of eyes. She blew gently on her stew and then took a mouthful.

As she chewed her food, her thoughts strayed to Cayden. Unconsciously, she touched the stone on the chain around her neck. It warmed to her touch and pulsed in her hand. He was alive, if not happy.

She sensed he was spitting mad at the moment. Not unexpected, considering what he had chosen to do. He would have a rough road ahead of him. But there was no reason why he shouldn't come out of it fine. She hoped.

Meal finished, they doused the fire and packed up their belongings, setting the horses off on a slow walk as the descent was as steep as the upward climb had been.

The thin scrub brush gave way to taller and taller trees. The heat of the day was undiluted on this side of the pass and the day warmed quickly. As they descended, the air grew thick with humidity due to the lower altitude on this side of the mountain range. Flowers appeared, dotting the hillside in pockets. Avery sniffed appreciatively and then pulled back on the reins abruptly.

That flower...it was the one she had smelled in her mind when she fell from Sunny's back. Avery leapt from her saddle and ran toward the now familiar scent. In the crevice of a rock a fragile orchid bloomed, its white flesh striped with thin veins of pink and blue. The flower bobbed on a bright green bulbous stem that continuously fed it rare nutrients to keep it blooming year around.

Avery dropped to her knees and gently cradled the flower in her hand. She *knew* this flower. How was that possible? She had never seen it before.

Sharisha watched from her mount, as Avery examined the flower. "It is called Heavensmist. The plant is known to have healing powers beyond the extraordinary. It is never to be moved. If you dig it up, it will die. This is the only place it grows naturally, here at the height of the pass. The plant is protected by our people. We harvest its seeds and grow a lesser, cultivated variety of it on our farms. The pure natural stock is sacred, however. It will cure you if you ingest it, if you are an inch from death, but at the cost of its own life. All of its offspring plants die too. We do not understand why."

Avery gently stroked the fragile petals. They quivered in response to her touch, the flower turning toward her hand. Sensation shivered through it, like a cymbal vibration. She felt life and spirit rush into her. She breathed deeply and felt completely rejuvenated.

"Come," Sharisha commanded. "We should reach the first Spirit clan village by nightfall."

Chapter 15

ZIONA CAUGHT UP TO THE LEGION when the sun was still about two hours in the sky. She was riding her mare named Seeker, after her task that had brought her to this area of the word, and leading a pack mule she had not yet named. Judging by the way it resisted doing any work, she was thinking Troll might be a good one.

When she caught up to the legion, she found them settling into a clearing bordered by cliffs on one side and a small tributary of the larger river on the left. The flats were usually flooded during the spring rains, but at this time, they were dry.

She joined the rest of the camp followers, riding up to a round woman sitting on the bench of a wagon loaded with goods.

"Good day, mistress," Ziona said politely. "Where might I find the supply clerk of the legion?"

The woman's eyes peered out at her from a dusty bonnet. "Quartermaster Higgs is the short, balding man other there." She pointed to the left side of the camp where it appeared a large tent was being erected. She eyed Ziona's packs with interest.

"Thank you, mistress." Ziona rode toward the edge of the camp.

A pair of soldiers stepped into her path before she was able to cross half the distance to the tent. "What is the nature of your business?" the larger of the two demanded.

"I have come to see the quartermaster, good sirs. I wish to offer my services to the camp as a seamstress of renown. I have experience creating army garments for the lowest recruit to the highest ranked officer. I assure you my prices are very reasonable."

"Very well, report directly to the quartermaster. He will tell you where you are permitted to set up camp."

Ziona nudged her mare forward and rode the short distance to the quartermaster's tent. She dismounted and then pulled a bundle of samples from her side pack. As she entered the tent, she observed a flurry of motion, as supplies were unloaded and stacked onto makeshift shelving. It appeared they intended to stay for a few days.

She approached the man who appeared to be in charge. "Good sir? May I speak with you a moment."

The hulking quartermaster, annoyed with the interruption, barked, "What do you want?"

"The good men at the entrance told me to come see you. Where should I set up my seamstress's tent?" She held out the samples for his inspection. "They are of the finest quality, I assure you."

He glanced at them and waved her away. "You can leave those here and set up your tent with the other merchants. I will come find you."

"Thank you, good sir." She left the tent.

On her way out of the camp, she spied activity on the back side, where a practice yard appeared to have been set up. A group of men were chasing a lad about Avery's age. He dashed here and there, trying to avoid their weapons. He glowed blue the entire time.

Smiling to herself, she searched for a place to set up camp.

∗∗

Cayden dodged to the left, rounding a tree which saved his head from being split open by the wooden mace swung into it. He had not been issued any weapons, not having earned the right by keeping his feet for ten minutes. He was at eight and a half minutes now by his reckoning. However, Sergeant Perez seemed to have a longer accounting of time.

Cayden had dropped one of the trainees, having kicked him as he swung his weapon, a staff, leaving is belly exposed. He had gained a weapon at last out of the exchange, but it was impossible to swing it in the trees where he had fled, the men chasing after him.

His eyes searched frantically for a spot from which to defend himself with his commandeered weapon. He spied an outcropping of rock too steep to climb. It would protect his back, however. He sprinted toward it, arriving just in time to spin into a defensive position.

He couldn't only defend. He had to attack. He had been the rabbit for two weeks now. The daily beatings were wearing him down. He was a mass of bruises and cuts even Laurista's administrations couldn't eliminate. Seven men were left and they formed up around him. Two were short, three were tall, and the other two were of medium height.

Cayden took a deep breath and calmed himself. He thought about the eagle he had called when carving its flute back home. Thinking of the eagle gave him an idea. He reached out with his senses and found an eagle nearby in the forest. He nudged it with his subconscious mind and the eagle responded, winging toward the camp.

The tall man on the left swung at Cayden with his sword. Cayden easily deflected it with the long staff. A man on his right dashed in with another sword, which was easily pushed aside. Suddenly, they rushed him at once, attempting to overwhelm him by sheer numbers. Cayden lay about with the staff, panic lending him speed if not accuracy. He knocked one on the head, dropping him to the ground, out cold. On his return swing, he took two more out at the knees. They fell on top of one another. A sword caught him, slashing a long cut down his upper arm. Thankfully the practice swords were left somewhat dull; however, they could still break bones and blood welled from the wound, dripping down to his hand and making the already slick staff, slippery in his grip. Cayden butted his attacker in the stomach while his sword completed its arc past his arm and he doubled over in pain, retching. He did not get back up. The remaining men backed off and reorganized. The two he had tripped got back to their feet. They moved a little more warily now, attempting to flank him.

Cayden breathed heavily, sweat pouring from his pores and mixing with the blood of his cut, causing it to sting and burn. Suddenly, he heard a screech from the sky. A lone eagle circled above him and then dived toward Cayden. The men glanced up at the sky, alarmed by the plummeting eagle.

Cayden swung his staff, clipping the nearest man on his ear. He fell to the ground, out cold. Cayden pulled back on his staff and rammed the butt end into the stomach of the man standing opposite. He clutched his stomach and spilled its contents, dropping to his knees. Cayden then swung at the third man who raised his sword arm in defence. Cayden rapped his wrist, causing it to go numb and drop the sword. Cayden then tapped the man in the head and he dropped.

The eagle clawed at the remaining two men, wings flapping, talons raking their backs and arms. Sergeant Perez, watching from the sidelines, cursed and called for archers. Cayden cried out to the eagle to flee. The eagle lifted back into the sky and vanished into the trees. Cayden lowered his staff. The remaining two men were no longer interested in fighting. Blood dripped from the shredded skin on their backs. Cayden breathed in heavily, trying to catch his breath. He had won for a change.

Sergeant Perez marched over to where the men lay groaning on the ground. He glanced at them and then frowned at Cayden. Cayden thought he saw a glimmer of respect in his eyes. Respect, yes, but hatred was reflected there too.

"So the rabbit has teeth at last. It's about bloody time. Lucky for you the eagle took a liking to their arms. You lot, up on your feet and off to the healer's tent. Since you helped cause this mess, you can help get them there, Cayden. Dismissed!"

Chapter 16

NELSON SQUEEZED HIS SKINNY FRAME into the gap, holding his lantern aloft as he shuffled sideways through the break in the stone wall. Hands took the lantern from him and then grasped his arm to give him a tug. He popped out of the crevice like a cork from a bottle, overbalancing on the landing.

He brushed his shirt and pants down and then examined his surroundings. He found himself in a rough, naturally formed cavern about the size of the stables of his inn. The ceiling was covered in stalactites at one end, close to a narrow stream of water that trickled through the rear of the cave. Matching stalagmites formed on the floor, giving the appearance of a tooth-filled jaw about to snap shut.

This limestone cave was promising. Of all the stones they had tunnelled through to date, this was the first that matched the stone construction inside the castle. The castle foundations were built on limestone, but the upper structure was of quarried granite from the mountain ranges to the northeast. Finding a limestone deposit was like finding gold. They were not far from their goal.

"Hector, how far does this cave extend? Have you had a chance to explore deeper yet?"

Hector rubbed his dark chin in thought, rough hand rasping across the stubble. "Yes, sir. However, we ran low on lantern fuel and had to turn back. If we follow the stream, it runs in a southeast direction that should bring us inside the castle walls. The stream is flowing away from the castle, which means there must be a water source up ahead. I suspect a spring of some sort."

Nelson nodded. The spring could be the one that fed the wells inside the castle.

"OK, let's work on widening this cleft. It needs to be wide enough for men and supplies to pass." Hector nodded his head in acknowledgement of the instructions. "I think this is a good place to set up a base camp. The cavern is wide enough to hold twenty men plus supplies. I'll head back and let Denzik know of our find. Erik, Hector, come with me and put together an exploration crew."

They squeezed back out through the crack and into the main tunnel. Men were busy clearing the debris from the latest tunnelling efforts. They were using pickaxes and water combined with fungus to soften the limestone wall. One of the men had discovered the pasty mixture easily dissolved the white powdery veins in the limestone rock, making it easier to knock out larger pieces of stone. The pickaxes clanked against the stone surface as they chipped away at the walls.

They exited the caves into the cellar of his basement. Nelson climbed back up into the inn and set off across the village square to Denzik's home. He found him out back tending to the vegetables in his meager garden. Denzik was bent over his hoe, chopping at the weeds attempting to take over the bed. Sweat glistened, streaking the dust coating his shirtless back as he hoed. Nelson stepped up to the side of a row of string beans, and peering over the laced stakes, he whispered, "The men have made a discovery. You need to come have a look at this."

Denzik straightened from his work, swiping his arm across his forehead and leaving a dirty smear. He nodded. He worried about what ears were about during the daylight hours. "I will share a pint with you as soon as I am finished here. I accept your invitation gratefully. There is nothing like cold ale after slaving away in the hot sun," he announced in a loud voice.

He nodded and Nelson headed off for the bakery.

Opening the door set the chimes to tinkling. His senses were overwhelmed by the sweet spicy scent of apple dumplings. He spied Fabian with his head emerging from a wall oven, a steaming tray of the sugary treats in his hands. At the sound of the bell, he spotted Nelson.

"Some great things are cooking in my kitchen too. Care to stop by for a bite after work?" It was his code to Fabian.

Fabian lips twitched. "I would be delighted to stop in. It beats going home for a lonely dinner. Around the usual time?"

"Certainly, I will save a table for you. In the meantime, I need fifty of your crusty dinner rolls for this evening."

Fabian rounded up the requested rolls and placed them in a paper sack for Fabian. "Cash or on account?" he enquired as he placed them on the counter.

"On account, if you please. See you at dinner." Picking up the bag of buns, Nelson walked out of the bakery and back down the dusty street to his inn.

The inn was a two-story wooden structure, framed by a verandah running the length of the front exposure. Rocking chairs were placed randomly along the front and were frequently used by guests to relax after their evening meal, lit pipe in one hand and a brandy glass in the other. The porch afforded a clear view of the highway, which did not disappoint for entertainment, day or night. A constant stream of traffic moved back and forth from the castle.

When Nelson had taken it over, the entire building had had a definite lean to the right. The wooden shutters were missing slats and the door creaked on hinges nearly seized up. The inside had been infested with mice and rats. Nelson walked up onto the porch and bent down to scratch his favourite cat, Sally, under her chin. She purred and wound around his legs, tail held rigidly in the air. He had found her, drowning in the rain barrel she had fallen into while attempting to get a drink. Scrawny and near dead, he had taken the kitten in. She had rewarded him by becoming a prime mouser, earning her keep every day. In fact, she was the best mouser he had ever had.

Entering the inn, Nelson waved to the assembled patrons who called out greetings. He stepped up behind the bar and put a note in the store's ledger about the bun purchase and then delivered them to the kitchen.

Inside he found his head cook, Tabitha, spoon in hand, tasting the broth from her soup pot. With a satisfied smacking of her lips, she gave the pot another stir and placed the lid back on it with a clatter. He handed off the rolls to her.

"There will be a few extra for dinner tonight. I hope you have made enough to feed everyone." She squinted at him and seeing his expression, nodded.

"I always cook for the regular crowd plus ten percent in case we have unexpected company like those soldiers that came through. Why don't you check the pantry and see for yourself? I will not be accused of slacking in my duties. Now let me get back to my work," she said primly. Scowling, she focused her attention on the large bowl of potatoes waiting to be peeled.

Nelson snorted a laugh then wandered off to the pantry. She really was the best cook he had ever had...along with being the main food supplier for their underground endeavors. It amazed him how she stretched the inn's budget to keep the underground crews fed. *I really must give her a raise some time,* he thought.

The pantry was located in a separate room from the kitchen. This was also where the trap door to his cellar was located. Usually, it was covered with a woven mat and a vat of potatoes sat on it to disguise its presence. The mat was attached to the door so it would settle back into place when someone pulled the hatch closed after lowering themselves into the cellar, effectively disguising the entrance on entering or exiting.

Hector and Erik were waiting for him when he entered the room.

"The men are assembled and the supplies are down in the tunnel. The crews are about halfway through the cleft. I would say it will be about another hour or two before they have it fully opened," Erik said.

"Good work. Head into the common room and get yourselves something to eat. It might be a long night."

The pair left as instructed. Nelson approached the left wall of the storage chamber. He stored his extra lamps next to a large barrel of lamp oil he kept for just this kind of occasion. He pulled out twenty lamps and began filling their bellies, trimming the wicks as he did so. Task completed, he placed them on a shelf near the entrance to the basement.

Next, he pulled a blanket off of a storage chest. Fishing his key ring out of his pocket, he searched for the brass key that matched the lock. He turned the key in the lock and it opened with a metallic click. Stored inside was a stash of weapons, swords and halberds, spears, and shields. He hesitated and then took out five of the swords and placed them beside the trunk. He locked it back up and replaced the blanket, concealing the trunk from curious eyes. Wrapping the swords in spare linen from the cupboard, he placed the bundle behind the lanterns and left the room.

Chapter 17

CAYDEN STRETCHED AND RELAXED HIS SORE MUSCLES as he lay on his pallet, idly rolling the stone his sister had given him between his fingers. The stone felt curiously warm, like it had been sitting in the sun of the south-facing garden of their cabin all day.

The tent flap opened and half of his tent mates clambered in, returning from dinner and flopping on their respective mats.

Darius dropped onto the pallet next to Cayden's, groaning in contentment. He rubbed his distended belly. "I don't know whether the eats were better than normal tonight or if I was extra hungry."

Pieter, the lad next to Darius, snorted and with a laugh flopped down on his own space. "If it wasn't for Cayden whooping us out in the practice yard, we wouldn't have been allowed those extra helpings. So kind of Laurista to send that note with us saying we required 'extra helpings' to assist with her healing...and so kind of the cook to oblige."

"Well, I for one do not plan to have Cayden 'whoop us' again anytime soon. He got lucky. That's all there was to it," said a third tent mate, James.

"How so? I was out cold from the beginning." Darius gazed intently at Cayden, his stare so intense that Cayden looked away.

"You missed the eagle attack," said James. "I've never seen such a thing before. That eagle dived from a clear blue sky and went straight for those of us who were attacking Cayden. Cayden didn't get a scratch from the bird. It was like it was protecting him." James stared at Cayden.

The others' eyes fell on Cayden too, watching his reaction. Cayden sat up, tucking the stone in his pocket. He stared back at the others, trying to think of what to say. A slow flush crawled up his neck. His ears heated.

"I can't explain what happened. I was as shocked as any of you when the eagle appeared." He dropped his eyes. This was stretching the truth, he knew, which only made the flush rise higher. "I'm not sad for its help, though."

Darius's toothy grin broadened, seeing his friend's embarrassment. "You beat us fair and square, Cayden. We all know it. We were curious about the bird, that's all. It did seem like it was protecting you or something. I know Perez was livid after you left. He felt you had cheated somehow. We can't see how that's possible, though."

The rest of the tent residents filed in at that moment, interrupting their conversation.

"Oh, before I forget," said Darius. "Perez says that you are to report to the supply tent first thing in the morning. You are to be fitted for a private's uniform like ours." Darius leaned over and whispered softly, "If you ever need someone to talk to, I am here for you."

"Thanks. I think I will sleep now." Cayden pulled his blankets up to his chin, rolled on his side. Before the lamps were dimmed, he was fast asleep.

***

The morning dawned cloudy and grey. A damp mist hung in the air, which soaked through Cayden's shirt long before he reached the supply tent. He wished he had pulled out his cloak, although it was really too warm for such a heavy garment.

He knocked on the wooden plate at the door of the supply tent, announcing his arrival. "Come!" Drawing aside the flap, he entered the tent he had visited on his first day. The supply clerk was seated at his makeshift table, scribbling in a ledger. He glanced at Cayden as he entered. "Name?"

"Cayden Tiernan, sir."

"Ah yes...seems you have completed your basic training. You are to report to the seamstress's tent which can be found in the merchant's camp outside our camp perimeter. You are to have three uniforms made." He tossed a coin purse at him. "Inside are your wages for the last two weeks. You are to pay her from your own pay, understand?"

"Yes, sir!"

"Then go. After meeting with her, you are to report back to your unit."

"Yes, sir. Thank you, sir!" Cayden saluted and left the tent.

Cayden stopped by the mess tent and grabbed a couple bread rolls and some cheese. He pocketed these and then headed for the perimeter of the camp. Dawn was breaking the horizon, flooding the sky with purple and pink. He had about an hour to run his errand before he was due back at camp. Quickening his steps, he jogged to the perimeter. Nodding to the guards, he passed through and out into the merchant's camp.

His spirits lifted as he left the military camp behind. He was free again for a short period. He breathed in deeply, smelling the earthy smells of springtime, his heart light. He gazed around at the landscape as he walked and munched on his cheese and bread, taking in the canopy of the great trees. A golden shaft of morning sun struck the leaves, the brilliant spotlight exploding his senses with the vibrant greens of new growth. Birds warbled and cooed, welcoming the day. It was a glorious morning and Cayden was happy to be alive in it.

Other than the few stolen moments alone with his flutes, he had not been able to escape his voluntary imprisonment. He wondered idly how Ryder was doing. He felt a pang of homesickness. The spring lambs would be coming soon. How would his father manage everything without him?

Cayden entered the merchants' camp and dropped to a walk, strolling along the makeshift road between the wagons. A man backing out of a covered wagon nearly bowled Cayden over. Cayden stepped out of the way just in time and then asked where to find the seamstress's tent. The man gestured down an aisle to the right.

At the end of the grass path, Cayden found a tent of bright green erected between two large maples. Smoke curled out of the center vent of the tent. He stepped up to the flap and knocked on the wooden shingle hung by the flap. "Mistress, would you be awake?"

A head popped out of the tent. Cayden found himself staring into the most beautiful eyes he had ever seen. Emerald green, almond-shaped eyes gazed at him from a heart-shaped face framed by curly wisps of hair. Cayden's heart stopped. Fumbling for speech, the words tumbled from his lips. "Sorry to disturb you. I need you to help me find my pants...No, to get some pants. I mean I have pants, but I need new pants. These are no good..." He stumbled to a halt, blushing, as he saw a grin split her face. Laughter sparkled in her eyes. Groaning, he took a deep breath to calm himself. "I sound like an idiot."

"Not at all," she laughed. Her laughter sounded like chimes dancing in a breeze. "I assume you are here for a uniform?"

"Yes." Cayden sheepishly tugged at his collar.

"Come inside then. What is your name?"

"Cayden Tiernan. I am a new private and I was told you made uniforms."

He followed her into the tent, noting the neatly arranged seamstress supplies. Bolts of cloths were stacked in piles along one wall. A table set with spools of threads in various colours, jars of buttons and zippers, scissors, measuring tapes, and other supplies Cayden didn't recognize lined the opposite wall.

At the back of the tent sat a small narrow cot and a banded flat-topped chest with an oil lamp set on top of it. A small fireplace was centered in the tent, a wisp of smoke curling out the hole from the banked coals.

"Please, sit." Ziona motioned to the chair set by the table of notions. "Tea? I made a pot a few minutes ago."

"Yes, thank you." Cayden gratefully sank into the chair indicated, wincing slightly. She poured tea into two ceramic cups and handing one to him and then perched on her table, one leg dangling over the side.

She studied him with interest. "I have been waiting for you to come see me. My name is Ziona Aspenwood." She studied him, taking dainty sips of her tea.

Cayden's studied her with curiosity. "You have? Why?" He met her frank gaze and, blushing again, dropped his eyes.

"So shy...," she murmured. "Do you know who you are?" The blue aura pulsed around him, rising and falling as his emotions swung between curiosity and surprise.

Cayden's eyes shot back to her. "What do you mean? I told you who I am."

"I see...well." Her eyes travelled up and down him. "I wish you could see what I see...It is all good. Believe me." Her appreciative eyes roved over him, taking in his lean torso, blond curly hair, and vivid green eyes. Cayden blushed again under the scrutiny, his heart galloping and a chill of excitement shivered down his back.

"We have been destined to meet. I am here not merely as a merchant seamstress. I am what they call a Seeker. My people have sent me to be of assistance to you. Of course, I had to find you first."

Cayden locked his eyes on hers. "You have been following me?" He frowned. "It was you! That day in the high pasture...I thought I saw something in the trees. Was that you?" He watched her eyes, gauging her reaction to his words.

It was Ziona's turn to be surprised. "I didn't think you had seen me." Her eyebrows rose in disbelief. "Human eyesight should not have been able to spot me at such a distance."

"I didn't see you, not exactly. It was more like I sensed where you were."

Ziona nodded her head, satisfied.

"Who sent you? What is a Seeker?" Taking another sip of his tea he tried to calm his racing heart. He was aware of her in a way he had never been before with any other woman. He inhaled her woodsy scent without thinking and then blushed again.

On impulse, Ziona reached up and unwound her braid from around her head, revealing her ears.

Cayden gasped, "You're Primordial! " His eyes searched quickly for spying eyes. "You shouldn't be here! It's extremely dangerous! They would hang you on sight, Ziona, if they ever found out what you are! You must go quickly!"

Ziona shook her head. She rewound her hair to hide her ears. "I am here for you. You are my destiny, Cayden. I set out with one other, Sharisha, seventeen years ago to find the prophesied children. We did not know where to go or even what they would look like. We only knew to watch for the signs. We have been searching for you and your sister for seventeen years. We are your guardians. And we are your friends."

Cayden clutched at his tea, trying to warm his suddenly chilled fingers. He shook his head, trying to clear it. "Wait...seventeen years? How old are you?" She appeared to be no more than a couple years older than him.

She again laughed. "We are a very long-lived race, but by Primordial reckoning, I would be of a similar age to you."

"Is this a safe place," Cayden asked, "to have this kind of conversation?"

"I have placed wards in the soil around the tent to prevent eavesdropping. It is part of my earth magic."

"You have done what?"

"A ward is an invisible barrier. In this case, it keeps sound from travelling in or out from the boundary it surrounds. It is centered on me."

"Oh. So why are you so interested in me? Frankly, I think you have it all wrong. I have never even seen a Primordial prior to this. I have barely been out of my village, except to go to the market in the next village over. What does my sister have to do with any of this?"

"Cayden, look at me." Cayden met her gaze with defiance and a trace of fear visible in his green depths. "You have special abilities, don't you?" His eyes widened, as fear leapt within him. "When I really look at you, I see a blue aura surrounding you. It pulses like waves lapping at a shoreline. We see it around your sister too."

Cayden's eyes locked on hers, searched hers, seeking her sincerity, examining her heart. Ziona shivered under the intense scrutiny. Here was someone she could not lie to. His eyes commanded truth.

"We believe you have abilities you are hiding, or perhaps are not aware of yet. The queen, if she were to capture you, would order your execution on the spot. She has searched her entire reign to find you and your sister for she is aware of our prophecies, even if she does not believe in them.

"She sends soldiers into our lands, in an attempt to wipe out our peoples so no one will be able to aid you. She makes war on our villages, and we have had to abandon our homes, retreating to a sanctuary she does not know of. Even now, a new assault has been ordered and her soldiers march for the three passes into the Primordial lands across the Great Spine. She does all of this to try and find you and Avery...and here you sit right under her nose. Your sister is on her way to the sanctuary as we speak." Cayden tried to absorb Ziona's words. He tried to deny what she said, but the words rang true in his head.

"Avery glows too," he murmured absently.

Ziona paused. "You can see her glow?"

"Yes. I have always been able to see her glow. Why do others not see it?"

Ziona nodded. "It is because they are not of the blood."

"What blood?" Cayden asked, pinning her with his bright eyes again.

"Primordial blood Cayden, Royal Primordial blood." She waited for the explosion. She didn't have to wait for long.

Cayden stood up abruptly. "There is no way I am Primordial! I know who my mother and father are and they are not Primordial! What kind of foolishness is this?"

"The prophecies foretell of a prince and princess who would be born to humans but are of the blood. We do not understand how this is possible either. The prophecies do not explain it. Finding you both with this sign makes it ironclad. There can be no doubt as to who you two are."

Cayden sank back into his chair shaking his head in disbelief. *It isn't possible...is it? It's outlandish and absurd!* He was not of royal birth; he wasn't even important in his village. He was a farmer playing soldier.

Your flutes are an unusual talent, his conscience whispered; *a very dangerous talent.* If news of that particular talent were to reach the wrong ears, it would put a price on his head. He knew he would be hunted day and night. He frowned. Maybe the hunting had already started?

He lifted his head to meet her eyes, hands clasped in front, arms resting on his thighs. "You wanted to know about my abilities. Would you know if they are related to this theory of yours?"

"What kind of abilities?" Ziona cocked her head to one side, studying him.

"It must be kept an absolute secret. No one must ever know about it. It would be very dangerous news to share, especially in our present company. I like to carve. Flutes are my specialty. But when I play them animals gather."

He watched her closely, gauging her reaction to his words.

Ziona frowned. "I have never heard of any Shamanic prophecies associated with you. Are these animals real?"

"Of course they are real. They seem to be called by the music of my flutes."

"I have no idea." She hopped off the table and walked over to him. "We need to get you measured for those uniforms. Stand, please?"

Cayden stood up and at her prompting, held his arms out parallel to the floor. Ziona picked up a tape measure and measured the under arm measurement, armpit to wrist. She then jotted this measure in a book at her side. Next she measured his bicep circumference, wrist, neck, and waist. She then measured from the lowest neck bone down his back to his waist and then from his waist to the floor.

"It will take me about a week to make these up. I would like you to come back for a fitting every day at dinnertime. Do not worry about getting dinner in the camp. You can share my dinner and we can talk further then in private."

Cayden nodded. "Would you sew some hidden pockets in my uniform? I'd like a place to store my flutes on my person."

"I will put a pocket right here," she tapped his chest, over his heart, "and in the pant right here." She said, pointing at his thigh.

"I should be getting back to camp." He glanced back at her. "I am not sure I believe anything you have told me. But I do know one thing, I am no hero. I couldn't kill an animal, let alone a person. I have no stomach for it."

"What do you intend to do when a battle comes? You're a soldier in the legion. How can you avoid hurting anyone in battle?"

"I don't intend to be here long. I never did. I volunteered for reasons I would rather keep private, but it wasn't because I wanted to serve."

Ziona fingered her list of measurements, thinking. "Then perhaps we should make plans to break from the legion. It would be easiest to slip away when the legion is on the move," she mused. "Let me think on it. We will talk tomorrow when you return for your fitting. I will have one set ready by then."

Chapter 18

CAYDEN FINISHED SKINNING THE BARK off the willow branch. The supple wood was easy to strip, the bark falling away in curls. He was seated on a rotting log at the edge of a meadow. Two deer grazed knee-deep in the pasture in front of him, their heads popping up from the lush grasses every once in a while to check on his position. Free time was a rare commodity but when the opportunity presented itself, he could not resist the lure of the woods and his hands itched to carve. Carving soothed his wounded spirit and took his mind off the residual aches and pains of training.

As he carved, the bark-less wood revealed veins of yellow, green and—of all colours—pink. He spit on the wood and rubbed it in. The colours glowed. Fascinated, he trimmed the length to six and a half inches and then began to hollow out the middle. The pliable wood bent under his ministrations, soft as butter in his hands. He flared the end of the pipe into more of a bell shape. He hollowed out several petite finger holes along the shaft.

Putting down his tools, he inspected his work. The flute seemed feminine to him somehow, as though he was carving a little girl's doll. He fancied the bell-shaped bottom looked like the billowing form of a child's skirt as she twirled. His fingers followed the coloured lines of the wood. At the base, he carved small wing-like symbols and the oak symbol.

He then took out a soft cloth and picking up a small pot with some beeswax he had secured from the cook, rubbed the soft wax into the surface of the flute. The colours glowed like a rainbow. His heart swelled with pride and a grin spread across his face.

Satisfaction oozed from every pore. He closed up the pot and put it and the cloth back in his pocket.

Closing his eyes, he put pipe to lips and gently blew. A tinkling sound like a child's laughter sprang from the flute and danced across the air. The deer raised their heads in unison, ears twitching in interest.

This time, no animal came to him. When he opened his eyes, a child was standing in front of him in a shimmering turquoise tunic. She smiled at him impishly, foot tapping to the music. Cayden spilled backward off the log in surprise, yelping as he hit the ground. Pain flared in his overtaxed body. He scrambled around on all fours to see if she was still there.

She waggled her fingers at him, mystery and mischief in her eyes.

Cayden, his mouth dry, croaked, "Who are you? How did you get here?"

"I am called Aossi and I live here. How did you get here?"

Cayden slowly sat back on the ground, afraid she would run away. He ignored the question.

"Why are you here?"

"You called me, didn't you?" She touched a hand to his flute.

"I called you? How can that be? My flutes have only attracted animals before." The words were out of his mouth before he realized he had spoken them aloud.

"Do you imagine only animals are attracted to your songs?" She tilted her head to one side, studying him. "Why play if not to have others enjoy it?"

Cayden shook his head, bemused. "Of course, I play for others to enjoy." He felt a twinge of guilt at the lie. He had never played his flutes for anyone. She winked at him, knowing it to be a lie. Cayden flushed in embarrassment.

"Let me tell you something, Cayden of the Cliffs. Music is a life force, a common well of unity that all may freely drink from. Music is a magic that can bind the worlds together. The soul of music is the very breath of life. All creation is bound together through this, yes?" She studied him further. "I think you know this already." Her mouth curved into an ear-splitting smile that lit up her face. "So why are you surprised that I came to hear you play?"

"But...what are you?" Cayden asked, bemused.

Aossi grinned and ignored his question. "That is a conversation for another day. For now, I must go, but know that I am only ever a song away." With a spin and a twirl of turquoise, she vanished right before his eyes.

Cayden gasped and slipped as he spun around, trying to see where she had gone. The deer lowered their heads and went back to munching on the grass. Cayden carefully placed the flute in the lined inner pocket Ziona had sewn for him.

He sat back down on the log, hands clasped and arms resting on his knees. Who was she and how did she vanish into thin air? He never had a person show up before. *Wait.* Was she a person? How had she known his name?

A harsh cry pierced the silence of the woods, and glancing up, he spied eagles soaring in lazy circles above his head. There were four of them, uncharacteristically grouped and circling in slow patterns above him.

He walked back over to the willow tree where he had found the branch. It was a huge tree, like the old oak tree back home, its crown high in the sky and its sprawling branches swooning back to the ground, its roots dug deeply into the bank of the river. It was ancient.

Suddenly, the deer's heads shot up and they froze. The eagles screeched, as one of their members plummeted from the sky. The eagle crashed to earth a short distance from where Cayden sat. The deer bounded away into the safety of the woods.

Cayden ran over to where the eagle was lying. It lay on its back, flapping its wings feebly. An arrow had pierced its body. Cayden knelt beside the dying bird. The eagle locked eyes on him and stopped flapping. Cayden *felt* its thoughts. It seemed at peace and glad of his presence. He placed his hand on the bird's breast, thinking to comfort it.

A jolt of searing pain ran up Cayden's arm like an electric shock. The bird arched its back and flopped back down, no longer breathing. At the same moment, Cayden saw a bluish mist rise from the bird. The mist gathered into a semi-transparent form of a bird with a wingspan as tall as a man. Its feathers were layered in blues and reds and purples. Its head was bald except for a small curl of feather on its crest. Cayden thought it resembled his mental picture of thunderbirds in the tales he had been told as a child.

The apparition steadied and Cayden felt thoughts being pushed into his head. The foreign intrusion made his head explode with pain. "Are you Mac Mak? The thunderbird of the stories?" He clutched at his head, trying to still the pain of the foreign communication.

"*Mick-mak*. My name is Mik'maq. In the old tongue, it means Allied Brothers. Thank you for aiding in my rebirth, young Cayden." Cayden didn't reply. His mind was foggy and slow with the pain in his arm and mind. "You and I are now brothers. You may call on me at any time and I will answer that call."

The thunderbird launched itself into the air, soaring over the clearing, and disappeared into the distance. The remaining eagles followed it. Cayden eyes followed the eagles' flight and abruptly he found himself seeing through the thunderbird's eyes. His focus narrowed and sharpened as he flew over the land. His stomach lurched as it dived steeply toward the ground. Cayden cried out in alarm, squeezing his eyes shut and throwing out his hands to stop his fall, landing on his hands and knees on the dirt. The thunderbird chuckled in his mind and then broke contact.

Cayden gulped and opened his eyes. He was still in the meadow on his hands and knees. He stood up, legs quivering and as he did so. Two men walked into view about twenty feet away from him. They both carried bows. Spotting Cayden, they walked over.

"You found the eagle! We weren't sure whether we had hit it or not!" The younger man picked up the eagle by its feet. "These feathers should be worth something in trade with the merchants. I guess it wasn't a complete waste of a hunting trip." They walked away, not waiting for a reply.

Cayden shivered. He felt chilled, as though he was catching a cold. His awareness of the eagles did not diminish. He felt stronger in aspects, his eyesight was sharper, his focus clearer, yet he shivered. *What is happening to me?*

Rubbing his arms, he headed back to camp. He couldn't help glancing at the sky.

Chapter 19

THE FOLLOWING DAYS SETTLED into a pattern for Cayden. Roll call at dawn, breakfast, sword training, archery training, pike drills, a break for lunch, and then hand to hand combat, flail and shields, and finally ending with halberds. Dinner would follow and then roll call before settling down for the night. He slipped off to Ziona's for his "fittings," sharing dinner with her on those evenings. He found her to be a smart and engaging companion, quick of wit and with a cheery disposition. He enjoyed her company immensely.

Cayden discovered he also enjoyed learning the forms of the sword and the pike drills. The flail drills usually left him heavily bruised as he was not as tall or as strong as the others in his training group. Some of those men reminded him of gorillas because their arms were so long. Cayden swore they would drag on the ground if they relaxed them enough. Cayden, however, was quick and light on his feet, perfectly suited to sword play. His skills improved rapidly.

Sergeant Perez never failed to set Cayden up to receive the worst positions with the worst equipment he could find. Sergeant Perez loathed Cayden. His narrowed eyes followed him everywhere, his hatred nakedly displayed on his face. Cayden found himself watching his back. Sergeant Perez had gathered a set of sycophants, who shadowed him like he was a lord.

Two weeks into this new routine, Sergeant Perez arrived at the training grounds with some older men of higher rank.

Sergeant Perez's evil grin split his fleshy lips, displaying yellowed teeth, and a satisfied expression spread across his face. *He looks triumphant.* Cayden broke out in a sweat, shivering in the breeze tugging his shirt. Someone had just walked across his grave.

"Line up, you lazy scum! Inspection!" Perez roared. They took their positions and snapped to attention.

The tall thin officer had a hooked nose that he stabbed into each of the men's faces, inspecting them with an intensity that frightened Cayden. Perez followed in his wake, re-inspecting the line of nervous men, as though attempting to read the secrets they hid. Perez, arms clasped behind his back, watched the reaction of the officer as he walked the line, intently examining each face. He paused when he reached Cayden, his narrow eyes searching his face.

"Bring the two guards who were with Sandez on guard duty that day." Perez's grin widened maliciously.

Two men jogged up to the group, dressed in scout's camouflage and saluted before Perez. Cayden had not seen them in the camp since their arrival. "Sir!" they snapped to the two officers.

"Do either of you recognize any of the men in this line up?"

The two scouts slowly walked past the line of men at attention and one paused directly in front of Cayden. His eyes roved over Cayden's features, studying him intently. Straightening, he turned to Sergeant Perez and said, "Yes! This man was with the heavier set man, who fought like a cornered badger. I do not know if he killed Sandez though."

It was enough for Perez, however.

"Cayden Tiernan, you are under arrest for murder!" He motioned to a couple of his cronies standing a little ways back. "Bind his hands and take him to the prisoner tents."

Cayden's tent mates roared their disapproval as he was roughly dragged out of line and his arms yanked behind him and tied securely with a length of rope.

"Back in line, you scum, unless you want to join him?"

Darius caught his eye, shock and sadness painted on his face. Cayden shook his head slightly, warning him to not get involved.

Cayden recognized the soldier who had identified him now. He was one of the three who had surprised him and Ryder that miserable day. The nameless soldier grinned as evilly as Perez did. "You thought to escape our justice by hiding in our midst? You will live to regret that day, boy. You will regret it very much, I think," he said softly. The threat in his voice made Cayden's mouth go dry. He did not answer.

The guard-turned-scout punched him hard in the stomach. Cayden doubled over, vomiting on the grass. He only kept his feet because his arms were being held by the two soldiers who had bound him. The soldier lifted his head and punched him in the face. Cayden's head snapped back and he felt his nose break. Blood spurted and ran down his face, dripping off his chin.

Rough hands jerked on his arms, hauling him away. A canvas sack was pulled over his head. He stumbled in his captor's grip, the uneven ground tripping his feet. His eyes watered with the pain of his broken nose. Twice more he was randomly punched in the stomach, eliciting a groan. Once they let him fall to the ground and then proceeded to kick him with sharp-toed boots. Cayden thought he heard Perez chuckle. Cayden felt a rib crack. Groaning, he could do nothing to stop the beating. He couldn't even protect himself with his hands tied behind his back.

Suddenly, it stopped and Cayden was hauled to his feet again. He collapsed as the world tilted around him. They dragged him the rest of the way and with a last shove, threw him into what felt like a cart. The bag was ripped from his head as he fell, still bound. A metal-sounding door clanged shut and there was a sound of a key being turned in a lock. Waves of nausea washed over Cayden as the world spun and he vomited. Everything receded from Cayden in a rush and he slumped, unconscious to the wooden floor.

Chapter 20

WHEN HE CAME TO, it was fully dark. He tried to move, only to find his hands were still tied. He felt around in his mouth with his tongue. All of his teeth seemed to be intact. He spit the blood out. The simple act of lifting his head caused searing pain in his ribs. He groaned out loud. He had definitely broken a rib or two. He moved his legs, moaning with the effort. *Nothing broken there,* he thought, panting with the exertion.

He peered around cautiously. He appeared to be in a metal cage of some sort outside of the camp. He thought it was one of the cages used by one of the butchers who supplied the camp with meat to haul livestock. Why was he outside the camp? This was not the prisoner tents. What was Perez playing at?

Cayden did not spot a sentry, which didn't mean there wasn't one. He tested his bonds, wriggling his fingers and trying to loosen the ropes. He felt around for the tied ends. His eyes searched the cage, looking for a nail or a sharp metal edge to fray the ropes on. There was nothing in his immediate line of sight. He tried to shift his position, but the flash of pain in his ribs made him suck in a deep breath and groan aloud.

"Cayden…Cayden, are you awake?" Darius's shadowed face appeared over the edge of the cage floor. "I came as soon as I could sneak past the patrol," Darius whispered.

"I am awake," Cayden whispered back.

"I went to the prisoner tents to see you, but they said you were not brought to them. Rather than hang around and ask questions that would raise suspicion, I left. On the way back to our tent, I saw one of Perez's cronies slip off in this direction. I decided to follow him and he led me straight to here. He was replacing another guard. Don't worry. He is out cold."

"That's great," Cayden croaked. He could barely speak; he was so thirsty. "He wouldn't happen to have had the key on him for this buggy?"

Darius grinned, holding up a round key ring. "Let's find out, shall we?" Darius reached for the lock on the back of the cage. Cayden lost sight of him, but he heard the key scraping in the lock.

It clicked open and Darius hopped in beside him. He produced a knife and quickly cut the ropes binding Cayden. Darius helped him to sit up. Cayden groaned and clutched his stomach. "You shouldn't have helped me. They will have no compunction about killing you for helping me."

"Never mind about that right now. Where should we go? You can't travel far in your current condition."

"Take me to Ziona's tent. She will know what to do."

Placing Cayden's arm over his shoulders, Darius helped Cayden get to his feet. Cayden bit down hard on his lip to keep from crying out. The cage spun crazily in his vision and he nearly fainted. Deep breaths were agony due to the broken ribs.

"Come on, Cayden, we have to get out of here. If you pass out, I will have to carry you."

Darius helped Cayden to the door and then gently lowered him to sit on the edge of the opening. Hopping down, he put Cayden's arm around his shoulders again and pulled him into a quick walk. Cayden stumbled and passed out twice during the short journey, ending in front of Ziona's tent. Ziona took his other side and helped bring him in, lowering him onto her cot. Cayden did not remember actually hitting the cot. Everything went black.

When he came to again, darkness was fading into dawn. Darius slumped in the chair, snoring softly. He appeared uncomfortable but slept on.

Ziona bent over Cayden, slightly out of focus. She pried one eye open and flashed the light from a tinder stick in front of his eyes. She then did the same to the other. Satisfied, she raised his shirt and examined the poultice she had placed on his ribs. She lifted the edge of the cloth and then placed it back down again.

"How are you feeling?" Her green eyes loomed large in his sight.

Cayden thought that her eyes were the eyes of an angel. His lips to curved in response or at least they tried to. His lip was too swollen to form the proper shape. Raising his hand to his face, he winced as he touched his nose. It felt like badly mashed potatoes to him, all lumpy and squishy.

"I have had better nights." He grinned crookedly. "Why did you let Darius stay? He should have snuck back into camp. Now everyone will know he is with me. He will be a wanted man too."

"He refused to leave. He said you two were a team and he had pledged himself to you a few weeks ago?" She raised her eyebrows in enquiry.

"Oh...that...well I didn't mean it literally. I didn't mean for him to follow me into trouble."

"That's what friends do, Cayden."

Ziona reached over for a pitcher of water and poured a glass for Cayden. She held up his head and helped tip the liquid into his mouth. He swallowed gratefully, washing the tinny taste of blood from his mouth.

Replacing the glass on the chest, Ziona sat down on the edge of the cot. "So, are you going to tell me what this is all about? Somehow I think I am going to learn why you decided to join the legion in the first place."

Cayden nodded and quickly told her about the incident with Ryder. Toward the end of the telling, he noticed Darius had woken and was listening intently also.

"So you didn't actually kill that soldier? Ryder did?" Darius asked.

"Yes. I had to hide him and protect the village."

"Then you are innocent," said Darius.

"Or guilty by association," said Ziona.

"None of this explains why they put me in a cage outside of the camp." Cayden eyes flicked from one set to the other. "If this was about that night, I should be standing trial for the legion. But they didn't even report they had found me. Something else is going on."

"I quite agree," said Ziona. "However, short of capturing and interrogating Perez and the mysterious second soldier, we cannot know what their motives are. What is certain is that there are parties interested in you, Cayden, outside of the legion itself."

Darius stared at Cayden, puzzled. Cayden felt equally mystified.

"I have done some healing to your ribs overnight. There were two cracked on the left side, but I think you will find they have mended now. Try to sit up, slowly now."

They helped Cayden sit up. The pain was still present, but it was a shadow of what it had been before.

"How were you able to heal my ribs so quickly?"

"I will explain another time," Ziona said with a glance at Darius. "Now, what do we do with you, young man?" She turned to face Darius fully, arms crossed over her chest.

"I'm not going anywhere without Cayden. I swore to help him and that is exactly what I intend to do." Darius scrubbed the toe of his boot on the soft ground. "That is, if you will allow me to stay, mistress. I go where Cayden goes."

"Well I think it is time we packed up and got away from this arena. It will be too difficult for you to be outside, Cayden. Too many people know you. You have approximately an hour and a half until dawn and an hour before roll call." Darius nodded. "I need you to slip back into camp and gather your and Cayden's satchels. Take only your satchels. Anything else will slow you down. Meet me back here in forty-five minutes. Be warned. If you are discovered, we will not be rescuing you nor will we wait for you."

"I understand, mistress." Darius left the tent.

"Now, we gather what we need. I have supplies stashed in other locations. There is nothing in this tent that I cannot carry in my satchel and leaving the tent up will give the appearance I am gone for the day and will return. I will leave word with a neighbouring tent that I have gone to the last village we passed to purchase some supplies. You will go into the woods out the back of my tent." She reached for a knife sitting on the cutting table and quickly slit the tent back at a seam. "Head out into the woods. I want you to make a wide circle around the camp and then join back up with the road about three miles west of here. You will find an ancient Primordial pine in the meadow off to the side of the road. Behind the great pine is a cave. I will meet you there in a day or two. There are supplies in the cave. You will stay there until I can meet up with you, all right? I want to be sure no one connects my disappearance with yours." *And I want to find out who is interested in you enough to try to kidnap you out of the middle of the legion,* she thought to herself.

Handing him a flask of water and slipping some bread and cheese into his pockets, she gestured towards the slit canvas. "I have put more medicine in the flask of water. It will heal you as you travel. Now go. I will send Darius after you as soon as he arrives, but you must go."

Cayden stood up slowly. His concern for her reflected in his green eyes. "Stay safe, OK?" He bent down and hugged her fiercely and then slipped out the back of the tent, disappearing into the trees.

Chapter 21

ZIONA GATHERED HER SATCHEL and flipped back the flap. In went the potions she had made for the journey, bandages, her Primordial clothing, and several human changes of clothes. She carefully packed anything that would reveal her true ethnic roots. She must remain anonymous. She gathered thread and a large stitching awl to repair the tent seam after Darius arrived. She burned the leftover dressings from tending to Cayden's wounds in the fire pit in the middle of her tent. The flames sparked and eagerly consumed the offering.

Her thoughts drifted back to Cayden. Who was after him? Did they know who and what he was? She shivered at the thought. She had suspicions as to who might be behind the kidnapping, for that was what it had been in reality. He had been kidnapped in broad daylight with over twenty witnesses. It was a boldly brilliant move by a dangerous adversary. She would have to stick as close as bark on a tree to him from now on.

She doused the fire with the last of the water from her basin and then pulled out several unfinished garments and laid them out on the table. She placed scissors and a spool of thread next to them, putting them down carelessly as though she had stopped in the middle of working on them. She partially straightened the blankets on the cot, mussing them enough to appear to have been slept in. With a last glance around, she buckled her travel bag and waited.

Five minutes later, Darius's head popped into the tent, followed by his body. He was not alone. Five of Cayden's tent mates filed into the tent behind him.

Darius carried his and Cayden's satchels. The other five men were likewise attired, carrying packs on their backs.

"What is the meaning of this?" Ziona snapped at him, frowning with displeasure.

"When I got back, these guys were awake and whispering in the tent. They had also gone to check on Cayden and had received the same response. They were trying to decide where to go searching when I arrived. I couldn't think of anything else to do but bring them along, seeing as they knew I had been out all night searching for Cayden."

"Mistress," piped up James, "Cayden is a good lad. He didn't deserve how they treated him. Something is wrong with Sergeant Perez. He didn't report back for roll call last night. It's like he disappeared right after he arrested Cayden." He shrugged at his companions. "Well, we figured there was something rotten in the camp and it was time we decided where our loyalties lie. We want to help Cayden escape." The others nodded their heads in agreement.

"All right, I don't have time for this. Darius, you are to take your companions and follow Cayden." She quickly went over the instructions she had given Cayden. "You are to hold at the cave and stay out of sight! Do not leave the cave until I arrive. Is that clear?" Heads bobbed in understanding. "Now go, it will soon be light. Be as silent as a hawk on the wing." She held back the cut canvas, and Darius led the way out the back of the tent. They were soon swallowed by the forest.

As soon as the last man exited, Ziona stitched up the slice in the canvas. It took about ten minutes to repair the damage, but in the end, it was completely invisible to the eye.

With a last inspection, Ziona picked up her travel bag and slung it on her shoulder. She went to her horse and saddled the mare quickly. Next, she threw a halter on the mule and led both animals away from her tent.

She stopped at the next tent and called out to the occupant. "Mandy, would you watch my tent for a few hours? I need to go back to Tintern to pick up some more supplies."

"No problem, Ziona. I will take care of things here till you get back."

"Thanks! I should be back before dark, but I may also stay over in the town. I fancy a hot meal and a bath."

"Not to worry!" Mandy hollered through the tent wall.
Ziona mounted her horse and with a gentle pat on her neck,
urged her into a slow walk, the mule following with a plod.
She took the road leading away from the camp. It disappeared
from view as the sun split the horizon. She was unsure if anyone was
watching her, so for that reason alone, she decided she must make
the journey all the way to Tintern. Her plan was to purchase some
supplies, book a room at the inn, and then quietly leave again after
dark and travel by night back to Cayden. If her suspicions were
correct as to who had attempted to kidnap him, then perhaps she
was being watched also. She kept her pace leisurely, as though she
didn't have a care in the world.

She reached the village about noon and dismounted at the inn, a
shabby establishment called The King's Ransom. *The cost lived up to
its name*, she thought, as she laid out the coin for her night's stay. The
innkeeper, a portly man with a balding pate, provided her a main
floor room by the rear door as requested so "she would have the
quietest room in the inn away from the rowdy late night crowd." She
picked up her key and nodded her thanks.

She gathered her horse and mule and led them around the back to
the stables. She handed them off to the stable boy and requested they
each get an extra measure of grain each and a good rubdown. She
flipped him a coin for his consideration and he grinned back in thanks.

She paused in thought. "Oh and when you are done grooming
my mare, please saddle her again? I may decide to go for a gentle
ride later this afternoon. Leave her in her stall, saddled." He nodded
and led the animals away.

Ziona carried her travel bag to her room. Opening the door, she
found a modest room, outfitted with a simple bed, a lumpy mattress,
a wash stand with a chipped bowl and mismatched pitcher. On the
wall hung a scratched silver mirror and a ladder back chair placed
under the window completed the furnishings.

She closed the door and locked it. She was weary and needed
rest. She had not dared to sleep after Cayden had arrived injured so
severely. Besides, he had been in her bed. She stretched out on the
lumpy mattress, fully clothed, and closed her eyes. It felt like heaven.
In less than a minute, she was fast asleep.

Chapter 22

SERGEANT PEREZ CRINGED as the deeply hooded figure paused in front of him. It was a full foot taller and Perez imagined cold slimy hands were hidden by the long full sleeves. Death stalked him and played with him.

"You let him escape," the voice hissed, not quite human sounding. "You had him tied and locked in a metal cage and he still escaped."

"No, my lord!" Perez trembled, afraid to gaze too deeply into the hood. "The boy was aided by friends. Our guard was knocked out. We do not know how they found out where he was being held. Please, my lord, I can find him." Eager to please, he implored the Charun, tenting his fingers in supplication.

"You failed," hissed the faceless voice, "and I have no use for defective tools." It reached out with scaly hands and grabbed Perez by the throat. Perez eyes bulged as his air was cut off. The spectral figure squeezed and bones snapped. Perez dropped to the dirt below like a practice dummy with its ties cut.

The figure seemed to float as it rotated. Three other eerie figures, similarly garbed, stood silently waiting. "Eliminate the humans. Leave none alive."

Heads bowed in acceptance of the order. They ghosted from the room, black phantoms of death descending on an unsuspecting foe.

***

Cayden wearily sank down onto a fallen tree blocking his path. He had been walking for several hours now. Dawn had arrived but the rising sun was not able to penetrate the dense vegetation surrounding him. He had stayed deep in the woods, using the fading darkness as a compass to keep him going west.

He pulled the flask of water from his pocket and took a swig. It was cool and minty tasting. His ribs ached still, but the pain was bearable. He shook his head, amazed. How had Ziona been able to heal him so quickly? His insides warmed as the liquid reached his stomach and he felt strength returning to his muscles. He took a deep breath. The pain in his ribs receded to a whisper. His nose had also returned to a normal shape and size.

A twig snapped. Cayden's head shot up, examining the forest to the west. He froze, his ears straining to catch any out-of-place sound. The brush quivered and parted, revealing a silver-haired wolf. The wolf sniffed the air then limped toward him. An arrow was jutting from her body. She sat down beside Cayden and looked at him, pain shadowing her eyes. The arrow had entered the right shoulder near the neck. The arrowhead and gone clean through and was sticking out from the underside of the shoulder blade.

Cayden, without giving it any thought to his actions, knelt beside the wolf. Blood stained her silvery coat. The wolf fixed her ice blue eyes on him and whined. Cayden reached for his water bottle and poured a small amount of the water into the lid of the flask. He offered it to the wolf, who slurped it up gratefully. The pain receded from her eyes.

"I can't take the arrow out here. Can you come with me to a safe place?" The wolf cocked its head, listening. Cayden felt her acceptance. She licked his hand and then grabbed his pant leg and started pulling on it. She walked a little ways away and then came back and pulled on his pant leg again. "You want me to follow you?" She sat down and waited, licking at her wound.

Cayden replaced the flask and stood up. "OK. Lead the way."

The wolf headed back into the trees in a westerly direction. They had pushed through the brush for a time when they came to a small clearing. A pungent odour assaulted his nose. It wrinkled in response. A wolf pack of about fifteen animals lay bleeding in the field. Flies buzzed and rose from the carcasses as Cayden walked through the slaughter field, examining the scene. The wolves had all been shot by arrows. Hoof prints mixed in with the blood had churned up a reddish mud. The attackers had been on horseback. Why would anyone attack a wolf pack? It made no sense.

The silvery wolf yipped to gain Cayden's attention. He walked over to her, where she pawed at a jet black wolf lying on its side, three black-shafted, black-tipped arrows piercing its body. This one was male. The one blue eye seemed to plead with Cayden. The wolf was still alive.

Hesitant, Cayden placed a hand gently on his head. A jolt of liquid fire shot up his arm and a conscience pressed hard on his brain. Cayden cried out as the wolf's essence was transferred to him. Cayden fell on his side, twitching, his limbs jerking uncontrollably. Slowly, the tremors left his body. The wolf took one last breath, trembled, and was still.

From the body of the wolf rose a form of a wolf but larger, three times the size of the wolf dead on the ground. The form solidified and unfolded as though in slow motion to stand on its hind legs. Hairy arms rippled with cords of muscles that flowed across to join an equally muscled chest matted with hair. The face of the dead wolf gazed at Cayden with long wicked teeth curling from its snout. It snorted and Cayden cringed back in fright. "Do not be afraid. You have given me the chance to live again. I have given you my mortal energy and spirit and you have given me my mythical form."

Cayden gazed back at the creature in shock. "What are you?" he croaked.

"I am a werewolf. We are often thought of as evil, just as the wolf is misunderstood. I and my kind will serve you. You need only to call." The werewolf glanced around at the killing field and a ferocious light blazed to life in his eyes. "Look closely at this scene for you can learn much about what hunts you. We were slaughtered to keep from bringing you warning." He gazed at the silvery wolf beside Cayden. "Take care of Sheba for she was my she-alpha."

With a final glance around, the werewolf bounded off and was soon swallowed in the trees. Cayden sensed his passing but still retained a connection to the werewolf and could sense his presence in his mind.

Cayden collected several of the arrows lying around, wrapping them in leaves and then tucked them in his pocket, careful to not touch the blackened tips. As he headed west again, he noticed a dead wolf with a piece of cloth clamped in its jaws. He pried the cloth loose and placed it in his pocket with the arrows.

He stroked Sheba's soft head. "Are you ready to go, girl?" She raised her head and then lowered it, nudging the dead black wolf, urging him to rise. When he did not move, she raised her muzzle to the sky and howled a long, sad call. The sound was so mournful Cayden's chest constricted. There was no answering call. Tears sparked in his eyes. She trotted off toward the west. Cayden followed.

***

Ryder gagged as vomit welled up into his throat, burning with the intensity of his disgust. He swallowed, the acidic lump burning a path back down into his queasy stomach. The tinny, maggoty smells of blood and body fluids clogged his nose and added a sauce to the bile attempting to escape his body.

The carnage was beyond his experience. His gaze took in a decapitated head sitting on top of a tent pole, blood staining the wooden shaft and pooling on the ground below. The tent was whole and untouched; however, the canvas surface was sprayed with pieces of entrails and bits of bone. The part of his brain protecting his mind from shock logically attempted to compute the amount of human residue needed to constitute an entire body. Whether a part or whole body, it was clear it had exploded on the side of the tent.

Gingerly, Ryder stepped around a corpse lying at his feet, careful not to step on the flayed remains.

This scene was repeated throughout the camp with little variation. The attack appeared to have been designed to create the maximum amount of carnage. Ryder could only think of one reason to do so: to elicit stark terror from any who viewed the scene. *It's working!* His limbs trembled as he fought them for control. Behind him, he heard noisy retching from his companions.

He forced himself to turn in a complete circle to survey the scene. Cayden could be in here somewhere, still alive. They had to search.

"Break into groups of two and search for survivors." He did not need to mention which survivor they were to search for.

The group of twenty men split into teams and fanned out through what remained of the legion. Ryder was joined by the baker's son, Joshua, who had begged to come with him when he had left home. Ryder had initially refused to take him along as he was only fifteen, but in the end Joshua had followed them out of town and continued to follow despite Ryder's repeated urgings for Joshua to go home.

Everyone with Ryder was a volunteer from the village. Rumours of Ryder's plan to help Cayden escape the legion had been whispered through town and one by one they had begged to come with him. Ryder now wished he had set out alone. This was not what he had expected to find. It seemed they had walked into the middle of a war...but what war? He had not heard any rumours the entire trip while following the path of the legion.

Joshua, swallowing heavily and wiping his mouth on the sleeve of his jacket, picked up a broken spear and prodded at the bodies they passed to see if any stirred. Flies buzzed around the carcasses, billowing up and resettling on the bodies after they passed. Vultures huddled in groups at one edge of the camp, squawking and fighting over a body. They had had to chase them off at first, but the vultures were overcoming their fear of the boys quickly.

Nothing moved except for the vultures and the flies. Nothing stirred.

The strange thing was Ryder did not see any enemy soldiers amongst the dead. *Surely they had killed some of the attacking force. Had the attackers carried off their dead then to hide their identities? If so, why was there no trail away from the camp?* They had scouted the perimeter to be sure there was no ambush waiting for them. There was no sign of a retreating army. Not even of fleeing soldiers.

Nothing about the scene before him made sense. He shivered, fear making his heart thunder in his head. He wanted to be away from this place. He wanted to run. But he searched on.

Joshua flipped over a tumbled water cart and jumped back in surprise. Huddled beneath the overturned wagon covered in mud and blood was a lad about Joshua's age. His eyes were wild in his ashen face. He was not wearing a uniform. The lad raised terrified eyes to Joshua and then cried out in relief, the flood of tears streaking his face.

Hearing the sound, Ryder strode over to the survivor. A witness had been found.

Ryder squatted down and gently gripped the lad's shoulders. "It's OK. We are here to help you. My name is Ryder. Who are you?"

The lad gulped and whispered, "Michale, sir."

"What has happened here, Michale? Who did this?" Joshua knelt beside Ryder, blocking the scene from Michale's eyes.

Fixing his gaze on Ryder, Michale whispered, "Black phantoms."

This was incomprehensible to Ryder. *What is this black phantom? A kind of ghost? Or an evil spirit?*

"Do you know Cayden Tiernan? Did you see him? Is he here in the camp still?"

"He was here, sir, but he left two days ago. Or maybe he was arrested. I saw some men taking him away. He was not here when the camp was attacked."

Ryder blew out the breath he hadn't realized he was holding. They did not need to linger on the dead, only confirm there were no other survivors.

He helped pull Michale to his feet and led him back to their horses on the west side of the camp. Michale kept his face averted from the scene surrounding him and allowed Ryder to blindly lead him out of the camp.

Reaching the horses, Ryder sat Michale on the ground. "Stay with him, Joshua. Get him something to eat from our packs and some water. I will be back shortly."

Relief flooded over Ryder as he went back into the camp turned graveyard, his steps a little lighter for the news. Cayden was not here when this happened. They would continue to search for him. He would find him.

His men were gathered on the eastern edge of the camp. When Ryder reached them, they confirmed they had found no other survivors.

"Gather up as many useful weapons as you can find. We will load them on the spare mule. Whoever did this may still be around and I, personally, would like to be armed if they return. In fact, I would rather not be here at all." The weapons would not help them repel such a foe, based on what had happened here. *Would any weapon be effective?*

"Also, gather any of the horses that are still nearby. We may need a change of mount along the way." Curiously, no horses had been harmed and they grazed in groups at the edge of the camp.

Twenty men had arrived at the camp that morning. Twenty-one left the camp heading along the western road in search of Cayden. The vultures resettled to feast as they rode away.

Chapter 23

CAYDEN REACHED THE CAVE just before dark. It was cleverly hidden. The entrance was a slit in the stone outcropping, the angle left the opening in perpetual shadow. One could walk within ten feet of the opening and not see it unless one knew to look for it.

Entering the cave, he found a large cavern hollowed back into the hillside. The cave was stocked with supplies. A racking system had been installed along one wall that contained thrush sleeping mats, blankets stacked in neat piles, lanterns and lantern fuel, and cooking utensils and pots on the top shelf.

The bottom shelf contained sacks of dried beans, corn and peas, ground flour, bottles of oil, bags of dried berries, fruits, and nuts. Dried meats rounded out the basic supplies. A small spring bubbled at the back of the cave.

Selecting a lantern already half full of oil, Cayden carried it over to the mud brick cooking oven already stacked with kindling. He gathered the flint and steel from the shelf and, kneeling, rained sparks into the fluffy starter. It leapt to life and caught the dried sticks above. Cayden added a couple of smaller pieces of wood from the stacked wood pile at the back to the fire. Soon a cheery blaze was burning in the hearth. He fetched a pot and a kettle and filled both at the spring then set them atop the cooking hearth.

Sheba watched all this from a position she had taken up at the cave entrance. Cayden knew she was guarding his back while he worked. He felt her presence in his mind and the other wolves distantly. None remained of Sheba's pack.

The water in the pot bubbled. Cayden added some dried salt pork, dried beans, and some dried onions. He gave the mixture a quick stir and the fetched the tin of tea from the shelf, sprinkling a hand full of leaves into the kettle.

He then joined Sheba at the mouth of the cave, satchel in hand. He sat down beside her, pulled out his flask with the healing water, a sharp knife, and some bandaging material. He stroked her fur. She rested her chin on his thigh.

"I need to take that arrow out now, girl." She lifted her eyes in response to his voice, trust in her eyes. "I will snap the shaft off as close to the entry point as I can. I need to pull on the arrow to get the rest out of you. OK?" He did not know if she understood his words or if it was the tone of his voice.

Gritting his teeth, he set to cutting the shaft of the arrow. Sheba growled and squirmed as the bolt shifted in her skin. The shaft broke off with a snap. "I am going to pull on the arrowhead here now. OK?" She panted, seeming to understand. Cayden gripped the arrowhead and quickly pulled. Sheba yelped and whimpered. The arrow pulled free. Fresh blood poured from the wound. Cayden quickly soaked two bandages in the water and pressed them to the wounds and held them. Sheba shuddered and lowered her head to her paws, panting. Slowly she relaxed as the water's soothing healing took effect. Cayden wrapped the cloths in place with more bandaging and tied them off. He then fetched a bowl from the shelf and poured the last of the water into it and placed it in front of Sheba. She thirstily drank it down.

Suddenly, Sheba's head came up and she growled a low growl. She stood up, hackles rising along her back. Cayden got to his feet and peered out of the cleft. Men were approaching on foot. The lead man paused and knelt examining Cayden's trail, and then their heads swivelled toward the cave.

"Do not move!" Cayden commanded, as he grabbed Sheba's scruff. He wished he had a weapon. Sheba would have to do. She growled low in her throat and shifted in front of Cayden, sensing his alarm.

"Cayden, it's me, Darius." Darius stepped forward, hands displayed for Cayden. He jerked his head towards his companions. "They wanted to come help you. They were waiting for me when I returned to the tent."

"It's OK, Sheba. They are friends." She continued to growl protectively and then licked his hand. He scratched her behind the ear.

They approached the cave and came to an abrupt halt as the wolf growled warningly at them from the shadowed entrance. Darius stopped in surprise. "What are you doing with a wolf?" Darius handed Cayden his satchel that he had retrieved from their shared tent. Sheba's lips curled back in warning at the movement. Darius snatched his hand away and backed up.

Cayden patted Sheba comfortingly. "We found we needed each other and joined forces. Never hurts to have an extra pair of eyes, especially ones as sharp as hers."

"Yes...but a wolf?" The others crowded in around Darius, leery of approaching Cayden while Sheba still rumbled warning.

Cayden shrugged. "Come on in. I have a stew cooking. With a few more beans, there should be enough for everyone." Sheba followed him back to the fire as the men filtered in and took up positions along the one wall. Her eyes followed them, marking their movements. She took up her position at the door again and lay down, clearly guarding the entrance once more.

The smell of the cooking stew drew the men like butterflies to nectar and they crowded around the pot, sniffing appreciatively. Cayden tossed in some more beans and some additional dried pork and let the stew cook while he sorted through the contents of his satchel. He felt around the base and found that all his essentials were there. He could feel his flutes in the bottom of his satchel, untouched.

Cayden gave the pot a final stir and then ladled stew into the wooden bowls. Famished, they set to eating, gobbling down the food without speaking.

After pouring a cup of tea for himself, Cayden brought a bowl with pork scraps to Sheba. He then settled with his back against the wall between the newcomers and Sheba. She thumped her tail and ate the offering hungrily.

"So tell me, Darius, how did you all come to be here?" Cayden's gaze took in all five men. *How well do I really know them?*

"We insisted on coming, Cayden." Pieter poured himself a cup of tea also. "We all felt bad about what went down back at camp. Sergeant Perez was completely out of line. When we couldn't find you or Darius later on, we knew something bad was going on. He acted strangely toward you from the first day. We all saw it."

Darius took up the story. "So they followed me back to where Ziona was waiting. Sergeant Perez never showed up for roll call, not the evening or the morning one. Ziona sent us on this way to catch up with you."

"Cayden, what's going on? Why did they accuse you of murdering a soldier?" Pieter asked. "The man with Sergeant Perez, he's not a regular soldier of the legion. He arrived a couple days before you did." The other men nodded in agreement.

"We were told he was sent by the queen. He roamed around the camp, checking out the younger recruits. We never saw him do much of anything else," said James. "I think he is some kind of military police or the queen's personal guard. He asked a lot of questions about everyone's background, where they were from, that kind of thing. Strange man, we all thought. It was like he was hunting someone though. We dubbed him 'the Inquisitor' as a nickname." He peered curiously at Cayden.

Cayden stared into his cup of tea. He had no idea who the officer was. He had not worn any insignia. If he had arrived just before Cayden volunteered, that would mean he was the lord that rode into town with the legion on the first day. Obviously, he was not searching for a murderer as that event occurred later. Cayden remembered the hatred in his eyes when he had glimpsed him outside of the inn.

He looked around at the silently waiting men. How much should he tell them? They deserved some of the truth. They had irrevocably bound their lives to his in deciding to follow after him. Foolish as it was, they had shown themselves to be friends and he decided they should not be left totally in the dark. He raised his head to find their faces staring at him.

"I did not kill anyone. My friend did." Leaving names out of the story, he told them what had happened that day. It seemed so long ago. Heads nodded as the story progressed. When Cayden finished speaking, silence descended on the cave. Cayden got up, retrieved another lamp from the shelf, and lit the wick.

"So this Inquisitor, what is his reason for being here? We assumed he was sent by the queen too," Darius said.

Cayden shrugged. He had no answer for them.

"You sure know how to make friends, Cayden," Pieter laughed. "I mean, we walk up and say hello while you cliff folk stick 'em with steel. Mind you, he probably deserved it, that one. Dangerous enemies to have though, I think."

"Now you know why you shouldn't be following me," Cayden urged. "I will be hunted, now they know I am out here. There are sure to be soldiers following me. If I were you, I'd sneak away and go back home. Best not to be found anywhere near me."

The others laughed.

"We are no longer farm boys, Cayden, any more than you are," Pieter said. "I fancy seeing a bit of the world, so I will stick around, if it's all the same." Heads bobbed in agreement.

Cayden shook his head, frustrated with their foolishness.

"I think I will turn in." Cayden tried to suppress the yawn in his voice. "I really didn't get much sleep last night." He grabbed a blanket and a mat from the rack and unrolled them near Sheba. Opening his satchel, he extracted his short knife and placed it within reach of his hand. He crawled under the blanket and Sheba nestled in beside him. They were asleep before the rest had finished their teas.

Cayden woke with a start about five hours later. Sheba's head came up at the same time. Someone approached the cave with a soft-booted walk. Strangely, Sheba did not growl. Cayden placed his hand on the knife. The moon silhouetted a figure, standing in the entrance of the cave. Ziona entered and spied Cayden. Sheba huffed and then put her head back down on her paws. Ziona placed her bag on the floor and, gathering a mat and blanket, stretched out near them with relief. She closed her eyes and fell promptly to sleep.

Chapter 24

DAWN LIGHT FILTERED into the opening of the cave, announcing a new day. Cayden sat up, rubbing his eyes. He stretched his ribs and found only a very slight tenderness remained. His ribs were fully healed, marvelling again at the potion Ziona had concocted for him.

He glanced over to see her eyes open and staring at him. She put a finger to her lips and then motioned for him to follow her outside. Sheba rose and followed, her limp much improved this morning. Cayden followed Ziona to the edge of the trees away from the cave, so as to not disturb the sleeping occupants. Cayden stopped in front of her, gathering her beautiful green eyes to his, and promptly became lost in them. He shook his head to dispel the spell.

"Thank you for helping me yesterday. What was in that water? It worked miracles."

Ziona stroked his face. "I will show you how to prepare it. It is a simple preparation but requires very rare ingredients. Sufficed to say, I made enough to keep us for a time if used sparingly. Your legion mates found you," she said, waving in the direction of the cave. "They made good time."

"Yes, they arrived late yesterday afternoon. Where have you been?"

"I had to make sure my back trail was clear before coming on to you. Rest assured no one has followed you to this site, other than those whom I have sent." She glanced down at Sheba. "Is she from the pack of dead wolves I found back in the woods?"

"Yes. I don't know who did this, but I did keep some arrows and a piece of a cloak one of the wolves had torn off in the fighting. Do you want me to get them?"

"Yes, let's take a look at them."

Cayden walked back to the cave and retrieved his satchel into which he had tucked the strange arrows. He extracted them and turned them over in his hands, examining the black fletching and shortened shafts. He handed them carefully to Ziona along with the torn piece of black cloth. Sheba whined and trotted off into the woods. Cayden didn't blame her; the memories were sad ones for him also.

Ziona examined the arrows. She frowned and then took the cloth from him. The fabric was light as gossamer silk yet resisted tearing or fraying. It must have taken the wolf a lot of strength to pull it free. Ziona's thoughts returned to a large male wolf she had spied in the forest, lying dead on ground. If the same wolf that tore this piece of cloth free, the three arrows in its body was a testament to his determination to not let go.

Ziona's brows drew down in a scowl. "Walk with me, Cayden." She strode away, stiff-backed from the cave. Reaching the woods, she ducked behind the large willow and spun to him. "Do you have any idea who hunts you?" she demanded.

Cayden frowned and shook his head. "No, there were none present when Sheba took me there. She led me to the site. I think she was the only one to survive. She had an arrow through her shoulder when she found me. Why do you assume they were hunting me?"

"You had better thank your lucky stars they were not around. They were hunting *you*. Of that there can be no question."

Cayden's eyes widened, meeting her earnest ones.

"What hunts you is called the Charun. They are the dead spirits of our land, Primordials who have been slain in battle and their souls received by the Goddess of the Dead, Helga. For them to walk the land again, they must be summoned by a Dark Primordial High Priest or Priestess. I did not believe that the legend had survived till this time, let alone the knowledge of how to animate them." She walked away and paced five stiff steps and then five stiff steps back, stopping in front of him.

She grasped his arms reading the fear in his green eyes. "The Seekers were taught about Charun by the Mother Priestess as part of our training. This knowledge is only passed to a few chosen ones. The knowledge of how to raise the Charun from the dead is kept strictly with the High Priestess, of course. The implications of them being here is worrisome."

Cayden struggled to get his lips to move. They had frozen in a perfect *O* shape of horror at her words. Charun! *But the Charun are a myth! Minions of the underworld; legendary creatures used by village parents to frighten disobedient children.* In all the old stories, they were described as loathsome creatures, terrifying to behold and now walking the earth...*hunting him.* Wait! Hunting him?

"Charun are, of course, already dead. It is very difficult, therefore; to kill one...or de-animate one would be a better description. One cannot kill what is already dead." She looked back when she realized he hadn't moved. He was frozen to the spot, horror freezing his limbs as though encased in ice.

Ziona took his hands in hers. She touched him this time, not to measure for clothes, not to heal, but to provide comfort and solace. She tugged on his hands pulling him close and wrapped her arms around him, drawing him into her embrace.

Cayden found it hard to unbend, to relax. He was shocked to his very core. Confusion had his thoughts running in all directions. Should he flee? Should he hide? Should he fight? But how? Where? Why? Above all, the question *why* was stuck in his mind. Why was this happening to him? Answers...he needed answers. Someone must know why!

He shuddered in her arms. Ziona soothed his back with a gentle hand. He met her eyes at last and asked the simple question, burning within him.

"Why, Ziona?"

"I don't have all the answers, Cayden. I know you are special and they seem to know it too. How knowledge of you reached their masters, I do not know either. I am glad I found you in time. And know this for a fact. I will protect your life before my own. From here on out, we will not be separated." She released him and checked the cave entrance again. All was still; the men slept on. "You are collecting quite a following. Something about you calls to the men around you. They sense something special about you, I think, greatness yet to fully flower. They are unconsciously answering that call. You will have to lead them."

Cayden snorted. "Lead them? Lead them where? If I am being chased by Charun, then I should tell them all to leave me and flee! It would be stupid of them to follow me, maybe even fatal!"

"You need them, Cayden. You cannot do this alone. They follow you out of choice. No man should take that choice away from them. You can explain the risk, but in the end the choice remains theirs."

"What is it I am supposed to do, Ziona? I don't understand what is happening. I don't know where to go."

Ziona gazed at him a long while. "I think you do know what to do. Where does your heart say to go? What are your instincts? Close your eyes and clear your mind. What feels right?"

Cayden closed his eyes. He slowed his breathing, stilling his racing heart. Ziona placed her fingertips at his temple and massaged in a slow circle. Peace flowed into him.

Where do I need to go? He let his mind float and suddenly there bloomed into his mind a castle wall surrounding tall towers of stone soaring above the ramparts. A flag snapped in the breeze...the flag of the queen.

His eyes jerked open. Ziona's were inches from his. He felt her sweet breath on his cheek. He stepped back, breaking contact. "I saw a castle. The queen's flag was flying there."

She frowned. "You are being drawn to the castle of she who is likely behind all of this?" Ziona shook her head in puzzlement. "What could possibly lie that way but death?" She hugged her arms around her middle as she paced. "Sharisha warned me not to interfere with your choices, but this hardly seems wise." She stopped in front of him, studying him again. "All right, we do it your way. We travel for the capital city of Cathair. It's time we roused the men. We need to keep moving." She headed back to the cave, Cayden following in her wake.

Sheba returned from her hunt with a rabbit clutched in her jaws. She trotted up beside Cayden and then growled a warning once again. Her eyes were fixed down the road to the east. Cayden squinted and saw a faint dust cloud rising to announce the presence of riders, multiple riders by the amount of dust in the air. He called out to Ziona and pointed in the direction of the cloud. By unspoken mutual agreement, they slid back into the trees to watch the oncoming riders.

The dust storm resolved into about fifty horses, only half of which were actually being ridden. Each rider led an empty-saddled mount. They were not soldiers. There were no wagons, which ruled out a merchant train.

The lead rider came into view and with a yelp, Cayden leapt from the trees and bolted out into the field and started waving his arms like a windmill. Sheba bounded after him and took up a defensive position in front of him. Ziona hissed and quickly followed, pulling a set of sharp knives from her sleeves and brandishing them.

Cayden stopped in surprise and then grinned. "It's my best friend, Ryder!" He swung back to the road and hollered, "Ryder, you big lump, I'm over here!" He wasn't sure if it was his hollering or if it was the flapping arms, but Ryder slowed and turned his mount toward him.

Suddenly, Ryder put boot to ribs and his horse bolted toward Cayden. Just as suddenly, the horse shied and Ryder nearly went straight over his horse's neck. His mount had spotted Sheba, who had grown to twice her normal size, fur distended from her body.

Ryder leapt down from his mount and continued on foot. Cayden patted Sheba and told her it was all right. She slowly relaxed but continued to growl softly. Ryder glanced at the wolf and stopped. "Is that you, Cayden?"

Cayden covered the distance between them and grabbed Ryder in a bear hug in response. Ryder crushed him back and then they were both talking at once. The men riding with Ryder halted on the road, watching the reunion.

Ziona walked up, tucking the knives back up her sleeves as she approached.

Behind her, the cave suddenly erupted with men, all brandishing weapons and running towards Cayden and Ziona.

Cayden held up his hand in a halting gesture with a quick glance over his shoulder. "These are friends. Please lower your weapons." Swords slowly dropped.

"Now that is what I call a welcoming party." Ryder grinned, surveying the partially clothed men. "There are strange things happening in the world." The grin slid from Ryder's face as he turned back to Cayden.

Cayden saw sadness touched with fear replace the joy of a few moments ago in Ryder's eyes. "We need to talk, Cayden." He looked at Ziona and raised an eyebrow in query.

Cayden reached back and took Ziona's hand, drawing her forward. "Ryder, this is Ziona. She has been a great help to me. Let's get your men settled and the horses picketed, and then we can talk."

Ryder motioned for the riders to approach and they filed in with their mounts.

"Why do you have all the extra horses?" Cayden was curious at the string of horse flesh being pulled along with the riders.

"I will explain in a minute."

They hobbled and picketed the horses, allowing them to graze. They remained saddled, however. Cayden noted the precaution.

"Please make these men comfortable and scrounge up a meal for them," Cayden instructed his companions. Ryder's men followed them back into the cave.

"Why are you here, Ryder?"

Ryder withdrew his waterskin from his saddlebag and leaned against a tree trunk. He uncorked it and took a long drink to quench his thirst and then described everything that had transpired up to their arrival a few minutes ago.

Ziona and Cayden took turns describing their flight from the legion's camp.

"We were so afraid you were lying dead in that horrible place." Ryder grimaced as the unwanted images passed before his eyes.

"One thing is certain." Ziona pinned Cayden with a look. "That camp was attacked because of you. You must take my warning seriously, Cayden. Men are dying for it."

Cayden raked his hands through his hair. He nodded. He looked to the south in the direction of Cathair. Something tugged at him, urging him to go in that direction.

That quickly, Cayden's band became thirty. There would be no more hiding their travels. From here on out, they would be riding in the open and much easier to spot.

Chapter 25

AVERY CROUCHED IN THE BUSHES between her father and Sharisha. The scene before them was eerily silent. A door swung back and forth in the breeze, creaking on rusting hinges. A lone chicken strutted across the empty street and disappeared into a flower bed to the right of the loose door. Nothing disturbed its passage.

The town seemed deserted. No smoke rose from the hearth chimneys. No children played in the warm sunshine. No laundry was strung from the drying lines in the backyards.

Sharisha stood up suddenly and strode forward into the village. Gaius and Avery followed, but at a much slower pace. Avery felt a great sadness about the town and a deep-rooted terror. Sharisha entered the dwelling with the creaking door. Inside was a comfortable living room. The chairs were covered with bright quilted pillow seats, the floors adorned with woven mats. Matching curtains fluttered in the windows.

The table in the kitchen was set with four bowls. A roast sat in the middle of the table, carving knife and fork resting on the side of the platter. Several slices had been carved from the roast and lay ready for serving. A bowl of potatoes and a bowl of peas were also on the table. The fly-covered food had spoiled as had the meat. There was no one home. The house sat empty.

Avery touched the tabletop and a flash of pure emotion assailed her. She gasped. For a second, she saw the family seated before her at the table. The woman wrestled two young children into their chairs. Her husband stood carving the meat. Suddenly, they both glanced toward the doorway. Horror sprang into their eyes and their mouths opened to scream. There was a sudden bright flash and everyone vanished.

Avery stumbled back from the table as the vision faded. Tears sprang to her eyes and she gasped, hands over her mouth. She collapsed to the floor. Sharisha bent down and eased her to a sitting position.

"What was it, Avery? What did you see?"

Avery described the vision, blinking away tears that misted her vision. Gaius frowned at the table.

"Was that an actual vision? Or was it my imagination?"

Sharisha helped her to her feet. "Oh, I think it was a true vision. As to what could cause people to vanish, I know of only one possibility." Sharisha strode out the door and continued to search the other dwellings. All were empty of inhabitants.

In the barn, they found a hay fork dropped beside a loose bale of hay. The stall door beside it was broken. The horse had kicked it down to get to the food. They searched the barn. None of the animal fodder had spoiled. Only the human and Primordial food was going bad. They found the horse out the back of the barn, happily munching on the flowers planted along the side of the inn next door.

"We need to leave this place," Sharisha said. They hurried back to their horses, which they had tied off in the woods. Mounting up, they skirted the village and continued on down the road.

The next three villages they reached were similarly abandoned, their inhabitants seeming to have disappeared midway through activities. The farms they found in between villages were also empty of human life.

They set up camp for the evening in the yard of one such farm, where they turned out the horses to graze. No one wished to sleep inside, even though it was obvious no one was returning to the houses. Settling down around their campfire, Avery turned to Sharisha. "Tell me what is going on. Where is everyone?"

Worry drew Sharisha's brows together. "These are villages of the spirit clans. The Primordial of this area have been taken by the Paimon. The Paimon is the king of the underworld who manages the armies of the dead for both the Mother Goddess and the Great Goddess of the Dark. Humans would know the armies of the Mother

Goddess as angels, the armies of the Dark as demons. It would appear the Paimon is recruiting for both armies."

Avery and Gaius gasped in unison.

"I think it is safe to say war is imminent, if not already occurring. Recruitment in this fashion is usually a result of unrest in the underworld." She addressed Avery. "The prophecies speak of a saviour to be born who will heal the land and its peoples and will lead the armies of righteousness against the forces of the Dark One, and who will unite all peoples in the final days." She looked away. "It seems those days are upon us now. It is time to rest. We will reach my people with one more day's hard ride."

Avery crawled under her blankets, her thoughts full of what she had seen. She eventually dropped into a troubled sleep, a sleep where she dreamed of Cayden in a cage and a ghostly hooded figure standing over him with a bloody knife. She cried out a warning, then rolled over and drifted back to sleep.

Chapter 26

CAYDEN AND RYDER assembled the men. They were a ragtag bunch in farmer's woolens and former legion uniforms. Joshua scratched at his arm where the itchy wool rubbed against his sweaty skin.

Silence fell as Cayden stepped forward to address them, Ryder at his side. Sheba took up a position on the other side of Cayden.

"We wish to speak to you about your presence here." Cayden glanced at Ryder, who nodded encouragingly. "I want you to know that I truly appreciate your care and concern in coming to rescue me." He gripped Darius on the shoulder. "Without your help, I would still be captured and possibly dead by now." Darius smiled, accepting the nod in his direction. "I must make you all understand the danger you are placing yourselves in by staying with me. Something is hunting me. I do not understand what or why. But understand this. Everything you have seen since leaving your homes is related to these enemies. They will not quit pursuing me. If you stay with me, there is every chance you will die doing so."

His gaze touched each of them briefly. "I cannot ask you to stay. There is no shame in going home after what you have seen these past few days. However, if you are willing, we would be glad to have your help and assistance. We will be travelling to the capital city of Cathair."

Ryder stepped in at this point. "If you choose to stay, the men who followed Cayden out of the legion will be training you all in battle and weapons techniques beginning today. You need to learn fighting skills if we are to survive. You have seen what we face. The legion was killed to a last man…except for those who had left earlier."

"What killed the men in the camp?" asked a pale-faced Joshua.

Ziona took over and painted a gruesome picture of the Charun for the men. Faces paled and many men swallowed, panic striking their hearts. Ziona then reached up and uncoiled her hair, revealing her Primordial features. The assembled men gasped in surprise. Murmuring arose from the crowd.

"Know this!" Ziona's voice rang out. "Cayden is not alone. He has the support of the Primordial people in this quest given to him. He does not fight alone! Do you stand with him?" She surveyed the men. "There can be no doubt in your decision. The world is changing and he is central to it. Choose now, but choose carefully for you will not be asked again. Stay and help; fight and die if necessary. Or leave. There is no shame in doing so. But you must choose now. If you leave later, it will be viewed as treason. There is no turning back."

The youths from Cayden's village shuffled their feet and as a man, looked to Ryder. Ryder nodded to them, feet spread wide and beefy arms crossed across his chest.

Michale stepped forward. "I think I speak for all the men here," he trembled, his voice breaking, "when I say we will stay. What hope is there for the souls of the living if things like the Charun are allowed to roam the world? We are all doomed if we do not take action. Stay or go home, but at least we know what is out there now. The people in the villages and farms across this land have no idea." He met Ziona's eyes and his hardened with determination. "If the Primordial people are willing to back Cayden, then I stand with Cayden." He stepped forward and knelt in front of Cayden, head bowed. "I pledge my life, body, and soul to you, Cayden Tiernan. I am your sword."

All of the men followed suit, going to one knee where they stood and repeated the pledge.

Cayden's jaw dropped open in surprise. Ziona nudged his arm. His jaw snapped shut.

Cayden cleared his throat. "Rise, men," he squeaked. They rose as one, flashing grins at each other. *It's like they think this is a grand adventure.* Cayden struggled to keep the grimace off his face. He felt completely foolish commanding them to rise, like some lord.

Cayden grabbed Ryder by the sleeve, hauling him around so their backs were to the men, their faces hidden. "We need to get going. We can't stay here. Can you organize them? Darius is a good man and well trained. He would make an excellent second-in-command for you."

"I will take care of it."

"Darius, step forward," Ryder commanded, turning back to the crowd. Darius took two strides forward and snapped a sharp salute. Ryder pulled his sword and in the fashion he imagined the knights of old would have performed this ritual, he commanded Darius to kneel. Darius sank to his knees and bowed his head. "Darius, you are hereby raised to the rank of captain and you are now my second-in-command." He lightly touched the blade to each shoulder then raised it straight, before dropping his arm to his side. His eyes took in all his men. "You will take orders from Captain Darius as you do me. Rise, captain."

"Your first task as captain is to get every man to a horse and to distribute the weapons we brought. Your men must be armed. Your second task is to arrange the men into fighting units. Choose a capable man to be in charge of supplies and have him gather men to secure provisions from the cave to be packed on the spare horses. We break camp in an hour. Dismissed!"

The men followed Darius back toward the cave and hobbled horses to begin preparations to leave.

Ziona moved closer to Cayden and Ryder. "We need maps. I will ride ahead and gather some maps in the next village. A lone woman will not be suspicious. Stay away from the main roads where ever possible. Try to keep the men on a parallel course to the road and use scouts to keep track of your relationship to the road. I will join back up with the band by sunset." She glanced at the sky. "The Charun prefer to move about in the darkness for they are creatures of shadow. Evening will be a dangerous time. Travel during the day should be relatively safe, provided there are no other forces out there hunting you, Cayden."

She retrieved her pack and sleeping roll and some basic supplies from the cave, gathered her horse and mule and with a quick hug for Cayden, mounted and rode off to the west.

Chapter 27

LAURISTA STUMBLED OUT OF THE BUSH, the gash on her head bleeding through the cloth she had hastily tied around her forehead. She limped slowly over toward the trembling horse. It was clearly terrified of her, nostrils flaring and eyes rolling back. It bared its teeth in warning.

She murmured soft words to it and held out the apple once again. She knew she would not survive unless she could ride for help. She stumbled and fell to the ground. The horse snorted and backed up further.

Her world spun. *Light-headed from blood loss*, her mushy brain told her. She reached up and applied pressure once again to her head wound. The world swam and she fainted.

A velvety soft muzzle nuzzling her hand roused her once more. The apple was gone. The horse snorted gently and took a step closer, searching her body for more apples. Laurista opened her eyes and stared it in the face. Slowly, she reached up her hand and patted its muzzle. Her hand closed on the bridle and she pulled herself up as the horse stepped back, pulling her to her feet.

She made a shushing noise, moving slowly to calm it. It stood still, permitting her touch. The gelding was still saddled. It had been one of the scouts' mounts. She gathered the reins and pulled herself into the saddle.

She pointed it west and nudged it into a walk, hanging on its neck to keep from sliding back to the ground.

***

Ziona paused, hearing the sound of movement in the bush. She faded back into the trees, watching the approach of some animal. Her horse whinnied in greeting. A grey gelding stepped out of the bush, carrying a rider slumped over in the saddle. Ziona urged her mount forward and approached the unconscious person. She dismounted and cautiously approached the woman whose blue dress was covered in blood, the once white sleeves stiffened in gore. The woman slid sideways out of the saddle, as her mount came to a halt. Ziona caught her and lowered her gently to the ground. She tied the horse with her own and retrieved her medicine bag, her precious potion, her skin of water, and soft rags.

Kneeling by the woman, Ziona forced some of their precious potion between her chapped lips. The woman swallowed it automatically, but her eyes remained closed. Ziona unstopped her water bottle and then unwound the hastily applied bandage around the lady's head. A large gash pulsed with blood, beginning to trickle down her forehead and into her matted hairline, remoistening the blood already soaking it.

Ziona washed the gash and then pulled a needle and thread from her pocket and stitched the large wound. It took forty stitches to close the gap. She examined her skull and was relieved to find no fracture. She knew that did not mean there was not some swelling under the skull.

She washed off the remaining blood and affixed a smaller bandage in place over the cut. She poured a little more potion down the woman's throat, which she swallowed again.

Next, she examined the rest of the woman. There were no other severe injuries. There was a slice in her sleeve, revealing a superficial cut on the arm that had long since stopped bleeding. Ziona cleaned that wound too.

Ziona leaned back to examine the woman. Obviously, the gore on her dress was not her own. She stripped the woman down to her smallclothes and then redressed her with a soft robe from her own pack.

As she finished her ministrations, the woman stirred. Her hazel eyes fluttered open and focused on Ziona's face.

"You are the seamstress from the merchant's camp," she croaked. She reached up and touched her forehead. Her eyes flew open. "You have stitched it already?" She struggled to sit up and Ziona assisted her. The woman trembled weakly. However, she felt herself strengthening dramatically. She peered closer at Ziona. "You are not what you seem, are you?"

"I am a friend. Now that I know where you came from, I understand the gore all over you. Come, we need to keep moving, those who attacked the camp are still nearby."

She helped her back onto her horse, repacked her supplies into her saddlebags, and mounted up beside the woman. "My name is Ziona."

"My name is Laurista. Your name is Primordial?"

"Yes. Let's go."

Laurista followed Ziona's retreating horse, eyes thoughtful.

They reached the village of Stonytrail about two hours later. Laurista donned Ziona's cloak to disguise her lack of proper clothing. They had stopped to bathe in a secluded bend of the river. Laurista joyfully sluiced away the gore and the stink of death from her skin and hair. They had not spoken much during the ride, Laurista too exhausted to do more than concentrate on keeping her balance in the saddle, Ziona deep in thought and planning.

They skirted the village and set up a meager camp on the western edge of the village in a small dense grove of cottonwoods. Approaching the town, they entered a dressmaker's shop and purchased two changes of clothing for Laurista. Ziona handed over the coins and nodded to Laurista's hastily whispered thanks.

"Is there a mapmaker in town?" Ziona asked the merchant.

"No mapmaker, but the village mayor keeps a stock of such items. He is the fifth house down on the riverside."

They made their way to the indicated dwelling and knocked on the red-painted door. A maid opened it and ushered them into a small waiting alcove. She returned a few minutes later with the mayor, a tall dark-haired man sporting a handlebar mustache that he twisted between his fingers as he listened to their request.

"I may have a map I can spare, but it was done for a mining survey, so it does not show the roads so much as the areas where caves are located. Would that suffice?"

"Yes, that would be fine, good sir." The mayor fetched the map and spread it out on a table before them. Ziona inspected it and then rolled it up tightly, slipping it into its protective sleeve. She handed over several coins in payment and thanked the mayor.

"Be careful in your travels, ladies. There are strange men and creatures afoot," he called to their retreating backs, closing the doors behind them.

Chapter 28

NELSON SET TWO STEAMING PLATES OF FOOD on the table,
one in front of Denzik and the other in front of Fabian. Fabian
rubbed his hands together, smacking his lips in anticipation. Thick
cuts of pork adorned his plate, dripping in rich gravy. Roasted
potatoes and freshly snapped peas were piled high in
accompaniment. Nelson carried three beer steins over to the table,
set them before the men, and then slid in beside Denzik at the
booth.

Forks and knives scraped and glasses clinked while they cleaned
their plates. Nelson sipped his beer, watching the room. No one
seemed to be paying any attention to them. His serving staff drifted
between tables and a happy hum hung in the air as the patrons ate
and conversed.

Nelson took another sip and then set down his mug. "We
discovered a promising cave this morning. It had too narrow of an
opening to get through, so I set the men to enlarging it. It is now
ready. Supplies have been brought down into the cavern and a crew
of eight men are waiting for us," he murmured in a voice low
enough to not carry past their table.

"As we get closer to our target, we will have to be careful about
when we are excavating. Sound travels far in tunnels and we do not
want to alert anyone on the inside to our presence," Denzik said.
"The patrols are at their thinnest in the early morning hours and we
should tackle the heavy excavation work then."

"It's also time we attempted to sneak someone into the castle
grounds to spy out the guards' schedules. For the final wall breach,

we may need an external distraction to take the guards away from the breach point," said Nelson.

"I agree," said Fabian. "And I think I know of just the person. The queen has a soft spot for my sticky buns. I believe we should send along my apprentice, Anthony, on the next delivery. He will be able to get right inside the castle and into the kitchens themselves."

Fabian dunked one of his rolls into the leftover gravy on his plate, smeared it around, and then popped the bite into his mouth. He chewed in satisfaction. "Excellent meal, as usual," he said in a louder voice to Nelson. "Please pass on my compliments to your splendid cook." He picked up his mug and drank deeply.

Nelson spoke up too. "Why don't you come back and compliment her yourself? She'd rather hear it from you than from me, I expect."

"Certainly, lead the way, good man!" They rose and followed Nelson through the back hallway to the kitchen. Warm fragrant air assailed them as the door opened, revealing a bustling room full of servers. Tabitha stood, waving her spoon toward a young girl, who was lifting a tray loaded with plates. "There's a good girl. Balance it on your shoulder and use the front hand to guide it. That's it. Now off with you!" They stepped back out of the way to give the girl a clear passage out the door. It swung shut behind her as she left.

Tabitha frowned at the intrusion and marched over to them. "You had better be bringing more supplies! I have been waiting for them for over a day now." She lowered her voice and nodded toward the small door at the back of the kitchen. "They are waiting for you out back."

"Thank you, kind mistress, for the delicious dinner. I would be honoured to unload the supplies for you. Carry on, my good woman!" Fabian smacked his middle in appreciation and headed off toward the rear door. Denzik followed with Nelson bringing up the rear. As they exited the kitchen, they found Erik standing in the back corridor.

"All is arranged, sir. The men are waiting for you below." He stood to the side to allow them to pass. They quickly entered the supply room and crawled down the ladder into the hidden cellar below. Erik pulled the trapdoor closed behind him.

Grabbing a lantern each, they trekked into the limestone cavern. The walk took about thirty minutes, during which Denzik admired their handiwork of the intervening seventeen years.

A great amount of time and effort and secrecy had gone into this project; but perhaps this evening would be the night they saw the fruit of their efforts. The tunnel was tall enough for them to walk fully upright and three abreast. Every hundred yards or so a side shaft had been cut, rising back to the surface for ventilation. Occasionally, during their excavations, they stumbled on another naturally formed cave and these were back-filled with the debris and stones chipped away during their tunnelling efforts.

Of course, the truly remarkable discoveries had come when they had uncovered the black rock in one of the side shafts. The men swore the stuff would burn better and longer than wood. It seemed strange to Denzik that a rock would burn, but the men assured him it was so. They gathered the flammable rock and separated it to be stored in an empty building in town. Perhaps they could sell some of it.

The end of the tunnel lightened and sloped slightly under Denzik's feet. Lanterns had been hung from pegs driven into the walls every twenty feet along the passage. The light resolved into a widened passage, where two men stood guard at the entrance they had widened.

Denzik stepped past the men and into the cavern. He stopped dead in amazement. The cavern, now lit by the twenty lanterns Nelson had prepared earlier, shone with an eerie beauty. The strangeness of the cave made Nelson feel as though he had stepped into another world. Perhaps he had.

He moved forward toward the men gathered in the center of the cavern. They all carried packs with shovels, picks, and gear to camp if necessary. Each carried a lantern and a walking stick to prod ahead and check their footing as they walked. No one wanted to step into a crevice or onto a fragile ledge that gave way underfoot.

They picked up the three spare packs waiting for them and slung them onto their backs.

"Lead the way, gentlemen," Denzik called to the men. One by one, they filed off down the cave, following the water source into the darkness. The cave narrowed and they followed the stream, the rocks slick and coated with an oily film. Nelson's booted foot slipped and splashed into the streambed. The footing was treacherous as they traversed the slimy, stony floor.

Half an hour later, the stream disappeared into a thin crevice in the wall and the tunnel they were following abruptly ended.

"Raise your lanterns and see if you can find any other openings in the rock face," Denzik called out.

They raised their lanterns, scanning the walls on either side of them.

Nelson raised his arm and pointed. Above the rocky face in front of them, about ten feet in the air, was a door-sized opening, obscured by deep shadows. Everyone raised their lamps, adding more light to flood the surface of the rock face.

There was an actual door in the opening. A thick iron-bound wooden door...a door that appeared very much like the doors found throughout the castle dungeons. They murmured to each other and searched to see if there were any other such openings. There was no ladder to the door and the face of the rock was smooth and unbroken. There was no door handle. It appeared it was meant to be opened on one side only.

Denzik scratched his day-old grey beard, eyes narrowed in thought.

"Have the men spread out. I want them to search this area. The door must have a purpose and I would prefer knowing what it is before we attempt to open it."

They scattered through the cave, searching for a clue to explain the door's presence.

One of the men wandered back into a shadowed corner and suddenly called out in alarm. They rushed over and found him staring down at a skeleton of a man in a Kingsmen uniform. The flesh had shrunk and shrivelled, covering the skull like a papier mâché mask. He lay on his back, head leaning against the rock, and clutched in his curled hand was a rotting leather bag.

Denzik reached down and picked up the bag, which crumbled to dust as he took it. Inside were twenty pieces of silver.

Denzik studied the door again. *This must be the Traitor's Gate*, he thought. At least he knew where they were now.

Denzik searched the body, but no clues were found as to his identity.

The others spread out and found five more bodies scattered in the area. They all appeared to have died around the same time. On the last one, Denzik found an insignia made of bronze, a captain of the King's Guard. He knelt down and examined the skeleton.

"There you are, Captain O'Reilly. I always wondered why you never came back to visit after your retirement. You never had a chance, did you?" he said softly. Denzik gazed around at the other men. He knew who they were now. The rest of O'Reilly's squad, the one he had taken over for all those years ago.

"I kept your secret safe all these years. Rest in peace, my friend." He stood up. He had missed Nelson and Fabian's approach. He gestured to the bones at his feet. "Captain O'Reilly." Nelson and Fabian nodded in understanding.

He raised his voice to encompass all the men. "This is the Traitor's Gate. I do not believe it has been used in decades. It may be unguarded. If so, it's good news for us. If not, we must be prepared for battle.

"We have found a path to the one door no one wants to be put out of." He ran his hand over the rough stubble on his chin, considering the wall. "We need to build a staircase to access that door and outfit it with a handle on this side."

Denzik reached down pulled out a silver coin from Captain O'Reilly's bag. Heads, they pushed on tonight; tails, they went back to prepare. He flipped the coin and it sparkled in the wavering light of the lanterns. He caught it and slapped against the back of his left hand. Tails.

"We are going back to our staging area. Be sure to leave no clues to our presence here. We will not even post a guard, until such time as we begin construction."

One of the crew began to take measurements of the area, preparing a checklist of materials needed at the staging site.

Denzik's gaze lingered on Captain O'Reilly's bones. "You will have a proper burial, my friend. We will be back for you."

He headed back up the passage, the men trailing in his wake.

Chapter 29

THE DENSE FORESTS GAVE WAY to rolling hills dotted with trees. The River Erinn broadened and slowed, its banks flattening. Fishing along its banks had been excellent and most of Cayden's evenings had been spent catching, cleaning, and roasting speckled trout over open cook fires. Fresh game and fish would help extend their supplies and so Cayden led the hunting party that morning. In truth, Cayden was leery about hunting animals for meat. His experiences with his flutes left him confused about the animals. He knew his men needed to eat meat to survive, yet the idea of killing an animal sickened him.

Peering around a large tree, he spied a group of five deer grazing at the edge of the bush line across the meadow. He waved his men forward and into bow range. They knelt and drew on their bows. Four arrows zipped away and two of the deer dropped. The other three bounded away into the forest cover.

Cayden's men whooped and ran forward to check on their kill. Cayden followed. The two deer had died instantly. His men pulled out hunting knives to skin them, keeping the deerskin, quartering the meat and leaving the bones and viscera behind for the scavengers to clean up. They hauled the heavy load back to camp on a makeshift sled they had brought along for that purpose.

A round-bellied man named Tucker from the village of Maiden's Head had been appointed the head cook of the camp. He met them and he took control of the deer when it arrived back at camp. He had been an apprentice to the butcher there and would see to its preservation and storage.

Cayden strode over to where Ryder was watching Darius run the balance of the men through training drills. Cayden joined Ryder and leaned against the broad tree trunk, eyes following the men's practice.

"Ryder, what are we doing out here? I don't understand why we are here."

Ryder watched the men training and did not reply.

"Surely this was all chance? We've had a run of bad luck, right? We are simple farmers. We are not soldiers. Why are we out here?"

Ryder shrugged his broad shoulders. "Do you think the fates leave everything to chance? Even fate has design. A tree toppled by the wind may think why me? Why now? But in the end, it still feeds the forest floor."

Cayden grinned. "When did you become a philosopher?"

Ryder shrugged again. "Probably about the time I let my best friend be dragged off by the enemy to save me from my fate. There is more to this than we realize, Cayden. Can't you see it? The world is changing and somehow you are central to it." He clapped Cayden on his shoulder. "We will face it together. I promise you that."

At that moment, Ziona entered the camp, accompanied by another woman, whom Cayden recognized instantly. He ran over to where they sat their horses.

"Laurista, you are safe!" Cayden reached up a hand to help Laurista dismount and then gently hugged her. She hugged him back.

"I am happy to see you are safe too, young Cayden!" She looked him up and down. Ziona raised her eyebrow in question at this greeting.

"Where ever did you find her, Ziona? Laurista is one of the best healers I have ever seen." Noting Ziona's expression, he added, "Next to you, of course." Cayden turned to hug Ziona next, but she held up her hand to stop him. Cayden blushed.

"We must keep moving, Cayden. This camp is too exposed. It attracts attention. How long have you been camped in this area?"

"We have kept moving." He frowned at her. "We haven't stayed long at any one spot."

"Your trail was as clear as if you had left me bread crumbs. If I can find you this easily, the enemies' spies certainly know where you are. We must move on quickly."

Ryder whistled for Darius, who came running over saluting.

"Advise the men we are breaking camp. We leave within the hour."

"Yes, sir!" Darius trotted back to the men he had been training. After an exchange of words, they dispersed through the tents, to break down the camp.

"I am sticking to you so closely you will think I am a tick on your back, Cayden," said Ziona. "I will not have you out of my sight again." Ziona raised her pointed eyebrows in challenge.

Cayden glanced at her in surprise. "What has happened, Ziona? You are wound up tighter than those sewing spools of yours."

She sighed, rubbing her arms. "I don't know, Cayden. Something isn't right. I feel like we are standing in quicksand and sinking, yet we can't see the bog."

She slapped at her neck as a bug bit her. She pulled away her hand, observing the squashed insect. "Spies can take many forms…" Her voice trailed off as she gazed at her hand, frowning.

Ziona's gaze took in the camp, watching the men. They worked with concentration, packing up tents and belongings and storing them on their horses, which stood saddled at the ready. Occasionally, one of the men would slap at their arms or neck as Ziona had done.

"I want you to put your cloak on and draw up your hood tight. Pass the same instructions to all the men. Despite it being a warm day, we need to not be instantly recognizable," Ziona said as she climbed back into her saddle, pulling up her hood and drawing it tight around her face.

Cayden pulled his cloak from his satchel and did as instructed. He quickly collapsed his tent and bound it to his saddle at the rear. Mounting his white mare, he rode over to Ziona.

They led the way out of the camp, taking a path that led away from the river and into some stands of scrub brush to the south. The river continued on to the west and soon was lost from view.

Over Cayden's shoulder the band strung out behind him, following his meandering path to the south. The land flattened into grasslands with an occasional tree or outcropping of rock to break up the flatness. Cayden shaded his eyes and squinted. The horizon stretched for miles in every direction. There was no way an enemy could sneak up on them. Yet, his nerves itched, along with his neck where a black fly had bitten him too. The sun was directly overhead when they stopped for a quick bite to eat and to rest the horses. Everyone sat on the ground by their mounts, eating some dried meat and washing it down with tepid water from their flasks.

As Cayden ate, he stared around at the unbroken flat expanse of sky in front of him. His gut pulled him south. It was getting stronger. He had absolutely no idea what it was, but still it called to him, tickling his mind. He pondered what was out there that could attract him so, eyes slightly out of focus as he searched inside himself. He was so self-absorbed that he didn't realize at first that the hazy black specks on the horizon were becoming larger.

Suddenly, Darius jumped up and yelled, "Riders!" Cayden jumped to his feet along with the rest of the men and quickly mounted. The specks grew and separated into what appeared to be a group of riders on the ground and some type of bird in the air following the riders.

Ziona hissed and heeled her mount. "By the gods! *Mount up! Now!*" she screamed at the men. "We must flee! It's the Charun! *Go now!* Scatter. Do not stay together!" The men, including Cayden, leapt into their saddles. Ziona reared her horse in urgency, causing the other horses to snort and begin to run in all directions.

Ziona grabbed Cayden's bridle and pulled his mount after hers, heading in a direction leading away from the main body of men. She bent over her horse's neck, urging it to greater and greater speed, murmuring to it in Primordial. The horse's ears were laid back as it ran, eyes wild. Cayden's mare kept her nose in the stallion's flank as if an invisible cord bound them together.

They ran into a gulley with a small stream trickling through its base. The lower terrain partially hid their silhouettes and allowed them to disappear in the grasses. They followed the gulley to an outcropping of rock jutting up from the flatlands. Ziona pulled her mount to a halt and dropped down to the ground. She handed the reins to Cayden and then climbed carefully to the top of the stone pile to check for pursuit. Cayden slithered up beside her to gaze down at the plain.

The Charun had reached the spot of their recently vacated campsite. There were three of them in total. They sat on black horses, examining the spot where Cayden's men had been. Overhead, half a dozen large black birds circled. Their heads were featherless, their large wings spiked with clawed tips. Vultures. Were they the same ones Ryder had seen in the legion camp?

A fourth black rider galloped up to the group, carrying a struggling person in its grip. Cayden felt alarm spike through his body. The man was dropped to the ground and as he tried to run away the creature grabbed him by the hair from horseback and held him still. A second rider dropped to the ground and floated up to the prisoner.

Cayden saw the prisoner shake his head in response to a question being asked. The Charun reached out with a clawed hand and hooked a digit into the prisoner's chest, causing him to scream. The first Charun hauled him back upright by his scalp, blood oozing down the man's chest.

Cayden felt his stomach roil, sickened by the scene. He recognized who the prisoner was. It was James. Ziona gripped his arm in warning. "Stay still," she hissed.

The second Charun hauled out a knife and sliced off the scalp of the prisoner while he screamed and screamed. Abruptly James fell to the ground as the scalp came free. Blood sprayed fountaining through the air.

Floating back to their beasts, the Charun mounted up and headed north. As they drifted away, the vultures fell from the sky, obscuring James's body from view.

Chapter 30

CAYDEN ROLLED OVER ONTO HIS BACK, eyes squeezed shut, trying to wipe out the scene behind him. It did not, unfortunately, stop sound from reaching his ears. The vultures screeched and fought over James's remains.

Cayden thought he was going to be sick, right there, right then. His stomach heaved and he broke into a sweat, trying to keep from throwing up. He failed. Rolling onto his side, he spewed his stomach's contents over the rocks at his side. Swiping the back of his hand across his lips, he panted, chest and belly heaving.

He sensed rather than heard movement at the base of the rocks. Sheba sat, staring up at them both and whined. He had almost forgotten about her in their recent flight.

Ziona edged back from the lip of the rock face and sat beside Cayden. Sheba crawled up onto the rock and rested her chin in Cayden's lap. He petted her soft head, drawing comfort from her presence.

"I can't rejoin them, can I, Ziona? I put them all in danger whenever I am near them."

Ziona nodded. "We cannot go back to them. The Charun are tracking us with black flies. Black flies can always find people, as they feed on blood. They are attracted to death and all life is slowly dying. They know what they hunt. If we leave, they will follow us. The others will be safer if we are not with them. They have no interest in them other than to find you."

Ziona crawled back up and checked the horizon. Nothing moved, except for the vultures. The others would not return as long as they were present.

"We need to go. I think James bought us some time, sending them off in the wrong direction. We need to use the time he bought us with his life," said Cayden.

"We will ride hard. We should be able to reach Cathair within two days if we do. We stop for short periods only and take shifts standing guard while the other sleeps."

They slid back down to their horses. Cayden took a swig of his water to rinse his mouth, spitting it out on the ground. He patted Sheba on the head and whispered, "Keep up, girl, and keep your eyes open, OK?" She licked his hand and tilted her head, listening. She trotted off ahead of them, seeming to lead the way.

They rode hard and by nightfall the area of the attack was far behind them. They did not see any sign of the band or any sign of their pursuers. The flies also disappeared. That evening they ate a cold dinner, not wishing to alert anyone to their presence. They hobbled their horses and allowed them to graze close to their camp, but they remained saddled. They slept under the open stars under a blanket, fully clothed.

Sheba sat with Cayden and watched with him while Ziona slept. All was still. She gnawed on the thigh bone of the rabbit she had caught for her dinner. Cayden pulled out his flutes and rolled them in his hands. He pondered their use, beyond calling the creatures to him. Was it possible they could help him in some other way?

He sensed Sheba's presence separately from the other wolves around them. He thought about his flutes tucked back under the grandfather oak tree back home. He wished he had brought them all along now.

If Ziona played the flute, would the animals come to her? He had never considered what would happen if others played them. He would have to have Ziona try it when she awoke.

Worried about what had happened to the others, Cayden unconsciously ground his teeth. *Surely they had escaped. There were only four of those creatures. The band would be OK. They had to be.* Cayden's frustration mounted as his ever-present worry about his friends came back full force. Was there anything to be done differently to protect them? They were dying because of him and he didn't understand why. He needed answers and he needed them now. His eyes were drawn south again toward that persistent nagging tug at his soul. Answers were waiting for him in Cathair and he was anxious to get there. He glanced at the sky and saw the moon was about three quarters gone. Dawn would be arriving in about three hours. He got up and shook Ziona awake, changing places. Crawling under the covers, he fell into a restless sleep in which werewolves stood guard while demons played his flutes and the dead clapped along.

***

Ryder huddled with the band members, midstream of the river. Their horses quivered with fear and exhaustion. The flies did not seem to like the water and refused to follow them into the streambed, a lucky break for them. Ryder took a quick head count. Everyone was accounted for except for Cayden, Ziona, and James.

Ryder prayed they were safe. "All right, here is what we are going to do. We will ride downstream toward Cathair for a couple of miles in this river. When we find a good location, we will exit the stream on the opposite side of where the Charun are located. Their flying spies should not be able to find us at least until the Charun cross over. Hopefully, they never do."

In their mad flight, they had headed north for a mile or so and then cut back to the river. The last few stragglers of the band had finally caught up to them. This had been the fallback plan Darius had discussed with the band in case they were separated. He had not shared this with Cayden or Ryder in the hope that if disaster struck they would leave on their own as the band led any danger away from Cayden. Ryder thought this plan rather brilliant of Darius. He would need to promote the man earlier than he thought.

"Let's head out!"

They splashed down stream for a few miles and eventually came to a sandbar extending out from the right-hand shoreline. The horses scrambled up out of the river happy to regain the solid ground of the riverbank, spreading out onto the grassland on the west side of the river.

Glancing at the sky, Ryder judged they had roughly three hours of daylight left to them. Their sidetrack had taken them another two hours off the path. Assuming Cayden, Ziona, and James headed due south they now had a five-hour lead on the band. Ryder's gut told him Cayden would push hard to reach Cathair now. He would not attempt to rejoin them.

Laurista rode up to Ryder and placed a hand on his arm. "The men are tired, my lord. They need to rest, as do the horses. To push on now would not be wise. There are injuries amongst the men I need to attend to."

He glanced down at her. "I am not a lord, Laurista. My name is Ryder."

She looked askance at him. "Of course, my lord."

He frowned, not understanding what she meant.

"Darius, have the men make camp, but they must be prepared to ride at a moment's notice. No cook fires, understand?"

"It will be as you command, sir." Ryder returned the salute from his captain and then followed Laurista back to her tent that was now acting as a field hospital. A small service tent had been set up to receive the wounded. Most injuries were not serious, cuts and scrapes and one arm broken when the man had tried to outrun the Charun. His horse had stumbled, throwing him, but he had managed to remount and escape. All in all, they had survived this first test and come through the other side relatively unscathed.

Ryder was sure it would have been worse if they hadn't discovered the flies' weakness. He was also sure they had been tracking them and would return to the hunt once the Charun discovered their prey had escaped once again. There was no doubt in Ryder's mind they were after Cayden, which meant he was in danger every second of every day.

Ryder strode over to Darius. "Captain Darius, I need you to select four men with demonstrated skills to perform as scouts."

Darius surveyed the men. "Gregory, Samuel, Phillip, and Macon, with me." The four soldiers walked up to him and Ryder. "These four have excellent horsemanship. Gregory and Samuel have served as trackers and scouts in the legion already. Phillip is from my village and can track a squirrel up a tree to its den. Macon can smell a rat even if it has been pickled and stuffed in a jar."

"Excellent." Ryder examined the four men. All were of a wiry build and short. "We need to know what we are riding into and who may be trailing us. Your job will be to continuously scout for enemies. I want one man out front as we advance and one checking our back trail as we march. The other two are your relief. You will scout day and night in six-hour shifts. I will leave you to arrange your scheduling, but it begins immediately. I do not want to be surprised ever again."

Ryder strode away, leaving the men to carry out his orders.

Chapter 31

THE WIZARD STIRRED ON HIS FILTHY PALLET on the floor. The cave-like cell was dank and damp, having been formed out of a natural occlusion in the limestone rock. In the corner stalactites and stalagmites, created by a steady drip of water, formed a jagged toothy cavity perfect for hiding small treasures he wished to keep out of sight of his hosts. He thought they were actually quite a bit longer than when he had taken up residence in the cave seventeen years ago.

The only reason he knew it had been seventeen years was because of the rough calendar he had gouged into the soft rock with a piece of calcite. That stone made a perfect chalk and it was plentiful in the cave. The difficult part was getting enough light to see to be able to write anything by. The few stubs of candles left behind by the guards soon sputtered and died, giving barely enough light to eat and perform his toilet once a day.

The door rattled and his usual jailer, Wendell, poked his head in.

"When are you going to die?" he puffed, dragging in a bucket and a plate with gruel. "You make me work so hard, hauling this slop up and down the stairs all the time."

"I am indeed sorry to inconvenience you, my good man. As luxurious as my accommodation is, I would hate to leave it empty. Now tell me, where would you ever find such an excellent tenant? Why, you would be retired and bouncing your grandkids on your knee before you could find a suitable replacement."

Wendell snorted and plopped down the bucket with an audible splash.

He set the lantern on a peg by the door, illuminating the cell for a short time. The old man sat on his pallet as always, long white hair flowing over his shoulders and onto his chest. It curled at the ends, reminding Wendell of a horse mane.

"Well, at least I don't have to shave you anymore, not that they ever checked on it. I need that shave more than you do. The lice are your buddies now, right? Bed bugs keep you company at night." He chuckled at his own dark humour.

"Alas, they certainly do," the wizard agreed pleasantly.

"Well here are your candle stubs." Wendell lit one and placed it on the ground. "I have a special treat for you tonight. Don't go expecting it every day, mind you. I had to sneak this in for you." He frowned at the wizard, suddenly unsure if this was a good idea after all. Shrugging, he tossed a package to the wizard. The small bag was made of old leather and tied with a drawstring.

"There is an extra candle strapped to the base of the water bucket. Enjoy your few extra minutes of light."

Wendell backed out of the cell with the full slop bucket and took up the lantern from the peg on his way out. The light dimmed and the key squawked in the lock. The sound of boots on stone faded with the light.

Mordecai Ben-Moses was a practical wizard. When materials presented themselves, there was no reason to flaunt one's powers. He retrieved the candle from under the bucket and set it aside so the wick would not be wetted by his ablutions.

He picked up the bag and tugged on the drawstring, dumping its contents onto his filthy robes. Out tumbled a multifaceted crystal, its cut surfaces sending rainbows of light flashing around the cell from the candle's flickering flame.

Mordecai grinned. Finally, his hard work was paying off. It had taken seventeen years of chit-chat and conversation to win the reticent Wendell over to his side. Now Mordecai had his focus stone back in his possession. The time was close; he knew it.

Mordecai felt him coming. *The bond was working. Gwen would be pleased that their plans of so long ago were coming to fruition.* His grin widened and then he set about bathing and eating his meal just as the liquefied stub of candle sputtered out.

He snapped his fingers and a flame danced to light on his fingertips. He checked another day off his chalk calendar and then lay back down to sleep. He snapped his fingers and the light extinguished. Closing his eyes, he reached out to the boy in his dreams, calling him to his destiny.

***

Cayden's band settled in a copse of trees nestled in a valley about half a mile off the main road. An animal trail had led back to the spot and, as Cayden had suspected, a small spring bubbled from the rocks near the trees.

A light rain continued to fall so they took luxury in putting up both tents, stretching a canopy between the two to keep their small fire dry and give them a spot to sit together.

Cayden scoured the underbrush to find kindling and dry wood for their fire. He located a very old birch tree, the white bark peeling in long curls. Perfect kindling lay at its base and he collected that along with some more substantial branches. One in particular was of great interest.

Arriving back at their campsite, he started a fire, while Ziona pulled food from their packs. She suspended a pot and a kettle from the arm of a tripod and added dried meat, beans, and water to the one and tea leaves to the other.

Cayden grabbed his satchel and lowered himself to the ground under the canopy, pulling out his carving tools.

Sheba trotted in from the scrub line, another rabbit clenched in her jaws. She settled on her belly beside Cayden and tore into her meal.

Ziona sat down beside him, watching. "Do you mind if I look at your flutes?"

Cayden reached into the bottom of his satchel and pulled out the three flutes he had stored there.

"These two, I carved back home and this one I made while I was in the legion camp." He hesitated before handing them over.

Ziona examined them, her slender fingers tracing the designs he had carved into them.

"Do you know what these symbols are?" Her nimble fingers followed the serpentine marks on the snake flute.

"They are designs, I imagine...aren't they? I carved whatever inspiration came to me at the time."

"I don't think so, Cayden. They look like runes to me."

Cayden paused halfway through reaching into his satchel again, eyes flashing to hers.

"Runes? I know nothing of runes. That is not possible."

"Nevertheless, it is what they appear to be." She smiled at him. "If you have discovered a talent for the ancient rune language, you are unique, Cayden. The knowledge of runes vanished over a thousand years ago. What do you want to do with them?" She held them up for his inspection. "Shall I play them for you? Or do you want to play them?"

Cayden studied her. Then he took back the ones he had carved at home, leaving the rainbow-barked one he had carved that day in the meadow in her hands.

"Play this one. I know what happens when I play it. You try it. Play any song that comes to mind."

Ziona put the flute to her lips and played. *The flute sounded...well, like a flute,* Cayden thought. The music was pleasant, the song pleasing. She played on for a few minutes. Then, she lowered the flute, eyebrows raised in enquiry.

Cayden shook his head. "Nothing happened, Ziona." He took back the flute, examining it. It was still the same as when he had played it. "It played nicely, but the song...the sound was different than when I play it."

Ziona did not seem surprised. "I think, Cayden, it is because this flute is bound to you. To anyone else, it will be a pretty flute. Only you have the ability to make it come alive. Come, you play it for me. Maybe I can see the effects, even if I can't make them happen."

Cayden put his lips to the flute and played. Instantly, the tone changed and laughter bounced out of the flute. The song giggled with light notes and a breeze gusted, swirling the leaves on the ground. This time when the child appeared in response to his playing, she was dressed in vivid green gossamer skirts and a halo of flowers nestled in her curls. She spun in a circle, dancing a jig to the music Cayden played.

Sheba raised her head and watched attentively. She did not growl or show any aggression at all. She seemed to accept the girl as normal. She went back to chewing on her rabbit.

Cayden lowered his flute and grinned at the familiar figure that appeared.

"'Tis a much better song than the last time, Cayden of the Cliffs," she said in a lilting accent.

Ziona, however, gasped and fell to her knees face down in the dirt in front of the child. "I am honoured and humbled by your presence, Great Aossi!" She pressed her forehead to the ground. Cayden was stunned. Aossi winked merrily at him again and skipped over to Ziona. She placed her hand on her hair and murmured something to Ziona in the Primordial tongue. Cayden thought it might be a blessing of sorts. He gazed at the scene in amazement. Tough, commanding Ziona on her knees to a child, albeit a magical one. Ziona rose from her subservient position and backed up beside Cayden. Her face was alive with joy.

"Tell us why you have come, ancient one?" Cayden's eyes jerked back to Ziona's at her words.

"Cayden has summoned us from our retreat." She twirled, her prismatic skirts swirling on feet floating above the ground. "Even we could not resist the spell of his music."

She danced over and placed a hand on the curve of Cayden's cheek. "He is so very special, even if he does not yet understand how. We know and we come as called." She grinned again and a finger tapped his cheek. He instantly felt a rush of joy swell in his chest. She soothed his worries and peace stole over him. She gazed into his eyes and they grew serious, a strange expression for her nature.

"Cayden, you are the one all creation has been waiting for. That we have been waiting for. Hidden within you is the ability to save this world, poised on the brink of destruction. You and your sister have great gifts, which you are only beginning to understand. You are prophesied to do great things. Many have sacrificed their lives to give the world this chance. We bow to you and are in your service." She knelt before him, head bowed. Ziona knelt beside Aossi also.

Cayden backed up in shock.

"Stop that! I don't understand any of this!" he croaked. "Would someone please tell me what is going on? Everyone seems to know far more than me." Frustration made his voice sharpen. "I need answers and I need them now!"

Aossi stood up and smiled at him. "That is the response I was waiting for. Take command, Cayden. Do not be afraid to lead. A king must be able to stand tall and with assurance. He must be able to make decisions sometimes with little or no knowledge. This is your destiny. The city you march toward is your home, Cayden. It is your heritage and your promise. The present queen is a usurper and must be deposed. There is one there, who is calling to you from within the city walls. It is so, yes?"

Cayden's eyes met hers and he nodded.

"Find him. He is a wizard of great power. He has been imprisoned there since your birth. He has been waiting for you. He has the answers you seek. You must free him and take back control of your capital."

"I am no king." Cayden rejected the charge automatically.

"You do not know who and what you are." Aossi studied him. "Find the wizard. He will help you to understand."

To Ziona, she said, "You are his guide, yes?" Ziona nodded reverently, bowing her head once again. "You must stay with him every minute of every day. There are many seeking him on behalf of the queen. She has entire legions of soldiers searching for him. She may even know you are coming. But they are not the only ones. There are deeper, darker stirrings."

Ziona nodded again. She straightened her posture, grim determination etching her face.

Aossi's smile dimpled her cheek, once again becoming the impish little girl.

"All you ever need to do, Cayden, is call for us. Protect that flute. Know that it works only for you. If you should ever lose it, you may also find us here." She poked his chest where his heart beat. "And here." She tapped his temple. "We will be watching over you too." With a swirl of green skirts that felt like a breath of warm spring air, Aossi vanished.

Ziona sank back to the ground, her eyes clouded over in thought.

Cayden placed the flute back in his satchel and then went over to the pot of stew bubbling and gave it a stir, his thoughts full of the conversation. At least now he knew who was calling him in Cathair. *But take the city?* He snorted to himself. How in heaven and earth would he accomplish such a task? It seemed ridiculous to contemplate. He laughed out loud. *I am no king. What a ridiculous concept.* He opened his mouth to say those exact words, but the look on Ziona's face stopped him.

She stared at him in fascination, and she was bowing before him once again. Cayden blushed deeply and reached down and pulled her to her feet. "Stop that. You are totally embarrassing me, Ziona! Get a grip on yourself, would you? She was just a little fairy person. What does she know about the future or about who I am?"

Ziona shook her head, marvelling at his innocence.

She sat down, drawing him down beside her. "Your Majesty." Cayden went to interrupt, but she plowed right over top of him. "You did not tell me you had summoned the Aossi."

Cayden frowned at her. "What is so important about them? They look like fairies to me."

"They are related to fairies, yes. But they are much, much more than mere fairies. They are of the Mother Goddess herself. They are the guardians of the spirits of nature; the chief stewards who protect the world and keep it in spiritual balance. It is said that they are immortal and exist on a plane between the mortal and immortal worlds. And…"—she raised a finger in emphasis—"they have not been seen in a millennium."

Cayden's mouth snapped shut. "So…they are…what? Angels? What do they do?"

"They maintain the status quo between good and evil, Cayden. Think of it this way. When the autumn comes and the leaves fall, what happens to them? They become part of the forest floor and in the spring the worms grind them into fertilizer to feed the tree, which in turn feeds the leaves of the new season. Death begets life and life falls to death. Harmony and balance are maintained in the circle of life that the Mother Goddess created. For good to exist, so must evil, for one cannot exist without the other. They are the balance."

"But why have they appeared to me?"

"You are significant to their plans or to their existence or both. You are somehow tied to them and them to you. They aid you because they must, because it is part of what was and what will be."

Cayden stood and went back to the pot. The stew was done. He ladled their dinner into two bowls and brought one to Ziona.

Ziona observed his stiff and jerky motions, frustration displayed in his every movement. "I know this is hard for you, Cayden, but you will find your answers in time. I am here to help you. At least we know one thing for certain."

"What do we know?"

"We know you were right to head to Cathair. And we now know why. Who is this wizard?" she mused.

"I have no idea. I have never met a wizard before." Cayden shrugged. "Can I ask you a favour?"

"Certainly, what is it?"

"Please do not call me 'Your Majesty' ever again."

Ziona shook her head, amused. "I cannot promise that, Cayden. However, I do believe it unwise to flaunt such knowledge to the common listener. Your secret is safe with me…for the time being at least." She regarded him once again. "I would never have believed starting out that this journey would bring me to this place and time. The Mother Goddess works in mysterious ways."

Cayden frowned, clearly not amused. They cleared up the dishes, working side by side, and then settled back with their tea. Curling his hands around the warm cup, he gazed into its murky depths. "I wonder why you couldn't summon the Aossi." He took a sip in contemplation.

"A good question. I believe those flutes are attuned to you and they will only respond to your touch in any magical fashion. Should anyone else pick them up, they will simply be what they seem, wooden flutes. I think it must have something to do with the runes. There is a magic in runes that is unique. The symbols have meaning beyond the actual shapes they form."

Cayden took another sip. "Maybe this wizard will know. Do you have any idea how to find him?"

"Well, if he is a prisoner, he is likely held in one of the prison cells, right?"

"That would make sense, yes. So do you have any ideas on how to go about breaking a wizard out of a prison cell? Why can't he break himself out?"

"I can think of many reasons why he might still be in that cell, Cayden, but none of them really help us. I think we need to enter the city and see what it is like before we try to form a plan to get him out. I know nothing about the palace and I assume you are equally in the dark about it?"

He nodded.

"Well then, we should get some rest, Your Majesty." She giggled and headed off to her tent. She glanced back over her shoulder and spied his look of consternation. Laughing, she let the tent flaps close behind her.

Chapter 32

NELSON AND FABIAN PAUSED, pulling Denzik to the side. They let the men pull ahead, so they were the last to leave the Traitor's Gate.

"This is the wrong opening," Nelson whispered.

Fabian nodded. "Yes, I think so too. A lucky discovery, but we were led to believe that the path to the proper insertion point would be more to the east."

"Then we must have walked right past it. Let's keep our eyes sharp on the way back." Denzik took the lead.

They headed off down the stream side path, keeping their eyes peeled for an opening in the rocky cavern face. The cave widened and narrowed in several places. About one hundred yards from the Traitor's Gate, Fabian pointed out a shadowed area partially concealed behind a stalagmite formation. From the other direction, the opening had been completely covered.

They scrambled up over the short rise of floor to the opening. It appeared to be high enough to allow a slightly stooped tall man to enter. Denzik and his companions, not being tall men, were able to stand straight, their hair brushing the stone above. Denzik shoved his lantern hand into the opening and a narrow passage opened up before them. It was not a natural formation. Small sharp grooves marked the surface of the tunnel.

"This may be it. Nelson, go inform our men that we are staying behind for a little while longer. We need to see where this path goes."

Nelson trotted off to do as bidden and returned a few minutes later, carrying an extra couple of lanterns.

Denzik led the way into the tunnel, which twisted around, its path seeming to follow the softer sections of the rock. After about ten minutes, during which they became completely disoriented, the path emptied onto a flat expanse of rock glowing with an eerie light. Some sort of fluorescent substance lined the cave, giving it a greenish glow. They spread out, approaching the wall in front of them. It was also plain but obviously made of limestone, and this time there was no question that it was man made. Large smoothed blocks of seamless limestone were stacked precisely, the stone quarried to the slightest of tolerances.

Denzik stepped up to the wall, searching its surface by lantern light. He ran his fingers across the surface, looking for anything to indicate they were at the right spot. The others searched alongside him. He moved down the wall, right into the corner where the massive foundation disappeared back into the natural rock. His fingers paused over an indentation about chest height shaped like a sword.

"Here, this might be it. Give me some more light." Nelson and Fabian raised lanterns, flooding the area with a flickering bright light.

Denzik rubbed the surface, scratching away years of dust and dirt to reveal the symbol. He backed up, eyes scanning the wall. "This must be it." He scratched at his beard in thought. "I have no idea what is on the other side."

"Why don't we tap on the wall and see if we get a response? After all, these are likely to be the deepest cells of the castle, correct? They must be prisoner cells."

"All right. I guess there is no way our tapping would alert any guards. Their stations are on the next level up." He gazed up the wall to where it disappeared into the cavern's ceiling.

"Here is a rock." Nelson pushed a stone into each of their hands.

"Let's tap the call to arms from the King's Guard. The current guard would not recognize it," Fabian suggested.

"An excellent idea." Denzik clapped Fabian on the shoulder appreciatively. It seemed fitting to attack the walls with sounds that had been banished from them.

They tapped out the bugle call, the rhythm coming naturally to them as though no time had passed. They paused at the end, waiting to see if there was any response.

Silence filled the cave...and then they heard a faint echo of their tapping. It was the same call, but coming from the other side of the rock. Someone was tapping in response.

Denzik switched over to the proper tapping code of the sentries and tapped on the wall, "Who are you?"

The reply, when it came, shocked them. "Mordecai Ben-Moses, First Wizard of the Fell. I have been waiting for you."

Chapter 33

THEY BROKE CAMP TO A FINE DRIZZLE that soaked the tents and ground. Ryder settled his cloak around his broad shoulders and drew up his deep hood to fend off the persistent moisture. The evening had passed peacefully. He tightened the girth on his horse, checking its catch. He tied his pack in place behind his saddle and mounted up.

The men were ready to go. *They have become quite good at this. Slowly, we are being transformed from a bunch of farmers into a real soldiering unit,* Ryder thought.

The once-boys-now-men laughed and joked as they went about their tasks, clearly happy to be in the band.

Last night around the campfire, they had finally chosen a name for themselves. They argued that all excellent fighting forces had a name. They approached Ryder for his permission to raise a banner in their chosen name. And so the Band of the Rebels' Land was formed. Darius led the name choice. Ryder had tried to talk him out of it initially.

"I don't know if it's such a good idea, Darius," Ryder said, the presence of the men standing behind him softening his words. "By choosing that name, you are announcing to the entire world that you are set against the queen and in open rebellion against her rule and her authority. You are painting bull's eyes on their backs."

"Exactly! Don't you see? By loudly proclaiming our allegiance to our homeland, we will attract like-minded men who are not organized but who wish to stand in revolt. We are not the only ones out here, Ryder."

Ryder scanned the eager faces around him and crossed his arms over his chest, pondering their choice. Yes, they would attract attention, but enough of the right kind to offset the expected whiplash when the queen learned of their presence and declared purpose? What if she sent her own forces against them? Experienced battle-trained troops!

"Then in the morning, we ride. We ride hard. For in announcing our intentions, we sacrifice the luxury of remaining hidden."

Laurista worked long into the night to fashion a banner. They located some royal blue cloth onto which they had sewn a circle embroidered with a bright golden eagle clutching a branch in its talons. The banner was hoisted into the air on a stout wooden pole they had foraged for in the woods. After arguing over who would have the first honour, Darius took it and rode up beside Ryder. The rest of the band formed up behind them to begin the long journey south, allegiance proudly displayed for all to see. They broke into song, singing a battle hymn of their own making:

"Hoist the flag and proudly fly
Our pride soars into the sky
War will find us come what may
Bring it on, we proudly say
We march no matter what the cost
In remembrance of what was lost
Our proud king stolen away
Will rise again on that day
Hoist the flag and proudly sing
Freedom comes on eagle's wings!"

Ryder hummed along as the drizzle dripped off his coat.

They followed the River Erinn for most of the day. Toward dusk, they came upon the outskirts of a small village set back from the river. A long stone arch bridged the river from shore to shore, wide enough to accommodate two wagons passing at mid-span.

The village was surrounded by farms, bordered with neatly trimmed hedge rows and low fieldstone walls. A dirt road opened up between the farms and led directly to the central village square. A sign announced the village as Erinnshire.

They rode into the village and stopped at the fountain in the center of the square. The new banner snapped in the wind announcing the band's arrival. Ryder gazed around and then dismounted. The villagers went about their business taking no particular interest in the newcomers.

Ryder spied the village inn on the south side of the square. It was a two-story structure, covered with mud plaster and peeling white paint. Wooden shutters painted a bright blue provided a splash of colour on the otherwise plain façade of the building. A sign hanging over the front entrance announced the name of the inn as The Frosty Mug. A tall glass of ale with a bead of moisture slipping down the side decorated the sign. The men eyed the sign and licked their lips in anticipation.

"Stay here," Ryder commanded, "while I seek out the mayor and ask him for a suitable location to set up camp. If he is agreeable to having the entire band in town, we will come back and fetch everyone."

Ryder was joined by Darius and Laurista as he entered the inn's dim interior.

A woman with a mass of curls piled high on her head straightened from wiping a table and inspected the newcomers. She wore a yellow ankle-length skirt and matching shirt, accented by a crocheted tan vest. Her friendly eyes greeted them.

"How may I help you, gentlemen and lady?"

"We have come with about thirty men and are planning to have them camp at the edge of town. Would the mayor be available to speak to us? We wish to ask where it would be the least intrusive to settle down for the night."

"I am the mayor. I am also the proprietress of this inn. My name is Simona."

"Pleased to make your acquaintance, madam. I am Ryder." He motioned to his companions and made introductions.

"I believe Old Man Jacoby has a field lying fallow this year. He may be willing to allow you to set up camp there for a small fee." She gave directions to the farm on the south side of town. "Will your men be coming into town later? I ask so I can let the cooks know of a larger crowd than usual." She glanced around her common room, which was presently about a quarter full.

"Yes, I believe they would be happy to avail themselves of your fine inn."

"Until then," she curtsied lightly, "gentlemen and lady." She marched off to the kitchens.

They left the inn and were surprised to find a small crowd had gathered around the band in the short time they were inside. Most were young men, but some were old gents, all speaking with the band and asking questions. As Ryder strode up, he heard one of the band say in a loud voice, "Yes, we have been travelling with a young prince. You would believe it too if you saw him. We got separated, but he is of princely seed. You know it to look at him. We are going to recover his throne for him. You'll see." Murmurs greeted these words as the crowd repeated the conversation to others too far away to hear.

Ryder mounted his horse again and motioned for the men to follow him. He glanced at Darius, who shrugged as if to say *don't look at me.* "They came to that conclusion all on their own."

A short ride brought them to the farm and an even shorter negotiation had them setting up camp in an empty hayfield with access to the farmer's well for watering their horses. The rain had let up and a watery sun poked through on the western horizon.

Darius set a few men to guarding the camp while the rest of the men found wash buckets and clean clothes. Then they walked back into town in threes and fours, hot food and cold ale on their minds.

Ryder, Darius, and Laurista strolled back to town also, drawn to the comforts of the village and also keen to hear some of the local gossip. Ryder knew their presence was being noted and he felt this would be the first true test of the band's acceptance or rejection by those they hoped to recruit in time.

They entered the inn and the band quickly filled the available tables, mixing in with the local men and beginning conversations. Ryder, Darius, and Laurista settled in at a table close to the door, so as to watch the people who entered.

A serving girl stopped at their table to place a basket of hot bread on the table. A barmaid stopped by next and took their drink order, retrieving three mugs of mulled wine for their table. Ryder spied the innkeeper who doubled as the town mayor and waved her over to their table.

"Simona, I was wondering if you would point out the local merchants. I find I am in need of a good tailor."

Simona peered around and then pointed to a pinched-faced, balding man sitting at a small table by the window. "He travels between villages and into the capital once a month to purchase supplies."

"That's great. Thank you." Ryder stood up and walked over to the man. He was absorbed in his plate of thinly sliced lamb and potatoes as Ryder paused by his table.

"Good evening. May I join you?"

The man shrugged and gestured to the chair opposite him. Ryder sat.

"My name is Ryder. I need to have some sashes made for me and my men. I am trying to locate someone who sews."

The man studied him. He did not give his name. "What kind of sashes?"

"They would be made to sit at the hip, solid colour with braiding along the edges, and a little embroidery on the front."

"The queen has forbidden the creation of any garment for armed men who have not received her seal sanctioning its making in advance." He squinted at Ryder, taking in his sword at his hip. "What you ask me to do might be viewed as treason."

Ryder frowned at the man. "I apologize. We are not from the area and we were unaware this law. Please forgive my impertinent request." Ryder stood, bowed stiffly to the man and withdrew back to his table.

He relayed the conversation to Darius and Laurista. She also frowned at the information. "If that is the case, there is a ban on selling materials that might be made into uniforms as well. It may be that this cloth is as strictly controlled as the sale of weapons. You might commission one sword, but you are sure to attract attention if you commissioned for, say, two hundred of them."

"Fortunately, we have a good number of those already courtesy of the legion. We will need to find a way to buy the proper cloth. Perhaps we can purchase some in several different villages, not enough in any one village to raise suspicions?"

"Why this sudden interest in uniforms?" asked Laurista.

"It occurred to me that in a battle, unless it is with the queen's forces, we would not be able to tell friend from foe. We need some way of identifying ourselves to one another, especially if our numbers grow."

"Good point." Darius picked up his fork, his stomach growling as the spicy meal arrived. They had taken no more than three bites when a large thud occurred, instantly followed by a flash of bright light and a shuddering crash. The windows of the inn blew in, glass shattering and spinning through the air. Screams of pain filled the room as those closest to the windows were impaled with the airborne shards.

Ryder leapt to his feet and drew his sword. The other band members, who had not been cut by the flying glass, also drew theirs. The windows filled with a howling rush of sound and then all went still.

Ryder ran out the door, followed by Darius and Laurista, who had a small sharp dagger in her hand.

The village square was strewn with debris. Trees had been snapped in two. The central fountain had been toppled, the basin cracked and water was flowing out onto the ground. Several people were getting slowly to their feet, while others did not move. In the center of the square, where their band had originally stopped, was a large blackened crater. Smoke curled from the edges of the depression and a flickering flame rose from the center.

Ryder strode up to the edge of the hole and looked down. A large glowing rock sat in the center of the depression, pulsing with the dull red of a horseshoe freshly out of the forge. The roughly shaped metal ball was about the size of a church bell. Ryder examined the hole, trying to gauge the direction the iron ball had come from. To launch a ball that large, it would take something larger than any catapult siege engine he had ever heard of. It would not have that long of a range, however. Puzzled, he found nothing in the area to suggest where the iron ball had come from.

Ryder bent to a nearby man and felt for a pulse. When none could be found, he moved on to a young child who was partially buried under the body of his mother. The woman's body was twisted in a grotesque form only possible if her back was broken. The child was stirring and crying, unable to push his mother's body off of him. Ryder rolled the woman over and picked up the child, ducking his head against his shoulder to shield his view of his mother's broken, bleeding body.

He sprinted toward the inn with the child clutched to his chest, meeting Laurista halfway. He pushed the boy into her arms without speaking. The child wailed for his mother. Laurista ran back toward the inn, the child's cries mingling with the moans of the injured.

Ryder saw the men of the band spread out, searching the carnage for survivors. Other people from the town were gathering on the square. Ryder followed Laurista back into the inn, where he found the mayor directing the serving girls to push the wooden tables off to the sides of the rooms, creating a triage area in the middle of the empty floor.

The cook appeared from the kitchen area with a virtual army of young men hauling buckets of water and what appeared to be the entire stock of towels and linens. They placed them on the tables at the side of the room.

Ryder walked over to the window where the glass had blown in. The merchant he'd been speaking to a few moments ago was slumped over his table, a chunk of glass from the window imbedded in his temple. Ryder turned him over. He was clearly dead. Ryder hoisted him onto his shoulder and his torso flopped over his back. He carried the dead man outside to the fountain area and laid him beside the other ten people who had been deposited there by the band in a makeshift morgue beside the fountain. As Ryder knelt to lay the man down, an object rolled out of the man's waistcoat pocket and dropped to the ground.

Ryder bent down and picked it up. It was a curiously shaped coin, octagonal in shape, and made of a strange silvery metal that seemed hot to the touch. On one side was a picture of the sun and on the other side what resembled a bear. Ryder pocketed the coin, not because it was valuable but because it seemed out of place. He quickly searched the man for identification but found nothing to tell him who the man had been.

Ryder straightened and walked back to the remains of the fountain. Something strange was happening and he itched to know what it was. He sent prayerful thoughts in the direction he hoped Cayden was riding.

Ride, Cayden, ride! I am not sure how long we can hold them from your back, whoever they are.

Chapter 34

THE FURTHER SOUTH CAYDEN AND ZIONA RODE, the more populated the area became. Grasslands gave way to rolling hills dotted with willowy branched trees that bent back to the earth. A fuzzy grey seemed to coat them. On closer inspection, Cayden realized moss was hanging from the branches, swaying in the breeze. Colourful birds flashed through the treetops, calling to each other as they passed.

As heat grew so did the humidity. The soil churned into ruddy clay that clung to their boots and to the hooves of the horses. Even though it was spring, the muggy air felt like midsummer at home.

They came to fields cultivated with a twiggy plant set in straight rows. They marched off in parallel green rows over the rise of the hill. Cayden examined them as he rode past. He had no idea what they were and his puzzlement must have shown because Ziona spoke up. "Those are cotton plants. They are native to this area, and it appears the local farmers are cultivating them rather than gathering and harvesting from the wild."

"If they are growing cotton in this quantity, then they must have a place to sell it. Who do you think is able to buy all this?"

"Likely local merchants buy it and ship it to the weavers on the southern coast. There is a large guild of wool and cotton weavers on the coast, and the most famous looms for these fabrics are to be found in the town of Seaside."

As they crested the hill, they came upon a small village. A weathered wooden sign hanging from a post announced the hamlet of Cottonham. The tidy fields were cultivated right up to the low stone wall. Past the wall, buildings sprung up and an assortment of people wandered about inside the town going about their daily routines.

"Should we go into the town?" Cayden enquired of Ziona.

She frowned, thinking. "It should be safe enough, but I think we should pose as a married couple. That way we can stay together without suspicion."

"We should be able to blend in fine, two simple travellers passing through."

Sheba shadowed them from the woods. She never entered the villages. She did not like large groups of humans. Ziona nudged her horse, encouraging a slow walk. They rode side by side and were soon entering the town.

Cayden sat tall, back straight and alert in his saddle. Ziona observed him from the corner of her eye. He sat like a monarch, even though he was simply dressed in his woolen cloak, tan pants, and boots. He did not realize his bearing screamed royalty. She saw his chin firm as his eyes surveyed the scene before him. A woman paused in the midst of pinning a blouse to a clothesline to watch him pass. Ziona hid her smile. *It was not every day you saw a king being molded and formed right before your eyes,* she mused.

Several men, gathered around what looked to be the local smithy's shop, watched them pass. They slowly followed after them, drawn to Cayden.

Cayden, completely oblivious to the attention he was attracting, dismounted in front of the inn, looping the reins over the railing. Ziona mirrored his actions and then stepped up onto the boardwalk beside him.

Cayden glanced down at her, wondering at his luck to have her beside him. He offered her his arm and she lightly placed her left hand on it. Together, they entered the tavern beneath a weathered sign announcing it to be the Cotton Gin Inn.

Inside the brightly lit interior, large quilts of cotton were proudly displayed on the walls and ruffled curtains of a similar fabric draped the windows. A round woman with grey hair secured in a tight bun on the top of her head greeted them as they entered. She took one look at the pair of them and dropped a deep curtsey.

"How may I be of service to my lord and lady?"

"We require lodgings and a hot meal served to our room. We would also ask the horses be given an extra measure of grain this evening."

"It shall be as you ask, my lord. Will your manservant be bringing your things?"

"We are travelling light. We will bring our own things up."

"Certainly, please follow me." She headed up the stairs to the right of the door. She led them to a room at the far end of the hall and around a corner. It was obviously the only room in this section, situated over storage rooms below.

She opened the door with a large iron key and then stepped back to allow them to view the room. A small suite was revealed, a large four-poster bed centered in the room with tall curtained windows flanking it. A tall boy dresser in a rich oak adorned one wall, while the opposite side held a petite ladies table with a wash bowl and pitcher. Fresh flowers sweetened the air with their perfume. "Our quietest and most private suite," she announced as they stepped across the threshold.

Ziona perused the room and dismissed the woman with "These rooms are suitable. Thank you." The plump proprietress curtsied roughly and then pulled the door closed behind her.

Cayden groaned and closed his eyes. "There is only one bed." The beginnings of a flush violently rose through the collar of his shirt. Ziona grinned at him, clearly enjoying his discomfort.

"Well, I suppose we do not have to worry about being cold tonight." She laughed as the colour climbed up into his cheeks. "Come, let us retrieve our gear and get a bite to eat."

They descended the stairs together to find a crowd gathered at the base of them. The villagers, including the women and men Ziona had noticed earlier, quieted as they spied Cayden and Ziona at the top of the stairs. Cayden instinctively placed his hand on his sword, eyes measuring the men and women in front of him. No weapons were visible, but it did not mean they were friendly.

They, in turn, doffed hats and made bows to him as he drew eye level with them.

"My lord," a man spoke up, drawing Cayden's attention. The man stared at Cayden with one wild eye that wandered when he tried to focus. A long scar ran from the corner of the wandering eye and disappeared into his rapidly receding hairline. "We could not help but notice your arrival. May we ask your name, sir?"

"My name is Cayden Tiernan." Cayden gazed at the men. There were a good twenty of them and about half as many women assembled. The innkeeper peeked from the door of the kitchen, listening with all her might. Cayden found it odd she would feel the need to sneak inside her own inn.

"And where are you from, my lord?" This came from a redheaded man not much older than Cayden.

"I am from the village of Sanctuary-by-the-Sea. Do you know it?" Cayden glanced around. The men shook their heads at the name. "Why do you ask?"

A middle-aged woman spoke up for the first time. Her blond hair liberally sprinkled with grey fell straight to her waist and her blue eyes were framed by thick eyelashes. She spread her skirts in a deep curtsey. "I'm Catriona, my lord." Peeking at him from under her lashes, she said, "You look like the king." Her voice trembled. "You are the spitting image of the king, may he rest in peace." She made a symbol with her fingers as she breathed a blessing, the crook of her fingers like an eagle's beak.

Ziona glanced sharply at the woman. "How would you know what the king looked like? He has been dead for over seventeen years. Where did you learn that sign? "

The woman cowered back as Ziona's gaze pinned her.

"Please, my lady. I worked as a maid in the castle when I was young. I was a maidservant to the royal family. Although I did not personally attend the king and queen, I had opportunity to see them in the halls. I was a servant to the prince and princess consort. Please, my lord, you have the same colouring and bearing as the king except for the eyes. They are different." The men around her nodded their heads in agreement. "These men, they also served in the castle. They served with the Kingsmen. All except Jakob; he was born here in the village. We beg you to tell us who you really are."

Cayden and Ziona gazed around at them all, stunned.

He had not expected to find people who would seem to recognize him, maybe even be able to identify him. These people appeared friendly, but what of his enemies? Would they be able to recognize him as well? *What am I saying? I am no king. This is foolishness!*

Ziona took control of the crowd by shouldering her way through them, dragging Cayden behind her by his sleeve. Gaining the open air outside the inn, they found an even larger group of people assembled. It appeared half the town was gathered; a good hundred people had congregated out front of the inn in less than ten minutes. Cayden and Ziona's horses had been swallowed up by the crowd but appeared untouched.

Cayden stopped cold, frozen in shock.

The crowd bowed and curtsied as he stepped onto the boardwalk outside the inn. The front row of men melted before him.

"My lord. My prince." A gnarled man in a worn and patched Kingsman uniform rose from the dirt and, with head lowered, spoke. "I pledge my life to your service. We have waited, watched, and prepared for this day as we were instructed to do." He bowed at the waist, his sword extended, grip toward Cayden. "My sword is yours. My life is yours to do with as you please."

The rest of the crowd kneeled behind the first row and repeated the pledge, man and woman alike.

Cayden found his tongue at last. "Stop!" he said, aghast. "What do you think you are doing? You have no idea who I am or where we are going."

Ziona placed a hand on his arm again and stopped his automatic rejection. She leaned over and whispered in his ear. "You are prophesied to save these people. Do you not think it is possible they have prophesies that speak of this day? Hear them out and ask them for their faith and knowledge."

Cayden gazed into her calm emerald eyes and his panic stilled.

He raised his hands to the crowd, who now stood in front of him and behind him, the group from the inn peering out the door.

He felt a feather-like touch along his cheek and heard a thunk. His mind had barely registered the fact that an arrow had imbedded itself in the door frame by his head, when a second arrow pierced his shoulder tossing him backward onto the boardwalk.

Ziona cried out and flung her body over his, shielding him from any more arrows. The first row of the sworn men scrambled upright and formed a human barricade around him, allowing no one access. One man pointed at the rooftop of the building across the street, where a man was seen running off toward the back of the building. Several men took off in pursuit.

Cayden groaned, blood gushing from his right shoulder and soaking his cloak and shirt. Ziona eased back off of him and glared at the men assembled around her. A sharp wicked knife with an obsidian handle gleamed in her hand.

"Be true to your oaths, gentlemen, or be prepared to pay this day with your life," she growled at them all. She flashed the knife and the men backed away slightly. The man with the wandering eye spoke up. He had pushed his way outside to help form part of the men protecting Cayden after he was hit.

"We have been sworn to defend the royal family since we were children. We will defend his life with our own. This we have always done and now that we have found him, this we will do with our last breath."

Ziona locked her eyes on his, dragging the truth from him. Seeing the honesty there, she nodded. "What is your name?"

"Tobias, my lady."

"Help me get Cayden back inside to our room."

Tobias gestured to another man beside him and together they lifted Cayden. He groaned in pain and his eyes rolled, sweat beading on his brow. They carried him back up the stairs as smoothly as possible and gently lowered his unconscious form onto the bed.

"Do you have a healer in this town?"

"We have a midwife, but she is used to setting bones. Perhaps she can be of assistance."

"Fetch her." The second man left.

"Tobias, I want a guard placed on this room, twenty-four hours a day. Do you understand me?" Tobias nodded. "Also, I want you to find the innkeeper and bring her to me. She is involved in this assassination attempt in some way."

"Yes, my lady, it shall be done. I will send up two men I trust to begin guarding the door immediately. I will also see to your horses, my lady." With that, he bowed and left the room, closing the door behind him.

Chapter 35

NELSON PEERED AT THE GLOWING GREEN WALL. Surely it was easier to build a ramp or a staircase to the suspended door than it was to assail the foundation wall of a tower that soared eight stories above the four stories buried deep underground, the fourth of which he was reduced to staring at as he attempted to form a plan to get through it. "Fabian has the easier of the two assignments," grumbled Nelson.

Nelson could try tunnelling deeper, but he suspected the foundation sat on bedrock. He could try blowing it up, but the resultant explosion would alert everyone inside the castle to his activities and most likely bring the upper four stories of natural caverns down on his head, and be insufficient to breach the wall in the end. There was insufficient water available to wear away the stone like he had done with his cold storage back at the inn in the village.

He ran his hand over his chin, scratching the day's growth of stubble. Absently, he reached for his cup of cold water sitting on a narrow stone ledge where he had placed it an hour ago.

The lad at his elbow spoke up. "Did you require anything more, sir?"

"Yes. I need a way to get through this section of wall, but I am stumped as to how to do it."

The lad peered at the limestone block in front of them. It was a faint pink colour and marbled with white veins. "We could use the same fungal paste we were using earlier, sir, if you are interested. You know it, the paste we used to widen the passageway. It worked quite quickly." He waved his hand in the general direction of the limestone block. "The mortar is made of the same substance as the veins of this block. We should be able to dissolve the white material completely."

Nelson smacked his head. Of course, how could he have forgotten? *Stupid old age is creeping up on me.* He frowned at the rock. "How long will it take?"

The lad paused, thinking. "Two days to make enough paste, I think…and maybe a week to dissolve the veins?"

Nelson clapped him on his shoulder. "Get it done in four days, and I have free ale for the night for you and your crew at the inn."

The lad whooped and ran from the cavern to gather his team.

***

Fabian sat back and munched on one of his sticky buns that he had brought along as an incentive to his crew. The icing oozed onto his fingers and he licked them, eyeing the proceedings.

The first stage was constructed, a wooden platform levelling out the bottom of the construct. Risers were being erected on the first stage and fastened in place. In all, they needed to rise about three stories to parallel the door of the Traitor's Gate.

Construction was going slower than he had hoped for. He had a shiny silver piece at risk, should his crew fail to gain entrance before Nelson's. He knew the old innkeeper was as stingy as a washwoman during a drought. He had to be in well ahead of time or kiss his coin goodbye.

Denzik strolled out of the mouth of the passage and paused beside him, watching the workers. He reached into the basket and picked up a sticky bun and bit deeply into its cinnamon center.

"I heard frum sum of the earz today," he mumbled around the delicious mouthful. He swallowed and continued, "There are rumours of a young man moving in this direction who is gathering quite the following." He popped in the last mouthful and chewed slowly. "Some say he has the look of our former king, although how that would be possible, I have no idea."

Fabian tore his gaze from his contemplation of the stairs and raised his eyebrows. "Is it possible, do you think? Is this the one?"

"Yes...yes I think so," Denzik said slowly. "So many things have been happening lately, fortuitous events. It's as if the fates or the Mother Goddess herself is taking an active hand. The ears are very active. Rumours are flooding into the system. Some speak of spirits on the move, haunting armies and laying waste to any that stand in their paths. Others speak of Nature herself rising up, wolves roaming, birds gathering, as though being called to battle. There are even rumours of Primordial warriors past our borders. Something is happening. We need to be ready."

Fabian nodded, thoughtful. "Have you alerted our branches to gather their men and prepare?"

"Yes, I did, as soon as we discovered the wizard. They are on high alert and sharing the watch, ready to respond. One village north of us has already gone silent. It is the area where the lad was rumoured to have been last seen. I can only hope it is positive news of them on the march."

"Time is short then."

Denzik nodded.

"Well we need a couple more days here, four at the most."

Denzik nodded again and then left to relay the news to Nelson.

Time is indeed short, Denzik thought. If this was the moment they had waited and prepared for all these years, they were actually out of time.

Chapter 36

CAYDEN WOKE TO A SOFT TONGUE lapping at his face. He opened his eyes to focus on two large ice blue eyes staring at him. Sheba was stretched out along the left side of his body on the bed. He attempted to sit up but immediately sank back in a groan, realizing for the first time that his right shoulder was swathed in bandages.

"She has not left your side. As soon as you were struck, she bounded out of the woods. I had to convince the men that she was your guardian also. She was frantic to get to you, so frantic that she has ignored her fear of men." Ziona sat in a chair to the right side of the bed observing Cayden. "She snapped at the hand of anyone who got too close. Remarkable restraint for a wild animal, I'd say." Ziona ruffled Sheba's fur.

They have worked out an understanding, Cayden thought.

"What day is it?" Sunlight streamed through the eastern-facing window.

"It's early the next morning. I thought it best to keep you sedated while we took the arrow out and healed your wound. It was deep and hit the bone. We had to remove some bone fragments that splintered, so you will be sore while it heals. I can speed up the process, but it still uses your body strength to heal, so the best thing is rest."

Cayden moved his right arm in a circle, rotating it carefully, testing its limitations.

"Did you catch the archer? Did you find the one who shot me?"

Ziona shook her head. "No. He seems to have had his escape route planned in advance. The innkeeper has disappeared also."

"What of all the people in the square? Are they all right?"

Ziona smiled. "I think I will let them tell you. It is very interesting what they have to say." She stood up and tucked his blankets in more closely to him. "I will go get you some food. Tobias is standing watch at your door. He has refused to rest until he saw you were fine with his own eyes. I will send him in to chat. He can be trusted."

She walked across the room to the door. Sheba's head swivelled to watch her go, eyes intent on the door and what lay beyond. She sniffed the air. Cayden stroked her fur and sensed her contentment at his touch.

Ziona was replaced by Tobias, who entered, closing the door behind him and then snapped to attention. "My lord, you wished to speak to me, sir?"

Cayden watched the man's lazy eye twitch in its socket. The scar was more pronounced this morning, possibly due to his tiredness at standing guard all night.

"How did you receive that scar?"

"I was in the Kingsmen Cavalry, my lord. I served during the Daimonic wars. During the Primordial uprising of Daimon Ford, I was speared by a Primordial soldier who had gotten inside the perimeter guard of the High Prince."

The door opened and another man walked in behind Tobias, the second man who had stood guard through the night. "My name is Stephanos, my lord. What he doesn't tell you is that he took down six other Primordial soldiers while having three arrows stuck in his body, saving the life of the High Prince."

Tobias shrugged. "I refused to allow them to hurt the prince." He bowed his head to Cayden. "But I have failed you, my lord, and I will accept any punishment you see fit. I should have seen the assassin on the top of the building." Tobias knelt by Cayden's bedside on one knee, hands clasped on his knee and head lowered. He looked like a condemned man waiting for the headman's axe.

Cayden struggled to sit up, gasped with the pain and sunk back. Sheba emitted a low growl but did not move.

"Don't be a fool," Cayden gasped, wheezing. *One of those bones the arrow struck must be related to my ribs*, he thought. "We had only arrived. There was no way to anticipate that attack. It must have been totally impromptu." Cayden frowned. "Rise, would you? You are embarrassing me. Besides, I can't see you on the floor."

Tobias scrambled to his feet, his face flaming. "I apologize again, my lord. I didn't mean to embarrass you."

Stephanos chuckled. "My lord, our friend Tobias here is a very literal person. I suggest you speak true every time and hold thoughts you may not wish taken to heart for he will see every word spoken as a command."

Cayden puzzled over what he was expected to do with the two men.

They were dressed similarly in tan pants made from a homespun cloth. Leather vests topped laced shirts with loose sleeves. Both men wore broadswords strapped to their backs. Stephanos's dark beard hid a pointed chin.

"I have the impression you were somehow waiting for me to come, although I cannot figure out any reason for a large contingent of king's soldiers to be holed up in this town."

"That is easily explained, my lord. We have been living our lives in this town since we were dismissed from the king's service seventeen years ago. The queen dismissed all those loyal to the king. We have raised families here." Stephanos fiddled with his bearded chin, nervously.

Tobias grimaced and spat on the floor and then realizing what he had done, shifted uncomfortably. "Sorry, my lord," he murmured. "The queen did not dismiss us. She rode us out of town on threat of death. What she did not realize is that our oaths are for life. She should have killed us." He made to spit again, but then thinking better of it he swallowed back his spittle.

"She did reconsider after the fact. We had to disband in order to not be hunted down like rabid animals. We dispersed," continued Stephanos, "settling in small villages and towns across the land, blending in with the locals, never together in numbers so large as to be noticed. But we did not disband. We have continued to work against the queen and have undermined her reign since the beginning. We have worked to sabotage her supply lines to make her forces ill. We have stolen horses, interrupted couriers, whatever came to mind to create mayhem for her legions. Many of these events she has blamed on the Primordials. All the while, we remained hidden and waited for the return of the prophesied king." He bowed to Cayden once again.

Cayden looked from one to the other and finally spoke what he dreaded saying, "And you think I am this king?"

Tobias caught his eye and grinned. "Of that, my lord, there is no doubt. You will see when we get closer to the capital. There are statues, my lord, in the central square that could have been molded from your form."

Cayden shook his head, dizzy as the implications washed over him. He could not move freely. He would be immediately recognized wherever he went. A part of him wanted to jump to his feet and flee, run as far and fast as he could as fate squeezed him to this path. He saw a great cage looming overhead, one he would never be able to escape, responsibility such as he had never wanted or known.

"My lord," Stephanos spoke this time. "We have heard it is prophesied you will free your people from the queen's grasp. We have waited these long years, working and preparing for this day. We have raised families and have sons and daughters pledged to your service. We are yours, as we pledged yesterday."

Cayden saw Stephanos was completely earnest in his words. Curious, he asked, "How many Kingsmen are we speaking of, Stephanos?"

"We are only one of many groups, my lord. The head of our organization is a man who is near the capital. We do not know his name, as we have only ever known those in our closest units to protect the others should some of us be captured. But at last count, your men totalled around twenty thousand troops, my lord."

Cayden sat bolt upright despite the pain. "*Twenty thousand*?" he exclaimed.

"Yes, my lord. They are scattered and would take time to assemble, but they exist, my lord."

"Oh sweet Mother of Earth," Cayden swore. What was he to do with so many people looking to him...to do what? He didn't even know what he was to do. He sank back to his pillows with a loud, extended groan. It was only partially due to the pain of his injuries, but the two soldiers believed he was tiring and backed out the door with low bows.

"We will leave you to rest, my lord. Have no fear; we are standing guard while you sleep." They withdrew with many more bows and closed the door behind them with a click.

Cayden flung his arms over his eyes, trying to hide from the cage closing on him, but there was nowhere to go.

Chapter 37

RYDER LED HIS MEN AWAY FROM THE TOWN two days after the attack. His men insisted on helping to bury the dead and making a start on repairing the damage to the inn and other buildings in the village. They could not stay for long, however, and after a couple days, they mounted up. As they rode away, Ryder found his ranks had swelled from their original thirty to nearly one hundred.

A sizeable portion of the villagers revealed themselves to be Kingsmen who had settled in the town around the time of Cayden's and Ryder's birth. The men had approached Darius and expressed their desire to assist with the young lord's adventure, as Darius had put it. Ryder suspected the men knew more than they were letting on.

For one, they had assembled on the morning of departure, fully outfitted and ready for a long campaign. Each man had brought his own mount, pack, supplies, and weapons. Each man had also donned his former King's Guard uniform. Some strained around girths that had realigned themselves south over the intervening seventeen years. However, all the men wore them proudly.

They rode into the camp and sat their mounts, waiting and expectant.

Darius had approached the lead man or who Ryder assumed was their leader. After a quick conversation, Darius had walked over to where Ryder had been saddling his mount.

"They want to join us."

Ryder had inspected the men. *It would be stupid to refuse such a well-trained group of soldiers who were not mercenaries, even if they were old enough to be his father. Their skills would be invaluable.*

"Let's make use of them. See that our men are mixed into their units. With their obvious military training, they should be able to teach cavalry charges and the like. They are to report to you as their superior. Select the men who are capable leaders and bring them to me. We will assign them rank."

Darius had done as instructed and now the reformed band had an orderly march, the men set in fighting units.

Ryder rode, flanked on one side by the chosen bannermen of the day and by Darius on his other side. He twisted in his saddle, gazing back at the band of men following him. They had not seen any fighting yet, but he knew deep down it was coming. There was no way for them to reach the capital city without bumping into the queen's legions. And then there were those Charun following them. He felt as though he was being squeezed through a cattle chute toward a dark and dangerous future.

His scouts patrolled ahead and behind the large body of men, now making its way south. Every few minutes, a rider would approach the band, sometimes in groups of twos and threes. More often than not, they also wore the King's Guard uniform. It seemed word was spreading of Ryder's band and the young prince they followed.

They kept moving, stopping for brief periods to sleep but for no longer than six hours at a time. They passed by smaller villages and towns, but they did not pause. Ryder sent teams of men into the towns to purchase supplies as they went. The gold they had brought from Ziona's cave gave them the funds they needed, however as their ranks grew, Ryder became more and more concerned about conserving their funds.

By the time they were two days distant from Devonshire, their numbers had doubled again, as more and more former King's Guard joined their ranks.

The annoying itch that had begun between Ryder's shoulder blades as they fled from the Charun grew worse, the closer they came to the capital city of Cathair.

On the third day, they reached the town of Pert Soaidh, which in the ancient tongue translated into "The Wooded Place of Heroes." Ryder gazed around in open interest as they approached the fringes of the town. It appeared to have been swallowed by a dense forest. There was only one road, split by the town, so that the one on which they travelled lead in from the north and formed again on the far side, departing to the south.

The town boasted the first true fortifications Ryder had seen. The wooden palisade surrounding the town was located on top of a steep-sided earthen mound that rose from a water-filled moat. A wooden drawbridge flanked by guard towers with archery slits adorned both entrance and exit. The middle of the town was split by a river flowing on its east-west axis.

This town would be able to withstand a siege, Ryder noted, as he rode through the gates and into the town proper. His men followed, arranged in precise units, trotted along behind him. No one challenged their entry.

The town was the largest they had seen so far. Wooden houses and shops lined the walls and dirt road, which curved to the right and followed the basic line of the palisade. Streets intersected the curving road like spokes of a wheel within a wheel. The spokes did not run straight to the center of the town but rather they were offset on the next wheel.

There was no straight line to the center of the town, which Ryder identified by a flag flying on top of the tallest structure. The ring roads of the wagon wheel offered the most direct approach. Ryder felt dizzy and confined within the curving streets.

The cobblestone was busy but not overly full, considering it was midday. Tall palisades cast deep shadows on the street below, creating a semi-permanent twilight. Shadows blurred the outlines of the buildings they passed. Ryder thought the design was brilliant; an invading force would be fighting in twilight conditions even in the full light of day, while the residents eyes were accustom to the gloom.

Indeed, as they rode past, they belatedly noticed the armed men watching them from the shadowed alleys between buildings. The itch between Ryder's shoulder blades grew.

As they rounded the curve on the far end of town, their way was blocked by row on row of armoured soldiers, pikes lowered to the oncoming horsemen. Archers stepped to the edge of the two-story buildings above, surrounding them, aiming down on their position. The shadowy figures from the alleys stepped forward. The rear of their procession closed with an equal number of pikes.

Ryder's men drew their swords, steel ringing as they slid them out of scabbards.

Ryder raised his arm signalling a halt and to hold position.

Ryder did not want to trigger a confrontation in the middle of the town. He nudged his horse in the ribs making it walk forward toward the waiting pikes.

"Who here speaks for you men?" He spoke loudly to the men gazing around. "I would speak to your captain."

The men remained in position, pikes lowered. Someone coughed in the group. A voice called from the side and a tall balding man, dressed in a red and blue tunic stepped forward. His blue pants were tucked into tall boots that clicked on the cobblestones as he walked forward. A large feather bobbed on the ornate hat he wore. He did not carry any weapons visible to Ryder.

"I do be the magistrate of this fair town," he announced in a bored voice, "and I do be afraid you intend to pass through without paying the customary levy for the use of our fine streets."

Ryder dismounted and approached the man on foot. "I apologize on behalf of myself and my men for the intrusion. We were unaware a toll had been set for the use of this road. If you could advise the appropriate fee, we will pay it and be on our way."

The magistrate looked Ryder up and down, taking in his dusty country garb. The corners of his mouth turned down in disgust. He ignored Ryder and addressed the eldest of the captains leading the team behind Ryder. "You, good sir, look to be a man of means, please instruct your servant here to remain silent in the presence of a lord."

The King's Guard, a man by the name of Lazaro, rode up beside Ryder. He removed his hat and bowed from the saddle. "You are mistaken, my lord. Sir Ryder is the lord of this band and it is to him you will answer."

The magistrate's eyes widened and his gaze swung back to Ryder. He bowed a short bow that was nearly an insult, for one of equal rank. "My apologies, my lord, I did not realize." He stepped back and gazed around at the tense soldiers on both sides. "Please, allow me to make up for my error. Let us talk over refreshments." He waved his hand and the pikes lowered. The archers eased back on their bows and relaxed.

Ryder nodded to Lazaro, who selected an honour guard for Ryder. Darius accompanied Lazaro and two other men. Laurista rounded out the group.

"Your men are to continue through town and may make use of the wagon staging grounds outside the palisade wall to the south. They will wait for you there."

The pike men separated and formed a gauntlet of steel down which The Band of the Rebel's Land continued to march.

Ryder followed the magistrate who was walking with his own contingent of guards toward a full log building set against an inner palisade wall. It was a two-story structure, the windows fitted with metal bars on the main floor. Stone steps rose to a set of carved double doors, which were opened at their approach by two ceremonial guards, dressed as flamboyantly as the magistrate.

The interior was lit by lamps hung from ornate metal arms, which were attached to the walls at even intervals. Long raised benches lined the back wall and a plain door was visible behind them. Smaller tables and chairs were scattered throughout the balance of the room with doors leading to other rooms on the side. Books lined the walls, their shelves reaching close to ceiling height. Between the doors, hung on the wall was an assortment of portraits of Queen Alcina. Ryder stared at the portraits as they passed.

"You admire my portraits of the queen? She graced me with her presence when she first came to the throne and privileged me with the opportunity to paint Her Grace. She was pleased to find that, as Pert is strategically placed on the road to the capital, her inhabitants are loyal to the throne." His lips curved into a smile that did not reach his eyes.

We have wandered into the mouth of the lion, thought Ryder. *Somehow I do not believe he intends for us to pass through his town.*

The magistrate led them through the end side door and into a room comfortably arranged with overstuffed couches that flanked a cold stone fireplace. Tall windows let in a gloomy light that passed for daylight in the shadow of the palisade wall.

"Please, gentlemen, lady, have a seat. I will call for refreshments."

The magistrate pulled on a silk cord and Ryder heard a bell ring in another room.

A maid dressed in blue livery entered and curtsied. "Please bring tea and scones for our guests, Sharona." She curtsied again and left the room.

"Let me introduce myself. My name is Samuel de Champagne and I am the magistrate and high official of this town." He gestured around at his surroundings. "This building is the courthouse and also houses the trade and taxation departments. Handy if someone do be trying to skip their duties. If they cannot pay their taxes, it do be but a short walk to their cell." He chuckled at the assembled men, who had not yet seated themselves.

"Please, please sit. We have things to discuss." He seated himself in a plush armchair. His guard took up position behind his back, watching the room and its occupants.

Ryder sat in a stiff-backed chair that allowed him free movement. The itch between his shoulders had not left with the disappearance of the town's soldiers. Laurista seated herself in a couch to his left and his escort arranged themselves similarly behind Ryder.

The maid re-entered and placed a tray with cups, teapot, and a plate of scones on a low table by the fireplace. She filled a cup of tea from the teapot and brought it over to Samuel, who took a sip of the brew. She did not serve the others.

"Come, help yourselves to tea." No one moved.

Ryder spoke for the first time. "We do not plan to linger in your town, my Lord Champagne. We intended to pass through on our way south. If you would advise the amount of the tariff, we will be on our way."

He sipped at his tea, considering eyes flicking over the audience in front of him. He set his cup down on the carved table beside his chair.

"Well, first I need to know the purpose of your journey. There are many different levies, depending on the purpose of passing through. For instance, if you are a merchant, moving wool to the looms of the coast, the appropriate levy may be a percentage of what trade you take away from the local wool farmers. If you are a trader in rare metals and coin, perhaps the appropriate levy is a donation to the fund of the poor as you are leaving nothing of value behind for my people.

"The law do be very broad in these areas, you see...and flexible to meet the need." He waved his hand at the books on the other side of the wall. "Our lawmakers have been very meticulous at recording every passerby and the levy imposed in order to keep the assessments fair. However, we have never had an army decide to ride through. They do normally take a route to bypass our fair town." He once again scrutinized the group. "Yes, indeed, you will make for a very interesting test case, I believe." He picked up his tea again, sipping it.

Ryder frowned at the floor, thinking. The magistrate demanded a levy yet he could not advise what was appropriate. Surely they were not the only travellers to pass through the town? Not all could be merchants. So how did they assess the levy against a single traveller or a family? Ryder shifted in his chair, wishing momentarily that he had chosen a softer one.

"We have nothing to trade. We are purchasing supplies as we travel. What would you have us give you?"

"Well you have hit the hammer right on the head, haven't you? You do be passing through and do be taking the supplies of the local farmers. You may even pay for them. If it had not been so, I am sure I would have heard of your band long before now.

"However, merely paying the farmer does not compensate this town for the use of the roads we maintain, so you can reach the farmer in the first place. It does not pay for the protection we give the farmer from bandits...or even rogue armies," he said with a languid smile that did not reach his eyes.

Laurista abruptly stood up and walked over to the cooling tea tray, pouring herself a cup of tea. She met Ryder's eyes and blinked as she took a sip. The magistrate's smile widened. She put it down and then brought Ryder a cup and returned to fetch hers.

She sat and sipped at her tea with Ryder doing likewise.

The magistrate froze, watching them intently. *So the tea was poisoned*, Laurista guessed. They continued to sip. Nothing happened.

The magistrate's eyes widened in shock as the poison appeared to have no effect.

"My Lord Champagne, poisoned tea is a very old ruse. Surely your healers have developed a counteragent to this particular kind?" She continued to sip her tea, as Ryder did his. "Obviously, your cup is not poisoned. Ours, I suspect, most definitely are."

"Perhaps"—Ryder pinned the magistrate with his hot glare—"we have found our levy."

The magistrate assessed him with roving eyes. "I do believe we have, my boy...I do believe, indeed."

Chapter 38

"HERE, PUT THE PRY BAR IN THIS WAY." Nelson flipped the bar over and wedged it back into the side slot of the limestone block closer to the top. A gap had appeared where the paste had done its job. "Now, give it a good heave and keep working it in the crack, back and forth. Then, alternate with the other side of the rock like this." Nelson handed the pry bar back to the Kingsman and stepped back out of the way.

They worked the pry bars, scraping aside mortar and wedging the steel under the lip of rock, shifting it by the tiniest of increments. The men had to take turns, working the block side by side, rocking it back and forth until a good three inches had been moved out from the face of the wall.

Suddenly, a tapping reply issued from the rock. Nelson flapped his arms, hushing the men. "Tap, tap...Tap, tap, tap..." went the message, repeating itself. Nelson listened intently. "Back...stand...back...," he murmured, sounding the code out. *Stand back?*

A great crash filled the cavern as the block popped out of the hole like the plug out of a dam. The one-hundred-pound rock fell to the floor and tumbled a couple of times before coming to rest. The men leapt back to preserve their toes as it rumbled past, churning centuries old dust into the air.

Nelson waved his hand in front of his face, coughing, and squinted at the now sizeable hole. A man stared back at him, white hair and beard streaming past his shoulders.

Nelson moved closer to the hole. "Mordecai Ben-Moses, I presume?"

"Alas it is I, or that was what I was called when I was locked away in here seventeen years ago."

"How did you do that?" Nelson said, peering at the old man as the dust from the collapse settled to the floor. He waved a hand to clear the lingering haze.

"Oh, a bit of this and a bit of that...some hocus pocus and there you have it." He grinned at the bewildered expression on Nelson's face. "Come, come surely the world has not forgotten about magic?" He tsked and shook his head sadly. "Magic surrounds us. All it needs is a disciplined mind, some focused intent and the will to see the thing through. This" —he held up his crystal—"also comes in useful."

Nelson's eyes squinted, more confused, not less.

Mordecai sighed. "I presume they did not announce my untimely death or any such thing in my absence? I would not relish having to explain how I am still alive when everyone who loved me has forgotten me and those who hated me are alive to hate me still."

Nelson chuckled. "No, they did not announce your death, although I think most have forgotten you existed. They never announced your capture. You were never spoken of again. Most thought you had died, so I suppose it is the same thing."

Mordecai chuckled softly. "Certainly, I can make use of being dead. Few souls have the opportunity to walk the land again in the same bodies that dressed them originally. I must admit, though, this cell has become quite wearisome in the intervening years. It is time I took up new residence elsewhere...but not quite yet. I am expecting a very important visitor shortly."

Nelson frowned. "They allow you company?"

"Certainly not—I don't exist, remember? No, this company will be dropped into my lap, quite literally, I believe." One eye stared through the crack. "Keep enlarging this hole for I foresee a time in the near future when it will come in quite useful. But you must replace all the stones at the end of the day. I will disguise the work from my side."

Nelson nodded. "I will bring Denzik to see you tomorrow. He's the brains of this outfit."

"Now, would you pass me one of those wonderful sticky buns I have smelled for the last hour? It's been so long." Mordecai sniffed the air in appreciation.

"I will never hear the end of it from Fabian," Nelson grumbled, passing the bag of sticky buns through to the grizzled old wizard.

***

Fabian grunted. The steps were finally in place and the door facing him at eye level. He ran his hand down the stubble on his unshaven chin and grunted again. He still had no idea how to open it. The thick oak door's hinges were covered in thick rust, proof positive of inactivity. He doubted if they had been opened since Captain O'Reilly and his men had taken up residence in the chamber. Fabian scratched his head, examining the problem.

Nelson must be close to getting through the block wall. Who would have thought he could chisel through a castle wall faster than I could assemble a staircase?

The lead carpenter squeezed past him, picking up his tools and dropping them into a tool belt strapped around his waist. Fabian grabbed his arm, halting him. "Tell me, how would you break open that door if it was up to you?"

The carpenter paused, glancing at the door. "You want to get into the next room?"

"Yes, I do."

"Well, why don't you have someone open it from the other side?"

"I don't know if anyone is on the other side."

"So, why don't you get someone to go and open it for you?"

Fabian stared at him. The idea wasn't as dumb as it sounded at first. "You do know who is on the other side?"

"Well, as this would be the prison section, I would assume some of the Queen's Guard."

"That is correct. Why would they help us?"

"They wouldn't...but one of the serving staff might. They feed the prisoners on a regular basis, right? So they have access to the prisoner cells." He headed down the stairs and back to the crew who were waiting below.

Fabian gazed after the man and then at the door again and laughed silently. It was time to arrange for a delivery of sweet buns to the castle. Nothing opens doors like the smell of food, and those sweet buns were a cinnamon-crusted golden key to the castle and to the corridors beyond.

Chapter 39

LAURISTA LEANED IN TOWARD RYDER as they walked down the steps of the government house. "Well played, my lord," she whispered, eyes darting around at the guards on either side of the double doors.

"So the tea was poisoned?"

"No, the cup was. The maid poured tea in his cup only to make sure he got the clean cup. I quickly rinsed your cup with the tea I poured, and then I combined it into mine while his attention was on you. I emptied the poison into my cup."

Ryder's head swung in her direction, alarm in his expression. "How are you still standing then?"

"I didn't drink any of the tea. I only pretended to. The tea never touched my lips."

The corner of Ryder's eyes crinkled in laughter. "Where did you learn to be so devious?"

She stepped along, raising her skirts to avoid the puddles left over from a passing shower. "I was the king's taster in my younger years."

Ryder's eyes widened, in response to her words. "You were in the royal court? Why did you leave?"

"I was reassigned to some country lord who was in charge of the legions in the outer territories. When he died during a siege, I ended up assisting the healer to the legion. Funny enough, everyone in the royal court was dead within a year of my dismissal from my post...with the exception of the queen, of course. I suspect they all died of poisoning, although it is considered treason to voice that opinion."

"Well, I am certainly happy to have found you. Do you really know the antidote to that poison?"

"Yes, I recognized the herb being used. I can make an antidote for it." She laughed. "The magistrate may not be pleased with its side effects, however, as unfortunately you find yourself with wicked cramps that require an inordinate amount of time spent in the privy."

Ryder laughed in response. He intended to be far away before the magistrate found the need to use that particular remedy.

***

Ryder and the band left the fortified town the following morning. Once the levy had been arranged and paid for, they were invited to trade openly with the townsfolk, who were happy to entice the soldiers with wares gathered from the four corners of the queendom. The men were allowed to return to the town in groups no larger than ten. They were required to sign in and out before the next group entered.

Despite the restrictions, the townsfolk were eager for news from the outside word. It seemed merchant caravans avoided the town due to the taxes levied. A vigorous smuggling trade was the result with an active underground component.

Ryder chose what was purported to be the best inn in the town, the Flaming Phoenix. They took a quiet booth in a corner away from the crowd of locals who appeared to be flocking into the inn for an evening of entertainment.

Ryder sipped on the house specialty, a spiced rum punch served in a mug decorated with a hand-painted phoenix. Ryder thought they looked like flamingoes with attitude. Laurista sat beside him, as did Darius and Lazaro who had insisted on accompanying them.

The inn's entertainment for the evening was provided by a man playing a dulcimer while a middle-aged woman sang. The townsfolk formed squares and began to perform a dance unfamiliar to Ryder. He watched while sipping his drink. People clapped along in time to the music.

A short muscular man took a winding path through the crowd to Ryder's table. He swept the hat from his head and then bowed to Ryder and said quietly, "My lord, I would speak with you, if it pleases you?"

Ryder nodded and motioned to the seat across from him.

"My lord, I have been told to enquire about your purpose in passing through our town?"

"We seek to catch up to some companions we were separated from."

The man nodded. "We have been commissioned to pass a message to the man who hails from the cliffs. Is this the man you seek?"

Ryder observed the man, trying to get his measure.

"Perhaps."

The man lowered his voice to prevent being overheard.

"Would you be headed for the capital?"

"It's possible."

"I have a contact in a village outside of the capital in a town called Lower Cathair. I have been instructed to advise the leader of the band from the cliffs when he passes through to find a man named Denzik."

The man glanced around again quickly, checking the crowd. The noise of the dancers drowned their voices and made listening in by normal means impossible.

"I am also to give you this." He slid a leather pouch across the table. "Do not open it here. Open it in private."

Ryder picked up the bag and tucked it into an inner pocket of his cloak.

"Please pass this message to Denzik when you see him. Tell him we stand ready to serve. The watchtowers are manned."

Ryder nodded.

The man stood up and without a backward glance walked away.

Laurista leaned her arms on the table to watch the man depart.

"Kingsman, do you think? Or a spy for the queen?"

"Could be both. What do we know of the politics in this area? It's time we moved on though. It's dangerous to stay in one spot for too long. Let's head back to camp."

Chapter 40

THE PEOPLE ASSEMBLED BEFORE CAYDEN were the ragtag remnants who had managed to flee before the legions descended on the outlying villages of Cathair. They had joined the Kingsmen's flight as they left the capital, blending into their ranks and fading into other villages, establishing new lives in order to protect their sons from the conscription teams. The light of rebellion shone in their eyes. Men and women alike were armed, the men donning pants and armour they had obviously created for themselves. Hand-tooled leather fashioned to fit each individual was proudly worn complete with leg chaps and arm guards.

The women had shorn their hair into a pageboy style that somewhat disguised their gender. They had fashioned linen amour that molded to their feminine forms, layers on layers of tightly woven linen, bound together and as thick as Cayden's thumb. Each woman's armour was specially made for her body and dyed vibrant hues of red, green, yellow, and blue. The amour made them look as intimidating as female dragons guarding their nest of younglings. To Cayden's eyes, they appeared every bit as fierce as the men.

Cayden nudged his horse into a slow walk. The sun had cleared the treetops. It promised to be a hot day.

Tobias advised they would reach the castle with two days of steady travel. He had sent runners ahead to scout the way and locate a promising area to camp their large band.

The wind rustled the treetops and played with the edge of his cloak. One of the women of the village had produced a fine silk cape made of a deep purple with golden crowns embroidered on the hem.

The crest of the king was embroidered over the right breast. It had been part of the ceremonial uniform of the King's Guard and the men had insisted Cayden wear it in their honour. Cayden had refused the gift, of course, but with Ziona's frown and the men's disappointment clearly etched on their faces, he had succumbed and now it was fastened around his throat with a fine golden clasp shaped like an eagle.

"I feel like a circus monkey," he said, tugging at the clasp.

"You are the image of the king. Yes, you are or soon will be." Ziona laughed as he grimaced.

His frustrated posture made her smile widen and she leaned over to straighten his collar. "Smile, the people are watching. You cannot let them see your insecurity or uncertainty. You must always display confidence and courage. They draw strength from you."

"Let's get this circus on the road," he said with a wobbly twist of his lips. He booted his mare to a trot, his guard spreading out around his mount.

They kept a steady pace throughout the day, catching up to the scouts about an hour before dark. The spot they had chosen for the camp was bordered by a stream on the west and the east was boarded by the road, which had been strangely empty all day. They settled in a meadow knee high in grass. The men and ladies quickly dismounted, hobbling their horses and giving them quick rubdowns before saddling them again. They set up a quick camp without tents, prepared to move quickly as they entered the area patrolled by the queen's guards. Small fires were lit, and as soon as the meal was prepared, they were doused and buried.

Cayden settled down in his blankets and gazed up at the stars glimmering above. He sensed the wolves nearby. Sheba was off meeting with the packs around their camp. He felt she was setting up her own guard, unbeknownst to the group surrounding him.

Ziona leaned over and checked his shoulder again. The arrow wound was a faint pucker now, the skin pink and healthy.

"Rest well, Your Majesty," she grinned and with a quick curtsey, dropped down, and buried herself in her blankets, giggling at his reaction.

Cayden grimaced and then a grin tugged at the side of his mouth. He chuckled as he relaxed, stretching an arm behind his head for a pillow. He drifted off to sleep, secure in the fact Sheba was watching out for him.

He jerked awake what seemed a short time later, to Sheba's howls combining with the howls of a dozen other wolves. He leapt to his feet, grabbing his sword as the urgency of her cries pierced his mind.

"To arms," he shouted before he even cleared his blankets.

Shadows flitted at the edge of his vision, as Ziona shot to her feet at his call. Cayden continued to holler and the camp erupted, the shadowy forms coalescing into soldiers brandishing swords and cudgels. Battle erupted around Cayden, who found himself in hand-to-hand combat for the first time since his arrest and attempted abduction from the legion. He scrambled to right himself then deflected a blow aimed at his head, the sword skidding along his blade and bouncing off his guard at the last second.

He shouldered the soldier, throwing him off balance and Ziona stabbed the fallen man. She backed up to Cayden and as a unit they battled the oncoming soldiers. Cayden's downward stroke sliced the wrist of the next soldier, as he attempted to stab Cayden in the thigh. Ziona's swing took the soldier in the throat and the man fell, blood spurting from his opened neck.

Cayden felt sickened. He did not want to kill. *I could not kill…not even to save myself.*

Ziona felt no such compunction. She fought like a cornered badger; her every intent to kill. Ziona shoved Cayden behind her, shouting, "Cayden! Do not worry about attacking to kill. Just wound. I will finish them."

The enemy soldiers surrounding them hesitated when the pair began fighting as a cohesive whole. Suddenly, all four soldiers attacked at once. Cayden's mind flashed back to his days as the rabbit and he sought a low center, his back guarded by the rock that was Ziona. Cayden dodged the first sword and ducked under the cudgel swung at his head. His sword arced, slicing through two sets of kneecaps, causing the two soldiers to stumble.

Ziona's sword decapitated the closest soldier, his head bouncing across the trampled grass, the soil darkening with his blood, even as she stabbed the second facing her in the shoulder causing him to curse and stumble away from her. He was lost from Cayden's view.

Cayden saw the two soldiers facing him pause, drawing back to reassess their opponents. Then they rushed him together and he sought to keep them at arm's length. He felt Ziona jerk behind him and heard the lone soldier facing her grunt.

The sounds of battle were suddenly muted under the howl of wolves. From the corner of his eye he saw multiple sets of glowing eyes, a second before the wolves attacked.

The air around them exploded as the snarling pack of wolves fell on the enemy soldiers. They fell back, attempting to guard their throats from the razor sharp fangs and curled claws. Men fell, hamstrung and ravaged by the savage attack.

Cayden stopped fighting, mesmerized. He could understand the communication between the pack members. He could *hear* what they were thinking. He knew where the wolves would attack next. His focus switched to an unfortunate soldier, who had been attempting to flank Cayden and Ziona, by taking advantage of the confusion caused by the wolves' arrival. The soldier realized his mistake a moment too late and with an agonized cry, disappeared beneath three large wolves.

The rest of the camp fought on, but the attacking forces were disorganized now, the wolves putting a panic into the defeated troops. Within a few minutes, all fell still, the few remaining legionaries retreating and disappearing into the trees on the opposite side of the road.

The wolves disappeared, silently sliding back into the shadows. Sheba padded up to Cayden and sat down at his side. She cocked her head to one side, panting at him. Cayden knew she was asking for confirmation she had done well. Cayden knelt beside her and hugged her. He cupped her wolf face between his palms. "You did great, Sheba. Well done!" Her tongue flopped out to the side for a second, and then she licked his hand. She trotted back into the woods, seeking her kin.

Cayden stood up and turned to speak to Ziona. It was only then he saw her swaying on her feet. Scarlet blood soaked the left side of her tunic. Cayden grabbed her as a surprised "Oh!" popped out and she collapsed in a heap.

Chapter 41

"ZIONA, YOU'RE HURT!" Frantically, Cayden pulled open her tunic to see a deep cut had opened up a belly wound, her intestines clearly showing through the open flap of skin. Cayden gasped and clasped his hand over the wound, attempting to keep her together.

Ziona's eyes glazed in pain. As she stared at Cayden, his silhouette glowed as blue and clean and clear as a summer sky. His silhouette shimmered and blurred as she struggled to focus on him. She knew it was blood loss, but in another part of her she saw his soul pulsing with life and comfort. She knew she was gazing at a god.

She smiled at him. "I am not afraid, Cayden. I see you clearly for the first time. I am yours; my soul is yours to do with as you please. I do not fear death when you are near." Her eyes drifted closed.

Cayden's heart burst within him. He shuddered and yelled, "Ziona, don't you give up on me. You cannot die! I need you. Please!" He shook her shoulder, begging. "Please, Ziona, stay with me!" Ziona did not respond. As he gazed at her, he saw a mist begin to rise from her body.

He pulled her body tightly to him, sheltering her in his strong arms. Hot tears slid down his cheeks as he gazed at her bloodied form. They dripped unchecked from the end of his nose and splashed onto her smooth alabaster cheek, sliding to join the dusting of black-tipped lashes feathered under her eyes. His soul was as parched as the desert, soaking up her life essence. Love, pure sweet love, slipped past his barriers, breaking free, gathering into a tempest that beat inside of him, an avalanche of feelings long resisted and buried deep. *Ziona, my heart, you cannot die! I will be lost*

without you! You are the completion of my soul. Please do not leave me.
Please, I beg you! I beg you!

Cayden shook, his body quaking, refusing to accept what he was
seeing. He threw back his head and howled, his soul screaming in
pain. He expanded his will and called frantically to the spirit of the
Aossi, his tears and his voice recreating the song of the flute, but this
time it played from his inner being. His lips formed words into a
chant he did not know the source of. Nonsense tumbled from his lips
as he prayed.

He opened his eyes and saw time had frozen around him. The
men who had reacted to his scream had slowed, as though they were
walking through air thickened by molasses. Surprise slowly spread
across their faces as they moved with the tiniest of increments. He
focused on Ziona and saw the mist had slowed also.

Aossi walked up to Cayden and placed a hand on his shoulder,
sharing his view of the still woman.

"It is not so easy to watch them die, is it, young one? Yet they
pass their spirit to you without a thought. They trust you to care for
them both before and after death. It is what being a god is about."

Cayden eyes filled with tears, his chest constricted in anguish so
tight he struggled to draw breath. He could not focus on her words.

"She cannot die. I need her, Aossi! She is my guide. I am lost
without her."

"Yes, she is your guide. You chose her long ago and you chose
well." She tilted her head observing the woman and then looked back
at Cayden. "I can do nothing for her soul. That is her gift to you. I can
return her body, heal her wounds, as she is not completely gone from
this world as of yet. But only you can return her soul to her."

Cayden looked away from Aossi, wiping tears from his face. "I
do not know how."

Aossi grinned impishly and tapped Cayden's nose with her
finger. "I think you do, young one. You stilled time so you would
have the time to save her. You also know how to return it. It is a
similar thing to return her soul to her body. But be warned, the
power of a god is not without repercussions. She will live in a half
world from this moment on. Half of her soul is bound to you in truth
as she had begun the process of the transfer. Return it to her now
and you are also bound to her. You will feel her near or far, forever

more." She fondly lifted his chin, meeting his eyes. "You already share such a bond, do you not...with your sister?"

Cayden considered her words, frowning. It was true. He could always tell where Avery was. He nodded his agreement with her words.

"Let us begin then." Aossi knelt down and replaced Cayden's blood-soaked hands with her own. She traced the line of the sword slash, humming a tune that brought a mental image of butterflies in a garden, lush with flowers, their wings sighing on the breeze. The skin knitted together. The mist remained frozen in time.

Cayden closed his eyes and concentrated on Ziona, seeking her essence in the air, gathering the pearls of her personality and tiny shards of her sensitivity, the wisps of her soul, and pulled them into a tight ball of bright being. Some of his own soul blended with the compact point of light, surrounding it and containing Ziona's spirit. He then pushed with his own soul, taking the point of life and forcing it back into the body lying on the ground. He didn't understand what he was doing, working with raw instinct as he searched for a spark to attach the light to. His soul touched her mind and prodded it to accept the blended essence.

Aossi drifted down and gently pumped Ziona's chest, forcing her heart to move and circulate its blood again. Cayden bent over and placed his lips on Ziona's and breathed a long soulful breath into her lungs. Her body jerked as his breath inflated her lungs and the heart took over pumping her blood.

Aossi grinned and pinched his cheek, laughing at the blush that grew there.

"Remember what I said, young one. " She winked at him one last time and disappeared.

The time bubble dropped and real time returned.

Ziona's eyes shot open and she gasped at the gentle pressure of Cayden's lips meeting hers.

The soldiers of the camp ran over form a solid barrier around them.

Cayden cupped Ziona's cheek and gazed into her eyes. "I nearly lost you."

Ziona cupped his cheek in response, holding him to her with the touch, her eyes searching his. "I am with you always to the end of days."

Cayden's eyes crinkled at the corners with joy. Vibrant green eyes locked onto hummingbird green and the bond flared between them.

Can you hear my thoughts? Cayden sent his thoughts to her with his mind.

Ziona's eyes widened in surprise and she sent back: *Yes, is that really you? I can hear your thoughts in my head!*

Yes, it's me, but I have no idea how I am doing it. Aossi said we would have a bond from this moment on, something about how we saved your life.

Aossi was here? She swivelled her head, her eyes searching for Aossi's form.

Cayden cleared his throat and resumed normal speech. "Can you sit up yet, Ziona?"

She stared down at her torso, observing the tattered clothing and the large pool of blood all around her. She ran her hand over the mended skin in wonder.

"I should be dead," she whispered.

Cayden helped her to a sitting position as Tobias arrived.

"My lord! My apologies, my lord! We were blocked by a large group of soldiers. We fought our way through them just now. They were intentionally delaying us." Tobias gasped as his gaze switched to Ziona for the first time. "My lady, you have been wounded!" He spun on his feet and bellowed, "Medic, get over here now!"

Cayden caught his arm. "It's OK, Tobias. I have tended to Ziona. She is fine now. She will need rest, but I am sure there are other more critically wounded."

Tobias took a closer look at Ziona. His hand trembled over the healed skin where her belly wound had been. He instantly dropped to his knees, bowing his head to the earth. "My lord, forgive me for my lack of faith. You are as great as we have been told. Praise to the king, the Protector of Souls! Praised be the Spirit Shield, true heir of Cathair!"

The soldiers around Cayden and Ziona instantly followed suit, picking up the chant and kneeling where they stood.

Cayden scrambled to his feet and held up his hands to quiet the men.

"Please, we have no time. Tend to your brothers and sisters in arms."

They rose and resumed their duties. As they did so, Cayden heard the whispering tale take flight amongst the troops.

In no time at all, word spread to every soldier and cook in the company or at least their version of it. The story would grow and evolve with the retelling, as all great tales do, but for those lucky few who were present for the event, there was no doubt in their minds they had witnessed the birth of a legend.

Chapter 42

THE CITY GATES WERE FLUNG WIDE OPEN under the brilliant sky. The curved gate was broad enough for three carts to travel side by side with ease. They dwarfed the farmers' and merchants' wagons moving in and out in a steady stream. Dust stirred in the air, brought in on the hooves of horses and wheels of the wagons, despite the smooth paving stones lining the road.

The dust is lesser here than on the open road beyond the two-mile marker, Fabian thought, *but still the buns are sticky and any dirt is unacceptable.* He glanced back into his covered wagon where sat three of his apprentices. They maintained a tight grip on the stacked trays of buns, adjusting the cloth covers to prevent the dusty air from settling on them. The heat of the day brought out the smells of cinnamon and the caramelized sugar glaze that was the hallmark of his recipe. Others had tried to emulate it but had failed. His were simply the best.

He drew up at the checkpoint and nodded to the officer who approached his wagon.

"Destination?" he yawned around the words in a bored voice.

"Castle cook's kitchen. I have a delivery of sticky buns."

The officer sniffed the air and then, in a voice filled with longing, groaned. "I have always wanted to try one of those."

"We don't often make the market these days. They are sold out long before I can get them here."

Fabian studied the officer for a moment and then snapped his fingers, as if a thought had just occurred to him. "Say, maybe we can make a deal. I need a guard till we reach the kitchens. Oh, not a real guard, someone to keep the crowds away from the wagon so these arrive fresh and hot, the way Her Majesty likes them. Spare a lad, say that one over there...to give us a hand?"

The officer motioned to the young recruit who was lounging against the wall, appearing as bored as his superior.

"Anthony!" he called.

The recruit marched over and snapped to attention. "Yes, sir!"

"Escort this wagon to the castle kitchens. They are not to be disturbed. Understood? Keep the crowds away. This is a delivery for the queen."

"Yes, sir!" Anthony took up position beside the horse team's head.

"Thank you, Captain, and please enjoy this with our compliments." He handed down a huge sticky bun oozing with caramelized sugar resting on a paper napkin.

The officer grinned and waved Fabian on. Fabian clucked to the horses and they clopped forward with a jingle of the harness.

Anthony temporarily slowed his gate, allowing Fabian to pull up beside him. Keeping his eyes forward, Fabian muttered in a low voice, "Good to see you again, Anthony. Is all prepared?"

"Yes, I have people in place within the castle with access to the dungeons. They are ready to act when we are."

"Excellent. Now let's see if we can get there safely without getting mugged for our load of sticky buns."

The cart horse plodded along, the way through the streets a familiar route for the old mare. As they approached the castle, she automatically turned down a side alley, cast in deep shadow from the wall of the castle on one side and a two-story building on the other. The alley narrowed to a width that barely allowed the cart through without scraping the sides. After three hundred paces, it opened into a small square. The castle wall was set with solid wooden doors, their heavy iron hinges recessed into the native limestone.

The square was a dead end. Directly ahead was the entrance to a set of stables. Two guards stood at the entrance. The horses of visiting lords and ladies were typically housed within these stables. The royal stables backed up to them through a common door in the castle wall that was never opened unless for an emergency and then only with the proper password.

Fabian halted at the gate and Anthony stepped forward to introduce the arrival to the guards posted at the kitchen receiving gate. He was greeted jovially and with much back slapping. Fabian overheard the words "...sticky buns?" and "...would be worth the lecture for a taste..."

The guards signaled to the watchman high on the wall and the gates rolled back on wheels set to assist the movement of their ponderous weight. The sunny inner courtyard slowly revealed women and men dressed in service livery, some carrying baskets balanced on their shoulders and others carrying pails or pulling small carts loaded with supplies. To the right, teams of horses and wagons were lined up, their owners waving their hands, instructing the servants on the delivery of their goods.

Fabian pulled up beside the last delivery and hopped down from his wagon. Anthony waited for Fabian at the back of the wagon and then whispered, "I can't remain here for long, but I can see you safely inside and to our contact." In a louder voice he said, "This way, please."

Fabian's assistants jumped down from the wagon bed and pulled out the sticky bun trays. They each carried two trays and left Fabian to pick up the last two and follow them.

The procession was keenly watched, as hungry workers caught a whiff of the delectable treats that drifted in their direction. Fabian glanced around and thought his plan for an escort was wise regardless of his other plans. He shook his head, bemused at the attention his wares were gleaning.

They reached the kitchen delivery doors without incident and crossed into the comparatively cooler interior. It took a moment for their eyes to adjust after the brilliant sunlight of the courtyard. They blinked, hastening the adjustment of their eyes to the dimmer setting. The main kitchen was a large three-sided stone room, the fourth set with large windows facing the courtyard. Long wooden shutters were thrown open to allow the heat to escape and to tease a breeze into the warm interior.

Three wooden tables ran parallel to the length of the room, stacked with plates and bowls and food in various stages of completion.

Large-bricked wall ovens flanked the end wall and in each open hearth, spits of meat sizzled as they were rotated, the metal spit attached to a wheel which was in turn was connected to a larger wheel set with handles. The spit boy cranked the wheel slowly, as he had been taught, wiping his sweaty forehead on a towel draped over his shoulder on one side. Fabian observed him crank the wheel five times, which set up the spring and the spit turned as it slowly unwound. The boy then moved to the next and then the next and by the time he finished the entire row, the first oven was ready to be wound again.

"Now isn't that efficient," said Fabian, gesturing to the lad.

"Sir, if you will follow me." Anthony marched away down a side corridor out of the main kitchen.

They followed Anthony down the corridor, the heat fading somewhat as they walked. At the end of the hallway, they entered a stone passageway that led to a set of circular stairs disappearing into the gloom. A hole in the wall displayed a wooden platform and a set of ropes alongside it. *A dumb waiter*, Fabian guessed.

They walked carefully down the curving staircase, eventually reaching the dim recesses below. A hallway led back underneath the main kitchen. A wooden door blocked the end of the dark hallway, which was lit by a couple of torches.

"This is the refrigeration room," Anthony explained. "You may store your baked goods here." He pulled on the door, swinging it open. Inside were wooden shelves lined with supplies; bags of potatoes and carrots, heads of cabbage, onions, and apples in bushel baskets rested on the floor.

Fabian found a spot on the far wall cleared for their trays. They placed them carefully on the rack.

"The queen requests that you stay and enjoy the hospitality of the castle." Anthony bowed to Fabian. "Your apprentices may join in with the other serving staff and enjoy the evening."

Fabian nodded to the staff, dismissing them. They grinned and trotted quickly out of the cold room, happy for an early beginning to a day in the capital. They quickly disappeared back up the winding stairs.

Once they were alone, Anthony dropped all formality.

"Come, we only have a couple hours before you will be expected to be in Her Majesty's presence. She has wanted to meet the creator of her favourite sweet for ages."

They pulled closed the cold storage door, and then Anthony led Fabian off down a side passage leading back toward the east end of the castle. He lifted a lantern from a wall stand and lit it, carrying it along in front of him. After about three hundred feet, they arrived at another set of stairs, carved directly out of the limestone which made up the base of the castle. They wound down the worn steps which opened out onto a railed stone landing. Fabian stepped up to the railing and gazed over the edge. Wooden doors with iron grills were set into either end.

Below a set of guards were seated with their booted feet up on a trestle table. Their swords were resting on the table beside their boots, reflecting the light of the lantern hung on a peg above their heads. Both guards held cards in their hands, intently studying the faces on each one. One guard leaned forward and tossed a card on the stack in the center on the table.

"Sire of hearts," he said. The other guard grunted.

"Squire of diamonds," he huffed, throwing his card on the pile.

"You know, they had better arrive soon. Our shift is almost over," said the first guard. The second grunted once more.

"Sire, consort, and bastard of diamonds. I win." The second tossed his remaining cards on the table.

The first growled and peered over his feet at the display, suspicious.

"You always pull that set. How is it you always get those cards?" The second guard shrugged, grinning.

Anthony harrumphed loudly from the landing.

Both guards shot to their feet, peering up at the balcony above. Spying Anthony, they relaxed.

"About time you got here! What took you so long?"

"There was a near riot in the courtyard for this guy's sticky buns. He attracts more flies than...well you know, that's not important now." Anthony opened the door on the left and headed down the stairs approaching the guards, Fabian trailing in his wake.

"When will the meal guard be around?"

"Soon. Wendell usually arrives about a quarter to the hour which should be any time now."

"You are sure he is on board?"

"Yeah, he has been doing this duty for twenty years. Sour to it, he is, always passed over for a promotion. He is keen to earn some gold though...and to get away from carrying chamber pots." He chuckled, while reaching for a lantern.

"This is Fabian, the one I told you about," he said, waving vaguely in his direction. "Come on. Let's find Wendell so we can get these cells open."

The second guard stood and produced a rusty keychain on which dangled around twenty long metal-toothed keys. It rattled as he searched for the correct key, and then he inserted it into the lock. With a creak of rusting hinges, the door opened to a gloomy interior hallway.

The wavering light fell immediately on a ruddy face, lips parted to reveal a swollen tongue. Glassy eyes bulged as the corpse's hands clutched the rope around his neck. The rope led up and over a crossbeam inside the doorway. His feet dangled as the body swayed mere inches from the floor.

Chapter 43

RYDER CHEWED HIS LOWER LIP AND THOUGHT. He chewed it some more and stewed over his choices. How does one hide five hundred plus soldiers from the eyes of the queen of the land as one descends on her city? His thoughts ran round and round in his head, but no answer presented itself.

The swelling band pushed their way slowly through a rough terrain consisting of scrub brush and rocky abandoned farmers' fields, keeping away from the main roads.

The recent rains had left flooded pockets of mud, their path clearly visible to any who wished to follow. He hoped no one was interested in them. He snorted in response to the absurdity of his own thoughts, as more people drifted into his ranks on a daily basis. He feared the news of their movements was far outstripping their progress.

Darius rode at his one shoulder, Laurista at his other. Both examined the shoreline ahead as they approached the banks of the river once more. They needed to find a good place to ford the river before they reached the capital proper.

One of the scouts appeared out of a stand of trees about two hundred yards ahead of their location. Ryder saw it was the young lad Michale they had rescued from the legion camp. Ryder hadn't realized Darius had recruited him into the scouting ranks.

The lad rode up and joined Darius to give his report.

"My lord, there is a good fording point not far from our location. The river widens and there are sandy shoals for about half of the river."

Ryder acknowledged the report with a nod. "Darius, alert the men and women and let the wagon drivers know we are going to attempt a fording of the river. They may need to lighten their loads."

"Yes, sir." He saluted and rode off to give the orders. Michale claimed a position out front, leading the way.

Laurista watched the young man ride away. "He is adjusting well to his new duties. I had feared for his sanity when he was first brought to me. He was barely coherent. He is still a boy, only now entering his manly years."

"Yes, but war and violence will make a man of a boy before he realizes what has happened. One cannot witness what he did and not have his innocence stripped from him." Ryder followed the lad's progress with his eyes. He reached into his pocket and fingered the pouch he had received from the mysterious man in Pert Soaidh. It contained a coin to match the one he had recovered in Cottonham and a brooch with the insignia of the Royal House of Cathair, a golden shield wreathed in blue spirits.

Laurista regarded Ryder. "Yes, it changes a boy into a man, doesn't it?" She lifted an eyebrow knowingly at him.

Ryder shifted in his saddle and chose to ignore her.

The Band of the Rebel's Land had swollen to over five hundred men. Ryder felt the weight of responsibility keenly. He had dreamed of becoming a knight, not the general of an army. He knew nothing of battle strategy or of fighting. Cayden had at least received some training. Ryder had none.

Yet Cayden was relying on him to help and he would do exactly that. *Cayden was changing too*, Ryder mused; they all were.

He had instructed Darius to search amongst the new volunteers for those men (and women) with battle experience. He had then seen them organized them into a rough command structure. He prayed it would be enough for he also realized they would be put to a true test one day soon. Every day they moved closer to the capital, and it pulled them closer to a confrontation with the Cathair garrison. He had no intention of riding up to the city gates alone. It would be suicide.

By the scouting reports, it appeared they would reach the outskirts of the town in about two days.

"Laurista, I plan to leave the band at our campsite this evening and go on ahead. I want to scout out this Denzik fellow and see what he has to say. I would like you to accompany me."

She nodded. "Yes, and we should take a couple of the old Kingsmen along. They may recognize this fellow."

They arrived at the shoreline of the river, the banks gently sloping toward the water's edge. The river slowed and almost stilled as it widened, and lily pads adorned with fuchsia blooms dotted the marshes formed by the sluggish flow. Frogs made plopping sounds as they launched themselves into the water and out of the path of the horse hooves. The trail led directly out onto a sandbar and disappeared off the end.

One of the scouts waved from the opposite shoreline where the trail picked up again after exiting the river. Ryder gazed up and down the river. It felt strange to be exposed after attempting to hide from enemies' eyes for so many miles. Shrugging his shoulders, he touched heel to flank and urged his mount into the waters. Laurista followed.

About halfway across, the sandbar ended and a rocky stream bed was exposed, the water tumbling over the slippery surface. The horses picked their way slowly across the river bottom and reached the other side without incident.

Darius crossed behind them with two other band members to join the scouts. Both men who had come with Darius were Kingsmen. Darius trotted up to Ryder as his horse climbed the bank, water streaming from her legs.

"Are you going on ahead, sir?"

"Yes, that was my intention."

"We would like to accompany you, if we may. You should not go off alone. There are those who would love to know who leads the band, I think. I fear for your safety."

Ryder frowned at the words. He did not like the idea of having a guard, in truth. He understood having an honour guard to create an image of power, but only in special circumstances.

"I think they are right, my lord," said Laurista.

"Very well, but you are *not* my guard, understand? We leave as soon as the band has safely crossed."

The band set up on the riverside for the evening, their tents sprawling in a semicircle from the banks of the river. The smell of roasting fish permeated the air.

Two hours later found the seven of them riding away from the camp. The scouts led the way, taking a direct route through the trees ending at the Cathair Road. An hour of such travel dumped them onto a rough stone and dirt roadway. They headed south, passing occasional wagons and the lone rider, but traffic was sparse, most having reached their destination before the sun stretched on the horizon.

Near dusk, they came upon a wagon train pulled off the road and under a grove of trees for the evening. Ryder motioned the others to stay back and dismounted, approaching the campsite on foot. A man and a woman tended a cooking fire and started at his sudden appearance.

"Good evening, kind sir and miss. What news from the road?"

"Good evening to you also. As we are travelling the same direction, how could you have not heard the news?"

"My companions and I have been travelling cross-country and only just arrived at the main road. We are curious as to the news in these parts."

The man and woman gazed back to Ryder's companions. "Would you like to join our camp this evening? We have some provisions to share."

"That is very kind of you. Perhaps we can share conversation and a meal, but we will be travelling further this evening."

Ryder tied his mount's reins to a low branch, allowing some slack for grazing then motioned the others to approach.

"My name is Mark and this is my wife, Joy. We are wool-dye merchants, bringing dyes to the mills on the coast." He motioned toward his wagons, their contents shrouded under large tan canvas tarps.

"I'm Ryder, and this is Laurista." He made introductions of the other men. "We are travelling to Cathair to meet up with a friend, who preceded us to town. We have heard talk of legions on the move and were wondering if there is unrest on the road ahead? Have you heard any news?"

Joy stirred their bubbling pot of stew and then moved over to make room for Laurista to sit beside her on the ground. Laurista smiled her thanks then settled in to listen to the men speak.

"There have been rumours of a great battle between a legion division and some rogue men. Some of the rumours say they are

Kingsmen although everyone knows they have been gone for near twenty years. Others say they are rogue bands from the north, come south to challenge Her Majesty's conscription laws. One such rumour, I credit more than the others. A wounded soldier stopped us by the roadside early in the morning today to beg water and a change of clothes. He was bloodied from head to toe and spoke of wolves attacking them in the midst of a battle." Mark frowned at the spoon in his hand. "One thing was certain. By the rips in his clothing and the scratches and gouges on his limbs, he did appear to have battled wolves. He spoke of an encampment of men who were being led by a dangerous young lord sought by the queen for treason. They had been sent to secure the peace, but then the wolves attacked and they fled."

Ryder sat up straight at the mention of the wolves. *Cayden*, he thought.

"Did this man speak of where this battle had occurred?"

"It was not far from here…a few miles ahead as the road goes."

"So this soldier was returning to his legion?"

"No, he was heading to the capital to gather reinforcements, I believe," said Mark. His wife nodded in agreement. "We had been considering turning around because of this news. War is never good for commerce, you know, unless you are a camp follower. Perhaps you would be so kind as to accompany us for as long as you can? An armed guard is not a bad thing in these troubling times and we can see by your posture and by the weapons on your mounts that you and your men are not unaccustomed to danger. There is greater safety in numbers."

Darius and Laurista exchanged glances. Ryder spoke in response to her affirmative nod. "We would be happy to have you journey with us. We are headed for a small village on the outskirts of the capital. Our friend's name is Denzik, perhaps you know him?"

"I can't say I do. However, there is a small village called Lower Cathair with a marvelous inn and the best bakery in the realm. We stay there often. Perhaps we can find your friend there if we ask around."

"How much further is this village?" Ryder scanned the horizon, judging the amount of daylight left.

"It is about a three-hour ride from here."

"I would prefer to continue on this evening then, if you are not too weary from your travels."

"It would be nice to sleep in a bed this evening, if one would be available," Mark said.

"And have a proper bath," piped up Joy.

"It is settled then. We leave as soon as we finish eating."

Chapter 44

THE CAMP AROUND CAYDEN STIRRED like a kicked anthill. Some men swarmed over the wounded, while others picked up their fallen comrades and carried them to the perimeter of the camp to prepare them for burial. The few dead wolves were also picked up and carried to the edge of the camp.

Ziona rested in her tent, having fallen asleep after sipping some of her potion. She had insisted the rest she had prepared be shared with the wounded men and it was being passed around from soldier to wounded soldier.

The decision had been made to not move the camp that night. Their presence was obviously known as was their destination.

The few soldiers who had escaped were no longer a threat. Whether they returned to their base camp or travelled directly to the capital to give warning and an account of the battle to their superiors, either meant they were no longer a direct threat.

Another attack was slim, yet they doubled the patrols, just in case.

Tobias became Cayden's self-appointed bodyguard by refusing to leave his side. He stood a short distance away from Cayden, legs spread, feet firmly planted, arms folded across his chest. His scar stood out lividly against his pale skin and his lazy eye jerked from the glare he shared with all who approached Cayden. *The effect was quite frightening,* Cayden thought, as he rested against a log outside of Ziona's tent.

Cayden picked up the branch he had found and turned it over in his hands, inspecting it, but for once carving held no interest for him. The peace he normally found in the familiar activity eluded him. *The events of the last few hours have unnerved me,* he admitted reluctantly to himself. He felt Ziona's presence behind him. He could almost see her dreams as she slept. Flashes of images crossed his mind when he focused on her, a wooded glade with tall ferns swaying and a door set in the trunk of a tree.

He shook his head to clear his thoughts and focused on Avery instead. It had been ages since he had thought about his sister. He felt worry and concern in the air and a spikey wave of fear assailed his senses. She was in trouble and he felt it as intensely as if he was standing beside her.

Avery? He called to her mentally, trying the same method of communication he had done with Ziona. Surprise and caution flooded back at him.

Cayden, is that you?

Yes. Are you all right? I sense fear in you.

After you left, Father and I left with a Primordial woman named Sharisha to go to the land of the Primordials. Right now, we are in the pass to the Primordial lands. There is a huge army camped at the foot of the pass, thousands of legionnaires. The Primordials are also massed in the mountains, and I fear that there will be an invasion soon. I will contact you later.

Stay safe! he whispered back with his mind, out of habit, and the connection broke. He sucked in a deep breath. The fear he felt through the bond was incredible. It made him itch. He felt an urge to leap to his feet and draw his sword, yet there was no enemy in range. Instead, he began pacing, back and forth in front of his tent. Five steps. Stop. Pivot. Five more steps. Stop. Pivot. Tobias kept pace with him, and sensing Cayden's distress, dropped his arms to his side, one hand resting on his sword hilt.

Cayden stopped pacing and stopped to stare in the exact direction of Cathair. That tugging was back, but stronger and more intense. He felt...well, it felt like a massive mind was pulling at his, calling to him. It was impossible to focus on any one thought; although he sensed a vast intelligence behind it.

He must get to Cathair. Further delay was pointless. *Whatever is pulling at me will not leave me alone, and delay would not assist Avery. I must continue on the path laid out for me and confront it.* It was time.

***

Mordecai sat in the semi-darkness, eyes partially closed. A flame danced on the upturned palm of his hand. He focused on the flame and observed the quality of the light, the prisms of colour in the flickering flame. The heat source pulsed, a heartbeat of light. Into the flame he poured his conscious thoughts and the flame expanded them, lightened them, causing them to drift to the roof of the cavern cell, up through the floors above and into the open air.

His will continued to expand, ever wider and wider, seeking the destination created in his mind. His thoughts searched, shifting on the winds, sliding here and there over man and beast, to finally settle on a young man asleep in his tent.

"Cayden," he whispered. "Cayden, you must come to me. Do not delay." Cayden rolled over in his sleep, mumbling. "You must hurry. Time is short. Seek out Denzik. He can be found in Lower Cathair."

"Lower Cathair," Cayden mumbled to himself, still asleep.

"I will be waiting for you here."

"Lower Cathair...Denzik..." Cayden snorted and then rolled onto his back and snored as his mouth dropped open.

***

The guards drew their swords and quickly checked the shadowed chamber. Anthony stepped up to the body and examined the middle-aged man. There was no wound visible on the body.

Anthony lifted the man as Fabian untied the rope from the lantern bracket, allowing the body to be lowered to the floor.

"Who is he?" Fabian asked the guards as they approached, having determined there was no one present in the hallway.

"This is Wendell. He is the meal and chamber steward that we bribed, the one we were supposed to meet. He must have come down early?"

The taller of the two guards shrugged as they exchanged glances. "We did not let him in though, so how did he get here?"

"If he was here to work, then where are the chamber pots he should be removing? Perhaps he had not reached his destination? In which case, where are the meals he was to deliver?" Fabian walked around the man, examining the body.

The guards noted the lack of any work-related objects. They frowned in unison, clearly perplexed.

"When did you two come on shift?" Anthony asked.

"We have been on since early this morning, our normal eight-hour shift, seven in the morning till three in the afternoon," said the shorter of the two.

"And you let no one into these access halls?" asked Fabian.

"No one has come down to the dungeons in the past eight hours. We have the keys right here for this door." He shook the key ring and the keys rattled. "The only other set is with the queen, but we would know if the queen came to inspect the prisoners."

Fabian frowned at the men. "You realize you are incriminating yourselves?"

The two guards frowned, consternation playing across their faces. "We patrol these halls every two hours," said the shorter one.

Fabian touched the dead man's body. He was cold, but rigor mortis had not set in yet. "His death occurred within the last two hours. It's odd, though; his body shows no sign of other injuries, no indication of a struggle. I believe he knew his killer."

Anthony walked around the body and nodded in agreement. "We need to check the prisoner cells and make sure he was the only victim."

The four of them spread out to search. The hallway was intersected in quick order by narrower halls, lined with cells, four on either side of their main hall.

The two guards took the first set of intersecting hallways and Fabian and Anthony continued on. The lantern light flickered in the cool ventilation breeze, a constant feature of the clammy dungeon. The two guards' shadows overtook them as they checked the cells at the next intersection to check the next section. Most cells were empty, and in the few occupied the prisoners were unhurt.

Eventually, Fabian and Anthony came to the hallway level with the Traitor's Gate doorway. This intersection had only one branch to the left with a spiral set of stairs winding deeper into the earth. With a nod, Anthony took the hallway toward the suspected location of the Traitor's Gate, drawing his sword as he left, lantern light bobbling in his wake.

Fabian held his lantern high to light the treacherous stairway. At the base of the spiral, he nearly tripped over a tray of congealed food and an abandoned chamber pot which had been hastily put down. The contents coated the stone floor.

Fabian stepped around the mess, wrinkling his nose, and then continued down the rough-cut passage. This deep in the dungeon, the corridor was roughly hewn as though it had been hastily chiseled as an afterthought. Only two cells were found this deep down in the passage and were reserved for the most heinous of prisoners. Fabian walked up to the left-hand cell and raised his lantern, light flooding the chamber. A white-haired elderly man blinked at him in the sudden light.

"I am relieved to find you well, Mordecai," said Fabian.

"Was there ever a doubt?" Mordecai rose to his feet and walked over to the door. "I fear my dear friend Wendell has not been so lucky. I heard a commotion at the end of the hallway as he left my chamber and a short while later I heard voices echoing down to my cell. They shone a light on me and then left. I am sure I recognized the voice. It has been many years and not nearly long enough since I heard it last."

"The guards' keys are accounted for, so unless someone copied them, there is only one other possibility," said Fabian.

"No doubt the keys have been copied, but I have not seen any recent use of them. No, I believe this was a random inspection by the queen, checking on her prize prisoner. Wendell is dead, I take it?"

Fabian unlocked the cell door. "Yes, he was found hanged inside the cell access chamber."

"Made to appear as a suicide?" Mordecai asked.

"Yes, I think that was the idea," said Fabian.

"Poor fellow, he was a good chap in the end. I am truly sorry he was on duty tonight. Queen Alcina felt the need on this particular evening to check on me. Unfortunately, Wendell spied her leaving my cell. I believe she did not want any witnesses to her interest in me. Would you see to it his widow receives this?" The wizard reached up into his sleeve and pulled out a leather purse, bulging with coins.

"How in the world did you manage to acquire all that in a prison cell?" Anthony's eyes widened, in surprise.

"The guards get as lonely as the prisoners do. What harm can come of relieving a poor prisoner of his coin?" Mordecai chuckled. "Fortunately, I am rather fond of cards and possess a keen eye, so I am rather lucky as a result."

"Aren't you leaving with us?" Fabian frowned at the wizard.

"No...no, not quite yet, I think. I believe it would give the game away and it appears Her Majesty is growing nervous and suspicious, hence her visit to me this afternoon. There is a secret passage from the royal suites to the prisoner cells. Did you know that?"

Fabian shook his head, bemused.

"She often visited me in the early years after my capture," mused Mordecai. "She thought she could torture a first wizard and have him tell his secrets. I am happy to report she was wrong." A smile lit his wrinkled cheeks. "Soon I shall leave these cells behind, but not quite yet. You, however, must be prepared. Gather the Kingsmen where ever you can find them. The time to reclaim the kingdom approaches. Let those loyal to the true House of Cathair know. Let the people of the Spirit Shield know their king has returned."

Fabian nodded in understanding. "Diversions have been set up within the castle, as we planned. Our people are in place." Fabian chuckled. "Nelson owes me some coins as I finished first." Fabian turned the key in the lock to Mordecai's cell and retraced his steps up the hallway to the stairs.

The voice of the wizard drifted up the passageway to Fabian. "Nelson asked me to pass on a message. He says dinner is on him when you get back and bring your coin purse. He arrived at the wall here about three hours ago."

Chapter 45

THE BALANCE OF THE JOURNEY to the outlying village of the capital was unremarkable. Few people travelled at night and the road was in use only by merchant trains running tight schedules of perishable goods.

Ryder peered at the indistinct forms as they approached and resolved into horse teams and wagons. Drivers raised a hand in greeting but did not slow as they passed.

They reached Lower Cathair as the moon broke the horizon. The area was suddenly bathed in a cool white glow, revealing low rugged fieldstone buildings with thatched roofs. A lower stone wall followed the road, guiding traffic to the main crossroad. Most traffic passed right by the village, focused on reaching the capital.

The windows of the houses were dark as they passed, the hour being late. The village slumbered. It wasn't until they left the road and entered into the village proper that they spied the inn tucked back against the river. Light spilled from the windows of the main floor illuminating the wooden front verandah.

They pulled up at the inn's entrance. Strains of music drifted out the door as a man and woman exited the tavern and walked off down the street, arm in arm.

Ryder and Laurista dismounted, leaving Darius to take the horses around to the inn's stable located at the side of the building. Mark followed Darius with his team and Joy accompanied them inside. The interior of the inn was warmed by two large stone fireplaces set at either end, crackling with a merry fire of dried logs. The locals were listening to a woman singing and playing a guitar situated on a raised platform to the right of the fireplace.

Joy placed a hand on Ryder's arm and pointed to a man standing behind the bar to the right of them. Ryder followed her to the barkeep and they each took a stool at the bar. A short wiry man stood polishing glasses in front of the bottles lined up under the etched mirror. He called a welcome over his shoulder without pausing from his work. "What can I get you all?"

"Mulled wine for me," said Ryder, peering at his companions and at a nod from Laurista and Joy: "and also for the ladies. We are also looking for information."

"Three mulled wines. An easy order to fill," he said as he pulled three mugs from under the bar and took up a pitcher of wine from the back counter, pouring as he spoke. "But as to information, well, that usually depends on who is asking and why?" His gaze finally rested on them, measuring.

Joy spoke up first. "We are looking for a gentleman named Denzik. We have business with him. It's important." Ryder looked at her, a quizzical look in his eyes.

The barkeep squinted at her and then looked at Ryder. "Your accent isn't from these parts. If I were to hazard a guess, I would say you hail from a village on the coast. Tell me why you are so far from home at such a young age?"

Laurista and Ryder exchanged glances then he shrugged. "We are looking for a friend of ours who was headed this way when we became separated. We have reason to believe he may seek this man named Denzik and wished to know if he has arrived yet."

"We also require rooms for the night," Joy said.

"A hot bath too," Laurista added.

"Now that is something I can arrange," said the barkeep. "A meal comes with the room, so why don't you eat and relax while we prepare your lodgings. I will see what I can do about your other request in the meantime." He flagged down a serving girl, who went off to the kitchens and returned with three steaming plates of roast chicken and potatoes. The barkeep wandered off into the back of the inn as they set about their meals. Darius and Mark soon joined them and two more plates arrived in short order.

***

Nelson let the door swing shut behind him and spoke to the head cook, Tabitha. "Keep that group at the bar busy. I have to go speak to Denzik. They asked for him specifically." He grabbed his coat from a hook by the back door to the kitchen and let himself out into the rear yard of his inn. He quickly found his way to a small gate set in the stone wall and briskly strode down the dirt path leading to the river.

Five minutes of energized walking brought him to Denzik's door. The lights were out. He knocked on his door and waited, fidgeting. His heart was thumping in his chest as though he had jogged the short distance.

A light flared in the window and then the door opened a crack and a sleepy-eyed Denzik peered out. Seeing Nelson standing there, he opened the door further to allow him to enter.

"What's up?" He walked back into his living room and sank down in his favourite chair.

"A group of out-of-towners are asking for you by name at the inn. They have accents from the coast…the northwest coast."

Denzik's posture straightened and Nelson imagined great mental gears whirling in his head. "What did they want?"

"They say they are searching for a friend who they were separated from and they thought he would come looking for you."

Denzik frowned. "I do not know anyone from that area of the province." He reached into his upper pocket and pulled out his pipe. With his left hand, he searched his other pocket for his pouch of tobacco. He pulled it out and packed the fragrant leaves into his pipe. The routineness of the action calmed his nerves and cleared his head.

"I doubt he is the one we seek. But he may have a connection to him. We need to speak to him privately, away from the villagers. The inn is no good. Go back, and after they are seen to their rooms, bring him along with you to my house here so we can talk privately. If it's nothing, I can spend a quiet hour or so sharing tea with a stranger from the coast."

Nelson nodded in agreement and left Denzik still packing his pipe and studying the patterns on the rug under his feet without seeing either of them.

***

Darius's room was at the far back of the inn, tucked under the roof line. The ceiling slanted to meet the walls about a third of the way down. His bed was pushed up against the wall, which suited him fine as who stood up on a bed anyways? He peered out his window which overlooked the back garden of the inn. Two shadows appeared in the garden below, hurrying toward the gate. One of those shadows resolved into Ryder, accompanied by the innkeeper.

He waited until they had disappeared from view, and then he donned his coat and picked up his saddlebags which sat on the floor beside him, still packed. He swung the pack over his shoulder and exited his room, quickly descending the back staircase and out to the stable where his horse was waiting in its stall, still saddled.

He flipped the groom a coin as he rode out of the stable and off into the night.

***

Denzik's kettle was boiling by the time Nelson arrived back at his doorstep with a stocky solid lad in tow. Tall of stature, the youth moved with a grace that spoke of confidence and grounding. *Now this is a good, solid soldier*, Denzik thought, as though measuring him up for a post in the Kingsmen ranks.

"Please, enter." He stepped aside for the lad, Nelson on his heels. He motioned to the chairs in the living room. "Tea?"

"Yes, thank you," said the stranger politely.

"I will take a cup too," said Nelson, leading the way into the living room.

Ryder inspected comfortable but sparse furnishings, noting the fine sword displayed over the fireplace mantle. It appeared to be sharp, and well used. Not a display piece at all. He frowned at it, studying it closely. *What was that marking on the hilt?*

"You are examining my sword very closely, lad. Do you know about swords?" Denzik set a cup of tea down in front of his two guests.

"I am an apprentice blacksmith. I have had the opportunity to work with steel such as this on occasion"—Ryder's head swung back to Denzik—"but never so fine a blade as that, sir. Where did you get it?"

"It's mine." Denzik lowered himself into his favourite chair and took a sip from his cup. "I am a retired Kingsman. It was my blade while in service to the king. I keep it polished and sharpened, but obviously it hasn't seen much action in the last twenty years. Still, old habits die hard. Tell me, why are you looking for me?" He studied Ryder over the rim of his steaming cup and noted the clear gaze he received in return. *This is an honest lad*, he thought.

Ryder took a sip of his tea. "I left Sanctuary-by-the-Sea roughly three weeks ago to catch up with a friend, who had been pressed into the queen's legions. By the time I caught up..." As Ryder recounted the tale of his travels, the words spilled from his lips in a torrent. He spoke of Cayden and their parting, and the men who followed him; the attack by the Charun, their separation, and his search since then to locate Cayden. He did not speak of Cayden's strange abilities but focused on the Kingsmen who had joined his ranks and his concern to reach Cayden before anything else happened to him. As he wound down his discourse, a stunned silence filled the room.

Denzik and Nelson exchanged glances and Nelson nodded.

"Son, we have been waiting for you and young Cayden for seventeen years."

***

It was predawn when Darius located them. As he suspected, their camp was located in the woods off of the main road. It seemed Cayden had acquired a bunch of soldiers, same as Ryder, but this bunch seemed less military and more like families. Darius marched up to the ring of guards and identified himself. He was escorted to Cayden immediately, who exited his tent and gave him a hug in welcome.

"I am so glad I found you! Have you been hiding here the whole time?" asked Darius.

"Nah, been trying to make our way south without running into the Charun. We ran into some legionaries recently. I am beginning to worry that our presence is known to the queen."

"Well, Ryder wants to talk to you. He's in the village ahead. Come with me for a quick ride?"

Cayden observed the quiet camp. Most of the men were bedded down. Ziona slept peacefully; he felt her nestled in his head. Tobias had finally gone to bed but set two guards for Cayden while he rested, as though it took two to replace him.

"OK, but I will need two escorts or there will be hell to pay when I get back."

Darius grinned. "OK. Grab your horses and personal guard, and follow me."

A short time later, Cayden and the two guards rode up to Darius, where he sat astride his horse. At Cayden's nod, they headed off into the woods, Darius taking the lead. The moon had fully risen now, and visibility was good for the horses. After about an hour of winding through the woods, they came to an opening in the forest wall and rode into a small meadow with knee-high grass. They rode out of the trees side by side and as they did so, the shadows of the forest elongated after them and resolved themselves into three tall, eerily still Charun. Three more glided out in front of them, encircling their small group. Cayden yelled and attempted to boot his horse into action, but the animal snorted and reared in fright at the sight of the Charun. His two guards, on either side, drew swords and booted their mounts, charging the Charun ahead of them. The Charun let them come.

The guards had almost reached the Charun when black arrows from the edge of the forest struck both rushing guards in the back, and they toppled off their mounts to the ground. Their horses bolted past the Charun and disappeared into the trees.

Cayden's eyes widened as he caught sight of Darius lowering his bow. A fourth black tipped arrow was notched in his bow and swung Cayden's direction. He sat calmly in his saddle, slightly behind Cayden, who had finally brought his mount under control.

"There is no sense fighting them, Cayden. You cannot win."

Cayden, seeing Darius's total lack of concern over the presence of so many Charun, felt his fear ratchet higher. "You brought them," he whispered, shocked. "You betrayed me! Why?"

Darius's lips twisted in a cold smile. "You didn't listen to what I said when we first met, did you? I joined the legion when they found me, but it was more than that. They needed a spy, someone to infiltrate the locals where ever we went with the sole purpose of finding you. The queen's bounty on your head has made me rich and I will live easy the rest of my days. I will finally be able to go home and help my family.

"Unfortunately for Sergeant Perez, he became rather greedy. He did not want to share the prize money for turning you in. So I had to steal you away from him...and what better way than by befriending and freeing you? Now I have tracked you all the way to the castle and will deliver you straight into the queen's waiting arms. I have you trussed tighter than a festive turkey. So much simpler to make sure I was the one who benefited in the end. Poor Perez. I doubt the Charun were very kind to him."

He turned his back on Cayden. "He is yours now," Darius said to the Charun. "Be sure to not harm him in any way. Take him to the queen whole and undamaged."

He spurred his mount and trotted back off into the trees. The Charun closed in on Cayden and claw-like hands reached for him. His horse snorted and shied away from the Charun. Refusing to wait to be captured, Cayden booted his horse in the ribs and it shot forward, galloping toward the oncoming Charun.

The Charun pulled out long hook poles and swung the loops forward, dropping two of them over Cayden's body even as he ducked to avoid them. The loops tugged tight, binding his arms to his side and yanking him out of the saddle to hang by the loops in midair. A third Charun, red eyes glowing from under its hood, glided forward and pressed an oily cloth to his face even as he struggled in their grip. The fumes stung Cayden's eyes and lungs, even as his senses faded into nothingness.

***

Ziona sat bolt upright on her cot. Terror spiked through her like a living thing, rioting her into motion. Sweat popped out in beads on her skin and she shivered as fear rolled over her waves through her connection to Cayden. She jumped to her feet and took three steps before exhaustion hit her like a club. She stumbled and grabbed on to the central tent pole to keep from collapsing to the ground. The room spun and she fought to keep her eyes open. "Help!" she cried out weakly. "Help!" she cried again, a little louder. She let go of the post and stumbled to the tent entrance, falling to her hands and knees and spilling out of the flap. She shivered again, dressed in nothing but her thin shift. The world spun and she slumped to the ground, helpless to stop herself from doing so.

Hands reached down and helped her to her feet, where she swayed in their grip, fighting to keep her eyes open. Bleary eyes attempted to focus on Tobias and another soldier, their grip on her arms the only thing keeping her on her feet.

"Let me help you to a seat, my lady," Tobias said.

Ziona shook her head and slurred drunkenly, "Its Cayden…He…" She swallowed past the dry lump in her throat. "He's in trouble…some kind of trouble…," she slurred. Ziona shook her head to try to clear it, but it only made things worse. "He's been drugged, I think." Her eyes drifted closed and she sagged in their arms.

Tobias bolted into Cayden's tent and found no sign of him. His fear mounting, he yelled for his men, who came running from all directions of the camp. "Search the camp and find him and his horse," he snapped to the guards stationed around him. "I want to know who is missing from this camp.

"Roll call *now*!" Tobias bellowed to the men standing around him. A bugle was brought forth and blared. Men tumbled from their tents to answer the summons.

Tobias lowered Ziona to the ground and grabbed one of the Kingsmen as he passed. "Take her back inside her tent and stay with her at all times. If she comes to again, I want to know immediately!" The soldier saluted and picked up the unconscious woman and carried her back to her tent.

Far away across the realm, Avery stumbled in her tent and fell to the ground, her voice slurring unintelligibly before she succumbed to the drugging fumes.

Chapter 46

THE SUN WAS PEEKING OVER THE HORIZON when Ryder, Laurista, Denzik, Nelson, and Fabian rode out of the village. They had waited as long as they could for Darius. If he had wandered off in the middle of the night without leave, he would be court-marshalled. They had been warned. It bothered Ryder, but he could find no answer for the strange behaviour. Nelson reported Darius's bed had not been slept in and the serving staff advised he had not been in the common room that evening.

Perhaps he had ridden on into the capital to find a greater selection of entertainments. Ryder tried to put it out of his mind. He had more important things to think about, but the absence weighed on his mind, making him uneasy.

The revelations of the previous evening still spun in his head. He had stumbled on, or been guided to, an underground movement of people with imbedded ties and loyalties to the former king. *He rode beside a knight...a real knight of the realm.* Ryder shook his head in wonderment, bemused by his thoughts, pushing down the giddy glee he felt.

They had explained their years of preparations and had given Ryder a quick tour of the beginning of the tunnel system to the capital. They had also been already aware of his and Cayden's bands—armies, they called them. Ryder thought it was going too far. His band of men and women were untested in battle and more of a rabble than a trained force. However, the drills were working and he did see improvement in them.

Denzik, Fabian, and Nelson were excited to meet up with Cayden and happy to lend their assistance in locating the other band through their eyes-and-ears network. Now that they knew what to look for, they were confident that someone would get back to them within a day as to the location of Cayden's camp. It was funny to think that Cayden had gathered a force of men and women in much the same way as he had.

They reached the camp about noon. As they rode in, Ryder looked around for Darius's cheery face. He could not locate him in the sea of faces saluting as they rode past. Cheers rose around him as he reined in at the command tent set up in the middle of the band.

Young boyish-faced Joshua, a familiar face from back home, came running forward to hold his and Denzik's bridles while they dismounted. Two other men stepped forward, and then they led the horses away to be cared for.

Denzik examined Ryder with interest as did Fabian and Nelson. The camp was filled with the sounds and smells of men and women sharpening blades, fletching arrows, and cooking meals over cook fires with the happy chatter of people who had found contentment in a common purpose.

Denzik nodded approvingly. "You run a fine camp here, Ryder. Yes, very fine indeed. I would like to do a walk about to inspect the camp." Ryder nodded and led the way out into the main body of his band.

The first section of tents housed a group of ladies who had joined them from the last village. Hair cut in the male fashion and dressed in tan pants and leather vests, it took Denzik and the rest a moment to realize they were women. When they did, they stopped dead. The women sat around their campfire, sharpening stones rasping along the blades of their swords. It was obvious they were well practiced at the skill. The closest woman tested the edge against her thumb and grunted in satisfaction as a small cut appeared across it.

Nelson approached the woman and paused beside her. "That's a fine edge you have put on your blade. Do you know how to use it?" The woman glared at him and then stood. She towered over him by a good eight inches. Nelson squinted up at her and the corner of his mouth twitched, holding back a grin.

She eyed him up and down. "I would not worry about my skills, little man, but more so about your reach." Ryder shook his head, making a mental note to speak to them about tact.

Nelson's grin burst on to his face. "What is your name?" he asked, laughing in earnest.

"My name is Candice, daughter of Sophia and Armando, knight of the realm, fallen in battle, may the gods bless them." She stood tall and menacing, evidently attempting to decide whether he was truly threatening, or just plain dumb.

Fabian walked up, chuckling. "Last time we saw you, Candice, you were but a babe in arms, but there is no mistaking your mother's good looks." Her eyes flickered over them all then settled on Denzik.

"I'm sorry, but you have me at a disadvantage. Should I know you?"

"No, my dear, we served alongside your father, and we are pleased to see you doing so well. Welcome to the fight."

Candice nodded with pride, winked at Ryder, and sat back down to resume her work.

Fabian wolf-whistled softly under his breath and strode away.

"You always did have a soft spot for Sophia. You never could keep your eyes off her legs," said Nelson.

Fabian's whistling stopped abruptly, like a cork plugging a bottle, and he quickly glanced over his shoulder to see if Candice had overheard. Denzik laughed out loud. Ryder found himself chuckling too.

They toured the laundry areas, the latrines, the kitchen, the small portable smithies, the supply tents, and the makeshift stables. Completing the circuit, Denzik ducked his head and entered the command tent. Spying a frosted pitcher and some glasses, he poured a drink and took a seat at a table consisting of three wooden boxes set close together in the middle of the room. Ryder joined him with his own glass.

"I am glad to be able to turn this venture over to your more experienced hands. Cayden asked me to help him, but I am sure he'd prefer to have someone in charge who knew what they were doing." He sat down and took a long drink of the cool lemonade.

Denzik studied him as did the other two. Ryder lowered his glass and his eyes travelled between the three men. "What?"

"We have no intention of taking over your camp or your men," Denzik said. "They are gathered together and are loyal to you. You and you alone are their leader. They would not do half as well under another's command."

Ryder frowned. "They are here because they wanted to help in recapturing the castle to oust the queen. It has nothing to do with me."

Nelson spoke this time. "I doubt that's true, lad, but you are the one who showed them the way and that makes you their leader. They trust you."

"But I know nothing of wars or battles. Sure, I once dreamed of becoming a knight, but it was a childish dream. I cannot captain these men, not in a real battle," Ryder protested.

"A true captain points the way. He doesn't do the majority of the battling. Fighting is what his troops do. And a wise general places many capable captains under his command. Do you have a title? What do the men call you?" said Fabian.

"I…well actually they call me 'sir' or 'lord.' Only those in command have titles and they are all captains."

"Then by your own command structure, you have assigned yourself the role of Captain General of the Band. Congratulations on your promotion, General." Denzik clapped him on the shoulder, grinning. Ryder groaned as the three men laughed at his stunned expression.

"Now, let us make plans for moving this army forward. By the time we are finished here, our scout should be back with the other band's location."

Chapter 47

CAYDEN WOKE SLOWLY, his mind fuzzy and his tongue dry as though coated in chalk. He tried to swallow, but his tongue stuck to his cheek with the gummy glue of his saliva. He dozed, the effort of lifting his head an impossible task. He dreamed he was surrounded by people, arms reaching out to him, begging him to hold them, yet he was only one man. How could he hold and comfort them all at once?

He jerked at a loud noise and began the climb toward consciousness, but then the sound went away and he succumbed to the darkness again.

"When is he going to wake?"

"You wanted us to keep him drugged. We have done exactly what you told us to do."

"We don't even know if he is the one we seek. I will not carry word of this man to Her Majesty without knowing for certain. You will discontinue the drugging and let him wake. The minute he does awaken, you will summon me and only me in person and with the utmost secrecy. Understood?"

"Yes, my lord. It will be as you command."

Cayden drifted in semi-consciousness. *Were those real people, real voices? Or were they more muddled dreams?* He wasn't sure. He thought he heard a key rattle in a metal lock, but maybe that was his imagination too. He had had so many dreams he couldn't begin to sort reality from fiction.

Yesterday—at least he thought it was yesterday—he had dreamed of a short fairy-like creature who had wanted him to dance a childish dance he didn't know to amuse the queen. When he had told her he didn't know the steps, she had grown to eight feet tall, her clothes had darkened and lengthened to black hooded robes. Her beady red eyes stared and she hissed at him from the dark depths. It didn't matter anymore. The party was over. His time was up, and this time he was going to die.

Cayden jerked awake this time to complete darkness. He tried to raise his head but found the effort more than he could manage. He stifled a groan, attempting to roll over, but his legs and arms were bound behind his back. He gingerly moved them to test if they were operational and a quick exploratory showed no obvious injuries or broken bones. He was lying on his right side on a stone floor. A green glow emanated from the rocky floor, walls, and ceiling, giving a faint but ghostly light. He lifted his head a fraction, trying to observe his surroundings, for he had no doubt where he was: in a prisoner cell deep under the castle of Cathair.

He was in trouble—big trouble—and this time there was no one around to help get him out of this jam. There was complete silence in the dungeon. He was unable to tell if there were other cells or other prisoners around him. The silence was complete. He attempted to move, to wiggle his fingers and toes as they were numb with cold. The ropes were tight, cutting into his skin, restricting the blood's circulation to his hands and feet. He did not know how long he had lain in one position. Cayden tensed and relaxed his muscles slowly and methodically, bringing circulation back into their lengths. His toes and fingertips burned as oxygen moved into muscles stiff from lack of use.

As he wiggled, his head bumped into an object placed on the floor. He strained around and found a ceramic bowl with some kind of gruel mixture and a second bowl with water. He wiggled his way around and lifted his head and slurped the cold water, much like a dog would. He lapped eagerly and then halfway through, stopped as a thought hit him. What if there were more drugs in the water? He grimaced and continued drinking. He would have to risk it. The bowl tipped as his head sagged against the rim and then clanked back down, spilling precious water onto the stone floor. He lapped it all, eager for every drop. Afterward, he relaxed back on the floor, resting for a second, letting the water soak into his parched throat and soothe his dry mouth. He felt the drugs' effects weakening their hold on him as the water flushed the remaining drugs from his system.

He reached out with his mind to Ziona. *Ziona, are you there?* He felt a stirring in the bond as though she was also asleep. *Ziona. Wake up, Ziona. Come on…*

Ziona's consciousness blurred and sharpened as she struggled against sleep. "Cayden?" Suddenly, her mind snapped into focused reality with the force of a bow string. *Cayden, you're alive! Where are you? Wait!* He felt her stop the communication with him for a second and he imagined her rushing from her tent to call the guards. Just as quickly, she re-entered his mind. *Cayden, can you tell me where you are?*

I think I am in a prison cell in the dungeons under the castle in Cathair. It has the look of a cell.

Are you hurt? Is anyone there with you?

No, I am alone, but I am bound hand and foot. I woke up a few minutes ago.

OK. Please do not do anything stupid. We are coming for you one way or another. Take care of yourself as best you can till we get there. OK?

I will. Are you OK? You seemed to be in a really deep sleep.

What you experience in the waking world affects me also. Did they have you drugged?

Yes. That is how the Charun took me.

Charun! He felt her shiver through the bond. *At least you are still alive. We are missing two guards here.*

Yes, they were felled by black arrows. Darius shot them. He betrayed us, me, to the Charun.

Darius! When did he arrive?

It was while you were resting. He was going to take me to Ryder, or so I thought. He said something about him being at the village on the outskirts of Cathair. I think that much of it was true.

We will see if we can find him. Stay safe, Cayden! Alert me should anything happen. I can hear your thoughts and will know. He felt a flood of warmth that felt a lot like love, flow through the bond. He sent it back to her.

"Cayden, are you awake?"

This voice was not in his head. It was whispered.

"Who are you? How do you know my name?"

"Finally," the voice whispered in relief. "I am Mordecai Ben-Moses. It has been I who has been calling you in your dreams. We have much to talk about," the disembodied voice said.

"Are you the one who can give me answers? Aossi said there was one who could help me located here in the castle."

"Ah, I see you have met Aossi already. Good, good. You are strong with your mother's blood I see. That is important, you know."

"My mother was born in Sanctuary-by-the-Sea. She died many years ago. You could not possibly know her? How long have you been here?" Cayden growled suspiciously.

"Oh...I would say for around seventeen years, give or take a few months. How old are you?"

"What does my age have to do with it?"

"A great deal I am afraid, seeing as you are the reason I have been here all these years."

"What foolishness is this?" Anger and a splitting headache sharpened Cayden's tone.

At that moment, the sound of boots scraping on stone reached their ears. "Play the fool, Cayden," Mordecai whispered urgently. "You know nothing and we have never spoken. You do not know me."

Cayden slumped back onto the floor of his cell and pretended to be sleeping again. He was facing away from the door. The boots drew closer and stopped at Cayden's cell. A light shone through the metal bars of the small window set in the door. Cayden could see the light swing crazily, the shadowy bars moving from one side to the other as the light moved.

The light receded and paused. Cayden wondered if—what was his name? Mordecai?—was faking sleep too.

The light followed the boot sounds back up the hallway and eventually faded away.

"Mordecai?" Cayden whispered.

"Yes, Cayden?"

"Who are you?"

"I already told you...just not in detail."

Cayden paused, and then said, "What you mentioned earlier, about my mother. What did you mean by that?"

"Exactly what I said, I was present at your birth. I assisted your mother when she gave birth to the pair of you. She was in need of magical assistance at the time."

"Why would you have been at my birth? What kind of assistance?"

"Not only yours but your sister's too."

"As she is my twin, how could it have been any other way?" said Cayden in an aggrieved voice.

"Cayden, we have much to talk about, but for now it is best that I do not reveal to you more than you need to know, at least until we are out of this mess, which will be quite soon. I am rather tired of this cell and the rats that frequent it. I will enjoy seeing the sun again."

Cayden pondered this silently from his cell. *What would it be like to waste away in a prison for seventeen years?* He shivered. He did not want to know.

"What do I do, Mordecai? I cannot continue to fake sleep" — Cayden's stomach rumbled — "and I am hungry."

"Eat, my boy, eat. First rule of any resistance is you must keep up your strength."

"OK, but this is going to get messy," Cayden said. "How about you talk to me while I figure this out?"

"Sounds good...yes...it's been so long since I have had someone to talk to. Tell me, can you see that green glow on the rocks? No, wait you should not speak with your mouth full, very bad for digestion. Hum, do you see that glow? It is more than a phosphorescent microbial. See how it pulses? Alas, another foolish question. It's quite impossible to answer while your mouth is full. I am sorry. I am rusty in the fine art of intelligent conversation after seventeen years of speaking to the same guard day in day out who has, unfortunately, run afoul of our dearly beloved queen."

Cayden snorted and licked at the bowl's meager contents. The man was really quite humorous and Cayden would have enjoyed his company if his situation hadn't been so dire. As Cayden licked his bowl clean, he let the old man ramble on. The food settling in Cayden's stomach stilled the spidery fingers that had been tickling his insides in hunger.

Licking his lips, Cayden relaxed back onto the floor. "I am finished."

"Oh, and in the nick of time, too! Tell me, what is your predicament there? I assume you are bound?"

"Yes, hand and foot."

"Dear me, that is quite unfortunate. I could be of assistance, but untying you would give the game away, certainly."

Cayden frowned again. He sensed he might do that a lot around this man. "You still haven't told me anything more than your name. How is it you know mine?"

"Once again my manners are appallingly lacking. My name is Mordecai Ben-Moses, First Wizard of the Fell."

Silence greeted these words. So this was the wizard Aossi had spoken of. Cayden had believed they were extinct in the realm, that they had been eliminated during the revolution.

"How can you be alive? I was told all the great wizards were dead."

"Alas this is true, for the most part. I, fortunately, was captured immediately after your birth, stripped of my powers, and imprisoned in this cell. My compatriots, they were not so fortunate."

Cayden found the mixture of being "imprisoned" and "fortunate" a very strange combination.

"So you have super magical powers, then?"

"Something like that, I suppose."

"So...how are we getting out of here?"

"The young are always so impatient. Jumping from one thought to the other. Patience, my young friend, I counsel patience. Your companions need time to prepare and spring their surprise."

"I am tired of surprises," Cayden grumbled. "That is how I ended up here tied like a holiday pig ready for the spit."

"Ahh...well as to that, it was prophesied."

"My betrayal by a friend was *prophesied*?" Cayden was stunned by this news. He was destined to suffer at the hands of a friend?

"I'm afraid so, Cayden. This is the beginning of troubled times for the world. You and your sister are being pushed along a path you were destined to travel since your birth. You know this to be so at least in part or you would never have found me."

Cayden fell silent. What reply was there?

Chapter 48

ZIONA RODE FROM CAYDEN'S CAMP with Tobias at her side and four more soldiers. The number of volunteers had soared with the news that they had discovered where Cayden was being held captive.

Riding into the capital with all of the men in tow would be tantamount to a declaration of war on the capital and they would tighten security around Cayden perhaps making it impossible to reach him or, worse yet, outright kill him before the band had an opportunity to rescue him.

Reaching Ryder was paramount and all she had to go on was Cayden's clue from Darius. Together, they might be able to mount a rescue that wouldn't endanger his life.

It was nearly noon when they reached the village of Lower Cathair. Men and woman tended their crops, cultivating the soil and picking produce for market. Children chased other children through the village square, laughing, while dogs nipped at their heels and raced ahead of them.

Ziona dismounted in front of the inn, flanked by quaint stone cottages that made up the majority of the dwellings of the village. The inn appeared to be the social center of the village as evidenced by the chatter that flooded over them as they pushed open the door to the common room. Ziona's glance around the room took in the two roaring fireplaces and the bustling staff, eventually pausing at a table, where a group of four men and a woman sat. From the breadth of the shoulders, there was no question that she had found Ryder.

She marched up to the table, interrupting their conversation. The others fell silent at her approach, studying her closely, but Ryder jumped to his feet and moved quickly to embrace her. "Ziona! It's great to see you! Where is Cayden?" She glanced back at his companions and frowned. "It's OK, Ziona. These are friends, Kingsmen of old."

"I need to speak privately, away from sharp ears. Is there such a place?" she asked of the men at the table.

Nelson stood up. "You may use the private library, my lady. This way please."

They all rose and Ziona followed Nelson to a comfortably furnished room off of the common room with padded chairs and shelves lined with books.

Ziona's companions remained standing, taking up positions to watch the door and the windows of the room. Two remained in the hallway to make sure they were not approached.

Denzik walked up to Tobias and stared him directly in the eye. Tobias never blinked. "Tobias Townsend. I never thought to see you alive."

Tobias's face broke into a grin. "It's good to see you too, sir!" He saluted the old general.

"You would be a Primordial Seeker...unless I miss my mark." Denzik said to Ziona. "I assume you are the one who has been assisting Cayden?"

"That is correct. Ryder has told you about Cayden? Or at least what he understands of Cayden?"

Denzik nodded.

"Cayden has been captured. He is being held in the prisoner cells of the castle as we speak." The blunt words galvanized the men, who were beginning to seat themselves. They shot back to their feet, all speaking at once.

Ziona held up her hands to quiet them. "Cayden is fine, at least as fine as he can be. We have formed...a special connection. I can sense what is happening to him. He is fine for the moment. I do not believe they are certain who he is or he would already be dead. We must reach him without delay. I can lead you directly to him."

"We have been preparing and planning for this moment for seventeen years, my lady. I assume you have acquired a following during your journeys?" Denzik nodded to the men standing guard.

"Yes, Cayden has managed to attract a large group of former Kingsmen, who have sworn allegiance to him. They are a few hours back, camped out of sight and waiting for our command."

Nelson nodded as did Fabian.

"Gentlemen, ladies, I believe it's time to implement our plan." Denzik walked over to the desk located under the window and pulled a small key from his pocket. Fitting key to lock, he opened the long flat drawer slid under the desktop. Inside were several long rolled scrolls, which he gathered up and brought over to the reading table in the center of the room. Everyone gathered around to view the scrolls.

Denzik selected one and then carefully unrolled it to show what appeared to be a maze of twisting lines that intersected in unpredictable ways.

"This is a map of the underground tunnel systems of Castle Cathair. This, my friends, is how we are going to retake the castle and drive out the queen forever. I would like you to go back to your respective camps and gather the ten most trusted men or ladies from your established captains. We need to familiarize them with the plan and move our troops into position. All the supplies we need are already in place for this attack.

"We are waiting for the heir to arrive and his men to gather. I must say, you both have done a fine job in pulling in the men. Our eyes and ears report that Kingsmen are streaming toward the capital in various disguises. Fabian, here"—he nodded at the plump baker—"has set up a series of distractions inside the castle itself and Nelson"—he nodded to the innkeeper—"will be redirecting the forces as they arrive into the tunnels."

At Ziona's look of confusion, Denzik quickly brought her up to speed about the tunnels dug between the river and the castle foundations. *Impressive that they planned and implemented such a grand design over the years, based on nothing but their belief that the king would return*, Ziona thought. They grinned at her surprised stare. "Very resourceful, gentlemen, I have to wonder who set these plans in place." She raised an eyebrow enquiringly, but the men all shook their heads refusing to speak of it.

"Meet back here in six hours with your captains."

Chapter 49

A BUCKET OF ICY WATER emptying over his prone form jolted Cayden awake. Gasping, he blinked his eyes and squinted against the sudden glare of the lantern held above him. The guard kicked Cayden in the ribs, and he cried out.

Cayden tried to clutch his stomach but, of course, this was impossible as his arms were still tied behind his back. He attempted to curl into a tighter ball, but then he felt a sharp knife slip between his wrists and ankles, slicing through the ropes holding him captive. He groaned as he rolled onto his stomach and moved his fingers and toes, trying to restore their circulation.

The guard reached down and hauled him to his feet by his hair. Cayden cried out again and then his eyes fell on the man holding the lantern. He was a tall steely-eyed man with short cropped hair and a grey goatee trimmed to a sharp point below his equally pointed chin.

"Lord Cyrus, this is the prisoner, my lord. He is awake now as ordered."

Cayden found his legs were weak after two days bound hand and foot. He wobbled and very nearly collapsed back onto the stone floor, but the guard's tight grip on his hair kept him upright. A spikey prickling ran from his feet and up through his legs as he put weight on his limbs. He was glad of the distracting pain on his scalp as the returning blood made his extremities burn.

The lord walked around Cayden, examining him. "I am to believe this skinny boy is to be feared? This poor farmer is the great prophesied threat to my queen's reign?" He stopped in front of Cayden and addressed him. "What is your name boy and where were you born?"

Cayden couldn't see a reason to lie so he answered truthfully.

"Cayden Tiernan. I was born in from a village called Sanctuary-by-the-Sea, on the northeastern coast of the realm."

"You have lived there your entire life?"

"Yes, I am born and raised there."

"Why do you travel to the capital?"

"I joined the legion when it came to our village, but the legion was attacked and everyone perished. I was out of the camp at the time of the attack and survived. I thought to join another legion if I could locate one."

Cayden wondered if his partial lie was convincing. He hadn't actually lied, at least until the end. He had only left out important parts.

The high lord stared at him. Cayden locked his legs and arms to keep them from trembling and betraying his nervousness and then met his eyes.

"You know what I think? I think you are a clever liar and a fraud. I think you do not have the brains to orchestrate a rebellion. Lord knows how many of your type have been tossed in these dungeons over the years, betrayed by beggarly men eager to claim the queen's bounty."

He walked around Cayden one more time and then paused in front of him, a puzzled expression on his cruel face. "And yet...there is something *familiar* about you...as though we had met on a previous occasion." He studied Cayden's features, searching them, and then turned away, tugging on gloves he had pulled from his vest pocket.

"Bind him in chains. I will have Queen Alcina inspect this one."

He left the cell as Cayden was dragged over to a set of leg and wrist irons affixed to chains imbedded in the stone exterior wall.

Chapter 50

THEY WRAPPED UP THEIR PLANNING SESSION around four o'clock in the morning. Birds were beginning to stir, sleepy twitters occasionally disturbing the silence in their wake. The captains rode off to their respective assignments, breaking camp and beginning the march back to the village.

Denzik's plan was to approach the village in units of ten Kingsmen from the dense woods on the opposite bank of the back of the inn. Once there, they would sneak men into the tunnels in small groups. Hopefully, their movements would be missed by the locals busy tending their fields and off to trade in the capital for the day.

Nelson's network of tunnels had expanded to include a riverside entrance, cleverly disguised to blend into the bank. While only he and a handful of trusted men needed access to the tunnels, hiding the entrance in the inn had made sense from a security point of view.

But as the tunnels expanded and the rumours from the ears heated up with whispers of the chosen one approaching, having only one entrance seemed foolhardy. *After all, how can I sneak in an entire army through the middle of my inn?*

As a result, three separate entrances had been established leading into the tunnels, all joining at different points along the underground passageways. Denzik had utilized some of those abandoned corridors and lengthened them. Now in addition to the river entrance, one was also to be found near the well on Denzik's land and a fourth in the storm cellar of the grain barn that Fabian used to store his flour sacks.

Nelson set up sentries posing as gardeners or workers doing repairs about the grounds to steer people away from the back of the inn. Sentries were also posted at the three other entrances. As they spied the men approaching, bluebird whistles would give the all clear signal to the units as they approached.

In the meantime, Fabian brought supplies in through the back door leading to the inn's kitchen plus an assortment of swords, arrows, and bows, all tucked neatly into the bottom of baskets of freshly baked bread, apples, and jerky. The baskets disappeared down the trap door and were hauled to the various staging areas within the tunnels, so that the men and women who arrived with no weapons would leave the tunnels armed.

Tabitha was the last line of defence, as she would disguise the inn's trap door once they had descended into its depths, standing guard with a cook's best tools, cleavers and knives, at the ready.

The first groups arrived, peeking over the horizon with the dawn, creeping through the trees as silent as a stalking mountain lion. They whistled the bluebird call to announce their presence, and the sentries whistled back confirmation that it was safe to approach. He motioned the first group of ten down into the tunnel entrance. Men and women scrambled down the inn ladder, dropped into the riverside stone shaft, slithered down a rope into the well, crawled out the side tunnel six feet above the floor of the well, and crawled into the space under the old mill stone, all intent on joining with their fellow Kingsmen.

The men continued to arrive all day and into the night, ten minute intervals between the groups, sixty men an hour. Twenty-four hours later, one thousand four hundred men in total had descended into the caves and settled into their assigned bands in the caverns and tunnels beneath the castle.

Denzik closed off and hid the riverside entrance, disguising it with an old wooden rowboat he pulled up in front of the entrance, leaning it on an angle and obscuring all the tracks. When he left, it appeared that the boat had been in storage there for a very long time.

He then returned to his home and removed the rope slung from the overhead crossbeam of the well and swept the area with a tree branch to erase the signs of booted traffic.

Denzik met Fabian as he entered the inn and together they wandered nonchalantly back to the library, which had become their makeshift command post over the last two days. The twenty captains, Ryder, Ziona, and Tobias stood or leaned against furniture, studied the maps pinned around the room on the walls, or conversed in low tones. Denzik felt their suppressed excitement, their eagerness to get on with the overthrow of the government and Cayden's rescue.

Denzik cleared his throat and the room fell silent.

"Tonight, the world changes forever. For seventeen years, we have planned, prepared, searched, and waited. But even more so, we have hoped. For seventeen years, we have endured the tyranny of a queen who murdered the royal family of Cathair down to the man, woman, and child. She attempted to wipe them from the earth...but she has failed."

Denzik reached for a box under the desk that had once held maps. He placed it on the tabletop and opened the lid. Inside were folded uniforms bearing the insignia of captains of the Kingsmen. They had been carefully folded and wrapped in bleached paper, the emblem of the Kingsmen stitched boldly onto the royal purple fabric. The men stood taller and snapped to attention at the sight of the uniforms.

"Tonight, we reclaim that which was taken from us. Tonight, we reclaim the throne for the rightful heir. Tonight, we throw off our disguises for tomorrow, and we declare our allegiance in battle." He gazed around at the men and smiled. The men cheered, saluted, elbowing each other aside as they rushed forward to collect their uniforms.

***

Mordecai lit the candles he had hoarded over the years with a flame conjured by his magic. The flames of twenty candles pushed back the gloom and spilled over into Cayden's cell.

Hanging on the wall as he was, Cayden could not immediately see the source of the light, but he was grateful for it nevertheless. The soft scurrying sounds of rats magnified in the dark until it sounded like there were hundreds of them in his cell. His imagination running riot, Cayden discovered a fear he never knew he possessed.

"Mordecai, get me out of here." A tremor of panic made Cayden's voice come out in a squawk. "There are rats here, Mordecai!" He shuddered and twisted in his shackles. "Hurry, please!"

"Just a minute, my boy!"

Cayden heard rustling from the cell across the way and a shadow moved across the wall, Mordecai passing in front of the candles.

Something ran across Cayden's foot, brushing against his pant leg. His leg shot out a whole two inches, in an attempt to kick off the rat, but instead of dislodging the creature, he felt its needle-sharp claws pierce the flesh of his calf. With a choked screech, Cayden thrashed in his bonds, the metal shackles cutting into his exposed skin.

"Mordecai!" he screamed, taking deep gulps of air to stem his rising panic.

"There, that should do it." With a popping sound, the cell door across from Cayden's swung open on squealing hinges.

"Mordecai!" Cayden gasped, as a second rat joined the first, its whiskered nose sniffing at the blood now trickling down from the abrasions on Cayden's leg from the manacles.

Mordecai's thin pale face flashed in the barred window of Cayden's cell, as he reached through the bars and stuck a guttering candle on the lantern shelf beside the door. In the weak light, the floor writhed and bubbled with small bodies that scurried here and there across the floor. Cayden found that actually seeing the rats, was far worse than fearing them in the dark and Cayden began to thrash again as his horror broke free. He screamed as a rat began to climb his pant leg.

"Oh my," said Mordecai. He pulled his focus stone out of his pocket, his balled fist clutching it tightly, and then thrust it back through the bars and murmured a few words that Cayden could not make out. There was a flash of brilliant white and the rats collapsed, slipping off of Cayden's legs as the life left their bodies.

Cayden, his heart pounding, sucked in several breaths, trying desperately to regain control.

Mordecai replaced the stone in his pocket and fished out the master key that he had stolen off of Wendell the last time he had visited his cell. He fit it into the lock, turned the tumblers, and hurried over to Cayden's limp form.

"Nasty business, rats," he said, gazing around while he worked on unlocking the manacles. "They are not normally active this time of day." He released Cayden's hands and then bent to release his ankles. "Ahh, I see now why they came in such numbers, look."

With a click the last shackle fell away and Cayden scrambled off the wooden platform on shaky legs, careful to not step on a dead rat. Rubbing his wrists, Cayden bent over to see what had attracted Mordecai's attention. Under the platform he spied a wooden trough full of rotting refuse. At either end, a hollow stone tube was visible. It connected to a long vertical drain in the floor of the kitchens many stories above. The garbage of the kitchens washed down and emptied into the trough.

"Ingenious," said Mordecai, examining the device. "Obviously, this particular cell is used to torture prisoners. The poor kitchen staff would have no idea that they are innocently aiding in this torture." He straightened then put his hand on Cayden's shoulder. "Are you ready to go? We need to hurry. I can't imagine we have much time. They will be back very soon to see what effect the rats have had on loosening your tongue."

"Let's get out of here," Cayden said fervently, shuddering, eyes averted from the floor.

He followed Mordecai back to his cell, locking the cell doors behind them. Mordecai tapped on a rock at the back of his cell. The sound of an answering knock filled the air.

Chapter 51

QUEEN ALCINA SLAPPED HER MAID'S HANDS AWAY
impatiently. "I told you, stupid woman, to fetch the emeralds, not
the pearls."

"But, Your Majesty, the emeralds do not compliment your lovely
dress." The maid smoothed the black silk and resumed buttoning the
high-collared back.

"I care not for your silly opinion, woman. Finish your duties.
Quickly! I do not have time to waste on your useless dribble."

The maid curtsied and quickened her movements, head bent to
hide the bloom of embarrassment on her cheeks. She fetched the
heavy silver collar set with emeralds and settled them around her
mistress's throat, fastening the heavy clasp at the back of her neck.
Next, she placed her thin pearl-studded crown on her hair and
secured it with combs. The combination was hideous, but she
clamped her lips shut, struggling to keep silent. With the queen's
current mood, voicing her opinion now would find her on the way
to the guillotine.

Alcina left the ridiculous woman behind, entering her sitting
room where Cyrus waited. He blinked at the combination but also
wisely said nothing. He knew Alcina was in one of her moods and
heads usually rolled when she was in a foul temper.

"Well? What is the news? You have a new prisoner in the cells.
Speak up, man. I have no patience for evasions this evening."

"We have an interesting prisoner below, my lady. You know I
would not impose on you to perform an inspection, but there is

something about this one. I can't put my finger on what it is, but he seems familiar somehow." He frowned in thought.

Alcina raised her severe eyebrows, like a hawk sighting a mouse attempting to hide. "That does not sound like much to go on, but I will humour you this time. Beheading that useless wizard might be just the thing to raise my spirits. Yes, I believe it is exactly what I need to relieve my stress." Her eyes glinted cold chips of blue ice in her pale face.

Cyrus opened the door and stepped back with a bow to let her pass. They made their way from the queen's apartments on the top floor of the main tower, down winding staircases, and through adjoining tapestry-draped corridors until they reached the upper walkway above the parade grounds.

They crossed to the other side of the castle housing most of the guest suites and the various meeting halls for dignitaries or noble petitioners. The kitchens were located in this section of the castle. They descended a broad-curved staircase to the pillared welcoming hall. The queen's coat of arms in a break with tradition was the sole decoration displayed on all the walls of the hall, all former monarch symbols having been removed.

They entered a hallway leading to the kitchens and then took a side corridor to a curving staircase that wound down deeper into the depths of the castle. Arriving at a landing, they spied two guards sitting at a table, playing cards. They snapped to attention on seeing the new arrivals and then bowed deeply at the waist.

"You are dismissed for ten minutes." The guards bowed again and left as ordered.

Cyrus pulled a key ring from his pocket and fitted it in the lock.

"Why did you choose to come down the main stairs this time, Your Highness?" Cyrus asked.

"That nosy maid is why. Unlike the other maids, she likes to hang around my apartments. I am suspicious of the reason why. The other maids are quick to leave my chambers. They understand that I do not want them around once they have performed their duty." She touched the emerald collar at her throat. "That one is too nosy by far. I do not want her to stumble on the secret passage entrance in the back wall of my closet. Secret passageways should remain secret, especially as that one leads all the way down to the cells—handy when I do not wish to be seen, but it would not do for others to know of its existence."

Cyrus lit a splint in the lamp hanging by the door and brought it to bear on the wicks of two unlit lamps. They flared to light, pushing back the shadows. He handed one to Alcina, the light flickering over her features. She stared back at him, a cruel twist of pleasure on her lips.

"Besides, it was a wonderful treat, surprising that servant who was currying favour with the wizard. Ahh, the look of surprise on his face when we popped out of the wall! That was to die for! Hanging him for his crimes was the only answer, of course. Smuggling supplies to the wizard is one thing, but failing to cut his hair was an unforgiveable mistake. One I intend to correct shortly."

Alcina preceded Cyrus down the hall, taking up a lantern from the wall and holding it aloft with one hand and picking up her skirts with the other. A cool breeze blew down the hall, bringing with it the odor of unwashed bodies. She wrinkled her nose in disgust but continued on to the end of the main hallway and then descending the curved rough-cut stone to the lowest of the dungeons. The *click-clack* of her boot heels echoed off the walls as she strode the short distance to the end where two cells flanked the stone corridor. Holding her lantern aloft, she let the light of it flood the interior of the cell.

It was empty.

Swinging the light around to the other cell, she flooded the interior with light, peering into it.

It was also empty.

At that precise moment, the alarm bells sounded. The castle was under attack.

Chapter 52

ZIONA GRABBED CAYDEN AS HE CRAWLED through the hole, pulling him out of the dusty passage, then hugged him, while Tobias crowded close, determined to not let Cayden out of his sight again.

Mordecai popped out of the hole behind him, surprisingly spry for one who had just been released from a seventeen-year imprisonment. He pulled out his focus stone and with a few murmured words, lessened the weight of the limestone block, thus assisting the rescue crews with the realignment of the stones into their original positions. They trowelled the mortar over the thin crack visible around the blocks and blended it seamlessly with the surrounding stones. When they were finished, it was impossible to tell the breach had ever occurred.

Nelson grinned pleased with the way the stones had slid out so easily with the lightest tug. The stone to Mordecai's cell had been used as an escape route in times past, secrets within secrets held silently by the ancient walls. Nice of them to mark the right stone, as it had sped up the process considerably. The dissolving paste was really quite the find, and the mortar had liquefied in a matter of hours. Now with the stones back in place, there was no evidence to show where the escape had occurred. Nor would the queen know where they had gone. They were safe...for now.

Ryder walked up and bear-hugged Cayden. Cayden groaned with the pressure on his sore ribs. Cayden's eyes wandered over the vaulted ceiling of the cavern and then onto the rescue team. "Where are we?" he asked.

"In caverns below the castle," Ryder said with a pleased smile. "Denzik here"—he waved Denzik over to him—"and his cronies have been mapping these passageways for years, ex-Kingsmen all. I think they expected you to come although I am not sure they expected to rescue you." Ryder bent over and whispered for Cayden's ears only, "Who's the old man?"

"A wizard and an old friend; a very old friend, if truth be told," Cayden said.

At that moment, Denzik arrived, and Ryder introduced him to Cayden. He bowed to Cayden and then shook his proffered hand. "Sire, I am so pleased to meet you! We have waited for a very long time for you to come, a lifetime, really. But we have not been idle, as you can see. You are pleased?" Denzik asked, just as the faint sounds of warning bells reached their ears, echoing through the cavern.

Ryder's head swivelled toward the sound and he glanced over at Nelson.

"We need to get back to our teams," said Ryder. "They have begun their assault through the Traitor's Gate. Anthony unlocked it from the inside and the teams are spreading out through the castle. Damn! The alarm has sounded too soon!"

Nelson walked over to Cayden, peering up into his face, as he towered above him.

"Sire, you are the spitting image of the late king, may the gods have mercy on his soul. It is an honour to serve under you once again." Nelson knelt before Cayden, head lowered.

Mordecai's eyes twinkled at Cayden's discomfort. Cayden reached down and pulled Nelson to his feet. "There is no time for this right now!" *I seem to say this a lot lately!* The thought flashed across Cayden's mind. "Didn't you say battle has commenced? Let's move!"

Both Nelson and Tobias snapped a salute as did Ryder. They gathered up the rest of the men and raced back to their respective units.

Ziona slipped back over to Cayden's side and held up a water flask for him to sip from. *More of her magic elixir,* he guessed and took a long swig. Ziona grinned up at him, hearing his thoughts. She slipped her hand into his.

Mordecai's smile broadened.

"Well, my boy, we now have a decision to make. The fight to retake this castle will rage above. But what truly concerns you at this moment in time is down here under the castle, under your ancestral home."

Cayden could feel it. The incessant tugging sensation on his soul made him restless, like his body was pumped full of adrenaline with no ability to burn it away. He now realized there had been a double pull happening, one to Mordecai, yes, but also another...deeper...somehow connected to him personally.

"How do you know this, Mordecai?"

"I was with you when you were born, but more importantly, I was with you before you *died.*"

"I died and then was born?" Cayden stared at Mordecai in confusion as did Ziona.

"Actually, you died and were born twice." Mordecai hummed to himself in satisfaction. "Cayden, what do you know of the prophecies? Ziona, perhaps you can help him with this? Your people must have similar ones."

She nodded, understanding. Mordecai closed his eyes, reciting the prophecy by memory.

"And it shall come to pass in the end of days that the Lord of All shall weep with sorrow for the destruction of his creation. Darkness shall cover the land and the Mother Spirit shall be crushed. Her tears flood the mountains, yet who listens? For her tears are consumed by the fires of Helga. Who can stand before her gates? The world is burning. Weep you souls of the earth for he must die and live again. On the wings of an eagle so shall your salvation be carried."

Something stirred with in Cayden awakening in him. A distant memory flashed across his mind...or had it been a dream?

Ziona tilted her head, a puzzled expression on her face.

"Come," said Mordecai, "there is something you need to see."

Chapter 53

MORDECAI LED CAYDEN AND ZIONA down a rocky path that narrowed into low ceilinged sloping tunnels and bent toward the center of the earth beneath the castle. The sweeping curves dug relentlessly into the dark, dank underground, deeper than anyone had ever gone before, if the layers of undisturbed dirt were any indication.

At first, a faint greenish glow seemed to seep from the rocks, but the closer they came to their destination, the colour became aqua and then took on deeper shades of blue. The blue intensified and Ziona, glancing at Cayden, suddenly gasped aloud. Cayden was glowing with the precise same colour that was emanating from the cavern ahead of him. His skin flickered, absorbing the blue, creating a celestial aura around him. He looked at her questioningly and then followed her eyes to look at his own hands. He stopped abruptly, shocked. Blue flames danced and swirled off his skin. Mordecai, hearing him pause, stopped walking also.

Cayden's skin glowed with the light of ten lanterns, dimming the light of their lamps to nothing.

"I suspected this would occur," said Mordecai. "It is nothing to worry about, Cayden. Come."

The cave mouth opened into an oblong cavern. Walls, slick with the dripping of ancient waters, morphed into quarried blocks of marble imbedded with heavy veins of quartz. The unpolished stone of the anteroom glinted dully in the light exploding from Cayden's skin. On the other side of the anteroom, an arched opening pulsed sympathetically with Cayden's glow, and crackling tendrils of cool flame flickered across the opening. Cayden felt his hair try to rise, as the blue lighting drew him forward. He was unable to resist the pull and his feet crunched across the anteroom to the main chamber. Mordecai and Ziona followed Cayden, their steps cautious.

Cayden reached out with his hand and touched the opening. Lighting snaked up his arm and wrapped around his body then melded with the blue mist emanating from his body. He stepped through into a cathedral of marble. The walls towered three stories above the chipped and cracked floor. Soaring buttresses ran from columns standing in each corner, meeting in the middle of the ceiling, where an inverted bowl clung to the ceiling, carved out of the marble of the cavern, and decorated with faces of men, women, and children. Windows that opened onto nothing dotted the walls, and long black scorch marks streaked across the marble. On one wall, a large crack spidered up and out of sight.

It was the simple limestone well directly below the inverted bowl of faces that drew Cayden forward. Perched on a rocky platform and decorated with runes, mist swelled and swirled over the sides, interspersed with more flashes of blue lightning, the source of which was the depths of the well. Cayden stepped up onto the ledge and peered into shimmering surface. The basin was fathomless. Cayden gripped the sides of the well, knuckles whitening, so strong was his grip on the lip. He swayed as a wave of dizziness washed over him. From the depths, faces twisted into the air and shimmered into a three dimensional shape then collapsed back into the foggy surface.

Cayden's eyes widened and he extended a hand toward its shimmering surface. Ziona stepped up beside him and gazed into the well.

The mists stirred and churned in reaction to his proximity and more and more wisps detached themselves from it, forming shapes.

One such shape pulled essence from his body, and steadied, rising out of the well and solidifying into the reflection of a beautiful woman with long curly brown hair and emerald Primordial eyes. Cayden and Ziona gasped at the same time, stumbling back from the well and slipping off the platform. Both recognized the woman, although for different reasons.

"Who are you?" Cayden croaked.

"Princess Gwen?" Ziona peered over Cayden's shoulder.

"My son," the image whispered. A ghostly hand curled toward Cayden's face, as though she longed to touch him. "I cannot maintain this form for long, so we must speak quickly. So long have I waited for your return to your ancestral home. You and your sister are the only hope for this dying world. The evil goddess has stretched out her hand to smother it. Even now, she squeezes the throat of the Primordials in a vice grip that pits family against family, clan against clan."

Ziona gasped audibly at this news.

"You and your sister are the key to stopping a war that will engulf both lands. You must go to the land of the Primordials and meet with the high elders. Time is short, my son. Do not delay! As always, our souls are yours." Her form faded back into the mists of the well.

Ziona, stunned, sank to her knees on the cold stone floor. Mordecai followed her lead.

"You are more than a king. You are the Lord of the Mists, the Seer of Souls!" Ziona gasped as she bowed to the floor, touching the cold stone with her forehead. Cayden looked at them both, a memory stirring at her words. He knew that title. He had been called it before, but it was in a different place, a different time.

"Ziona is correct. This is the Well of Souls, Cayden. You are the Lord of the Mists and the caretaker of the souls within it." Mordecai straightened from his prone position, still kneeling. "You placed these souls here, Cayden. Do you remember?"

Cayden rubbed his head. Vague images flashed through his brain, but he found it impossible to make them settle into an actual memory.

He shook his head. "I do not know. There is something there, but I cannot seem to access it." He stepped back onto the ledge and peered over the edge, suddenly realizing the voices of his dreams were before him. They had not been dreams at all, but real souls calling out to him in his relaxed state. He dipped his hand into the pool and the mist clung to him, enveloping his arm and then his entire body in a lover's embrace.

"How many souls are in here?" Cayden asked, gazing unfocused at the surface as he listened to the whispering of voices only he could hear; the faces of tens of thousands of souls glimpsed in the swirling mists.

"These are all the departed souls who have ever lived, Cayden, at least all those who have not been snatched away by the shadow and not now inhabiting living bodies. You are their guardian, Cayden. You guard their rest until they are reincarnated, until they are blessed to be reborn as infants. That is why they are attracted to you. I think you see why this place had to be protected," Mordecai said. "I have been guarding the Well of Souls until your return, keeping the minions of Helga from discovering its location and from snatching away the future of mankind. Though they have searched long and hard, they have not found this place. It was for this reason the tunnels were created under the castle.

"The Royal Family of Cathair has ever been its protectors, the Spirit Shield of the Cathairs providing a blood shield and a spirit shield for the souls of humanity. Now I give this sacred duty back to you. This is why you must fight for this castle. It is your heritage and your birthright, but beyond that it is a sacred trust to protect, not only for you but for the entire world."

Chapter 54

CAYDEN, MORDECAI, AND ZIONA entered the castle through the Traitor's Gate and slipped up the passage to the parade grounds where the battle was at its fiercest. Soldiers from both sides lay bleeding and dying on the field. Cayden was shocked at the carnage, bodies broken and twisted, some barely recognizable as human.

His footsteps slowed and he hesitated. *This is insanity. There is no reason for this bloodshed. These people fight each other when they should be at peace. They are not each other's enemies. The queen is the enemy; she is the one who pits friend against friend, human against human. I must put an end to this.*

Around the injured and dying soldiers, auras pulsed, as they teetered on the cusp of death. Cayden walked out into the sea of bodies and knelt beside one such man from the Queen's Guard. His eyes were glassy and clouded in pain. Cayden gripped the man's hand. Cayden felt a shiver in his arm and the man went limp. A bright glow formed around Cayden. He visited soldier after soldier, friend and fallen foe alike, giving comfort and solace with a touch at the last moment of their existence on earth. Their souls passed to him like a feathery sigh. Instinctually, he sent them to the Well of Souls to their rest.

Mordecai walked behind him, anxiously scanning the various battles going on around them, searching for signs that someone was taking an interest in their proceedings. Ziona gripped her knife tightly in her hand and scanned the milling crowd of soldiers, spinning when the battle stumbled too close.

Cayden stood and Mordecai grabbed his arm, steering him to the other side of the courtyard and out of harm's way, ducking into the open doorway at the base of a tower leading to the very highest point of the castle. They launched themselves onto the skinny spiral staircase, the clash of steel and screams of the wounded pursuing them as they raced up the stairs. Occasional flashes of battle were glimpsed through arrow slits in the block, but they did not pause.

At the first landing, a shadow detached from the wall and a guard stepped forward to challenge them. "Halt!" he yelled, drawing his sword. Mordecai raised his hand and with a blast of magic, sent the man flying backward to strike the wall on the other side, sliding to the floor. More palace guards spilled from either end of the hallway as Ziona grabbed Cayden by the sleeve and hauled him up the stairs. Fear gave their feet wings, spurring them to greater speed, the whoosh of air and muffled thumps from Mordecai's fight, chasing them as they fled.

It had been a bold plan. They had been outnumbered, their success in no way assured. As he climbed, Cayden caught a glimpse of Ryder battling two opponents who, due to his size, made it a reasonable match. His tunic was torn and multiple cuts to his face left blood dried in patches on his cheek. Cayden paused, wanting to call out to him, but Ziona grabbed his sleeve and tugged him back into motion.

"Don't stop," she hissed. "They are battling for you. Your fight is not their fight. Keep going!"

As Cayden ran up the steps, Ziona heard steps echoing on the staircase behind them. Someone must have slipped past Mordecai. She turned and ran back down the staircase to confront the new threat.

Reaching the top, Cayden spilled out onto a flat-topped spire with a wide stone walkway circling the finial, rising another twenty feet into the air. He panted, hands on knees, catching his breath. Grey stone gargoyles, evenly perched on the waist-high stone wall, caught his eye. Cayden walked slowly around the circle, the wind whipping his tunic and tugging at his sleeves, as he surveyed the entire battle playing out below…a battle being fought for him.

He leaned out over the merlon to check the progress of the battle below when suddenly he felt the cold touch of sharpened steel at his throat.

"Careful now," she *tsked*, "don't want to lose your pretty head, now do you? Move slowly back from the wall. That's it."

Cayden eased away from the merlon, moving so as to not accidently slit his own throat on the fine edge. Beads of blood swelled against the sword despite his careful movements. As he straightened, head arching back away from the sword, Queen Alcina curved around him, inspecting him.

"Is this the upstart from the cellars, Cyrus?"

With his eyes pinned on Cayden, Cyrus said, "Yes, my queen. He is the one I was bringing you to see." His eyes glinted with anger. "Slit his throat right now and we can be done with this."

"Wait!" Alcina raised her hand to stay his swing. "Where is your sister?" She stopped in front of Cayden.

"My sister?" Cayden thought furiously. "I have no sister."

"Liar!" the queen hissed. She grabbed a hand full of hair, pulling his head back and further exposing the taut flesh of his throat. "I merely need to give the word and your head will be bouncing down this wall walk like a child's toy. Where is she?" she hissed again.

"I do not know. I haven't seen her in weeks," Cayden gasped, trying to swallow without moving his Adam's apple, the sword moving with the action.

"Bind his hands, Cyrus. We will take him with us. The castle is lost, but we have our prize. The Great Mistress will be pleased."

Alcina handed her sword to Cyrus and pulled a short knife hidden inside a pocket of her cloak then tightened her grip on Cayden's hair. "To make sure you do not run again, I am going to gouge out your eyes." She raised the short dagger and brought it flashing down. Cayden closed his eyes, shuddering with the anticipated impact.

At that moment silvery fury, in the form of Sheba, flashed through the air. Howling with rage, her paws landed on Cyrus's chest, knocking him back across the merlon. The sword clattered off the top of the wall and spun out into the air, falling to earth. Cyrus slipped between two of the stone teeth, great canine tusks missing his throat by inches as the wolf rolled past.

Ziona's battle cry was no less intense. She screamed and launched herself from the stone archway at Alcina. The queen spun around, ducking Ziona's blade and slashed with her own catching Ziona's arm as she passed. The cut was not deep but blood oozed all the same. Ziona flinched back from the next slash and then both Cyrus and Alcina were dashing for the staircase, disappearing into the opening. Sheba chased after them, snarling and snapping in full blood lust.

Cayden gasped for breath as Ziona reached him. She ran her hands up his arms over his shoulders and finally cupped his head to turn it gently, inspecting the sword cut at his throat.

"Thank the gods! You are OK," she gasped, fear etched into her beautiful face. She sagged with the release of adrenaline and hugged him tight, trembling. Cayden wound his arms around her and folded her close to his body, taking deep breaths to calm his fear.

"It's OK. We're OK. We're OK," he murmured into her hair.

Gently pushing her away, he looked down into her fear-soaked eyes. "Come, we have a job to do. Let's end this."

Chapter 55

THE CASTLE WAS IN AN UPROAR. Armed men fought battles on every level, insurgents against Queens Guard, farmers against innkeepers, milk maids against kitchen staff.

Marcia, Queen Alcina's maid, silently cheered the rebels on from her hiding place in the closet of the queen's chambers. The soldiers had materialized out of nowhere in spots throughout the castle. They were not attacking any servants, not that she noticed anyways. Those they came across they ran straight past without a glance. If servants raised a hand against them, though, they were quickly dispatched. She witnessed one of the cook's staff attack a soldier with a cooking knife and the soldier had not hesitated to run him through.

After that, the invading men gave fair warning, asking the staff to stand down and stand aside, this was not their fight.

Marcia heard the door to the queen's apartments open and stealthy footsteps sounded. She peeked through the keyhole to see who had entered. Alcina ran across the room, grabbed a travel bag and started shoving a random assortment of things into it. Clothing followed shoes followed jewels. The door opened again and Cyrus entered, his jacket sleeve torn, blood running down his arm from a deep jagged wound. His sword dripped onto the hand-knotted silk carpet at his feet. He grabbed the queen roughly by the arm and shook her.

"We don't have time for this, Alcina!" In his panic, he forgot the royal honorific. "If they capture you, they will behead you! We must leave *now!*" he hissed. Grabbing her by the arm, he pulled her toward the closet.

Marcia's heart leapt to her throat. *If they discover me, they will run me through with a sword!* She knew it. She shied back into the gowns and crouched in the corner. The door next to her opened and Cyrus and Alcina pushed past her to the back of the tall storage closet. They pried open a panel on the back wall, which swung open on hidden hinges and disappeared into the black hole beyond the closet wall, leaving it ajar in their haste.

Chapter 56

CAYDEN STILL DID NOT UNDERSTAND the complete how and why of it, but he did understand his aid was needed.

He reached into his pocket and pulled out his flutes. They warmed in his hand, a comforting joyous reunion with his trembling fingers. Ziona had retrieved them from his tent and brought them along. During their walk back up from the Well of Souls, she slipped them into his pocket, reverently, seeming to understand their purpose for the first time.

He hoped she was right. He hoped he understood them half as well as she did.

He selected the one he had carved the day Aossi had appeared. He placed it to his lips and began to play. The air around him shimmered and warped, the sky a rippling sound wave.

At first, the sound of battle drowned the sound of the flute, but as he played, it grew louder and louder. The other flutes in his pocket warmed and vibrated in sympathy. Suddenly, sound burst from those flutes, a chorus of music even though he was not directly playing them. The songs melded into one and swelled like a trumpet call, blasting out over the grounds below.

Soldiers from both sides took startled notice, pausing in their battles to gaze up at a sky suddenly in turmoil, boiling and bubbling with silver grey clouds laced with rainbows. Then a piercing shaft of light split the nighttime sky, blinding the soldiers on the field below.

At the same time, bright spots randomly popped onto the field below. The glowing spots resolved themselves into wolves and snakes, running out of doorways and around the corners of buildings, spilling through archways, slithering and skulking out of drain pipes, sliding out of cracks and crevices in the stone, and rising from the ground in answer to the call of Cayden's song. The men paused in mid-battle, great cries of alarm rising and falling from all who spotted the creatures.

The wolves snarled and snapped at the men; the snakes hissed and danced, rattling tails and flaring hoods, drawing the battling men's attention away from each other as friend and foe turned as one to face this new, unknown threat. Confusion reigned in the milling crowd below.

Thunder boomed and rumbled. Forks of brilliant lightning split the sky, cracking open the clouds.

The soldiers cried out, falling to their knees and clasping hands over ears ringing with the concussion of the thunder. They squeezed their eyes closed against the blinding brilliance of the lightning.

The thunder, the lighting, the snarling wolves, and the slithering snakes were nothing compared to the ghostly forms that rode into the commons, phantom souls riding rainbow-hued chariots pulled by great white-winged Pegasus, their shining armour blinding, commanding the allegiance of the soldiers below.

The great generals of old, Kingsmen whose faces were familiar to all, paused to gaze at the combatants. As one, they pulled flaming swords from sheaths and raised them into the air. The message was clear. Cease this battle now or we will finish it, permanently. Denzik spied Captain O'Reilly and grinned.

The combatants cried out and confusion reigned. Some, crazed at the sights before them, tried to fight the ghosts. On contact, their swords became a flaming inferno that spread from weapon to clothing. Screaming, the flaming beacons of rebellion ran through the crowd, panicking the balance of the Queen's Guard. Some scrambled for the exits, only to find the exits blocked by wolves and Kingsmen. No one was leaving the area.

Cayden lowered his flute, aghast at the stampede that was occurring below. He could not discern friend from foe. All he knew was that people were dying. To his vision, a misty blue fog rose from the ground as more and more men and women departed this life.

"Help me, Ziona! I don't know how to stop this! They are going to kill each other to the last person! Help me stop this madness!"

Mordecai put a gentle hand on his shoulder and squeezed it. "Now is the time, Cayden. Now is the return of the king, the true heir of Cathair, the true Spirit Shield. Claim your heritage. Claim your birthright. Speak to them."

Ziona slipped her arm around his waist from the other side and leaned her head against his shoulder. "I believe in you, Cayden." She gestured to the milling people below. "They believe in you too, if you will allow them to. Speak to them."

Cayden looked from one to the other. "I do not know what to say." he murmured, his eyes roving over the scene below him.

"Speak what is in your heart. They will hear it," said Mordecai, stepping back out of sight of the crowd. Ziona returned to the staircase, guarding his back as he mustered the courage to speak.

Cayden stared sightlessly at the scene before him, blocking out the scene as his mind wandered back over the events since leaving Sanctuary-by-the-Sea. He sorted and slotted his experiences, turning them over, examining them. He thought of Avery, how she had looked the last time he had seen her, the concern in her eyes at his decision to leave. She knew nothing of what had transpired since joining the legion nor did he know what adventures she had stumbled into. Surely her path was a smoother one than this? He smiled slightly, thinking what her reaction would be when they could finally sit down and talk as brother and sister again. *I miss her so much!* he thought, his heart lurching painfully in his chest in that part he reserved just for his twin.

His mind wandered down familiar paths, back into his earliest childhood memories of the pair of them, playing in the pastures around their farm. They had always known they were special, accepted that they were unique. They shared an ability to talk to each other telepathically, but they had innocently believed it to be part of that special, indescribable bond that twins share. They had never thought of their magic as dangerous or deviant, but Queen Alcina had thought it so and she was correct. Her fears had turned out to be a real and justified danger to the queen and to her reign. They'd been physically hidden from the world. *Now the world knows about my magic, and soon it will know of Avery's too, at least amongst the Primordial clans.*

He had not heard the Primordial Prophesies as a child, but the children's games they'd played with the other villagers' children and stories told by the villagers themselves had hinted at the belief in a saviour of souls; that the Lord of the Mists was a real person, a Seer of Souls. *I am a true heir of the powers that belong to a Spirit Shield of Cathair, of this there can be no doubt...but Avery must also be a Seer of Souls.* He tested this newly minted thought in his mind and knew it to be true in his heart of hearts. *We are both Seers of Souls, the pair of us, twin Seers.*

If this is the truth of the matter, then the rest must also be true. With a grimace, he tucked the flute in his pocket and resigned himself to his destiny. *Mordecai has a lot of explaining to do, starting with our family line. I will make him cough up those prophesies, even if he chokes on them. I must learn everything I can, for both my life and Avery's depend on it.* He gazed out over the top of the castle walls and to the north, straining his eyes to see the grey haze that was the mountains of the Highland Spine, dividing his lands (his mind tried to shy from the thought) from the Primordial lands. *I am coming, Avery, and I will be armed with information when I do. Stay safe!*

With a deep breath and a sigh, Cayden raised his voice to speak to the milling army of bewildered and discontented men scattered throughout the castle grounds, still looking for a way to escape the prowling animals blocking all the exits. His voice swelled and moved over the surrounding countryside, magnified by the magic of the flutes.

"Lay down your weapons, immediately! This battle is ended. I have returned to claim my birthright, the throne of the Spirit Shields of Cathair. My sister and I are the rightful heirs of Cathair and the heavens bear witness to this. The usurper has been ousted. The royal line is being restored. Hear me now and obey!"

The Queen's Guard quieted during his speech, which could be heard in every corner of the kingdom. Sword arms dropped and a murmuring replaced the screams of moments ago. The ethereal chariots drifting inches above the ground rose into the air, causing the soldiers to shy back. Leading the chariots, in the most brightly coloured one of all, sat Aossi, grinning like a schoolgirl, feet propped up on the felly rim. She winked at him and waved.

Cayden managed a weak smile and lifted his hand in acknowledgment of the greeting.

"The Kingsmen will gather your weapons. There will be no more fighting. Hear me and obey! Choose to disobey and your time on this earth will be an unpleasant one. There are plenty of dungeons waiting to be filled. I know, as I have seen them."

The few soldiers who remained on their feet slowly lowered their weapons and as one raised their hands in surrender. The wolves prowled the edges of the battle, tongues lolling, giving every appearance of grinning. Snakes slithered onto rocks and back into the crevices they had exited.

Slowly, the fighting ended. A silence fell over the scene, broken only by the moans of the injured. Suddenly, cheers erupted from the Kingsmen, a great ground swelling roar of victory. The Kingsmen moved amongst the Queen's Guard, securing weapons and herding those of the former Queen's Guard still standing into the center of the battlefield, ringing it with the steel of their swords,

"The Kingsmen will escort you into the holding cells on the first level of the dungeons. Once there, you will be offered proof of my lineage and an opportunity to swear allegiance. Those who refuse will be tried as traitors to royal house of Cathair. I suggest you ask many questions of the Kingsmen. Satisfy yourselves as to the truth of this matter."

One belligerent guardsman yelled up at Cayden, "Where is the queen? Where is Queen Alcina! You cannot be king while she lives."

Murmurs broke out from the circle, and the Kingsmen tightened their grips on their swords, in warning.

Ziona crossed back over to stand beside Cayden and he slipped his arm around Ziona's shoulders, giving her a squeeze. She hugged him and stared down at the scene, mouth open in awe.

It was done...for now.

***

In the woods outside of the castle grounds, two figures in heavy travelling cloaks hurried away from the battle. Suddenly, the skies opened up and a piercing ray of light flooded the area. Rays of pure energy pierced the gloom of the forest canopy, silhouetting the trees. Alcina saw ghostly chariots materialize and slide through the solid castle walls. She swore a very un-queenly word and ducked behind a tree. Cyrus paused.

The gaunt trees writhed as light flooded the forest driving back the gloom and stabbing into Charun hiding amongst the trunks of the trees like a red hot poker. The light scoured the forest and the Charun burst from cover, screaming with the touch of the light as it sliced through the darkness. Flames leapt from their withered skin as they writhed and thrashed and burned. Exposed to the light's purity, they shrivelled and smoked as they died.

Cyrus and Alcina bolted, the shrieks lending speed to their flight. *What power was able to destroy a Charun?* Alcina shuddered. She wasn't about to wait around to find out.

Chapter 57

MORDECAI LEANED BACK ON THE CRENELLATED WALL
and crossed his arms under his bushy white beard studying Cayden.
Cayden sighed and turned his flute over in his hands before tucking
it back into his pocket. His mind was spinning with all that had
transpired in the past twenty-four hours.

"Cayden."

Cayden lifted his head in response to Mordecai's call, meeting his
eyes. He was surprised to feel tears welling in his own. He swiped a
sleeve across his eyes to disguise their wetness.

"Was she really my mother?" The question burst from his lips,
unbidden. Of everything he had seen, everything that had happened,
this was the one piercing thought, the one overwhelming need he
had...to know the truth.

"Yes," Mordecai said softly.

Ziona passed a hand across his back in comfort.

"Tell me now. Tell me it all. I want to know the truth. And now,
before I have to face everyone below."

Mordecai sighed. He pulled Cayden over to sit beside him at the
base of the wall. Ziona eased herself down beside him, to listen in.

"Seventeen years ago, a Primordial princess fell in love with a
handsome young prince of Cathair. Tall, blond, and fair, he sat his
stallion with a bearing that commanded attention, as the prince and
heir to the throne of Cathair should. This was at the peak of the
Daimonic wars, which I am sure you have heard of?"

Cayden nodded his head, still staring at his hands.

"The battles between the kingdom and the Primordial forces at
Daimon Ford were long and protracted affairs with heavy raiding

occurring back and forth across the river and many casualties on both sides.

"During a break in one of the skirmishes, a raiding party was sent out on a mission to kidnap your mother. They sneaked into the Primordial lands and managed to get right into the sacred capital city of Faylea, a feat accomplished by few. It was a bold but desperate attempt to end the fighting. I think the original plan was to merely hold her for ransom and force the Primordial warriors, who are the fiercest of all fighters, to cease battle and retreat.

"Your father, however, took one look at Gwen when she arrived in Cathair as a prisoner and his heart was lost. Rather than return her to her people, he set about convincing his father that their marriage would be best for the kingdom, arguing that it would unite the lands forever more.

"Obviously, the Primordial peoples were in an uproar over the disappearance of their beloved princess and the battles resumed with an even greater fervour. Many, many lives were lost on both sides in the battles that followed.

"Princess Gwen was never mistreated; in fact, she was pampered and given every consideration and freedom to explore the castle at will, but she was forbidden to leave the grounds. Prince Alexander was often seen escorting her on walks, and as their love grew, so did his demands that they be allowed to marry.

"Alcina, your father's sister, secretly harboured the ambition to succeed her brother to the throne. Indeed, the laws of Cathair encouraged her in this, as they state that a ruling king or incumbent male heir must be married prior to ascending to the throne or the next closest married female relative to the reigning king would be crowned.

"As Prince Alexander had not shown the remotest interest in any of the eligible young female nobles paraded before him, Alcina had convinced herself that the throne would be hers.

"Gwen's sudden appearance and the attention lavished by the Cathair prince on the guest captive flared her anger and jealousy. As the next in line to the throne, she was unwilling to see a Primordial princess within reach of the throne. Unbeknownst to the rest of the royal family, she hatched a plan to overthrow the entire royal line, beginning with the murder of her brother." Mordecai sighed heavily, his mouth drooping; his eyes troubled.

"The king's death appeared to be the result of natural causes, but I found traces of heart leaf in his salad the night he died. He had supped in his suite that dreadful night, alone. I could never pinpoint who delivered his meal that evening.

"His son, Prince Alexander, had left two days prior on a routine patrol with a group of young men in training to be Kingsmen. He was killed, once again, under suspicious circumstances and never returned.

"You see, your grandfather had agreed to their marriage, just hours before Prince Alexander left on patrol. The wedding was being arranged in secret via pigeon messengers sent between the Primordial chieftains and the king.

"Your father and mother, so very anxious to be together, had begun to see rather more of each other than is proper for the unwed. Gwen became pregnant and attempted to hide her condition from the rest of the royal family, but Alcina discovered the pregnancy. It was then that I realized the royal family was in grave danger, but I had no proof.

"One day, as they strolled through the secluded gardens near the library, Gwen and Alexander were approached by the fairy Aossi who had been sent as a messenger from Alfreda, the Mother Goddess herself and her brother Caerwyn, the Spirit Shield.

"Aossi knew of the plan to kill the royal family and also of Gwen's pregnancy. She convinced your parents that the only way to save their respective kingdoms and the world was for the godlings, Alfreda and Caerwyn, to be born to humans and walk the world as mortals once more. The catch was that they needed to join with Gwen's babes as hosts.

"You see, the veil, or the shield between the living and the dead, has been weakening, and the minions of Helga are snatching away the souls at rest, and enslaving them in the netherworld. Helga, as you know, is the ruler of the underworld, banished to rule the souls of the condemned in that torturous place by the gods of old with the blessing of her siblings, Alfreda and Caerwyn.

"Fearing for their lives and for yours and Avery's by extension, your father and mother agreed to the plan." Mordecai paused for a moment, checking to make sure that he hadn't lost Cayden along the way. "There are several things that are required to invoke magic such as was being proposed by Aossi.

"Firstly, you need a wizard's Will. This is the essence of what makes a wizard's magic work. Secondly, you need a focus; a tool with which to compact and combine the elements of the spell. I use this stone as my focus." Mordecai reached into his pocket and pulled the smooth focus stone out to show Cayden. It lay flat and smooth, a pearly sheen coating its surface. "With a focus stone, my wizard's Will, and your parent's co-operation, the final element was the soul of a god. With these, we could give human form to the gods. With an archaic incantation not used since the beginning of time, we bound the souls of the immortals to human flesh."

And suddenly, as though buried beneath an avalanche, a memory floated up out of a crack in his being. Cayden's eyes glazed over as he fought to remember, to bring the memory to the forefront of his mind...and then it was gone.

"For an instant," Cayden said, "I remembered...something," he frowned, "but now it is gone." He stood up and started to pace.

Tears of frustration glistened in Cayden's eyes and he did not check them as they slowly made tracks in the dirt on his face.

Mordecai continued the story, politely ignoring Cayden's distress.

"Your mother summoned me to her chambers, the evening after the news of Prince Alexander's fall. When I arrived, it was obvious that she was gravely ill by the deathly pallor of her skin. Her overriding concern was for the babies dying inside her as the poison ran its course. She was desperate to save her royal children, who were conceived to bring peace and a flesh bond between the two warring factions of the earth, a united royal family spanning both nations."

He told Cayden of the magic of the Primordials, how they were attuned to the spirits of the land and the animals that resided in it, of how the mythical creatures of the earth were in tune with the Primordial spirits.

"Your flutes are a conduit of magic that speaks to the spirits of the beasts. The magic you possess calls them and your magic could also act as a trigger for their souls to reincarnate into their mythical form." Cayden nodded, knowing this from his encounter with the werewolf form of Sheba's alpha.

"But what you need to understand most of all, Cayden, is that you and Avery volunteered to do all of this."

Cayden's head shot up at his words. Ziona leaned in closer, to listen.

"If Princess Gwen is my mother and Prince Alexander is my father then who are the people who raised me?" Cayden slipped his hand into Ziona's, seeking comfort. She squeezed his in return.

"The man and woman who raised you, in Sanctuary-by-the-Sea are also your parents, Cayden, in every sense of the word. You are a merging, a blending of both of those babes whose bodies you inhabited. The binding of your godling essence to the physical bodies conceived by your royal parents merged you into a new being. When I triggered the magic that pulled you from your dying infant bodies and into the infants being born in Sanctuary, your mortal and immortal essences merged with those children's bodies.

"As you know now, being the Seer of Souls, no soul had yet been delivered to those infants, so you delivered your own soul to the host baby waiting for this bonding. You and your sister are truly the children of both parents."

Mordecai reached over and grasped Cayden's shoulder in his right hand and squeezed it. "I know you love your parents very much. Surely it is a comfort to know they truly are your parents in every sense of the word?"

Cayden smiled a small smile, the pain of the truth receding from his eyes as he absorbed Mordecai's words.

"I will show you the ancient texts that are stored in the castle library vaults," Mordecai said. "But of this there is no doubt. You are the Seer of Souls, the godling that is the caretaker of the souls of the deceased. You willingly divested yourself of your divinity in order to wage this battle, in order to bring unity to creation. But understand this: as you are now human, it also means that you can die. And for you, young Cayden, there is no rebirth. If you die in this form, you are dead, wiped from existence in any form. For you, death is final."

Cayden shivered. He had suspected that he could die, but not that it would be...forever. Everyone knew about the rebirth of the souls of the dead. It was the basis of their legends.

"What about Avery?" he asked.

"Avery is also a godling. I think you already know who she is."

Ziona gasped. "Is Avery the Goddess Pinesi, the Goddess of the Woodlands?"

Mordecai nodded. "Yes, that is one of many names used by the Primordial people. She is the goddess of the woodland creatures, the mother goddess of nature and guardian of mythical souls. She is also your sister, Alfreda."

"Then she is in danger too?" Cayden asked.

"Yes. Yes we must find her and soon." Mordecai stood up and brushed off his ragged robes, still filthy and torn from his imprisonment. "Now, if you will excuse me, I'd like to find some real clothes and a bath. I haven't had one of those in, oh...seventeen years I believe?" He trotted off to the stairwell and disappeared.

Cayden reached out to Avery with his mind. *Avery, where are you?* He received no response.

Chapter 58

IN THE DAYS FOLLOWING THE RECAPTURE OF CATHAIR, Cayden and his new subjects struggled to settle to a new routine. The town swelled with migrants who flocked in from the countryside on the strength of rumour and a chance to glimpse the new king. The scattered Kingsmen slowly trickled back into the city, bringing their families with them, anxious to offer their services even though many were now past their prime fighting days.

Cayden cornered Mordecai early on and pestered him to teach him his family history, and they spent many long days in the squat, stone library, shaped like a flat topped stone turret, in the center of the walled gardens, pouring over the books contained there.

The royal ascent was on everyone's mind, and both ex-Queen's Guard and Kingsmen alike joined together to celebrate the coronation of the royal missing heir, King Cayden. A simple ceremony was held in the public square the following day out front of the palace amidst great security. It was at Cayden's insistence that all people should be allowed to attend. Commoners crowded the square, hung out of windows and perched on rooftops to cheer as the crown was placed on his head. A week of celebration was ordered, and the festivities lasted for the better part of two before life returned to normal.

Denzik, Nelson, and Fabian were reinstated as captains of the Kingsmen and promoted to Captain Generals. The band was incorporated into the Kingsmen as a new and highly specialized unit, dedicated to service as Cayden's personal guard and allowed to retain their chosen name. Similar units were formed within the Kingsmen, reflecting regional areas and homes, uniting the scattered former guard into familiar bonded units.

Of Cyrus and Alcina, no trail was found to indicate where they had fled. A frightened maid brought to them in the early hours after the cessation of the battle had led them to a hidden passage behind Queen Alcina's closet and gave witness that they had fled through it. A large contingent of Kingsmen ducked inside and followed the hidden passage until it emptied into the tunnels under the castle. They searched but could locate no further clues as to the direction they had fled.

A bounty was set of one hundred thousand gold crowns on the head of Alcina and ten thousand gold crowns for Cyrus for their capture and return. A bounty of five hundred gold crowns was set on Darius's head and Ziona, still furious over Cayden's kidnapping, matched the bounty from her personal purse doubling the sum, so keen was she to capture the traitor. The Kingsmen searched the woods where the ambush had occurred, to no avail.

Denzik was given the charge to map out the underground tunnel system to prevent exactly the type of unseen ambush attack they had engineered on the castle.

Ryder was awarded a knighthood and as his first duty, commissioned to find more like minded people to expand into a full order of Cathairian knighthood. He set off immediately to search the realm for the bravest and most loyal men and women of all the lands, both human and Primordial. His mandate was to forge a unique peacekeeping force, starting with the knights of Cathair. Once the initial shock of his commission wore off, Ryder begged for a training facility. With a broad grin, Denzik deeded his farm to Ryder. Lower Cathair would soon become known as the home of the Royal Knight's Guild.

On the second evening after their victory, Cayden took Ziona for a walk through the rose gardens, hand in hand. He stopped at a secluded stone bench and pulled her down beside him. Once seated, he took up her hand, kissing it lightly.

"We need to talk about this bond. What do you want to do about it? Where do you see this—us going? I know I am attracted to you"—Cayden's ears pinked as his heartbeat quickened—"but how do you feel about us being able to read each other's minds? I mean, what if you want to, you know, date someone?"

Ziona laughed, and Cayden's ears reddened even further.

"You do not need to worry about such things," she said, smoothing his hot cheek with her cool palm, "there is no one here I would consider mate worthy...except for you." She quirked an eyebrow in his direction, and his thoughts instantly winged back to their first meeting in her tent back during his legion stay. "Why don't we take it slowly, see what develops? There is much to be done and I need to return to my people and let them know what has transpired here. There is much to be told that the elders need to hear. I fear that the war between our peoples is about to escalate. Who knows what plans Alcina and Cyrus are about to implement?

"One thing is certain, however. Whether as mates or as very deep friends, we are bonded as no other two people have been in the history of this world. In that sense, we are true soulmates, now and forever."

Epilogue

THE SMELL OF ROTTING EGGS PERMEATED THE AIR as the lava spluttered and splashed over the cracked edges of the pool. The little light shed by the glowing basin was quickly dispersed by shadowy creatures that slithered on the floor of the cavern. The darkness was not threatened by the light, but instead it swallowed the feeble attempt to define the shape of the space.

All of this was lost on the two shivering forms prostrated on the rough stone floor, afraid to lift their faces to gaze on the goddess before them.

"You have crawled here to ask my forgiveness when the stench of your failure has reached my nostrils long in advance of your arrival?"

"Great Mistress of the Dark," Alcina gushed in a rush to be heard, "we hurried all the way to your fortress to bring you the news that the boy has finally revealed himself and we now know which one he is! Surely we can destroy him now if you would loan us the aid of your creatures. We will not fail again." Alcina hazarded a furtive peak out of the corner of her eye at the ethereal shadow swarmed form before her and then, gasping in fear, pressed her forehead back to the stone floor once again.

"What say you, Cyrus? Is your failure as complete as Alcina's? What excuse do you bring to try and persuade me that I shouldn't end your worthless lives right now and feed your souls to my pets here?" The goddess gestured to the mindless, formless milling swarm of minions at her misted feet.

Cyrus stirred and with gaunt face still pressed to the floor, whispered, "Great Mistress, your plan has not yet failed. We know of his weakness now. Our spies report that he will not raise a hand to destroy life, whether that life is for good or for evil. It will be his undoing. He will not be able to stand against our armies or against your greatness. Please lend us the assistance of your servants. I promise when we meet them on the field of battle, none shall remain standing and their souls will serve your glory for all eternity as it is prophesied."

Silence met his plea and he shivered at the icy touch both he and Alcina felt slide into their minds; as a cold and clammy spectral hand clutched at the heart of their souls' essence. They involuntarily cried out at the stroking, empty feeling of the soulless. The goddess stripped their minds bare and weighed their souls, examining their intentions. Shivering uncontrollably, their bodies thrashed on the icy surface of the audience chamber. Suddenly, the touch withdrew and they lay panting, dragging in raged breaths as they fought their terror.

"I find your intentions aligned with mine and so your souls are not forfeit...yet. Do not fail me again. My patience is growing thin. Here is what you will do." The goddess bent down and touched a spectral finger to each of their temples, placing her instructions in their minds.

"Now leave me. Do not return unless you can report success. If you slink back in failure, I promise you will beg for death; a death that will be denied, forever."

Suddenly a sharp cold wind swept the chamber, like a door opening onto a blustery winter's day. As abruptly as the wind began, all stilled. Cyrus and Alcina lifted their faces from the stone floor. Helga was gone.

SPIRIT SHIELD – BOOK TWO

Prologue

THE ARMY ROLLED OUT OF THE SOUTHERN PLAINS and into the short hills, a river of red-coated lava swirling through the valley base, splashing up onto the hillsides, coating the passes with a crimson crust of soldiers, clogging the narrows.

The Primordial runners peered down at the roiling mass of men from their perch high atop an abandoned eagle's nest in a towering deciduous tree which clung to the northern edge of the pass. The crown of the treetop camouflaged their lookout while providing an unimpeded view of the undulating scene below.

As one, the runners shimmied down from their perches and ghosted into the dense cover of squat pine, the thick carpet of needles providing silent footing as they ran. Of all the passes to approach, this was the worst, the most feared by the Primordial Chiefs, as the civil war left the defending clans stretched to the limit.

Indeed, some defenders had abandoned their posts; their fear over the rumoured fate of their families overcoming their desire to fight. Whispers of villages emptied. Entire families snatched away by unknown forces had caused a swelling defection within the forward units of tribal defenders. It was so rampant that the chieftains now arrested those who attempted desertion and handed them over to the priests rather than admit that the Flesh clan defenders were cowards.

The Primordial priests were only too happy to receive the disaffected clansmen as they had their own mandate to fulfill.

Their hands were bound and then they were marched in a seemingly never ending stream of clansmen to a solitary camp perched high on the side of the Wailing Mountain, deep within the pass. The guards assigned to this duty delivered their prisoners swiftly and without delay, wishing to be away from the encampment full of shivering, wild eyed priests. The priests' camp never slept except during the daylight, the time from dusk to dawn alive with the scurrying holy men.

Late into the night, the screams of the sacrifices howled through the encampment, flooding down to the tents below, the souls of the sacrifices dancing in the flames of their campfires, confirming the transfer to those who would continue the fight.

Primordial High Priests, clothed in cloaks comprised of leathery-patched skin imbedded with eagle feathers, raised bloody knives to the sky and chanted. The bleeding of the sacrifices was a delicate thing. Too little bleeding and the sacrifices would go into shock before the transfer was complete; too much bleeding and the soul would be lost.

A bare-chested apprentice with only one eagle feather bound to each tattooed arm dipped a hollowed gourd into a basin of potion warming on hot rocks at the edge of the fire pit. Carefully, he carried the gourd, brimming with liquid, over to a woman, naked except for her blindfold, staked out spread eagle on the ground at the edge of the flickering light.

With one hand, he pinched her cheeks so that her mouth was forced into an O shape and then tipped the contents of the basin into it. He plugged her nose, forcing her to swallow convulsively while she thrashed in her bonds. The blindfold slipped and the woman's eyes stabbed into the apprentice. Then with the last of her strength, she spat the remains of the potion back at his face. With a scream, he stumbled away from the woman, frantically wiping it off. Everywhere the potion landed, it bubbled and hissed. Blisters erupted, large red swellings bubbling on the skin. They popped and oozed, drying instantly. Within seconds the skin withered, curling into drifts that feathered to the ground, even while the woman's eyes rolled back in her head.

Blood bloomed under the curls, to run in rivulets that joined larger flows. The High Priests crowded around the corpse and caught the blood in gleaming bone vessels and began a rhythmic chant, waving a hollowed rain stick carved with runes over the bowls, seducing the spirit of the blood sacrifice, binding it to the blood for transfer into a new vessel.

The woman's heart pumped valiantly as the last of its life force seeped to the surface. With a final shudder, she relaxed in her bonds, sagging limply in the ropes suspending her body.

The priests turned their backs on the empty shell and the chanting rose in pitch, calling forth the spirit of the dead woman. Wisps of movement danced on the surface of the bowls of blood, thickening, then dissipating, and formed once again a shadowed impression of a red face floating above the surface of the bowls.

They walked past the line of shivering men, kneeling at the edge of the fire light, arms bound behind their backs, awaiting their turn to serve the High Priests. All averted their eyes, hoping to not be chosen, hoping that they would be executed in the normal fashion. Beheading was preferable to being bled to death in their eyes. A whimper escaped the mouth of one of the deserters as his courage failed once again. With a jerk on his bindings, he was hauled to his feet by two burly apprentices, howling as he was dragged towards the sacrificial pit.

The High Priests paid no attention to the commotion, transfixed on the process at hand. Their chanting grew louder once again, as they approached a small animal tied to a metal stake driven deep into the ground. On closer inspection, a bear cub peered up at the approaching priests, licking its lips hungrily. The priests placed the bowls before the cub, chanting in a sing song voice that soothed the bear cub.

Once the priests backed away, the cub sniffed at the offering and then began to lap up the blood thirstily. The priests' song shrieked, assailing the ears of the watchers and the bear drank until all the blood was gone.

Suddenly, the song ceased. A gong was sounded once, twice, three times. As the sound faded from the third gong, the cub roared.

A vortex formed around the cub, spinning and swirling, dragging soil into its maelstrom as it arose, faster and faster, tiny bolts of energy sparking within the cloud, which grew into a funnel then into a tornado that picked up the cub and whirled it about. Bolts of lightning stabbed the ground and the priests stepped back, hands covering their faces as the sand stung their skin, whipping their eagle feathers until they mocked flight.

With a great clap of thunder and a blinding flash of light, everything stilled.

As the dust cleared, a body was revealed, curled into a ball on the ground. Slowly it unfurled, and rose to its feet.

A muscular woman stood before them, ten feet tall, with the face of a bear. Long brown hair curled past her muscular shoulders. She was clad in a tight-fitting leather jerkin and leggings, a great sword strapped to hip.

Artio sniffed the air and with a feral toothy grin rumbled, "BOW TO ME."

As one, the Primordial clansmen and High Priests fell to the ground, faces pressed to the earth.

Artio drew her lips back and bared her long incisors in a parody of a smile and then roared her pleasure.

About the Author: Susan Faw

Professional by day, book nerd and fantasy champion by night, Susan is a masked crusader for the fantastical world. Championing mythical rights, she quells uprisings and battles infidels who would slay the lifeblood of her pen. It's all in a night's work, for this whirlwind writer. Welcome to the quest.

VISIT SUSAN ONLINE:

http://www.susanfaw.com

http://www.facebook.com/SusanFaw

http://twitter.com/susandfaw

http://www.pinterest.com/susandfaw

FIND OUT HOW IT ALL BEGAN! DOWNLOAD THE FREE PREQUEL, SOUL SURVIVOR AT THE LINK BELOW!

http://susanfaw.com/soul-survivor-prequel-free-download/

CPSIA information can be obtained
at www.ICGtesting.com
Printed in the USA
LVOW13s1108300617

539915LV00001B/2/P